GRACE HARLOWE'S FIRST YEAR AT OVERTON COLLEGE

JESSIE GRAHAM FLOWER, A. M.

Grace Harlowe's First Year at Overton College

Jessie Graham Flower

© 1st World Library, 2009
PO Box 2211
Fairfield, IA 52556
www.1stworldlibrary.com
First Edition

LCCN: 2009923480

Softcover ISBN: 978-1-4218-8856-9
Hardcover ISBN: 978-1-4218-8955-9
eBook ISBN: 978-1-4218-8757-9

Purchase *"Grace Harlowe's First Year at Overton College"*
as a traditional bound book at:
www.1stWorldLibrary.com/purchase.asp?ISBN=978-1-4218-8856-9

1st World Library Literary Society

Giving Back to the World

"If you want to work on the core problem, it's early school literacy."

- James Barksdale, former CEO of Netscape

"No skill is more crucial to the future of a child, or to a democratic and prosperous society, than literacy."

- Los Angeles Times

"Literacy... means far more than learning how to read and write... The aim is to transmit... knowledge and promote social participation."

- UNESCO

"Literacy is not a luxury, it is a right and a responsibility. If our world is to meet the challenges of the twenty-first century we must harness the energy and creativity of all our citizens."

- President Bill Clinton

"Parents should be encouraged to read to their children, and teachers should be equipped with all available techniques for teaching literacy, so the varying needs and capacities of individual kids can be taken into account."

- Hugh Mackay

CONTENTS

CHAPTER I

OFF TO COLLEGE

"Do you remember what you said one October day last year, Grace, when we stood on this platform and said good-bye to the boys?" asked Anne Pierson.

"No, what did I say?" asked Grace Harlowe, turning to her friend Anne.

"You said," returned Anne, "that when it came your turn to go to college you were going to slip away quietly without saying good-bye to any one but your mother, and here you are with almost half Oakdale at the train to see you off to college."

"Now, Anne, you know perfectly well that people are down here to see you and Miriam, too," laughed Grace. "I'm not half as much of a celebrity as you are."

Grace Harlowe, Miriam Nesbit and Anne Pierson stood on the station platform completely surrounded by their many friends, who, regardless of the fact that it was half-past seven o'clock in the morning, had made it a point to be at the station to wish them godspeed.

"This is the second public gathering this week," remarked Miriam Nesbit, who, despite the chatter that was going on around her, had heard Grace's laughing remark.

"I know it," agreed Grace. "There was just as large a crowd here when Nora and Jessica went away last Monday. Doesn't it seem dreadful that we are obliged to be separated? How I hated to see the girls go. And we won't be together again until Christmas."

"Oh, here come the boys!" announced Eva Allen, who, with Marian Barber, had been standing a little to one side of the three girls.

At this juncture four smiling young men hurried through the crowd of young people and straight to the circle surrounding the three girls, where they were received with cries of: "We were afraid you'd be too late!" and, "Why didn't you get here earlier?"

"We're awfully sorry!" exclaimed David Nesbit. "We had to wait for Hippy. He overslept as usual. We threw as much as a shovelful of gravel against his window, but he never stirred. Finally we had to waken his family and it took all of them to waken him."

"Don't you believe what David Nesbit says," retorted Hippy. "Do you suppose I slept a wink last night knowing that the friends of my youth were about to leave me?" Hippy sniffed dolefully and buried his face in his handkerchief.

"Now, now, Hippy," protested Miriam. "If you insist on shedding crocodile tears, although I don't believe you could be sad long enough to shed even that kind, we shall feel that you are glad to get rid of us."

Jessie Graham Flower

"Never!" ejaculated Hippy fervently. "Oh, if I only had Irish Nora here to stand up for me! She wouldn't allow any one, except herself, to speak harsh and cruel words to me."

"We shan't be able to speak many more words of any kind to you," said Miriam, consulting her watch. "The train is due in ten minutes."

When Grace Harlowe and her three dear friends, Nora O'Malley, Jessica Bright and Anne Pierson, began to make history for themselves in their freshman year at Oakdale High School, none of them could possibly imagine just how dear they were to become to the hearts of the hundreds of girls who made their acquaintance in "Grace Harlowe's Plebe Year at High School." The story of their freshman year was one of manifold trials and triumphs. It was at the beginning of that year that Grace Harlowe had championed the cause of Anne Pierson, a newcomer in Oakdale. Then and there a friendship sprang up between the two girls that was destined to be life long. The repeated efforts of several malicious girls to discredit Anne in the eyes of her teachers, and her final triumph in winning the freshman prize offered to the class by Mrs. Gray, a wealthy resident of Oakdale, made the narrative one of interest and aroused a desire on the part of the reader to know more of Grace Harlowe and her friends.

In "Grace Harlowe's Sophomore Year at High School" the girl chums appeared as basketball enthusiasts. In this volume was related the efforts of Julia Crosby, a disagreeable junior, and Miriam Nesbit, a disgruntled sophomore, to disgrace Anne and wrest the basketball captaincy from Grace. Through the magnanimity of Grace Harlowe, Miriam and Julia were brought to a realization of their own faults, and in time became the faithful friends of both Anne and Grace.

During "Grace Harlowe's Junior Year at High School" the

famous sorority, the Phi Sigma Tau, was organized by the four chums for the purpose of looking after high school girls who stood in need of assistance. In that volume Eleanor Savelli, the self-willed daughter of an Italian violin virtuoso, made her appearance. The difficulties Grace and her chums encountered in trying to befriend Eleanor and her final contemptuous repudiation of their friendship made absorbing reading for those interested in following the fortunes of the Oakdale High School girls.

Their senior year was perhaps the most eventful of all. At the very beginning of the fall term the high school gymnasium was destroyed by fire. Failing to secure an appropriation from either the town or state, the four classes of the girls' high school pledged themselves to raise the amount of money required to rebuild the gymnasium. In "Grace Harlowe's Senior Year at High School" the story of the senior class bazaar, the daring theft of their hard-earned money before the bazaar had closed, and Grace Harlowe's final recovery of the stolen money under the strangest of circumstances, furnished material for a narrative of particular interest. After graduation the four chums, accompanied by their nearest and dearest friends, had spent a long and delightful summer in Europe. On returning to Oakdale the real parting of the ways had come, for Nora and Jessica had already departed for an eastern city to enter a well known conservatory of music. Marian Barber and Eva Allen were to enter Smith College the following week, Eleanor Savelli had long since sailed for Italy, and now the morning train was to bear Miriam Nesbit, Grace Harlowe and Anne Pierson to Overton, an eastern college finally decided upon by the three girls.

"Last year we left you on the station platform gazing mournfully after the train that bore *me* away from Oakdale," remarked Hippy reminiscently. "How embarrassed I felt at so

Jessie Graham Flower

much attention, and yet how sweet it was to know that you had gathered here, not to see David Nesbit, Reddy Brooks, Tom Gray or any such insignificant persons off to school, but that I, Theophilus Hippopotamus Wingate, was the object of your tender solicitations."

"I expected it," groaned David. "I don't see why we ever woke him up and dragged him along."

"As I was about to say when rudely interrupted," continued Hippy calmly, "I shall miss you, of course, but not half so much as you will miss me. I hope you will think of me, and you may write to me occasionally if it will be a satisfaction to you. I know you will not forget me. Who, having once met me, could forget?"

Hippy folded his arms across his chest and looked languishingly at the three girls.

A chorus of giggles from those grouped around the girls and derisive groans from the boys greeted Hippy's sentimental speech.

Suddenly a long, shrill whistle was heard.

"That's your train, girls," said Mr. Harlowe, who with Mrs. Harlowe, Mrs. Nesbit and Mary Pierson had drawn a little to one side while their dear ones said their last farewells to their four boy friends. The circle about the three girls closed in. The air resounded with good-byes. The last kisses and handshakes were exchanged. Reckless promises to send letters and postcards were made. Then, still surrounded, Grace, Miriam and Anne made their way to the car steps and into the train. Grace clung first to her mother then to her father. "How can I do without you?" she said over and over again. Tears stood in her gray eyes. She winked them back bravely. "I'm going to show both of you just how much I appreciate going to college by doing my very best," she whispered. Her father patted her reassuringly on the shoulder while her mother gave her a last loving kiss.

"I know you will, dear child," she said affectionately. "Remember, Grace," added her father, a suspicious mist in his own eyes, "you are not to rush headlong into things. You are to do a great deal of looking before you even make up your mind to leap."

"I'll remember, Father. Truly I will," responded Grace, her face sobering.

"All aboard! All aboard!" shouted the conductor. Those who had entered the train to say farewell left it hurriedly.

"Good-bye! Good-bye!" cried Grace, leaning out the car window.

From the platform as the train moved off, clear on the air, rose the Oakdale High School yell.

"It's in honor of us," said Grace softly. "Dear old Oakdale. I wonder if we can ever like college as well as we have high school."

Jessie Graham Flower

CHAPTER II

J. ELFREDA INTRODUCES HERSELF

For the first half hour the three girls were silent. Each sat wrapped in her own thoughts, and those thoughts centered upon the dear ones left behind. Anne, whose venture into the theatrical world had necessitated her frequent absence from home, felt the wrench less than did Grace or Miriam. Aside from their summer vacations they had never been away from their mothers for any length of time. To Grace, as she watched the landscape flit by, the thought of the ever widening distance between her and her mother was intolerable. She experienced a strong desire to bury her face in her hands and sob disconsolately, but bravely conquering the sense of loneliness that swept over her, she threw back her shoulders and sitting very straight in her seat glanced almost defiantly about her.

"Well, Grace, have you made up your mind to be resigned?" asked Miriam Nesbit. "That sudden world-defying glance that you just favored us with looks as though the victory was won."

"Miriam, you are almost a mind reader," laughed Grace. "I've been on the verge of a breakdown ever since we left Oakdale, and in this very instant I made up my mind to be brave and not cry a single tear. Look at Anne. She is as calm and unemotional as a statue."

"That's because I'm more used to being away from home," replied Anne. "Troupers are not supposed to have feelings. With them, it is here to-day and gone to-morrow."

"Yes, but you were transplanted to Oakdale soil for four years," reminded Grace.

"I know it," returned Anne reflectively. "I do feel dreadfully sad at leaving my mother and sister, too. Still, when I think that I'm actually on the way to college at last, I can't help feeling happy, too."

"Dear little Anne," smiled Grace. "College means everything to you, doesn't it? That's because you've earned every cent of your college money."

"And I'll have to earn a great deal more to see me through to graduation," added Anne soberly. "My vacations hereafter must be spent in work instead of play."

"What are you going to do to earn money during vacations, Anne?" asked Miriam rather curiously.

"I might as well confess to you girls that I'm going to do the work I can do most successfully," said Anne in a low voice. "I'm going to try to get an engagement in a stock theatrical company every summer until I graduate. I can earn far more money at that than doing clerical work. I received a long letter from Mr. Southard last week and also one from his sister. They wish me to come to New York as soon as my freshman year at college is over. Mr. Southard writes that he can get an engagement for me in a stock company. I'll have to work frightfully hard, for there will be a matinee every day as well as a regular performance every night, and I'll have a new part to study each week. But the salary will more than compensate me for my work. You know that Mary did dress-making and worked night and day to send me to high school. Of course, my five dollars a week from Mrs. Gray helped a great deal, but up to the time Mr. Southard sent for me to go to New York City to play Rosalind I didn't really think of college as at all certain. Before I left New York for Oakdale, Mr. and Miss Southard and I had a long talk. They made me see that it was right to use the talent God had given me by appearing in worthy plays. Mr. Southard pointed out the fact that I could earn enough money by playing in stock companies in the summer to put me through college and at the same time contribute liberally to my mother's support.

"The home problem was really the greatest to be solved. I felt that it wouldn't be right for me to even work my way through college and leave Mary to struggle on alone, after she had worked so hard to help me get a high school education. So the stage seemed to be my one way out after all. And when once I had definitely decided to do as Mr. Southard recommended me to do I was happier than I had been for ages."

"Anne Pierson, you quiet little mouse!" exclaimed Grace. "Why didn't you tell us all this before? You are the most provoking Anne under the sun. Here I've been worrying about you having to wait on table or do tutoring and odds and ends of work to put yourself through college, while all the time you were planning something different. We all know you're too proud to let any of your friends help you, but since you are determined to make your own way I'm glad that you have chosen the stage, after all."

"I think you are wise, Anne," agreed Miriam. "With two such people as Mr. Southard and his sister to look after you, there can be no objection to your following your profession."

"I am glad to know that you girls look at the matter in that light," replied Anne.

"Suppose we had offered any objections?" asked Grace.

"I'll answer that question," said Miriam. "Anne would have followed the path she had marked out for herself regardless of our objections. Am I right, Anne?"

"I don't know," said Anne, flushing deeply. "You have all been so good to me. I couldn't bear to displease my dearest friends, but it would be hard to give up something I knew could result in nothing save good for me." Anne paused and looked at Grace and Miriam with pleading eyes.

"Never mind, dear," comforted Grace. "We approve of you and all your works. We are not shocked because you are a genius. We are sworn advocates of the stage and only too glad to know that it has opened the way to college for you."

"Shall you let the fact that you have appeared professionally be known at Overton?" asked Miriam.

"I shall make no secret of it," returned Anne quietly, "but I won't volunteer any information concerning it."

"I wonder what our freshman year at Overton will bring us," mused Grace. "I have read so many stories about college life, and yet so far Overton seems like an unknown land that we are about to explore. From all I have heard and read, exploring freshmen find their first term at college anything but a bed of roses. They are sometimes hazed unmercifully by the upper classes, and their only salvation lies in silently standing the test. Julia Crosby says that she had all sorts of tricks played on her during her first term at Smith. Now she's a sophomore and can make life miserable for the freshmen. I am going to try to cultivate the true college spirit," concluded Grace earnestly. "College is going to mean even more to me than high school. I don't imagine it's all going to be plain sailing. I suppose, more than once, I'll wish myself back in Oakdale, but I'm going to make up my mind to take the bitter with the sweet and set everything down under the head of experience."

"To tell you the truth," Miriam said slowly, "I am not enthusiastic over college. I value it as a means of continuing my education, and I'll try to live up to college ideals, but I'm not going to let anyone walk over me or ridicule me. I'm willing 'to live and let live,' but, as Eleanor Savelli used to say when in a towering rage, 'no one can trample upon me with impunity.'"

"I wonder when we shall see Eleanor again," said Anne, smiling a little at the recollection called up by Miriam's quotation.

"That reminds me," exclaimed Grace. "I have a letter from Eleanor that I haven't opened. It came this morning just before I left the house." Fumbling in her bag, Grace drew forth a bulky looking letter, bearing a foreign postmark, and tearing open the end, drew out several closely folded sheets of thin paper covered with Eleanor's characteristic handwriting.

"Shall I read it aloud?" asked Grace.

"By all means," said Miriam with emphasis.

Grace began to read. Anne, who sat beside her, looked over her shoulder, while Miriam, who sat opposite Grace, leaned forward in order to catch every word. They were so completely occupied with their own affairs, none of them noticed that the train had stopped. Suddenly a voice shrilled out impatiently, "Is this seat engaged?" With one accord the three girls glanced up. Before them stood a tall, rather stout young woman with a full, red face, whose frowning expression was anything but reassuring.

"Yes—no, I mean," replied Grace hastily.

"I thought not," remarked the stranger complacently as she stolidly seated herself beside Miriam and deposited a traveling bag partly on the floor and partly on Grace's feet.

"These seats are ridiculously small," grumbled the stranger, bending over to jam her traveling bag more firmly into the space from which Grace had hastily withdrawn her feet. Then straightening up suddenly, her heavily plumed hat collided with the hand in which Grace held Eleanor's letter, scattering the sheets in every direction. With a little cry of concern Grace sprang to her feet and, stepping out in the aisle, began to pick them up. Having recovered the last one she turned to her seat only to find it occupied by their unwelcome fellow traveler.

"I changed seats," commented the stout girl stolidly. "I never could stand it to ride backwards."

Grace looked first at the stranger then from Miriam to Anne. Miriam looked ready for battle, while even mild little Anne glared resentfully at the rude newcomer. Grace hesitated, opened her mouth as though about to speak, then without saying a word sat down in the vacant place and began to rearrange the sheets of her letter.

"I'll finish this some other time, girls," she said briefly.

"Oh, you needn't mind me," calmly remarked the stranger. "I don't mind listening to letters. That is if they've got anything in them besides 'I write these few lines to tell you that I am well and hope you are the same.' That sort of stuff makes me sick. Goodness knows, I suppose that's the kind I'll have handed to me all year. Neither Ma nor Pa can write a letter that sounds like anything."

By this time Miriam's frown had begun to disappear, while Anne's eyes were dancing.

Grace looked at the stout girl rather curiously, an expression of new interest dawning in her eyes. "Are you going to college?" she asked.

"Well, I rather guess I am," was the quick reply. "I'll bet you girls are in the same boat with me, too. What college do you get off at?"

"Overton," answered Grace.

"Then you haven't seen the last of me," assured the stranger, "for I'm going there myself and I'd just about as soon go to darkest Africa or any other heathen place."

"Why don't you wish to go to Overton?" asked Anne.

"Because I don't want to go to college at all," was the blunt answer. "I want to go to Europe with Ma and Pa and have a good time. We have loads of money, but what good does that do me if I can't get a chance to spend it? I'd fail in all my exams if I dared, but Pa knows I'm not a wooden head, and I'd just have to try it again somewhere else. So I'll have to let well enough alone or get in deeper than I am now."

The stout girl leaned back in her seat and surveyed the trio of girls through half-closed eyes. "Where did you girls come from and what are your names?" she asked abruptly. "Partners in misery might as well get acquainted, you know."

Grace introduced her friends in turn, then said: "My name is Grace Harlowe, and we three girls live in the city of Oakdale."

"Never heard of it," yawned the girl. "It must be like Fairview, our town, not down on the map. We live there, because Ma was born there and thinks it the only place on earth, but we manage to go to New York occasionally, thank goodness. Ever been there?" she queried.

"Once or twice," smiled Miriam Nesbit.

"Great old town, isn't it?" remarked their new acquaintance. "My name is J. Elfreda Briggs. The J. stands for Josephine, but I hate it. Ma and Pa call me Fred, and that sounds pretty good to me. Say, aren't you girls about starved? I'm going to hunt the dining car and buy food. I haven't had anything to eat since eight o'clock this morning."

J. Elfreda rose hurriedly, and stumbling over her bag and Grace's feet, landed in the aisle with more speed than elegance. "You'd better come along," she advised. "They serve good meals on this train. Besides, I don't want to eat alone." With that she stalked down the aisle and into the car ahead.

"It looks as though we were to have plenty of entertainment for the rest of our journey," remarked Anne.

"I prefer not to be entertained," averred Miriam dryly. "Personally, I am far from impressed with J. Elfreda. She strikes me as being entirely too fond of her own comfort.

Now that she has vacated your seat, you had better take it, Grace, before she comes back."

Grace shook her head. "I don't dislike riding backward," she said, "if you don't mind having her sit beside you. Perhaps some one will leave the train by the time she comes back; then she will leave us."

"No such good fortune," retorted Miriam. "She prefers our society to none at all. I think her advice about luncheon isn't so bad, though. Suppose we follow it?"

Five minutes later the three girls repaired to the dining car and seated themselves at a table directly across the aisle from their new acquaintance. J. Elfreda sat toying with her knife and fork, an impatient frown on her smug face. "These people are the limit," she grumbled. "It takes forever to get anything to eat. If I'd ordered it yesterday, I'd have some hopes of getting it to-day." Then, apparently forgetting the existence of the three girls, she sat with eyes fixed hungrily on the door through which her waiter was momentarily expected to pass. By the time that the chums had given their order to another waiter, J. Elfreda's luncheon was served and she devoted herself assiduously to it. When Grace and her friends had finished luncheon, however, the stout girl still sat with elbows on the table waiting for a second order of dessert.

"Good gracious!" remarked Miriam as they made their way back to their seats. "No wonder J. Elfreda is stout! I suppose I shouldn't refer to her, even behind her back, in such familiar terms, but nothing else suits her. I'm not charitable like you, Grace. I haven't the patience to look for the good in tiresome people like her. I think she's greedy and selfish and ill-bred and I wouldn't care to live in the same house with her."

"You're a very disagreeable person, Miriam, in your own estimation," laughed Grace, "but fortunately we don't take you at your own valuation, do we, Anne?"

"Miriam's a dear," said Anne promptly. "She always pretends she's a dragon and then behaves like a lamb."

"What time is our train due at Overton?" asked Miriam, ignoring Anne's assertion.

"We are scheduled to arrive at Overton at five o'clock," answered Grace. "I wish it were five now. I'm anxious to see Overton College in broad daylight."

At this juncture J. Elfreda made her appearance and sinking into the seat declared with a yawn that she was too sleepy for any use. "I'm going to sleep," she announced. "You girls can talk if you don't make too much noise. Loud talking always keeps me awake. You may call me when we get to Overton." With these words she bent over her bag, opened it, and drew out a small down cushion. She rose in her seat, removed her hat, and, poking it into the rack above her head, sat down. Arranging her pillow to her complete satisfaction, she rested her head against it, closed her eyes and within five minutes was oblivious to the world.

The three travelers obligingly lowered their voices, conversing in low tones, as the train whirled them toward their destination. Their hearts were with those they had left, and as the afternoon began to wane, one by one they fell silent and became wrapped in their own thoughts. Grace was already beginning to experience a dreadful feeling of depression, which she knew to be homesickness. It was just the time in the afternoon when she and her mother usually sat on their wide, shady porch, talking or reading as they waited for her father to come home to dinner, and a lump rose in her throat as she thought sadly of how long it would be before she saw her dear ones again.

Far from being homesick, self-reliant Miriam was calmly speculating as to what college would bring her, while Anne, who had quite forgotten her own problems, sat eyeing Grace affectionately and wondering how soon her friend would make her personality felt in the little world which she was about to enter. And J. Elfreda Briggs, of Fairview, slept peacefully on.

CHAPTER III

FIRST IMPRESSIONS

"Overton! Overton!" was the call that echoed through the car. After handing down the hats of her friends, Grace reached to the rack above her head for her broad brimmed panama hat. Obeying a sudden kindly impulse, she carefully deposited J. Elfreda's hat in the sleeping girl's lap, touched her on the shoulder and said, "Wake up, Miss Briggs. We are nearing Overton."

J. Elfreda sleepily opened her eyes at the gentle touch, saying drowsily, "Let me know when the train stops." Then closed her eyes again.

Miriam shrugged her shoulders with a gesture that signified, "Let her alone. Don't bother with her."

At that moment the train stopped with a jolt that caused the sleeper to awake in earnest. She looked stupidly about, yawned repeatedly, then catching a glimpse of a number of girls on the station platform, clad in white and light colored gowns, she became galvanized into action, and pinning on her hat began quickly to gather up her luggage. "Good-bye," she said indifferently. "I'll probably see you later." Then, rapidly elbowing her way down the aisle she disappeared through the open door, leaving the chums to make their way more slowly out of the car. As they stepped from the car to the station platform Grace caught sight of her at the far end of the station in conversation with a tall auburn-haired girl and a short dark one. A moment later she saw the three walk off together.

"J. Elfreda found friends quickly," remarked Anne, who had also noticed the stout girl's warm reception by the two girls. "I wonder what we had better do first. What is the name of the hotel where we are to stop?"

"The Tourraine," replied Miriam.

The newcomers looked eagerly about them at the groups of daintily gowned girls who were joyously greeting their friends as they stepped from the train.

"I had no idea there were so many Overton girls on the train," remarked Grace in surprise. "The majority of them seem to have friends here, too. I wonder which way we'd better go."

"By the nods and becks and wreathed smiles with which those girls over there are favoring us, I imagine that we have been discovered," announced Miriam, rather sarcastically.

Grace and Anne glanced quickly toward the girls indicated by Miriam. A tall, thin, fair-haired girl with cold gray-blue eyes and a generally supercilious air occupied the center of the group. She was talking rapidly and her remarks were eliciting considerable laughter. Amused glances, half friendly, half critical, were being leveled at the Oakdale trio of chums.

Grace flushed in half angry embarrassment, Anne merely

smiled to herself, while Miriam's most forbidding scowl wrinkled her smooth forehead.

"I think we had better inquire the way to our hotel and leave here as soon as possible," Grace said slowly. A sudden feeling of disappointment had suddenly taken possession of her. She had always supposed that in every college new girls were met and welcomed by the upper classes of students. Yet now that they had actually arrived no one had come forward to exchange even a friendly greeting with them.

"Well, if this is an exhibition of the true college spirit, deliver me from college," grumbled Miriam. "I must say—"

Miriam's denunciation against college was never finished, for at that juncture a soft voice said, "Welcome to Overton." Turning simultaneously the three girls saw standing before them a young woman of medium height. Her hand was extended, and she was smiling in a sweet, friendly fashion that warmed the hearts of the disappointed freshmen. She wore a tailored frock of white linen, white buckskin walking shoes that revealed a glimpse of silken ankles, and carried a white linen parasol that matched her gown. She was bareheaded, and in the late afternoon her wavy brown hair seemed touched with gold.

"I am so glad to meet you!" exclaimed the pretty girl. "You are freshmen, of course. If you will tell me your names I'll introduce you to some of the girls. Then we will see about escorting you safely to your boarding place. Have you taken your examinations yet?"

"No," replied Miriam. "We have that ordeal before us." Her face relaxed under the friendly courtesy accorded to them by this attractive stranger. She then introduced Grace and Anne. Their new acquaintance shook hands with the two girls, then said gayly, "Now tell me your name."

Miriam complied with the request, then stated that through a friend of her mother's they had engaged a suite of rooms at the Tourraine, an apartment hotel in Overton, until their fate should be decided.

"The Tourraine is the nicest hotel in Overton," stated Mabel. "I am always in the seventh heaven of delight whenever I am fortunate enough to be invited to dine there."

"Then come and dine with us to-night," invited Miriam.

Mabel Ashe shook her head. "It's very nice in you," she said gravely, "but not to-night. Really, I am awfully stupid. I haven't told you my name. It is Mabel Ashe. I am a junior and pledged to pilot bewildered freshmen to havens of rest and safety."

"Do you consider freshmen impossible creatures?" asked Anne Pierson, her eyes twinkling.

The young woman laughed merrily. "Oh, no," she replied. "You must remember that they are the raw material that makes good upper classmen. It takes a whole year to mould them into shape—that is, some of them. Now, come with me and I'll see that you meet some of the upper class girls."

As they were about to accompany their new acquaintance down the platform, a tall, fair-haired girl walked toward them followed by the others upon whom Miriam had commented. "Wait a minute, Mabel," she called. "I've been trying to get hold of you all afternoon."

"You're just in time, Beatrice," returned Mabel Ashe. "I wish you to meet Miss Harlowe, Miss Nesbit, and Miss Pierson, all of Oakdale. Girls, this is Miss Alden, also of the junior class."

Beatrice Alden smiled condescendingly, and shook hands in a somewhat bored fashion with the three girls. "Pleased to meet you," she drawled. "Hope you'll be good little freshmen this year and make no trouble for your elders."

"We shall try to mind our own affairs, and trust to other people to do the same," flashed Miriam, eyeing the other girl steadily.

Grace looked at her friend in surprise. What had caused Miriam to answer in such fashion? There was an almost imperceptible lull in the conversation, then Mabel Ashe introduced the other girls. "Now we will see about your trunks, and then perhaps you would like to walk up to the college," she said briskly. "It isn't far from here. Some of the girls prefer to ride in the bus, but I always walk. I can show you some of the places of interest as we go."

"Come over here, Mabel, dear," commanded Beatrice Alden, who had moved a little to one side of the group. Mabel excused herself to her charges, and looking a little annoyed, obeyed the summons. Beatrice talked rapidly for a moment in coaxing tones, but Mabel shook her head. Grace, who stood nearest to them, heard her say, "I'd love to go, Bee, and its awfully nice in you to think of me. I'll go to-morrow, but I can't leave these poor stranded freshmen to their own homesick thoughts to-day. You know just how we felt when we landed high and dry in this town without any one to care whether we survived or perished."

"If you won't go to-day, then don't trouble about it at all," snapped Beatrice. "I know plenty of girls who will be only too glad to accept my invitation, but I asked you first, and I

Jessie Graham Flower

think you ought to remember it. You know I like you better than any other girl in college."

"You know I appreciate your friendship, Bee," returned Mabel, "but truly I wish you cared more for other girls, too. There are plenty of girls here who need friends like you."

"Yes, but I don't like them," snapped Beatrice. "I'm not going to make a martyr of myself to please any one. My mother is very particular about my associates at Overton, and I don't intend to waste my time trying to make things pleasant for the stupid, uninteresting girls of this college. I did not come to Overton to take a course in doing settlement work. I came here to have a good time, and incidentally to study a little."

"Now, now, Bee, don't try to make me believe you haven't just as much college spirit as the rest of us," admonished Mabel in a low tone. "Don't be cross because I can't go to-day. Come with me, instead, and help look after these verdant freshmen. There was a positive army of them who got off the train."

Without replying Beatrice turned and walked sulkily away toward the other end of the platform. Mabel looked after her with a half frown.

"I am afraid we are causing you considerable inconvenience," demurred Grace. "Please do not deprive yourself of any pleasure on our account."

"Nonsense," smiled Mabel. "I am not depriving myself of any pleasure. Oh, there goes one of my best friends!" Putting her hands to her mouth she called, "Frances!" A tall slender girl, with serious brown eyes and dark hair, who was leisurely crossing the station platform, stopped short, glanced in the direction of the sound, then espying Mabel hurried toward her.

"Good old Frances," beamed Mabel. "You heard me calling and came on the run, didn't you? This is the noblest junior of them all, my dear freshmen. Her name is Frances Veronica Marlton. Doesn't that sound like the heroine's name in one of the six best sellers?" Mabel introduced the three girls in turn. "Now let us be on our way," she commanded, looking up and down the station platform at the fast dissolving groups of girls. "I don't see any more stray lambs. I think the committee appointed to meet the freshmen has fulfilled its mission. And now for your hotel. It is past dinner time and I know you are hungry and anxious to rest."

Picking up Grace's bag she led the way through the station followed by Grace and Miriam. Anne walked behind them with Frances Marlton. The little company set off down the main street of the college town at a swinging pace. It was a wide, beautiful street, shaded by tall maples. The houses that lined it were for the most part old-fashioned and the wayfarers caught alluring glimpses of green lawns dotted with flower beds as they walked along.

"It makes me think of High School Street in Oakdale!" Grace exclaimed. "If ever I feel that I'm going to be homesick, I'll just walk down this street and make believe that I'm at home! That will be the surest cure for the blues, if I get them."

Mabel Ashe, who was now walking between Grace and Miriam, looked at Grace rather speculatively. "You won't get them," she predicted. "You'll have so many other things to think of, you won't think of yourself at all. Here we are at the college campus. Over there is Overton Hall."

The eyes of the newcomers were at once focussed on the stately gray stone building that stood in the center of a wide stretch of green campus, shaded by great trees. At various points of the campus were situated smaller buildings which Mabel Ashe pointed out as Science Hall, the gymnasium, laboratory, library and chapel. In Overton Hall, Mabel explained, were situated certain recitation rooms, the offices of the president, the dean and other officials of the college. Around the campus were the various houses in which the more fortunate of the hundreds of students lived. It was very desirable to secure a room in one of these houses, but somewhat expensive and not always easy to do. Rooms were sometimes spoken for a whole year in advance.

"Do you room on the campus?" asked Grace.

"Yes," replied Mabel. "I live at Holland House. I was fortunate enough to have a friend graduate from here and will me her room. I entered Overton the autumn following her graduation."

"One of our Oakdale girls is a junior here," remarked Grace. "Her name is Constance Fuller. She graduated from high school when we were sophomores. We do not know her very well, and had quite forgotten she was here. This afternoon on the train, Anne, who never forgets either faces or names, suddenly announced the fact. I wonder if she has arrived yet. We came early, I believe, but that is because we are obliged to take the entrance examinations."

"Now I know why the name, Oakdale, seemed so familiar!" exclaimed Mabel Ashe. "I have heard Constance mention it. She is one of my best friends. Does she know that you are to be here?"

"No," replied Grace. "We haven't seen her this summer. We were away from Oakdale." Grace did not wish to mention their trip to Europe, fearing their companion might think her unduly anxious to boast. One of the things against which Julia Crosby, her old time Oakdale friend, and a senior in Smith College, had cautioned her, was boasting. "Avoid all appearance of being your own press agent," Julia had humorously advised. "If you don't you'll be a marked girl for the whole four years of your college career. The meek and modest violet is a glowing example for erring freshmen."

"I'll remember, Julia," Grace had promised, and she now resolved that she would think twice before speaking once, whatever the occasion might be.

"Constance has not arrived yet," said Mabel. "I heard her roommate say this morning that she expected her to-morrow. She rooms at Holland House, too. I shall tell her about you the moment I see her. This is the Tourraine," she announced, pausing before a handsome sandstone building and leading the way up the steps that led to the broad veranda, gay with porch boxes of flowers and shaded by awnings.

"Won't you come up to our rooms?" asked Miriam.

"Not to-night, thank you," replied Mabel. "Frances and I will be over bright and early to-morrow morning to pilot you to the college. Then you can find out about the examinations. Good-night and pleasant dreams." Extending their hands in turn to the three girls and nodding a last smiling adieu, the two courteous juniors left them on the hotel veranda.

"I must admit that I have been agreeably disappointed," said Miriam Nesbit as the three girls stood for a moment before entering the hotel to watch the retreating backs of their new acquaintances.

"I, too," replied Grace. "I can't begin to tell you how dejected I felt while we stood there on the station platform and no one

Jessie Graham Flower

came near us or appeared to be aware of our existence."

"It was enough to discourage the most optimistic freshman," averred Anne.

"I wonder who J. Elfreda Briggs's friends were," commented Miriam. "She never said a word about knowing any one at Overton. I imagine she is a thoroughly selfish girl, and the less I see of her in college the better pleased I shall be."

As their suite of rooms had been engaged in advance it needed but a word to the clerk on Grace's part, then each girl in turn registered and they were conducted to their suite.

"This suite seems to be supplied with all the comforts of home," observed Miriam, looking about her with satisfaction. "I am thankful to have reached a haven of rest where I can bathe my grimy face and hands."

"So am I," echoed Grace, setting down her suit case and sinking into an easy chair with a tired sigh. "I am starved, too. Let us lose no time in getting ready for dinner. After dinner we can rest."

For the next half hour the travelers were busily engaged in removing the dust of their journey and attiring themselves in the dainty summer frocks which they had taken thought to pack in their suit cases.

"I'm ready," announced Grace at last, as she poked a rebellious lock of hair into place, and viewed herself in the mirror.

"So am I," echoed Anne.

"And I," from Miriam. "Why not walk down stairs? We are

on the second floor, and I never ride in an elevator when I can avoid doing so."

The trio descended the stairs and made their way to the dining room, where they were conducted to a table near an open window which looked out on a shady side porch.

"So far I haven't been imbued with what one might call college atmosphere," remarked Miriam, after the dinner had been ordered and the waiter had hurried off to attend to their wants.

"I felt a certain amount of enthusiasm while those upper class girls were with us, but it has vanished," said Anne. "I am just a professional staying at a hotel."

"I imagine we won't begin to regard ourselves as being a part of Overton College until after we have tried our examinations and found an abiding place in some one of the college houses. I hope we shall be able to get into a campus house. I have always understood that it is ever so much nicer to be on the campus. We really should have made arrangements before-hand, and if we hadn't waited until the last moment to decide to what college we wished to go we might be cosily settled now."

"Perhaps we are only fulfilling our destiny," smiled Miriam Nesbit.

"Perhaps," agreed Grace in a doubtful tone. "Once we are in our hall or boarding house I dare say we will shake off this feeling of constraint and become genuine Overtonites."

"Had we better study to-night?" inquired Grace as they made their way from the hotel dining room.

"I think it would be a wise proceeding," agreed Miriam. "I want to go over my French verbs."

"So do I," echoed Grace. "Let's study until ten, and then go straight to bed."

Ten o'clock stretched well toward eleven before Grace put down her text book with a tired little sigh and declared herself too sleepy for further study.

It had been arranged that Miriam should occupy the one room of the suite while Grace and Anne were to share the other, which had two beds. The long journey by rail had tired the travelers far more than they would admit. For a few moments, after retiring, conversation flourished between the two rooms, then died away in indistinct murmurs, and the prospective Overton freshmen slept peacefully as though safe in their Oakdale homes.

CHAPTER IV

MIRIAM'S UNWELCOME SURPRISE

The two days that followed were busy ones for Grace, Anne and Miriam. The morning after their arrival Mabel Ashe and Frances Marlton appeared at half-past eight o'clock to conduct them to Overton Hall. There they registered and were then sent to the room where the examination in French was to be held. Examinations in the other required subjects followed in rapid succession and it was Friday before they had settled themselves in Wayne Hall, the house in which they were to live as students of Overton College.

Wayne Hall was a substantial four-story brick house, just a block from the campus. It was looked upon as a strictly freshman house, but occasionally sophomores lived there, as the rooms were well-furnished and the matron, Mrs. Elwood, had a reputation for looking out for the welfare of her girls.

To their delight Grace and Anne had been allowed to room together, while Miriam had by lucky chance secured a room to herself across the hall.

"If that poor little yellow-haired freshman hadn't failed in all her examinations I shouldn't be rooming alone," said Miriam rather soberly as she dived into the depths of the now almost

Jessie Graham Flower

emptied trunk.

"Did you meet her?" asked Grace, who, seated on the bed beside Anne, watched Miriam's unpacking with interested eyes.

"No," replied Miriam. "One of the freshmen at the table told me about her. She said that the poor girl cried all day yesterday and last night. She didn't dare write her father, who, it seems, is very severe, that she had failed. He won't know she's coming until she reaches home."

"What a pity," said Anne sympathetically. "It must be dreadful to fail and know that one must face not only the humility of the failure, but the displeasure of one's family too."

"If I had failed in my examinations neither Father nor Mother would have said one reproachful word," said Grace.

"Of course I'm sorry for her," said Miriam, "but considering the fact that I am now going to room alone, I shall write to Mother and ask her to send me the money to furnish this room as I please. I'd like to have a davenport bed, and I want a chiffonier and a dressing table to match. There's room here for a piano, too. I'll have it over in this corner and then I'll—"

Rap, rap, rap! sounded on the door.

"Come in," called Miriam frowning at the interruption.

The door opened to admit Mrs. Elwood, and following in her wake, laden with a bag and two suit cases, her hat pushed over her eyes, a half-suspicious, half-belligerent expression on her face, was J. Elfreda Briggs.

"Well I never!" she gasped in astonishment, dropping her belongings in a heap on the floor and making a dive for the nearest chair. "You're the last people I ever expected to see. Where have you been, anyway? I supposed you'd all flunked in your exams, given up the job, and gone back to Glendale, Hilldale—what's the name of that dale you hail from?"

"Oakdale," supplemented Anne slyly.

"Yes, that's it. Oakdale. Foolish name for a town, isn't it?"

During this outburst Mrs. Elwood had stood silent, looking at J. Elfreda with doubtful eyes. Now she said apologetically, "I'm very sorry, Miss Nesbit, but could you—that is—would you mind having a roommate after all? My sister, Mrs. Arnold, who manages Ralston House just down the street from here, took Miss Briggs because she thought one of her girls wasn't coming back. Now the girl is here and she has no place for Miss Briggs. Of course, if you insist on not having a roommate, my sister and I will see that Miss Briggs secures a room in one of the other college houses." Mrs. Elwood paused and looked questioningly at Miriam, who stood silent, an inscrutable expression on her face. Grace and Anne, remembering Miriam's dislike for the stout girl, wondered what her answer would be.

The settling of the question was not left to Miriam, for during the brief silence that followed Mrs. Elwood's depre-catory speech J. Elfreda had been making a comprehensive survey of her surroundings. "It's all right, Mrs. Elwood," she drawled. "Don't worry about me. I like this room and I guess I can get along with Miss Nesbit. You may telephone the expressman to have my trunk sent here. I'm not going back to Ralston House with you. I'm too tired. I'm going to stay here."

Mrs. Elwood looked appealingly at Miriam, as though mutely trying to apologize for J. Elfreda's disregard for the rights of others.

Miriam's straight black brows drew together. She stared at their unwelcome guest with a look that caused a slow flush to rise to the stout girl's face. Suddenly her face relaxed into a smile of intense amusement, and extending her hand to J. Elfreda, she said, "You are welcome to half this room, if you care to stay."

"Well, I never!" exclaimed the other girl for the second time, as she shook the proffered hand. "Honestly, I thought you were going to give me a regular freeze out. You looked like a thunder cloud for a minute. I expect it won't be all sunshine around here, this year, for I'm used to having things go my way, and I guess you are, too."

"Then perhaps learning to defer to each other will be good practice for both of us," suggested Miriam.

"Perhaps it will, but I doubt if we ever practise it," was the discouraging retort.

"I'll notify my sister that you are to be here, Miss Briggs," broke in Mrs. Elwood. "Then I'll see that this room is made ready for two. Thank you, Miss Nesbit." She turned gratefully to Miriam.

"All right," answered J. Elfreda indifferently. "You can fix it up if you want to, but I warn you that I'll probably buy my own furniture and throw out all this." She waved a comprehensive hand at the despised furniture.

"You are at liberty to make whatever changes you wish," Mrs. Elwood responded rather stiffly, and without further remark left the room.

"She didn't like my remark about her furniture," commented the stout girl, "but I'm not worrying about it. It's funny that I should run into you girls, though. What kind of a time have you been having here, and did you pass all your exams?"

The girls replied in the affirmative, then Grace asked the same question of Elfreda.

"Of course," was the laconic answer. "I had a tutor all summer, besides I told you on the train that I wasn't a wooden head."

"Where did you stay until you went to Ralston House?" asked Anne. "We saw you go away from the station with two girls when you left the train, and we've seen you twice at a distance during examinations, but this is the first chance we've had to talk with you."

J. Elfreda stared at Anne, her eyes narrowing.

"Do you want to know just what happened to me?" she asked slowly. "Well, I'll tell you three girls about it, because I've got to tell some one and I don't believe you'll spread the story."

"We won't tell anyone," promised Grace.

"How about you two?" asked the stout girl.

"I'll answer for both of us," smiled Anne.

"All right then, I'll tell you. Now remember, you've promised."

The girls nodded.

"Well, it was this way," began Elfreda. "When I left the train I hadn't gone six steps until two girls walked up to me and asked if I were a freshman. They said they were on the committee to meet and look after the girls who were entering college for the first time. I said that was very kind of them and asked them to show me the way to Ralston House. They picked up my suit cases and we started out. They asked me my name and all sorts of questions and I told them a little about myself," continued the stout girl pompously. "They seemed quite impressed, too. Then one of them said she thought I had better see the registrar before going to Ralston House, for the registrar would be anxious to meet me. They both said I was quite different from the rest of the new girls, and made such a lot of fuss over me that I invited them into that little shop across from the station to have ice cream."

"And then?" asked Miriam.

"Then," said J. Elfreda impressively, "after they had had two sundaes apiece, at my expense, they played a mean trick on me. They took me into a big building a little further down the street, down a long hall, and left me sitting on a seat outside what I supposed was the registrar's office. They said I must wait there and the registrar's clerk would come out and conduct me to the registrar. They said that it was against the rules to walk into the office and that it was the business of the clerk to come out every half hour and conduct any one who was waiting into the registrar's private office.

"Well, I sat there and sat there. It made me think of when I was a kiddie and used to watch the cuckoo clock to see the bird come out. But there wasn't even a bird came out of that door," continued Elfreda gloomily. "People passed up and down the hall, and every once in a while a man would walk right into the place without knocking, or seeing the clerk, or anything else.

"After I had sat there for at least two hours, I made up my mind to go in even if I were ordered out the next minute. I marched up to the door and opened it and walked into the office. There was no one in sight but a young woman who was putting on her hat. 'Where's the registrar?' I asked. 'He hasn't been here to-day,' she said. 'I thought the registrar was a woman,' I said. She seemed surprised at that and asked what made me think so. I said that two of the students had told me so. Then she looked at me in the queerest way and began to smile. 'Do you want to see the registrar of Overton College?' she asked. 'Of course I do,' I said, for I began to suspect that something was wrong. Then she stopped smiling and said it was too bad, but whoever had sent me there had played a trick on me and brought me to the office of the Register of Deeds. Instead of Overton Hall I was in the county court house. Now can you beat it?" finished Elfreda slangily.

"I should say not," cried Grace indignantly. "I think it was contemptible in them to accept your hospitality and then treat you in that fashion. No really nice girl would do any such thing, even in fun."

"I should say not," sympathized Miriam, forgetting that she did not yearn for J. Elfreda as a roommate. "What did you do after you discovered your mistake?"

"I left the Register's office, his deeds, and all the rest of that building in pretty short order," continued Elfreda. "When I reached the street I went straight back to the station and hired a carriage to take me to Ralston House. Mrs. Arnold gave me my supper even though it was late, and the next day I saw the registrar in earnest. I told her the whole story and described the girls. I didn't know their names, but she said she thought she knew who they were from the description. So I suppose she'll send for me before long to identify them."

"But you're not going to?" questioned Grace in astonishment.

"Why not?" returned the stout girl calmly. "Do you think I'll let slip a chance to get even with them? I guess not."

"But this will be carried to the dean and they will be severely reprimanded and the whole college will know it," expostulated Grace.

"Well, the whole college should know it," stoutly contended Elfreda. "I'll show those two smart young women that I'm not as green as I appear to be."

Grace was on the verge of saying that J. Elfreda would have shown more wisdom by keeping silent, but suddenly checked herself. She had no right to criticize J. Elfreda's motives. To her the bare idea of telling tales was abhorrent, while this girl gloried in the fact that she had exposed those who annoyed her.

"I'm sorry you told the registrar," she said slowly. "Perhaps in the rush of business she'll forget about it."

"She'd better not," threatened Elfreda, "or she'll hear it from me. When it comes to getting even, I never relent. I'm just like Pa in that respect. However, let's change the subject. Now that I'm here, show me where I can put my clothes," she added, addressing Miriam. "Do you keep your things in order? I never do. The morning I left home Ma said she felt sorry for my future roommate."

Elfreda kept up a brisk monologue as she opened one of her

suit cases and began hauling out its contents. Miriam made a gesture of hopeless resignation behind the stout girl's back.

"I must go to my room and get ready for dinner," said Grace, her eyes dancing. "Coming, Anne?"

Anne nodded and the two girls beat a hasty retreat. Elfreda's calm manner of appropriating things and Miriam's resigned air were too much for them. Once inside their room they gave way to uncontrolled merriment.

"I knew I'd laugh if I stayed there another second," confessed Anne. "Poor Miriam. I heartily agree with Ma, don't you?"

"Yes," smiled Grace. Then, her face sobering, she added, "I am afraid she is laying up trouble for herself. I wish she hadn't told."

CHAPTER V

AN INTERRUPTED STUDY HOUR

The first two weeks at Overton glided by with amazing swiftness. There was so much to be done in the way of arranging one's recitations, buying or renting one's books and accustoming one's self to the routine of college life that Grace and her friends could scarcely spare the time to write their home letters. There were twenty-four girls at Wayne Hall. With the exception of four sophomores the house was given up to freshmen. Grace thought them all delightful, and in her whole-souled, generous fashion made capital of their virtues and remained blind to their shortcomings. There had been a number of jolly gatherings in Mrs. Elwood's living room, at which quantities of fudge and penuchi were made and eaten and mere acquaintances became fast friends.

The week following their arrival a dance had been given in the gymnasium in honor of the freshmen. The whole college had turned out at this strictly informal affair, and the upper class girls had taken particular pains to see that the freshmen were provided with partners and had a good time generally. At this dance the three Oakdale friends had felt more at home than at any other time since entering Overton. In the first place, Mabel Ashe, Frances Marlton and Constance King had come over to Wayne Hall in a body on the evening before the dance and offered themselves as escorts. Furthermore, the scores of happy, laughing girls gliding over the gymnasium floor to the music of a three-piece orchestra reminded Grace of the school dances in her own home town. J. Elfreda had also been escorted to the hop by Virginia Gaines, one of the sophomores at Wayne Hall, who had a great respect for the stout girl's money, and it was a secret relief to Grace that she had not been left out.

Now the dance was a thing of the past, and nothing was in sight in the way of entertainment except the reception and dance given by the sophomores to the freshmen. This was a yearly event, and meant more to the freshmen than almost any other class celebration, for the sophomores, having thrown off freshman shackles, took a lively hand in the affairs of the members of the entering class. It was sophomores who under pretense of sympathetic interest wormed out of unsuspecting freshmen their inmost secrets and gleefully spread them abroad among the upper classes. It was also the sophomores who were the most active in enforcing the standard that erring freshmen were supposed to live up to. The junior and senior classes as a rule allowed their sophomore sisters to regulate the conduct of the newcomers at Overton, only stepping in to interfere in extreme cases.

Grace and her friends had met nearly all the members of the sophomore class at the freshman dance, but in reality they had very few acquaintances among them that bade fair to become their friends.

"I don't suppose we'll have the honor of being escorted to the reception by sophomores," remarked Grace several evenings before the event, as she and Miriam strolled out of the dining room. "We'll have to go in a crowd by ourselves and look as though we enjoyed it."

Jessie Graham Flower

"Why not stay at home?" yawned Miriam. "I'm not as over-awed at the idea of this affair as I might be."

"No," replied Grace, shaking her head. "It wouldn't do. We ought to go. The dance is to be given in honor of the fresh-men, and it's their duty to turn out and make it a success. Are you going to study your Livy to-night, Miriam?"

"If I can," replied Miriam grimly. "It depends on what my talkative roommate does. If she elects to give me another instalment of the story of her life before she came here, Livy won't stand much chance. We have progressed as far as her twelfth year, and I was just on the point of learning how she survived scarlet fever when the doctor didn't expect her to live, last night, when she happened to remember that she hadn't looked at her history lesson and I was mercifully spared further torture."

"Poor Miriam," laughed Grace. "But you could have said you didn't want her the day Mrs. Elwood brought her here. What made you decide to let her stay? I saw by your face something interesting was going on in your mind."

Miriam looked reflectively at Grace. "I don't know I'm sure just why I let her stay. It wasn't because I wished to please Mrs. Elwood, though she is so nice with all of us. I had a curious feeling that I ought to take J. Elfreda in hand. If it had been you whose room she invaded you wouldn't have hesitated even for a second. Ever since you and I settled our differences back in our high school days I've always held you up to myself as an example. Now, honestly, Grace, you would have taken her in without a murmur, wouldn't you?"

"Ye-e-s," said Grace slowly, her face flushing. "I would have said she might stay, I think. But, Miriam, you mustn't hold me up as an example. I couldn't be more generous and loyal and broadminded than you."

"In the words of J. Elfreda, 'let's change the subject,'" said Miriam hastily. "Where's Anne?"

"Anne is out visiting the humblest freshman of them all," replied Grace. "Her name is Ruth Denton. Anne singled her out in English the other day, scraped acquaintance with her, and found that she has a room in an old house in the suburbs of the town. She takes care of her own room, boards herself and does any kind of mending she can get to do from the girls to help her pay her way through college. Anne only found her last week, but I have promised to go to see her, too, and I want you to go with me."

They had paused at the door of Miriam's room. Her hand on the door, she said earnestly, "I'd love to go, Grace. I might know that you and Anne couldn't rest without championing some one's cause."

"What about you and J. Elfreda?" questioned Grace slyly.

"Oh, that's different," retorted Miriam. Opening the door she glanced about the room. Her own side was in perfect order, but J. Elfreda's half looked as though it had been visited by a cyclone. The cover of her couch bed was pulled askew and the sofa pillows ornamented the floor. Shoes and stockings were scattered about in wild disorder. Her dressing table looked as though the contents had been stirred up and deposited in a heap in the center. From the top drawer of the chiffonier protruded a hand-embroidered collar, and a long black silk tie hung down the middle of the piece of furniture, giving it the effect of being draped in mourning.

Catching sight of this Grace pointed to it, laughing. "It looks as though she were in mourning, doesn't it?"

"For her sins, yes," replied Miriam grimly. "Isn't this room a mess, though? I've picked up her things ever so many times, but I'm tired of it. Come in here to-night, Grace. I want to see how it seems to have my dearest friend in my room, all to myself."

"All right," laughed Grace. "I'll get my books."

Five minutes later she reappeared and, cosily establishing herself in the Morris chair that Miriam insisted she should occupy, the girls began their work. For the time being silence reigned, broken only by the sound of turning leaves or an occasional question on the part of one or the other of the two. Finally Miriam closed her book triumphantly. "That's done," she exulted. "Now for my English."

"I wish I was through with this," sighed Grace, eyeing her Livy with disfavor. "I never do learn my lessons quickly. I have to study ever so much harder than you and Anne. Now, if it were basketball, then everything would be lovely. Still, you're a champion player, too, Miriam, so you've more than your share of accomplishments. Anne, too, excites my envy and admiration. She can act and stand first in her classes, too, while I have to work like mad to keep up in my classes and am not a star in anything. Perhaps during this year I shall develop some new talent of which no one suspects me. It won't be for study, that's sure."

Miriam smiled to herself, but said nothing. She knew that Grace already possessed a talent for making friends and an ability to see not only her own way clearly, but to smooth the pathway of those weaker than herself that was little short of marvelous. She knew, too, that before the end of the school year Grace's remarkable personality was sure to make itself felt among her fellow students.

"What are you smiling to yourself about, Miriam?" demanded Grace.

But at this juncture the door was burst violently open and J. Elfreda Briggs dashed into the room, threw herself face downward on her disordered bed and gave way to a long, anguished wail.

CHAPTER VI

A DISTURBING NOTE

Miriam and Grace sprang to their feet, regarding the sobbing, moaning girl in blank amazement.

"What on earth is the matter, Elfreda," said Miriam.

The answer was another long wail that made the girls glance apprehensively toward the door.

"She'll have to be more quiet," said Grace, "or else every girl in the house will hear her and come in to inquire what has happened." Going over to the couch, she knelt beside Elfreda and said almost sharply, "Elfreda, stop crying at once. Do you want all the girls in the house to hear you?"

"I don't care," was the discouraging answer, but in a lower tone, nevertheless; but she continued to sob heart-brokenly.

"Tell me about it, Elfreda," said Grace more gently, taking one of the girl's limp hands in hers. "Something dreadful must have happened. Have you had bad news from home?"

"No-o-o," gasped the stout girl. "It's the sophomores. I can't go to the reception. They won't let me." Her sobs burst forth afresh.

Grace rose from her knees, casting a puzzled glance toward Miriam. "I wonder what she means." Then placing her hands on Elfreda's shoulders she raised her to a sitting position on the couch and dropping down beside her put one arm over her shoulder. Miriam promptly sat down on the other side, and being thus supported and bolstered by their sympathetic arms, Elfreda gulped, gurgled, sighed and then said with quivering lips, "I wish I had taken your advice, Grace."

"About what?" asked Grace. Then, the same idea occurring to them simultaneously, Miriam and Grace exchanged dismayed glances. Elfreda had come to grief through reporting the two mischievous sophomores to the registrar.

"About telling the registrar," faltered Elfreda, unrolling her handkerchief from the ball into which she had rolled it and wiping her eyes.

"I'm so sorry," Grace said with quick sympathy.

"You're not half so sorry as I am," was the tearful retort. "I'll write to Pa and Ma that I want to go home next week. They'll make a fuss, but they'll send for me."

"Are your father and mother very anxious that you should stay here?" asked Miriam.

"A good deal more anxious than I am," responded Elfreda. "Ma picked out Overton for me long before I left high school. She thinks it the only college going and so does Pa."

"Then, of course, they will be disappointed if you go home without even trying to like college."

"I can't help that," whined Elfreda. "I can't stay here and have the whole college down on me, and that's what will happen. You girls don't know how serious it is."

"I think you had better begin at the beginning and tell us everything," suggested Miriam, a trifle impatiently.

"It was the night of the freshman hop that they began to be so mean," burst forth Elfreda. "I went to the dance with Virginia Gaines, that sophomore who sits next to me at the table."

"Who do you mean by 'they'?" asked Grace.

"Alberta Wicks, the tall red-haired girl, and Mary Hampton, the short dark one. They took me over to the court house," was the prompt answer. "The registrar reported them to the dean. She sent for them the very day of the dance and gave them an awful talking to and they were perfectly furious with me for telling. They found out that Virginia had invited me to the dance, and told her the whole story. She was horrid to me, and hardly spoke to me all the way to the gymnasium or coming home. They must have told every girl I know, for not one of them would come near me. I had to sit around all evening, for I didn't know half a dozen girls, and you three were too busy to look at me. You can imagine I had a slow old time, and I was glad to get home. Maybe you noticed I wasn't very talkative that night after we got back to the house, Miriam?"

Miriam nodded.

"After that, Virginia and I didn't speak. I didn't care much anyhow, for she made me tired," continued Elfreda. "But when the talk about the sophomore reception began I saw that they were going to hand me a whole block of ice. It was bad enough to have them cut me in classes and on the street, but I had set my heart on the reception and wrote to Ma to send me a new dress. It came yesterday. It's pale blue with pearl trimmings and it's a dream. But what good does it do me now?" She stared gloomily ahead of her for an instant, then went on:

"Of course, I knew no one would invite me, but I made up my mind to ask if I could go along with you folks, and I was going to ask you to-night, when just before dinner a boy came here with this note." From the inside of her white silk blouse she drew forth an envelope addressed to "Miss J. Elfreda Briggs." Handing it to Grace she said briefly: "Read it."

Grace drew a sheet of paper from the envelope, unfolded it and read:

"Miss Briggs:

"In reporting to the registrar two members of the sophomore class you have offended not merely those members, but the class as well. You have shown yourself so entirely incapable of understanding the first principles of honor, that Overton would be much better off without you. Do not attempt to attend the sophomore reception. If you are wise you will leave Overton and enter some other college.

"The Sophomore Class."

Grace handed the note to Miriam.

"What do you think of it?" asked Miriam, looking up from the last line.

"I don't know what to think," rejoined Grace. "It doesn't seem as though a whole class would rise up to settle what is really a personal affair. Even though the sophomores are angry, they have no right to threaten Elfreda and advise her to leave Overton. If the dean knew of this affair I am afraid there would be war indeed."

"Shall I tell her?" asked Elfreda eagerly. "I think I'd better; then they won't dare to make me leave college."

"Listen to me, Elfreda," said Grace firmly. "No one can make you leave college unless you fail in your studies or do something really reprehensible, but there is one thing you must make up your mind to do if you wish to stay here, and have the girls like you."

"What is it?" inquired Elfreda suspiciously.

"You mustn't tell tales," was Grace's frank answer. "No matter what the girls do or say to you, don't carry it to the officials of the college."

"Do you mean that I'm to submit to all kinds of insults and not take my own part?" demanded Elfreda, forgetting her grief and assuming a belligerent air.

"You are not fighting your own battles when you carry your grievances to the dean, the registrar, or any other member of the faculty," said Grace gravely. "You are merely giving them unpleasant information to which they dislike to listen."

"Humph!" was the contemptuous ejaculation. "The dean made it hot for the girls just the same. I guess she didn't object much to hearing about it."

"You are not looking at things in their true light, Elfreda," put in Miriam. "I'll venture to say that when the members of the faculty were students they were just as careful not to tell tales as are the girls here to-day. Of course, if students are reported to them, they are obliged to take action in the matter, but I'm sure that they'd rather not hear about the girls' petty difficulties."

"'Petty difficulties!'" almost screamed Elfreda. "Well, I like your impudence." Jerking herself from the girls' embrace she stood up and walked to the other side of the room. Stumbling over one of her shoes she kicked it viciously aside, then, leaning her head against the door, her sobs broke forth afresh.

In a twinkling Miriam was beside her. "Poor Elfreda," she soothed. "You are tired and worn out. Take off your hat and coat and bathe your face. You'll feel ever so much better after you've done that. You mustn't be cross with Grace and me. We are only trying to help you. While you are bathing your face, I'll make some chocolate and we'll have a cozy little time. Won't that be nice?"

Elfreda nodded, winked back her tears, and slowly drawing the pins from her hat, flung it on the foot of her bed. Her coat followed, and seizing her towel from the rack she stalked out of the room and down the hall to the bath room.

"Miriam, you're a darling and a diplomat!" exclaimed Grace, closing the door, which the stout girl had left wide open. "Chocolate is the one thing calculated to reduce J. Elfreda to reason. We will feed her, then renew our lectures on tale-bearing. Never call me a reformer. I am certain that before the year is over J. Elfreda won't know herself."

"Nonsense," scoffed Miriam. "She is an interesting speci-men, and furnishes variety, of a certain kind," she added with an impish grin, glancing comprehensively at the disordered room. "As long as I have taken her unto myself as a roommate I might as well do what I can for her. What seems so strange to me is that with all her money she is so crude and slangy. She doesn't seem to have any ideals or much principle either. Yet there is something sturdy and frankly independent about her, too, that makes one think she's worth bothering with after all."

"How did her father make his money?" asked Grace.

"Lumber," replied Miriam. "They own tracts of timber land in Michigan. Elfreda can have anything she asks for."

Grace sat down on Miriam's bed, her chin in her hands. She was thinking of the note she had just read and wondering what had better be done. Miriam, despite her avowal that she was tired of picking up her roommate's scattered clothing, busied herself with reducing Elfreda's half of the room to some semblance of order. Going to the closet, she took down an elaborate Japanese silk kimono and laid it across the foot of Elfreda's bed.

"What had we better do about this note?" Grace asked, picking it up from the table and re-reading it.

"What do you think?" questioned Miriam.

"I think we had better ask the advice of some upper class girl," said Grace. "I'm going to see Mabel Ashe to-morrow morning. I'll tell her about it. Elfreda mustn't be cheated out of her right to go to the reception."

"But if the whole sophomore class objects to her, what then?"

"I don't believe the whole sophomore class does object to her," returned Grace. "I have a curious conviction that not many of them know her even by sight. I think that this note was written for spite."

"Do you think Miss Wicks and Miss Hampton wrote it?" queried Miriam.

"I don't want to accuse any one of writing it, but they are the only students who would have an object in doing so," declared Grace. "I hear Elfreda coming down the hall. Don't say anything more about it just now," she added in a lower tone.

"My goodness, I forgot all about the chocolate!" exclaimed Miriam, scurrying to a little oak cabinet in one corner of the room and taking out the necessary ingredients. "Here, Grace, open this can of evaporated cream with the scissors. You can use that paperweight for a hammer."

Fifteen minutes later, wrapped in the folds of her kimono, J. Elfreda sat drinking chocolate and devouring cakes as though her very existence depended upon it.

"You girls are ever so much nicer than I thought you'd be," she said reflectively, between cakes. "I must say that I'm agreeably disappointed in you, Miriam. I was pretty sure you were a regular snob, but you're nothing like one. I couldn't help thinking about what you said, Grace, while I was bathing my face," she continued. "It made me mad for a minute, but I've come to the conclusion that you were talking sense, and from now on the faculty will have to go some to get any information from me."

CHAPTER VII

GRACE TAKES MATTERS INTO HER OWN HANDS

"We have had, what might be considered by some people, a momentous evening," remarked Grace as Anne Pierson walked into their room shortly before ten o'clock. Having left the now almost cheerful Elfreda to the good-natured ministrations of Miriam, Grace had said good night and returned to her own room for a few more minutes of silent devotion to Livy.

"What happened?" asked Anne as she hung up her wraps, took down her kimono, and prepared to be comfortable.

"What might be expected," returned Grace, and briefly recounted what had transpired in Miriam's room.

"Wasn't it nice of Miriam to make a fuss over her, though?" said Anne warmly.

"Yes, of course, but it isn't Miriam's amiability that I'm thinking about at present. It's what we'd better do to straighten out this trouble for Elfreda," said Grace anxiously. "I felt glad when I came to Overton that I did not have to worry about any one but myself, and now I'm confronted with Elfreda's troubles."

"I think it would be best to see Miss Ashe first," agreed Anne, after a brief silence.

"That settles it, then, I'll go. Tell me about your new freshman friend, Anne."

"She's a very nice girl," Anne replied, "and has lots of the right kind of courage. She lives in a big, bare room in the top of an old house, clear down at the other end of the town, and the way she has made that room over to suit her needs is really wonderful. She has one corner of it curtained off for her kitchen and has a cupboard for her dishes, what there are of them. She cooks her meals over a little two-burner gas stove, and does her own washing and ironing. Every spare moment she has she devotes to doing mending. She does it beautifully, too. Ever so many girls have given her their silk stockings and lingerie waists to darn."

"Poor little thing," mused Grace. "I suppose she never has a minute to play. I don't see how she manages to do all that work and study, too. I wish we could do something to help her."

"I don't know what we could do," returned Anne thought-fully. "I imagine she wouldn't accept help. She strikes me as being one of the kind who would rather die than allow her friends to pay her way."

"There must be some way," Grace said speculatively, "and some day we'll find it out."

"Sometimes I feel as though I had earned my college money too easily," confessed Anne. "The work I did on the stage wasn't work at all, it was pure pleasure. Ruth Denton's work is the hardest kind of drudgery."

"But think how hard you worked to win the scholarship," reminded Grace.

"That was work I loved, too," replied Anne, shaking her head deprecatingly over her own good fortune.

"Never mind," laughed Grace. "Just think of how hard you might have had to work if you hadn't been a genius, and that will comfort you a little."

"Grace, you are too ridiculous," protested Anne, flushing deeply.

"Anne, you are entirely too modest," retorted Grace. "Come on, little Miss Nonentity, let's go to bed or I won't get up early enough to-morrow morning to see Mabel Ashe before my first recitation."

"All right," yawned Anne. "To-morrow night I must stay in the house and write letters. I've owed David a letter for a week. I wonder why Nora and Jessica don't write."

"They promised to write first, you know," said Grace.

"If we don't hear from them by Saturday we'd better send them a postcard to hurry them up. Let's go down to that little stationer's shop to-morrow and see what they have. I must find one that will suit Hippy's peculiar style of beauty."

Laughing and chatting of things that had happened at home, a subject of which they never tired, Grace and Anne prepared for bed.

The next morning Anne awoke first. Glancing at the little clock on the chiffonier she exclaimed in dismay. They had overslept, and there was barely time to dress and eat breakfast before chapel.

"Oh, dear," lamented Grace as she slipped into her one-piece gown of pink linen, "now I can't go to see Mabel until after luncheon. How provoking!"

But it was still more provoking to find, when she called at Holland House, late that afternoon, that Mabel Ashe had made a dinner engagement with several seniors and had just left the house. "What had I better do about it?" Grace asked herself. "Shall I put it off until to-morrow or shall I take matters into my own hands? It's only four days now until the reception, and those girls may do a great deal of talking during that time." She paused on the steps of Holland House and looked across the campus toward Stuart Hall. "I'm sure I heard some one say that both Miss Wicks and Miss Hampton live there," Grace reflected. "I don't like to do it, but it's the only thing I can think of to do." Squaring her shoulders Grace crossed the campus, a look of determination on her fine face. Mounting the steps of Stuart Hall she deliberately rang the bell.

Miss Wicks and Miss Hampton were both in, the maid stated, ushering Grace into the big, attractively furnished living room. A moment later there was a scurry of footsteps on the stairs and Alberta Wicks, followed by Mary Hampton, entered the room.

Grace rose from her chair to greet them. "Good afternoon," she said pleasantly. "I shall have to introduce myself. I am Grace Harlowe of the freshman class. I saw you at the dance the other night but did not meet you."

"How do you do?" returned Alberta Wicks in a bored tone, while the other girl nodded indifferently. "I remember your face, I think. I'm not sure. There was an army of freshmen at the dance. The largest entering class for a number of years, I understand."

"Freshmen are perhaps not important enough to be remembered," returned Grace, smiling faintly. Then deciding that there was nothing to be gained by beating about the bush she said earnestly, "I hope you will not think me meddlesome or presuming, but I came here this afternoon to talk with you about something that concerns a member of the freshman class. I refer to Miss Briggs, whom I am quite certain you know."

"Miss Briggs," repeated Alberta Wicks, meditatively. "Let me see, I think we met her—"

"The day she came to college," supplemented Grace.

"How did you know that?" was the sharp question.

"I saw you and Miss Hampton when you approached her, and also when you walked away from the station with her," Grace said quietly. "Miss Briggs rode part of the way on the train with us to Overton."

A deep flush rose to the faces of both young women at Grace's indisputable statement. There was an uncomfortable silence.

"I know also," continued Grace, "that you conducted her to the county court house instead of the registrar's office and left her to find out the truth as best she might."

"Really," sneered Alberta, "you seem to be extremely well informed as to what took place. It is quite evident that Miss Briggs published the news broadcast."

"She did nothing of the sort," retorted Grace coldly. "She did tell my roommate and me, and I regret to say that she also told the registrar, but she now realizes her mistake in doing so."

"Her realization comes entirely too late," was the sarcastic reply. "She should have thought things over before going to the registrar with anything so silly."

"Ah!" ejaculated Grace. "I am glad to hear you admit that the trick you played was silly. To my mind it was both senseless and unkind. However, I did not come here to-day to discuss the ethics of the affair. Miss Briggs has received a note forbidding her attendance at the sophomore reception and advising her to leave Overton. It is signed 'Sophomore Class.' It states her betrayal of two sophomores to the registrar as the cause of its origin. What I wish to ask you is whether the sophomores have really taken action in this matter, or whether you wrote this note in order to frighten Miss Briggs into leaving college?"

"I do not admit your right to interfere, and I shall certainly not answer your question, Miss Harlowe. You are decidedly impertinent, to say the least," replied Alberta in a tone of suppressed anger. "I cannot understand why you should take such an unprecedented interest in Miss Briggs's affairs and I shall tell you nothing."

"Very well," said Grace composedly. "I see that I shall have to go to each member of the sophomore class in turn in order to find out the truth. I cannot believe that these girls are so lacking in college spirit as to ostracize a newcomer, even though she did act unwisely."

"You would not dare to do it!" exclaimed Mary Hampton excitedly. She had hitherto taken no part in the conversation.

Jessie Graham Flower

"Why not?" asked Grace. "I am determined to go to the root of this matter. I don't intend Miss Briggs shall leave college, or be sent to coventry either. She has acted hastily, but she will live it down, that is, unless word of it has traveled too far. Even so, I hardly think she will leave college. I am sorry that we have failed to come to an understanding."

Grace walked proudly toward the door. Inwardly she was deeply disappointed at having failed, but she gave no sign of feeling her defeat.

"Come back!" commanded Alberta Wicks harshly, as Grace stood with her hand on the door knob. Grace turned and walked toward them. Her face gave no sign of her surprise.

"Do you really intend to take up this affair with every member of the sophomore class?" demanded Alberta, eyeing Grace sharply. There was a faint note of dismay in her voice, despite her attempt to appear unconcerned.

"Yes," answered Grace firmly. "The only alternative would be to take it to the faculty, and that is not to be thought of. I shall make a personal appeal to each sophomore for Miss Briggs."

"Then I suppose rather than bring down a hornet's nest about our ears, we might as well tell you that the majority of the class know nothing of this. A number of sophomores, with a view to the good of the college, decided themselves to be justified in sending the letter to Miss Briggs. We do not wish young women of her type at Overton, and Miss Briggs will do well to go elsewhere. She will never be happy at Overton."

"Is that a threat?" asked Grace quickly.

Alberta merely shrugged her shoulders in answer to Grace's question.

"You may call it what you please," remarked Mary Hampton sullenly.

"Thank you," said Grace gravely. "I think I have a fair idea of the situation. I believe I know too, just how many sophomores were concerned in the writing of the letter, and am sure that their adverse opinion will neither make nor mar Miss Briggs. Good afternoon."

With this Grace walked serenely out of the house, leaving behind her two discomfited and ignominiously defeated young women.

"Do you believe she would have kept her word and put the matter before the class?" asked Mary Hampton after Grace had gone.

"Yes," responded Alberta, frowning. "She wouldn't have hesitated. She meant what she said. She is one of those tiresome persons who is forever advocating fair play. She only does it as a pose. She imagines, I suppose that it will attract the attention of the upper class girls. I should like to teach her a lesson in humility, but it is dangerous, for with all her faults she is by no means stupid, and unless we were very careful we would be quite likely to come to grief."

CHAPTER VIII

THE SOPHOMORE RECEPTION

It was the night of the sophomore reception and the gymnasium was ablaze with light and color. All day the valiant sophomore class had labored as decorators. Sofa cushions, portieres, screens and anything else that might add to the beauty of the decorations had been begged and borrowed from good-natured residents of the campus and nearby boarding houses. There were great branches of red and gold leaves festooning and hiding the gymnasium apparatus, and the respective sophomore and freshman colors of blue and gold were in evidence in every nook and corner of the big room. There was a real orchestra of eight pieces from the town of Overton, seated on a palm-screened platform which had been erected for the occasion; while a long line of freshmen in their best bib and tucker crowded up to pay their respects to the receiving line of sophomores, headed by the class president.

The freshmen of Wayne Hall had elected to go together, and Ruth Denton had also been invited to take dinner and dress with Anne, then go with her and her friends to the reception. At first Ruth demurred on account of her gown, which was a very plain little affair of white dotted swiss. Then Grace had come to the rescue and insisted that Ruth should wear a very beautiful white satin ribbon belt with long, graceful ends, belonging to her, which quite transformed the simple frock. There was also a white satin hair ornament to match, and Miriam's clever fingers had done her soft brown hair in a new, becoming fashion. Even Elfreda had insisted on lending her a white opera cape and praising her appearance until the little girl was in a maze of delight at so much unexpected attention. Grace, Anne, and Miriam had put on their graduating gowns and Elfreda was arrayed in all the glory of the gown she had ordered for the occasion and afterward entertained so little hope of wearing.

Just as they were ready to start the door bell rang. There was a sound of laughing voices and the patter of slippered feet on the stairs, and Mabel Ashe, accompanied by Frances Marlton, Constance Fuller, and two other juniors, appeared on the landing.

"Better late than never," announced Mabel cheerily, as Grace appeared in the doorway. "We've come to take you to the reception. We weren't invited until the eleventh hour, but we're making up for lost time."

"Why, I didn't know juniors were invited to the reception," exclaimed Grace, taking Mabel's extended hand in both her own. "Judging from all outward signs I suppose you are going to the reception, else why wear your costliest raiment?"

"Your deduction is not only marvelous but correct," returned Mabel. "We were invited because the sophomores found themselves lacking not in quality, but quantity. There weren't nearly enough sophomore 'gentlemen' to go round, so we juniors were pressed into service.

"I'm so glad," returned Grace warmly. "We know nearly all

Jessie Graham Flower

the freshmen, but we know only a few sophomores. We were lamenting to-night because we expected to be wall flowers."

"Not if Frances and I can help it," promised Mabel. "Girls, I want you to meet Miss Graham and Miss Allen, both worthy juniors. You already know Constance."

The "worthy juniors" nodded smilingly as Mabel presented Grace and her friends.

"Get your capes and scarfs," directed Mabel briskly. "We must be on our way. I'm sure it's going to be a red-letter affair. The sophomores have nearly worked their dear heads off to impress the baby class. Do you girls all dance, and how many of you can lead?"

"Miriam and I," answered Grace. "Anne is not tall enough. Elfreda and Ruth will have to answer for themselves."

Ruth Denton confessed to being barely able to dance. Elfreda, who looked really handsome in her blue evening gown, answered in the affirmative. Grace noted with secret satisfaction that the stout girl was keeping strictly in the background and making no effort to push herself forward. "If she only behaves like that all evening the girls will be sure to like her, and if anything comes up later about this registrar business there won't be such fuss made over it," Grace reflected.

"Come on, Grace!" Frances Marlton's merry tones broke in on Grace's reflections. "I'm going to be your faithful cavalier. I'll offer you my arm as soon as we get downstairs. We never could walk two abreast in state down these stairs."

Grace followed Frances's lead, smiling happily. Julia Graham, a rather stout, pleasant-faced young woman in pink messaline, bowed to Miriam. Anne found herself accepting the arm of Edith Allen, while Constance Fuller took charge of Ruth Denton. The crowning honor fell to J. Elfreda, for Mabel Ashe walked up to her, slipped her arm in that of the astonished girl, saying impressively, "May I have the pleasure, Miss Briggs?"

The little party fairly bubbled over with high spirits as they set out for the gymnasium in couples, but to Elfreda the world was gayest rose color. To be escorted to the reception by the most popular girl in college was an honor of which she had never dreamed. Only a few days before she had resigned all hope of even going, but through the magic of Grace Harlowe she was among the elect. For almost the first time in her self-centered young life, she was swept by a wholly generous impulse to do the best that lay within her in college if only for Grace's sake. While she listened to Mabel's gay sallies, answering them almost shyly, her mind was on the debt of gratitude she owed Grace, who, without mentioning her visit to Alberta Wicks, had assured her that she had made inquiry and found that the letter was not the work of the sophomore class as a body. Grace had refused to voice even a suspicion regarding the writer's identity, but had so strongly advised Elfreda to pay no attention to the cowardly warning, but attend the reception as though nothing had happened, that the stout girl had taken her advice.

Grace was now quietly jubilant over the way things had turned out. She was so glad Mabel had chosen Elfreda. "I wonder how she knew," she said half aloud.

"How who knew, and what did she know?" inquired Frances quickly.

"Nothing," replied Grace, in sudden confusion. "I was just wondering."

Jessie Graham Flower

"I know what you were wondering and I'll tell you. A certain junior who is a friend of a certain sophomore told Mabel certain things."

"Frances, you are a wizard!" exclaimed Grace in a low tone. "How did you know of what I was thinking?"

"The question is," replied Frances, "do you understand me?"

"I think I know who the sophomore is," hesitated Grace, "but I don't understand about the junior."

"And I can't tell you," replied Frances gravely. "I can only say that Mabel likes you very much, Grace, and that a certain junior who is fond of Mabel is jealous of your friendship. Both Mabel and I admire your stand in the other matter. You are measuring up to college standards, my dear, and I am sure you will be an honor to 19—."

Frances finished her flattering prediction just as they stepped inside the doorway of the gymnasium. Before Grace had time to reply they found themselves among a bevy of daintily gowned girls that were forming in line to pay their respects to the president of the sophomore class and five of her class-mates who formed the receiving party. After this formality was over the girls walked about the gymnasium, admiring the decorations. Mabel Ashe was fairly overwhelmed by her admirers. It seemed to Grace as though she attracted more attention than the receiving party itself. It was: "Mabel, dear, dance the first waltz with me;" "Come and drink lemonade with us, Queen Mab," and "Why, you dear Mabel, I might have known the sophomores couldn't get along without you."

"She knows every girl in college, I believe," remarked Anne to Edith Allen, as Mabel stood laughing and talking animatedly, the center of an admiring group.

"Every one loves her from the faculty down," replied Edith. "She hadn't been here six weeks as a freshman until the whole class was sending her violets and asking her out to dinners. She was elected president of the freshman class, too, and had the honor of refusing the sophomore nomination. They want her for junior president, but she will refuse that nomination, too. She is as unselfish and unspoiled as the day she came here and the most sympathetic girl I have ever known. We are all madly jealous of Frances."

Anne smiled at this statement. "It is nice to be liked," she said simply. "That is the way it is with Grace at home."

"I'm not surprised," replied Edith, regarding Grace critically. "She has a fine face. That Miss Nesbit seems nice, too. She is a beauty, isn't she?"

Anne replied happily in the affirmative. To her praise of her two dearest friends was as the sweetest music.

"Shall we dance?" said Edith, rising and offering her arm in her most manly fashion. A moment later the two girls joined the dancers, who were circling the floor with more or less grace to the strains of a waltz.

"What kind of a time are you having?" asked Grace an hour later as she and Miriam met in front of one of the lemonade bowls.

"I'm enjoying it ever so much," was the enthusiastic answer. "I've met a lot of sophomores that I've been wanting to know, and they have been so nice to me. Have you seen Elfreda lately?"

"No," said Grace with a guilty start. "I've been having such a good time I forgot her. Let's go and find her now."

The two began a slow promenade of the room in search of the missing girl. Suddenly Grace clutched her friend's arm. "Look over there, Miriam!" she exclaimed.

Seated on a divan beside Mabel Ashe and surrounded by half a dozen sophomores was J. Elfreda. She was talking animatedly and the girls were urging her on with laughter and cries of "Now show us how some one else in Fairview looks."

"What do you suppose she is saying?" wondered Miriam. "Let's go over." They neared the group just in time to hear Elfreda say, "The president of the Fairview suffragist league." Then her round face set as though turned to stone. Her eyes took on a determined glare, and drawing down the corners of her mouth she elevated her chin, rose from the divan and shrilled forth "Votes for Women" in a tone that fairly convulsed her hearers. Then suddenly catching sight of Grace and Miriam she sat down abruptly and said with an embarrassed gesture of dismissal, "The show's over. I see my friends are looking for me. I'll have to go."

"You funny, funny girl!" exclaimed Mabel Ashe. "What a treasure you'll be when we give college entertainments. You'll make the Dramatic Club some day."

"Nothing like it," returned Elfreda, resorting to slang in her embarrassment.

"Where did you ever learn to mimic people so cleverly?" asked one sophomore.

"Oh, I don't know," replied Elfreda almost rudely. "I've imitated folks ever since I was a kid—little girl," she corrected. "You said you'd waltz with me to-night, Miriam, so come on. That's a Strauss waltz, and I don't want to miss it. Please excuse me," she said, turning to the assembled girls. She was making a desperate effort to be polite when she preferred to be rude.

"Mabel Ashe, you're the dearest girl," Grace burst forth as the little crowd dissolved and strolled off in different directions. "You have been lovely to Elfreda, and instead of her evening being spoiled, you know what I mean, she has actually made a sensation."

"I am not the only one who has been looking out for J. Elfreda's interests," reminded Mabel. "I am glad that she has this talent. It will help her to make friends with the girls, and if nothing more is said about the registrar affair she will soon have a following of her own."

"Do you think anything more will be said?" asked Grace anxiously.

"Not if I can help it," was the response.

It was almost midnight when, after seeing Ruth Denton home, the four girls climbed the steps of Wayne Hall.

"It was lovely, wasn't it, Anne?" declared Grace as she slipped into her kimono and began taking the pins from her hair.

"Yes," said Anne with a half sigh. She was deliberating as to whether she had better tell Grace a disturbing bit of conversation she had overheard. After all it wasn't worth repeating. She had simply heard one freshman say to another that she had been prepared to like Miss Harlowe, but something she had heard had caused her to change her mind. Anne suspected that in some way Elfreda's troubles had been shifted to Grace's shoulders.

CHAPTER IX

DISAGREEABLE NEWS

"Hurrah!" cried Miriam Nesbit gleefully, coming into the living room of Wayne Hall where Grace sat at the old-fashioned library table absorbed in writing a theme for next day's composition class.

"What's happened?" asked Grace curiously, looking up from her writing.

"We're to go over to Exeter Field to-morrow for a try out in basketball. I do hope we'll both make the team."

"So do I," agreed Grace promptly. "But there are so many girls that we may not be even chosen as subs. Besides, our playing may not compare with that of some of the others."

"Nonsense," returned Miriam stoutly. "Your playing would stand out anywhere, Grace, even on a boys' team. I consider myself a fair player, too," she added, flushing a little.

"I should say you are!" exclaimed Grace. "Who told you about the try out?"

"It's on the bulletin board. I don't see how you missed it."

"I didn't look at the bulletin board this morning. I meant to, then something else took my attention, and I forgot all about it." The "something else" had been the extremely frigid manner in which two freshmen she particularly liked had greeted her as she caught up with them on the way to her Livy class that morning. Grace wondered not a little at this cavalier treatment, but could arrive at no satisfactory conclusion regarding it. She finally tried to dismiss the matter by ascribing it to over-sensitiveness on her part, but every now and then it haunted her like an offending spectre.

"I always look at the bulletin board, no matter what happens," declared Miriam emphatically. "I must hurry upstairs and impart the glorious news to Elfreda. We had elected to spend Saturday afternoon in moving our furniture about, hoping to gain a few square inches of room space, but we'll have to postpone doing it. We can do it the first rainy Saturday. Hurry along with your paper and come upstairs. I'm going to make tea, and I've acquired a new kind of cakes. They're chocolate covered and taste like home and mother."

After Miriam had gone upstairs Grace sat staring at her theme with unseeing eyes. Disagreeable thoughts would come, and try as she might she could not drive them away. She had been snubbed and she could not forget it. Giving herself a little impatient shake she turned her attention to her theme and went on writing rapidly. Half an hour later she folded it neatly, placed it inside one of her books, and went slowly upstairs. She found Miriam, Anne and Elfreda seated on the floor deep in tea drinking. Before them was a plate piled high with the new kind of cakes, and a five-pound box of candy that Elfreda had received from New York that morning.

"Sit down here, Grace," invited Anne, making room for her friend. "Give her some tea this minute, Miriam. She is a working woman and needs nourishment. Did you finish your theme, dear?"

Grace nodded. Then taking the cup Miriam offered she dropped two lumps of sugar in it, and began drinking her tea in silence.

"What's the matter, Grace?" asked Anne anxiously.

"Nothing," replied Grace. "I feel reflective. I suppose that's why I haven't anything to say. Did Miriam tell you about the basketball try out on Exeter Field?"

"Yes; but not for mine—I mean—I'm not interested in basketball," amended Elfreda, hastily. "I tell you this trying to cut out slang is no idle dream."

There was a shout of laughter from the three girls.

"Now, see here," bristled the stout girl. "You needn't laugh at me. What I meant was that—that it is very difficult to refrain from the use of slang," finished Elfreda with such affected primness that the laughter broke forth afresh.

"Humph!" she ejaculated disgustedly. "I don't see anything to laugh at. Goodness knows I'm trying hard to break myself of the habit."

"Of course you are," sympathized Anne. "We aren't laughing at you. It was the funny way you ended your last sentence."

Elfreda's face relaxed into a good-natured grin. "I am funny sometimes," she admitted calmly. "Even Pa, who doesn't smile once a year, says so."

"I must go," said Anne, rising. "I haven't looked at my

history lesson, and it is frightfully long, too."

"I'll go with you," announced Grace. "I must mend my blue serge dress. I stepped on it while going upstairs this morning and tore it just above the hem. I had to change it for this, and was almost late for chapel."

"I waited for you in the hall as long as I could," said Anne. "I meant to ask you what happened, but forgot it. Grace, what do you suppose Elfreda said before you came upstairs?"

"I can't possibly guess," rejoined Grace. "J. Elfreda's remarks are varied and startling."

The two girls were now in their own room.

"These are nice ones," averred Anne. "She said that you and Miriam and I were the first girls she'd ever cared much about. She said that she had never tried to do anything to please any one but herself until she came here. Then when you stood up for her, and fixed things so she could go to the reception, she said she held up her right hand and swore to herself that she'd try to be worthy of our friendship. That's why she's trying not to use slang, and to be more generous. She keeps her things in order, too. You noticed how nice everything looked to-day."

"Miriam, not I, is responsible for the change," said Grace. "She is a born diplomat. She knows exactly how to proceed with J. Elfreda. I hope there won't be anything more said about the registrar affair, though. I want Elfreda to like college better every day."

"Grace," said Anne hesitatingly, "if I tell you something, will you promise not to worry over it?"

"What do you mean?" asked Grace quickly, a puzzled look in her eyes. "I can't promise not to worry until I know that there's nothing to worry over. If you have heard something disagreeable about me, I'm not afraid to listen."

"I know it," said Anne. Then she went on almost abruptly. "I heard two freshmen talking about you the other night at the reception. One of them said that she had been prepared to like you, but had heard something that had caused her to change her mind." Anne looked distressed.

For a moment Grace sat very still.

"Oh, dear!" lamented Anne. "I'm sorry I told you. Now I've hurt your feelings."

"Nonsense!" retorted Grace stoutly. "It will take more than that to hurt my feelings. I am beginning to see a light, however. At the reception the other night Frances told me that Mabel had heard about my call at Stuart Hall from a senior who is a friend of a certain sophomore. Now, that sophomore is either Miss Wicks or Miss Hampton. It looks as though these two girls were not willing to let bygones be bygones. I haven't the slightest idea what they may have said about me, but I am sure they must have circulated some untruthful report among the freshmen. I don't like to accuse any one of being untruthful, but I am quite sure that I have done nothing reprehensible. Now that you have told me I'm going to watch closely. If a number of the girls snub me, I shall know that it is serious."

"Then you will fight for your rights, won't you?" pleaded Anne. "It isn't fair that you should be misjudged for trying to help Elfreda."

"I don't know," replied Grace doubtfully. "It might not be

worth while. I have a theory that if one is right with one's conscience nothing else matters."

Anne shook her head dubiously. "That won't protect you from unpleasantness unless the girls think so, too. Our freshman year is our foundation year, and if we allow any one even to think that we are not putting our best material into it, the shadow is likely to follow us to the very threshold of graduation. It is easy enough to start a rumor but once let it gain headway, it is almost impossible to check it. Nearly all of your sophomore year in high school was spoiled through standing up for me. That's why I'm so determined to make you look out for your own interests."

While Anne was earnestly urging Grace to action, Grace was frantically rummaging in her closet for her blue dress. It was several minutes before she found it. If the blue dress could have spoken it would have borne witness to the fact that its owner dashed her hand suspiciously across her eyes before emerging from the closet with it over her arm.

CHAPTER X

THE MAKING OF THE TEAM

Saturday dawned clear and sunshiny. It was an ideal autumn day, and luncheon at Wayne Hall was eaten rapidly. Everyone was eager to give an opinion regarding the basketball try out, and with one or two exceptions each girl cherished the secret hope of making the team. Anne was one of the exceptions. She had no basketball yearnings. She was ready and willing to be an enthusiastic and loyal fan, but aside from walking and dancing she had no desire to take an active part in college sports. She was extremely proud of Miriam's and Grace's fine playing, however, and never doubted for an instant that both girls would make the team. "I'm sure you and Miriam will be chosen," she asserted to Grace, as the latter stood before her mirror, viewing herself in her new felt walking hat, that had arrived that morning.

The two friends had run up to their room after luncheon to hurry into their coats and hats, preparatory to going to Exeter Field. Anne eyed Grace admiringly. "Your new hat is so becoming," she said.

"I think yours is ever so pretty, too," returned Grace. "It looks like new. No one would know that you bought it last season. You take such good care of your clothes, Anne. I wish I could take as good care of mine. I hang them up and keep them in repair, but somehow they just wear out all at once."

"Don't stop to mourn over wearing out your clothes on this gala day," laughed Miriam Nesbit, who had appeared in the open door in time to hear Grace's plaintive assertion. She was wearing a becoming suit of blue and a blue hat to match.

"Where's Elfreda?" asked Grace. "She's going, too, isn't she?"

Miriam nodded, then said slyly, "If she ever gets ready."

Just then an anguished voice called out, "Miriam, please come back. That pin you fastened in the back of my waist is sticking me and I can't reach it."

Miriam flew to the rescue, smothering an involuntary laugh as she ran. Five minutes later she and Elfreda, in a new brown suit and hat, wearing the expression of a martyr, joined Grace and Anne on the veranda, and the four set out for Exeter Field.

"I'm not going to talk about certain things to-day, Grace, but did you notice that all the girls at our table were as nice with you as ever?" said Anne in a low tone.

"Yes; I noticed it," returned Grace. "If they continue to be the same, I shall think that we have been making a mountain of a molehill."

"Look at that crowd ahead of us," called Miriam.

A veritable procession of girls wound its way up the hilly street to Exeter Field. There were big girls and little girls, all talking and laughing happily, until the still October air rang with the sound of their gay, young voices. The majority of them were well-dressed, although here and there might be seen a last year's hat or coat that no one seemed to notice or to mind. Overton had a reputation for democracy in spite of the fact that most of its students came from homes where there was no lack of money.

Arriving at the field the four girls followed the crowd, which for the most part made for a long, low building at one end of the field.

"Where are they going?" asked Grace.

"For ice cream, of course," replied a young woman who stood near enough to overhear Grace's question.

"Oh, I want some ice cream," piped up Elfreda.

"Very well, my child, you shall have it," said Miriam in a grave, motherly tone.

The young woman who had answered Grace's question glanced at Miriam with twinkling eyes. Then she smiled broadly. That smile warmed Grace's heart.

"Won't you come with us?" she asked.

"Thank you, I believe I will," she replied. "I think I have the advantage. I know you are Miss Harlowe, but you don't know me. My name is Gertrude Wells, and I am a freshman, too. Now, suppose you introduce your little friends, and we'll go over to the club restaurant. I was waiting for my chum, but she has evidently deserted me."

Grace decided that she liked Miss Wells better than any

other freshman she had met. She had a dry, humorous way of saying things that kept them all in a gale of laughter. Elfreda, too, seemed especially interested in her, and exerted herself to please. After their second ice all around they strolled over to where the manager of the college athletics association was marshaling the candidates for the try out. Grace and Miriam hurried off to the training quarters at one end of the field to put on their gymnasium suits.

The girls who wished to play were formed into teams and tried out against one another and the most promising of the players ordered to step off to one side after having lined up for play three times. It was after four o'clock when Grace and Miriam were called to the field. The long wait had made Grace rather nervous. Miriam, however, was cool and self-possessed, and played with snap and vigor.

"I don't know what ails me," said Grace despairingly, as she and Miriam stood waiting for the next line up. "I didn't play my best. I tried to, but I couldn't."

"You're nervous," rejoined Miriam. "Just make yourself believe you are back in the gym at home and you can show them some star playing."

"I will," promised Grace. "See if I don't."

It was after five o'clock before the last ambitious freshman had been given a chance to display her basketball prowess or lack of it. Grace had made good her word and forgetting her nervousness had played with the old-time dash and skill that had won fame for her in her high-school days. Her playing had elicited cries of approval from those watching and she had the satisfaction of hearing, "You play an excellent game, Miss Harlowe," from the manager. Miriam, after her third trial, also received her full measure of applause, and flushed and happy the two girls clasped hands delightedly when they received word that they were to report for practice at four o'clock Monday afternoon. As they were leaving the field to go to the training shed Gertrude Wells hurried toward them. "Miss Harlowe," she called, "please wait a minute."

Grace paused obediently while Miriam and Anne walked on ahead.

"Will you and your friends, Miss Nesbit, Miss Briggs and Miss Pierson, come over to Morton Hall to-night at half-past seven o'clock. I have invited a number of my freshmen friends, and I'd love to have you come, too. It's Saturday night you know, so you won't have to worry about recitations to-morrow."

"Thank you," replied Grace. "I will come with pleasure. Girls," she called to the three ahead, "come back here."

Gertrude repeated her invitation, which was instantly accepted. "Be sure to come early," was her parting admonition.

"This is our first freshman invitation," remarked Grace after Gertrude had left them. "I'm so glad. I had begun to think we would never get acquainted with the rest of our class."

"I understand that 19—is the largest class Overton has ever had," said Anne.

"All the more reason why we should be proud of it," declared Miriam quickly.

"I wonder what they'll have to eat,' said Elfreda reflectively.

A derisive giggle greeted this remark.

"Well, you needn't laugh," retorted Elfreda good-naturedly. "I didn't say that because I'm so fond of eating. I was just wondering whether it would be worth while to eat supper or not."

"Take my advice and eat your supper, Elfreda," laughed Anne. "I have an idea that we shall be fed on plowed field, fudge or something equally nourishing."

"Humph!" commented Elfreda. "That's just about what I thought. I hope we have something sour for supper to-night. I'm getting tired of sweet stuff. It's frightfully fattening, too."

"What on earth has come over you, Elfreda," laughed Grace. "I thought you were devoted to chocolate and bonbons."

"I was," confessed Elfreda, "until I saw you and Miriam play basketball this afternoon. I was crazy to play, too. But imagine how I'd look on the field. I couldn't run six yards without puffing. I'm going to try to get thinner, and perhaps some day I can make the team, too."

CHAPTER XI

ANNE WINS A VICTORY

The pleasurable excitement of making the team and receiving the invitation to the spread had driven all thought of the conversation overheard by Anne from Grace's mind. Above all things Grace wished if possible to establish friendly relations with every member of her class. Now that she and her friends were invited to Morton House they would meet a number of new girls. The Morton House girls had the reputation of being both jolly and hospitable. Grace had the feeling that so far they had made little or no social headway among their classmates. Aside from Ruth Denton and the students at Wayne Hall they knew practically no other freshmen.

"This spread will help us to get in touch with some of the girls we don't know," she confided to Anne while dressing that night for the party.

"I hope so," replied Anne. "We seem to be rather slow about making friends here at Overton; that is, among the freshmen. We really know more upper class girls, don't we?"

"Yes," assented Grace. "But after to-night things will be different."

It was only a few minutes' walk to Morton House and the four girls enjoyed the brief stroll.

"I wonder if we're too early," said Grace, consulting her watch. "It lacks three minutes of being half-past seven. That's Morton House, isn't it?" pointing at the substantial brick house just ahead of them. The little party climbed the stone steps. Miriam rang the bell. Almost instantly the door opened and Gertrude Wells smilingly ushered them into the hall. "So glad you have come," she said. "All the other girls are here."

"We need not have been afraid of being too early, then," laughed Grace.

"Hardly," smiled Gertrude, "the majority of us live here. There are twenty freshmen in this house, and we invited ten more from outside. Thirty girls in all, but the living room is large enough to hold us, and Mrs. Kane doesn't mind if we make a good deal of noise. Come upstairs to my room and take off your wraps. Then we'll join the crowd." A little later they followed their hostess downstairs to the big living room, that seemed fairly overflowing with girls. The buzz of conversation ceased as they entered. Gertrude introduced them one after another to the assembled crowd of young women, who received them with varying degrees of cordiality.

Anne's observant eyes noted that one group of girls in the corner barely acknowledged the introduction. She also noted that the two freshmen whose conversation she had overheard at the reception formed the center of that group. The four girls found seats at one end of the room and the conversation began again louder than ever. Grace and Miriam found themselves surrounded by half a dozen girls who were eager to know where they had learned to play basketball. Elfreda

Jessie Graham Flower

espied two freshmen who recited history in the same class with her and was soon deep in conversation with them. Anne, being left to her own devices, sat quietly watching the throng of animated faces around her. With her, the study of faces was a favorite pastime, and she furtively watched the little knot of girls, whose lack of cordiality had been so noticeable to her.

They were carrying on a low-toned conversation among themselves, and by the frequent glances that were being cast first in the direction of Grace, then Elfreda, Anne knew that the story of Elfreda's report to the registrar was being talked over. Anne felt her anger rising. Why should Grace be made to suffer for Elfreda's mistake, and why should Elfreda have her freshman year spoiled on account of that mistake. Of course, no one liked a tale bearer, but Elfreda would never again tell tales. Besides, why should the freshmen undertake to champion the cause of two sophomores, unless the latter had entirely misrepresented things?

Anne could never tell what prompted her to rise and stroll over to the group. The young women were so busily engaged in their conversation that they did not notice her approach. Anne heard one of them say in a disgusted tone, "I can't understand why Gertrude invited them. She knows we dislike them."

"She seems very friendly with them," grumbled another girl. "If I had known they were to be here I should have stayed upstairs or gone out rather than meet them. They showed extremely bad taste accepting Gertrude's invitation."

"Perhaps they don't know that we are down on them," suggested a pale-faced girl rather timidly.

"Of course they know it," sputtered one of the two

disgruntled freshmen. "Nell and I almost cut that Miss Harlowe the other morning. Don't try to stand up for her, Lillian. She and that Miss Briggs are beneath the notice of the really nice girls here. Overton doesn't want bullies and tale-bearers. They're not in accordance with college spirit."

The contempt with which these words were uttered stung Anne to action. Stepping forward she said quietly, although her eyes flashed, "Pardon me, but I could not help hearing what you said. Will you permit me to speak a few words in defense of my friend, Grace Harlowe?"

An astonished silence fell over the group of girls. Before one of them had time to recover from her surprise at Anne's intrusion, she began to speak in low tones that attracted no attention outside themselves, but whose earnestness carried conviction to those listening:

"You are evidently not in possession of the true account of what happened to Miss Briggs the day she came to Overton. You know, perhaps, that two sophomores took advantage of her verdancy and hazed her. Perhaps they neglected to state, however, that they accepted her invitation to eat ice cream before they returned her hospitality by conducting her to the hall of a public building where they left her to wait for the registrar. Considering the fact that she was tired from her long ride, and had had no supper, I think it was an extremely poor exhibition of the much vaunted Overton spirit. It was late that night before she reached her boarding house. She was naturally indignant and next day reported the matter to the registrar. This, I must admit, was unwise on her part. She is very sorry, now, that she did so."

"All this is not news to us," snapped Marian Cummings, one of the two freshmen Anne had overheard at the reception. She stared insolently at Anne.

"But what I am about to tell you will perhaps surprise you," Anne answered evenly. "Miss Briggs received a note purporting to come from the whole sophomore class. The writer of the note threatened her with vague penalties if she attended the sophomore reception, and practically ordered her to leave college."

The girls looked at one another without answering. This silence showed only too plainly that this was indeed news.

"Miss Briggs showed the letter to Miss Nesbit, her room-mate, and to Miss Harlowe," Anne continued composedly. "She was heartbroken over it and would have left Overton if Miss Harlowe had not persuaded her to stay. Miss Harlowe did a little investigating on her own account. She suspected two sophomores of being responsible for the letter, believing the rest of the class knew nothing about it. She called on the two young women and forced them to admit their knowledge of the note. Both denied writing it. It is evident that they have misrepresented matters among their friends. As far as Grace Harlowe is concerned she is utterly incapable of doing a mean or dishonorable act. We were classmates in high school and she was beloved by all who knew her."

Anne paused and glanced almost appealingly around the circle of tense faces. Then Elizabeth Wade, the other hostile freshman, said slowly: "Girls, I am inclined to think we have been imposed upon. Miss Pierson, I will be perfectly frank with you. We knew nothing about the note. Personally, I consider it an outrageous thing to do, and in direct violation of what we are taught regarding college spirit. Briefly, what we did hear was that Miss Briggs had reported two sophomores for playing an innocent trick on her, and that Miss Harlowe had urged her to do so. Also that Miss Harlowe had visited the two upper classmen and, after rating them in a very ill-bred manner, had ordered them to apologize to Miss Briggs."

Anne smiled. "I can't help smiling," she apologized. "If you knew Grace as I know her, you'd smile, too."

Marian Cummings's face softened. "I do wish to know her, now," she smiled. "After what you've told us I think the rest of us feel the same. I'm glad you made us listen to you, Miss Pierson."

"So am I," "and I," agreed the other girls.

Anne's face flushed with joy at her victory. "I hope 19—will be the best class Overton has ever turned out," she said simply, "and I hope that any misunderstandings that may arise will be cleared away as easily as this one has been."

"Suppose we go over and congratulate Miss Harlowe on her playing this afternoon," proposed a tall freshman, "and we might incidentally pay our respects to Miss Briggs. We must help her to live up to her good resolutions, you know," she added slyly.

Anne was in a maze of delight at her success. The other guests had been so busily engaged with their own little groups, no one of them had overheard Anne's defense of her friend. Grace, who was giving an eager account of the famous game that won her team the championship during her sophomore year at high school, looked up in surprise at the crowd of merry girls which suddenly surrounded her. For an instant she looked amazed, then smiled at them in the frank, straightforward fashion that always made friends for her.

Gertrude Wells, who, with three other freshmen, had been in the kitchen preparing the refreshments, appeared in the door just in time to see the girls surround Grace. She smiled contentedly, and nodding to the fluffy-haired little girl standing beside her said gleefully: "What did I tell you? Look in there."

The fluffy-haired little girl obeyed. "How did you do it?" was the quick answer.

"They did it themselves. I just did the inviting and they did the rest. Of course there was a certain amount of chance that they wouldn't get together, but it was worth taking. After meeting her this afternoon I felt sure that the girls were wrong, but I wished them to find out for themselves. How it happened, I don't know, but we are sure to hear the story after the party is over."

While Gertrude Wells was congratulating herself on the success of her experiment, Grace Harlowe was remarking to Miriam Nesbit that she thought Gertrude Wells would be an ideal president from 19—and that she intended pointing out this fact to the freshmen of Wayne Hall.

CHAPTER XII

UPS AND DOWNS

At breakfast the next morning Grace began her campaign, and she continued to sing Gertrude Wells's praises when she encountered a group of her freshmen friends after the services. Then Anne, Miriam, Elfreda and she went for a stroll down College Street and into Vinton's for ices. Here they encountered quite a delegation of girls from Morton House, among whom was Gertrude herself, and a great deal of mysterious intriguing went on behind that young woman's back, who, quite unconscious of the honor about to be thrust upon her, was telling her chum that she thought Grace Harlowe would make a good president for 19—.

On her way home Grace exclaimed delightedly: "Look across the street, girls! There is Mabel Ashe. Let's go over and speak to her."

Suiting the action to the word the four girls hurried across the street to greet their favorite. Mabel smiled pleasantly, stretching forth a welcoming hand, but the young woman with her regarded their presence as an intrusion and glared her displeasure at the newcomers.

"How do you do, Miss Alden?" ventured Grace politely, but

Miss Alden stared over her head and with a frigid, "Really, Mabel, under the circumstances, you'll have to excuse my leaving you," she turned and marched off in the other direction.

"I suppose we are the circumstances," said Grace, with a faint smile. She was furiously angry at the unlooked-for snub, but refused to show it. Anne looked distressed, Miriam was frowning, while Elfreda glowered savagely.

"Don't mind what she says," soothed Mabel. "She feels awfully cross this afternoon because she has met with a disappointment. She has an invitation to a Pi Kappa Gamma dance and she has been refused permission to go. Result, she is in a raging, tearing humor."

"But I thought one could always go to a fraternity dance if properly chaperoned," remarked Grace innocently.

"One can," mimicked Mabel, "if one doesn't ask permission to go too often, and if one has no conditions to work off. Now, you see why Mistress Beatrice is obliged to languish at home while the man who invited her will no doubt have to invite some other girl, who is lucky enough to have no conditions."

"Isn't it rather early in the year to be conditioned?" asked Miriam.

"Yes, but Beatrice has been cutting classes ever since she came back this year," confided Mabel. "I am not betraying a confidence in telling you this. She admits that she neglects her work. She says she is going to settle down after mid-year's exams and work."

"I think she's about the most snobbish proposition I ever

came across," announced Elfreda. "It would serve her right if she did flunk in her examinations. I hope with all my heart she falls down with an awful bump."

Elfreda had forgotten her former aspirations toward cultivating the true college spirit.

"You mustn't wish even your bitterest enemy bad luck," smiled Mabel Ashe. "Superstitious people say that the bad luck will be visited on the head of the one who wishes it."

"I'm not superstitious," retorted Elfreda. "Of course, I believe that pins cut friendship, and that it's bad luck to see the new moon through the window, or to walk under a ladder. It's a sure sign of death to break a looking glass or dream of white flowers, too, and to drop a spoon means certain disappointment, but aside from a few little things like that, I certainly don't believe in signs."

"Oh, no, you don't believe in signs," chorused the girls, in gleeful sarcasm.

"Well, I don't," reiterated Elfreda. "That is, not a whole lot of them."

"Good-bye, children, I must leave you at this corner," announced Mabel. "Come and see me soon. I'll look you up the first evening I have free."

"I should think that Miss Alden would hate herself," remarked Elfreda scornfully, as she marched along beside Grace. "She hates you, that's sure enough."

"Nonsense, why should Miss Alden hate me? You are letting your imagination run away with you, Elfreda," laughed Grace.

"Don't you believe it," declared Elfreda doggedly. "She doesn't like you, because Mabel likes you, and she likes Mabel. Some one told me the other day that she can't bear to have Mabel look cross-eyed at any other girl here. She claims that it's because she loves her so much, but I think it's because she wants to have the most popular girl at Overton for her friend," finished the stout girl shrewdly.

"What shall we do this afternoon?" called Miriam Nesbit over her shoulder.

"Go on boosting our candidate," laughed Anne. "Let us go for a walk after dinner. We will call on Ruth Denton. Then we'll take her with us to Morton House. That will be a nice way for her to meet the Morton House girls. While we are there we can find out how the land lies. Then we will take Ruth home with us for supper and the rest of the evening, if she doesn't have to study."

At the dinner table that day Grace again introduced the subject of the class election and was pleased to note that her suggestion regarding Gertrude Wells as the best possible choice for class president had borne fruit. The two sophomores at the table who had been through two class elections, having just elected their president, smiled tolerantly at the excitement exhibited by the "babies," and advised them not to elect in haste and repent at leisure.

"Why don't you children find out something about what the rest of the class think before you rush into electing Miss Wells, just to please two or three girls?" asked Virginia Gaines, the sophomore who had assiduously cultivated the acquaintance of Elfreda—then dropped her at the first sign of trouble. "We sophomores wouldn't allow ourselves to be influenced by cliques. We consider the good of the class of more importance than the good of any individual member."

She smiled disagreeably at Grace, who looked at her steadily, then said, "Was your remark intended for me and my friends, Miss Gaines?"

"Not necessarily," flung back the sophomore, "unless you feel that it applies to you and to them."

"No, I don't believe it does," declared Grace with a quiet smile. "In fact, I quite agree with you in saying that the good of the class should always come first. That is why we are all anxious to nominate Miss Wells for president of 19—."

A dull flush rose to Virginia Gaines's sallow face. She was not quick-witted and could think of no reply. The other freshmen at the table were taking no pains to disguise their glee at Grace's retort. Virginia's sarcastic comment had proved a boomerang and she had gained nothing by launching it. She hurried through with her dessert and left the table without another word, casting a half malignant look at Grace as she went.

"Virginia's mad,
And I am glad,"

sang a freshman softly as the door banged.

"Please, don't," said Grace soberly. "I'm sorry she's angry, but I couldn't help it. I seem always fated to arouse sophomore ire."

"I wouldn't mind a little thing like that," comforted Elfreda. "I'd rather be the enemy than the friend of some girls."

"But I don't want to be the enemy of any girl," declared Grace, looking almost appealingly about the table.

Jessie Graham Flower

"Of course you don't," soothed Emma Dean, a tall, near-sighted girl at the end of the table, who had the reputation of making brilliant recitations. "You couldn't antagonize the rest of us if you tried. That is, unless you deliberately broke my glasses."

A shout of laughter went up from the table. Virginia Gaines, who had lingered in the hall, heard it, and her face darkened. In spite of Grace's declaration for peace she had made an enemy.

CHAPTER XIII

GRACE TURNS ELECTIONEER

Directly after dinner that afternoon, the four girls, looking very smart in their new fall suits and hats, set out for Ruth's. They found her seated at her little table eating a very humble dinner of her own cooking. "I'm sorry I can't offer you anything to eat. I have 'licked the platter clean,' you see. But won't you have some tea? I think I have cups enough to go round, only I'm afraid I haven't enough saucers."

"Thank you," began Elfreda, "but—" then a warning pinch from Miriam caused her to eye the latter reproachfully and subside.

"We'd love to have tea with you," smiled Miriam. "Wouldn't we, girls?"

Elfreda, who had divined the reason for the pinch, said "yes" with the others, and Ruth bustled about with pink cheeks and a delicious air of importance. She took down from the cupboard shelf a box of Nabiscos that she had been treasuring for some such occasion as the present, placing them on a little hand-painted plate, the only piece of china she possessed. When the tea was made the guests emptied the little tea-pot and ate all of the Nabiscos, to the intense

Jessie Graham Flower

satisfaction of their hostess, to whom entertaining was a new and delightful pastime.

"Now, you must put on your wraps and go with us," commanded Grace, setting her cup on the table. "We are going to Morton House to make our party call. The future president of 19—lives there. That is, we think she is the future president and we hope to make others think so, too."

Ruth obediently went to the closet where her plain little hat and shabby, old-style coat hung. She looked hesitatingly from the smartly tailored suits of her guests to her own well-worn coat, then with a proud little lifting of her head, she took it down and began putting it on.

During their walk to Morton House the girls met several freshmen they knew, and these were faithfully interviewed as to their preference in the matter of 19—'s president. To Grace's delight none of them had made any choice in regard to candidates, so her glowing remarks as to Gertrude Wells's ability to make a good president fell on fertile soil. Fortune favored them, for when they reached Morton House they found Miss Wells out and two-thirds of the girls downstairs in the living room listening to the new songs that the curly-haired little girl at the piano had received from New York the day before. She was in the middle of one when the girls entered the room. Grace held up a warning finger and pointed to the piano.

The song ended several notes short and the little girl turned her head toward her audience, saying, "I knew some one came in."

"Won't you sing for us?" asked Anne, who loved music. The little girl's voice reminded her of Nora O'Malley's, and Nora's singing had always been a source of delight to Anne.

"Not now," smiled the singer. "I wish to talk, but I'll sing for you later."

"We came over this afternoon," said Grace to the girl sitting next to her, "to find out who Morton House wants for president. We would like to have Miss Wells—"

Grace was interrupted by a little cry of delight. The girl sprang to her feet and cried, "Hear! hear!" Then she took Grace by the shoulders and laughingly commanded, "Arise, occupy the center of the room and tell the girls what you have just told me."

Before she knew it Grace was standing in the middle of the room, earnestly advocating Gertrude Wells's cause, while the Morton House girls were making as much demonstration as was considered decorous on Sunday. Grace concluded with, "I'm quite sure that every girl at Morton House will vote for Miss Wells and every freshman at Wayne Hall, too. Before class meeting next Friday I hope to be able to convince the majority of 19—that they will make no mistake in voting for Miss Wells."

Grace sat down amid subdued applause, and every one began talking to her neighbor about the coming election. Ruth Denton listened to the gay chatter with shining eyes. She had forgotten all about her shabby suit. Presently the curly-haired little girl came over and sat down beside her, asking her if she liked college. Ruth looked admiringly at the little girl, whose dainty gown, silk stockings and smart pumps bespoke luxury, and answered earnestly that she liked it better every day. "You must come and see me," said the curly-haired little girl, whose name was Arline Thayer. "We recite Livy in the same section, so we have something in common to grumble about. Isn't the lesson for to-morrow terrific, though?"

"I haven't looked at it to-day," confessed Ruth happily. "I study hard on Sunday as a rule, but to-day is the first time, you see—" Ruth hesitated.

"I see," said Arline kindly. "Hereafter you mustn't study all day on Sunday. You must come and take dinner with me next Sunday and stay all afternoon. Promise, now, that you'll come."

"Oh, thank you. I'd love to come," stammered Ruth. She could scarcely believe that this dainty little girl who wore such pretty clothes had actually invited her to dinner at Morton House.

"Did you have a good time, Ruth?" asked Miriam, as they started for home late that afternoon.

"Don't ask her," interposed Anne mischievously. "She forsook me and hob-nobbed openly all afternoon with that curly-haired girl, Miss Thayer. I am terribly jealous, and there is a deadly gleam in my eye."

"Please, don't think, Anne—" began Ruth nervously, looking distressed.

"I am past thinking," retorted Anne melodramatically. "The time for action has come. I shall challenge my rival to a duel the first time I see her. We will fight with—"

"Brooms," grinned Elfreda. "I once fought a duel down in our orchard with my cousin Dick. Brooms were the chosen weapons. We certainly did great execution with them. They were new ones and the brushy part kept getting in our way until we happened to think of cutting it off and fighting with the handles. After that things went more scientifically, until Dick hit me on the nose by mistake. I wailed and shrieked and had the nose bleed, and Ma whipped Dick and sent him home. That was about the only duel I ever fought," concluded the stout girl reflectively, "but if there's the slightest possibility of either of you choosing brooms for weapons, I'll give you the benefit of my experience by training you for the fray."

"Shall I take her at her word, Ruth?" laughed Anne.

"No, I'm not worth all that trouble," returned Ruth half shyly.

"We won't have time to escort you home, Ruth," remarked Grace, looking at her watch. "We must leave you at this corner. Be a good child and don't sit up all night to study. Come over Tuesday evening to dinner, and we'll all study together."

"Thank you, I will if I don't have too much mending on hand," replied Ruth. "Good-bye. I can't begin to tell you how much I've enjoyed being with you."

"Don't try," advised Elfreda laconically. "We've had just as much fun as you have."

Miriam and Grace exchanged glances. Elfreda was making rapid strides along the road to fellowship.

"I like that girl," she announced as Ruth disappeared around the corner. "She has lots of pluck. When we asked her to go out with us to-day she looked at her old coat and hat, then at us. I could see that she was ashamed of them. But she wasn't ashamed for more than five seconds. She straightened up and looked as proud as a princess. I could see—"

"A great deal more than we did," finished Miriam. "I believe you have eyes in the back of your head, Elfreda."

Jessie Graham Flower

"I don't miss much," agreed Elfreda modestly. "I saw you and Grace look at each other when I said we'd had just as much fun as Ruth," she added slyly. "I know what you were both thinking, too. You were thinking that I wasn't so selfish as when I came here. You needn't color so because I caught you. I am selfish, but I'm beginning to find out, just the same, that there are other people in the world besides myself."

CHAPTER XIV

AN INVITATION AND A MISUNDERSTANDING

The class elections went off with a snap. Grace nominated Gertrude Wells for president. There were two other nominations, and after the three young women had gone through the ordeal of inspection before the class, the votes were cast. Gertrude Wells was elected president by an overwhelming majority, and the nomination and election of the other class officers quickly followed. The next night Grace and Miriam gave a dinner in honor of her election at Vinton's, to which twelve girls were invited, and for a week the new president was feted and lionized until she laughingly declared that a return to the simple life was her only means of re-establishing her lost reputation for study and avoiding impending warnings.

The class of 19—soon became used to being a regularly organized body and held its class meetings with as much pride as though it were the most important organization in college. Thanksgiving plans now occupied the foreground, and as the vacation was too short even to think about going home, the girls began to make plans to spend their brief holiday as advantageously as possible at or at least very near Overton.

Jessie Graham Flower

"There's a football game over at Willston, on Thanksgiving Day," remarked Grace, looking up from the paper on which she was jotting down possible amusements for vacation. Miriam had run into Grace's room for a brief chat before dinner. "We don't know any Willston men, though. I think football is ever so much more interesting when one knows the players. If we were nearer the boys we might attend a fraternity dance once in a while."

"David says in his last letter that he is waiting impatiently for the holidays. Just think, Grace, won't that be splendid to be back in dear old Oakdale again?"

"It seems years since I kissed Mother and Father good-bye," said Grace, rather wistfully. "How I'd like to be at home for Thanksgiving."

"Don't think about it," advised Miriam. "I was as blue as indigo last night. Let's keep our minds strictly on what we're going to do with our holiday. What have you put down?"

"The football game first. Then I have tickets for a play that the Morton House girls intend to give. We might go to Vinton's for supper on Thanksgiving night. If we have a Thanksgiving dinner here that day it's safe to say supper won't amount to much. I think—"

Grace did not finish with what she was saying. A quick step sounded down the hall and an instant later Anne ran into the room waving an open letter in her hand. "Girls, girls!" she cried, "you never can guess!"

"What is it? Tell us at once," commanded Grace, springing from her chair. "You've received good news from some one we know."

"Yes," replied Anne happily. "My letter is from Miss Southard. She wishes us to spend Thanksgiving with her and her brother in New York City. Isn't that glorious, and do you think we'll be allowed to go?"

"Hurrah!" cried Grace. "Since we can't go home, it's the very nicest sort of plan. I think we'll be allowed to go. We haven't any conditions to work off, and I haven't planned to do any extra studying either. Thank goodness, my allowance had an extra ten dollars attached to it this month. Mother wrote that she thought I might need the money, and I do. I couldn't possibly have stretched my regular allowance over this trip."

"I have money enough, I think," said Miriam. "I am a thrifty soul. I saved ten dollars out of my last month's allowance. It was really extra money that I had asked Mother for. I intended to buy a sweater and then changed my mind."

"The expenses of my trip will have to come out of my college money," confessed Anne, a trifle soberly, "but I'd be willing to spend twice that much to see the Southards. Mr. Southard is playing 'Hamlet' and so we shall have the opportunity of seeing him in what the critics consider his greatest part."

"Remember, we haven't asked permission to go, yet," remarked Grace.

"The registrar couldn't be so cruel as to refuse us," said Miriam cheerfully. "Let's besiege her fortress in a body."

"When shall we make our plea?"

"To-morrow morning after chapel," suggested Anne. "Then we'll have more time to plan our trip."

The registrar's office was duly besieged the next morning, as agreed, and the three girls hurried off to their classes with beaming faces. When they returned to Wayne Hall after recitations that afternoon it was to find Elfreda hanging over the railing in the upstairs hall, an unusually solemn expression on her face.

"Are you going?" she called down anxiously. "Yes," nodded Grace. "At three o'clock Wednesday afternoon."

Elfreda gave a smothered exclamation that sounded like, "What a shame," and disappeared into her room, slamming the door.

"I'm coming into your room for a while," said Miriam. "Elfreda will open the door before long."

"Yes, do," returned Grace hospitably. "Is she angry because you are going away over Thanksgiving?"

"No, not angry, but awfully disappointed. She almost cried last night when I told her about it. I suspect she is crying now. She's like an overgrown child at times."

"I'm sorry we can't take her with us," deplored Grace. "Does she know where we are going?"

"Yes," returned Miriam. "She was practically thunderstruck when she learned we were to visit the Southards. The queer part of it is this. She saw Mr. Southard and Anne in 'As You Like It' last year. She thinks Mr. Southard the greatest actor she ever saw, and she even spoke of Anne's cleverness as Rosalind; she doesn't know it was Anne who played the part."

"Anne doesn't wish her or any one else here to know it,"

cautioned Grace. "Do you suppose any other girl here saw Anne as Rosalind?"

"Goodness knows," replied Miriam, with a shrug. "There's an old saying that 'murder will out.' If any one here did see her, sooner or later she'll be identified and lionized."

"That's just why I don't wish the girls here to know," protested Anne, who had been listening to the conversation of her friends, a slight frown puckering her smooth forehead. "I don't care to be patronized and petted, but secretly held at arms' length because I am a professional player. If the girls find out that I played Rosalind in Mr. Southard's company I'll never hear the last of it." In her anxiety Anne's voice rose above its customary low key. In fact, all three had been talking rather loudly, and the entire conversation had been carried straight to the ears of the girl who stood outside the almost closed door. Elfreda had come across the hall to hear the details of the proposed visit, but had remained outside the door transfixed at what she heard. Then she found her voice.

"So that's your idea of true friendship, is it?" demanded an angry, choking voice that caused the surprised young women to start and look toward the door. Elfreda stepped into the room, her face flushed with anger, her blue eyes fairly snapping. "You make a great fuss over me when there's nothing going on, but none of you would invite me to go with you to New York, when you know I'm crazy to go. And that's not enough, you can't get along without talking about me. I heard every word Anne said. I know now that it was she who played Rosalind in 'As You Like It' last winter, because I saw her with my own eyes. If you girls had been as honorable as you pretend to be you'd have told me about it and I never would have said a word. But, no, Anne was afraid to tell, for fear she'd 'never hear the last of it,'" sneered Elfreda, mimicking Anne. "She's right, too. She never will.

I'll not stop until I tell every girl at Overton the whole story. When you come back," she went on, turning to Miriam, "you'll find that I've moved. I thought you were nice and I tried to be like you, but now I don't care to live in the same house with you, and I don't intend ever to notice any of you again. With that she rushed across the hall, slammed the door, and turned the key.

"Locked out," said Miriam grimly. "I hope she'll let me in before the dinner bell rings. I'd like to change this grimy blouse for a clean one. I'll try to reason with her, once she opens the door."

"Shall we go in, too, and try to explain matters?" asked Anne. "I didn't say that she would tell the girls about my stage work. Surely, she understands, too, that we are not at liberty to invite her to go with us. I'll tell you what I will do. I'll telegraph the Southards and ask permission to invite her. They will be perfectly willing for us to bring her."

"That might be a good plan," reflected Grace. "Don't waste another minute, Anne, but telegraph Miss Southard at once."

"Yes, go ahead," counseled Miriam, "and while you're gone I'll try to pacify Elfreda."

But all Miriam's efforts to restore peace failed. When a little later she knocked gently on the door, Elfreda unlocked it, but received her roommate's friendly overtures in sulky silence. After dinner, for the first time since the sophomore reception, she spent the evening in Virginia Gaines's room and that night the two girls prepared for sleep without exchanging a word.

Meanwhile Anne telegraphed, "May we bring friend? Will explain later. Anne," and was anxiously awaiting a reply. It came the next morning while they were at breakfast and read: "Your friends always welcome. Telegraph train you will arrive. Mary Southard." Anne passed the telegram to Grace, who sat next to her. After one quick glance at it Grace passed it to Miriam. Elfreda, who sat directly opposite her, watched the passing of the telegram with compressed lips. Miriam, raising her eyes from the yellow slip, found those of her angry roommate fixed on her in mingled curiosity and disdain. Ignoring the look she said quietly, "I should like to see you for a moment after breakfast, Elfreda. I have something to tell you."

The stout girl's eyes narrowed. She glanced about the table and saw Virginia Gaines watching her with a disagreeable smile. The sophomore raised her eyebrows and shrugged her shoulders as though to say, "So, you are going to allow her to order you about." Elfreda's face grew dark with angry purpose. She leaned well forward across the table and said in a tone of suppressed fury: "Kindly keep your remarks to yourself. I don't care to hear them."

"Very well," replied Miriam coldly, although her eyes flashed and the temper that had been all but uncontrollable in days gone by threatened to burst forth in all its old fury. Several girls smiled, and Virginia Gaines laughed aloud.

"A new declaration of independence has evidently been signed," she jeered. "Too bad, isn't it, Miss Harlowe? You'll have to begin all over again on some one else."

"I am not likely to trouble you, at any rate, Miss Gaines," returned Grace pointedly.

This time the laugh was at Virginia's expense. A dull flush overspread her plain face. Her angry eyes met Grace's steady gray ones, then fell before the honest contempt she read there. During that brief instant she saw herself through Grace's eyes and the sharp retort that rose to her lips remained unuttered.

In the next instant Grace was sorry for her rude retort. It would have been far better to remain silent, she reflected. By answering she had shown Virginia that the latter's taunt had annoyed her.

"I wish I hadn't answered Miss Gaines," she confided to Miriam as they were leaving the dining room. "It doesn't add to one's freshman dignity to quarrel."

"I am glad you did," returned Miriam. "It was a well-merited snub, and she deserved it."

CHAPTER XV

GREETING OLD FRIENDS

To spend their brief holiday with the Southards was the next best thing to going home, in the opinion of the Oakdale girls. Mr. Southard met them at the station with his automobile, and a twenty minutes' drive brought them to the Southard home. Miss Southard met them at the door with welcoming arms. She was particularly delighted to see Anne, for the few weeks Anne had spent in their house had endeared her to the Southards and made them wish her their "little sister" in reality rather than by fond adoption.

"What shall we do after dinner to-night?" asked Miss Southard, as she showed her guests to their rooms after the first affectionate greetings had been exchanged. "Everett, as you know, is appearing as Hamlet, and wishes you to see him in the part. However, he has engaged a box for us for to-morrow night. To-night we will go to some other theatre if you wish."

"To tell you the truth," replied Anne, slipping her hand into that of the older woman, "we'd rather spend the evening quietly with you. That is, unless you care particularly about our going out."

Miss Southard's face revealed her pleasure at this announcement. "Would you really?" she asked. "I should like to have you girls to myself rather than go to the theatre, but I supposed you would prefer seeing a successful play to staying at home with me."

"Nothing could drag us from the house after that confession," laughed Grace. "For my part I think it would be much nicer to stay at home. We have so much to tell you."

Dinner was a merry meal. Mr. Southard, who in the meantime had come in from the theatre, became so absorbed in the conversation of his young guests that both he and his sister forgot the time. The entrance into the dining room of James, his valet, with his hat and coat, and the warning words, "Ten minutes past seven, sir," caused him to spring from his chair, glance at his watch with a rueful smile, and hurry out to where his car stood waiting for him.

"It's nice to be an idol of the public, but it's hard on the idol just the same," sighed Grace, as the door closed after him. "Shall we see him again to-night?"

"You may stay up and wait for him if you wish," returned Miss Southard, "but it will be after midnight. 'Hamlet' is a long play."

"I saw Mr. Southard in 'Hamlet' long before I knew him," remarked Anne. "My father and I were in New York rehearsing the play in which I afterwards refused to work. The manager of our company was a friend of Mr. Southard. One night he asked me if I would like to see the greatest actor in America play 'Hamlet.' I said that Everett Southard was the only man I ever wished to see in the role. I shall never forget how I felt when he handed me a slip of paper. It was in Mr. Southard 's handwriting and called for two seats at the theatre where he was playing. He said he had asked Mr. Southard for the passes purposely for me, because," Anne flushed slightly, "he insisted that in me lay the making of a great artist, and that I ought to see nothing but the great plays, enacted by great players."

"How interesting!" exclaimed Grace. "You never told us anything about your stage days before. What did you think after you saw 'Hamlet'?"

"I went about in a dream for days afterward," confessed Anne. "Then, I began to hate the play we were rehearsing, and finally ended by refusing to stay in the company. Mother was with my sister in Oakdale, so I went to them. I felt that there was no chance for me to ever become great. I had no faith in my own ability, and I was determined not to waste my life as a second or third rate actor. So I gave up the stage and decided to try to get an education, then teach. You know the rest of my story. Now comes the hardest part. After giving up all idea of the stage, the door that I thought was barred has been opened to me. The unbelievable has come to pass, and I have in a measure achieved what once seemed unattainable. Do you think that I ought to bury my one talent when my college days are over and become a teacher, or do you believe that I should put it to good use by becoming an exponent of the highest dramatic art?"

Anne paused, looking almost melancholy in her earnestness.

"My dear child," said Miss Southard gravely. "You are straining your mental eyes with trying to look into the future. Wait until graduation day comes. By that time you will know what is best for you to do. As far as your work in the theatre is concerned, I consider that it is far more to your credit to use the talent God has given you to help yourself through college, than to wear yourself out doing tutoring or servants' work. There is no stigma attached to my brother's art, why should there be to yours?"

"Good for you, Miss Southard," cheered Grace. "I'll tell you a secret. Anne thinks just as you do, only she won't say so."

"While you are here, Anne, Everett wishes you to meet Mr. Forest, the manager of the stock company he wrote you about," continued Miss Southard.

"He is a playwright, producer and manager all in one, isn't he?" asked Miriam. "I have seen ever so many pictures of him, and read a great deal about him. They say he is always on the lookout for material for stars."

"Yes," returned Miss Southard. "He was in Europe during Anne's engagement here last winter. Nevertheless, he heard of her and asked Everett a great many questions about her. I think he will offer her an engagement for next summer with a certain stock company which he controls."

"How can I ever repay you and Mr. Southard for all you have done for me?" said Anne earnestly.

"By accepting the engagement," laughed Grace.

"Grace is right," agreed Miss Southard. "Everett and I are trying to help Anne in the way we think best."

"Then I will be pleasing myself, too," confessed Anne. "For I love my dramatic work as well as I do that of the college. Now, let us talk about Oakdale and all our friends. We have so many things to tell you."

It was after eleven o'clock when the girls retired. They had decided not to stay up until Mr. Southard's return. Once in their rooms they found themselves too sleepy for conversation and five minutes after their lights were out they were fast asleep.

They were up in good season the next morning, as it had been agreed that they should be present at the morning service in the church the Southards attended. Thanksgiving dinner was to be served at exactly half past twelve o'clock, instead of at night, for Mr. Southard had a matinee as well as an evening performance to give and never left the theatre for dinner during this short intermission.

In church that morning as she sat listening to the beautiful service, Grace felt that she had everything for which to be thankful. In her heart she said an earnest little prayer for all those unfortunates to whom life had grudged even bread. She resolved to be more kind and helpful during the coming year, and prayed that she might see the right clearly and have the courage always to choose it.

"I felt as though I wanted to be superlatively good all the rest of my life," confessed Miriam on the way home. "That minister preached as though he loved the whole world and wished it to be happy."

"He does. He is a very fine man," said Miss Southard, "and does splendid work among the very poor people. It will perhaps surprise you to know that he was at one time an actor of great promise in Mr. Southard's company. Then he received the conviction that his duty lay in entering the ministry and he left the stage, entered a theological institute and after receiving his degree came back to New York as the pastor of a small church on the East Side. Everett and I were among his most faithful parishioners. Then later on he received an appointment to the church we just left, and has been there ever since."

"That will be an interesting story to tell the girls when we go back to college," said Grace thoughtfully. "He is a wonderful man, he made me feel as though it paid to do one's best."

"That is the reason he has been so successful in his work, I suppose," remarked Anne. "He makes other people feel that it pays to be good, too."

From the subject of the actor-minister the conversation drifted to Overton. Miss Southard listened interestedly to Grace's vivid description of the college, the various halls and even the faculty.

"Then you are satisfied with your choice? You never wish that you had entered Vassar or Smith or any other college?"

"Yes, I am satisfied," declared Grace, while Miriam and Anne echoed her reply, but Grace might have truthfully added that there were times when even the glorious privilege of being an Overton freshman had its drawbacks.

CHAPTER XVI

THANKSGIVING WITH THE SOUTHARDS

Thanksgiving dinner was served at exactly half-past twelve o'clock, and eaten with much merriment and good cheer. At half-past one Mr. Southard was obliged to leave his sister and guests, and at two o'clock they were getting into their wraps, preparatory to accompanying Miss Southard to another theatre to see one of the most successful plays of the season. That night they saw the actor in "Hamlet," and his remarkable portrayal of the ill-fated Prince of Denmark was something long to be remembered by the three girls as well as by the rest of the enthusiastic assemblage that witnessed it.

"I shall never forget the awful look in his poor eyes," said Grace solemnly. Then she joined in the insistent applause that Everett Southard's art had evoked. Presently the actor appeared and bowed his appreciation of the tribute. Then he made his exit nor could he be induced to appear again.

Anne sat as though turned to stone. She could not find words to express the emotions that had thrilled her during Mr. Southard's marvelous portrayal of the role. His own person- ality was completely submerged in that of the melancholy ghost-ridden youth, who, dedicating his life to the purpose of avenging his father's murder, welcomed death with open arms when his purpose had been accomplished. She had seen a great play and a great actor. The first time she saw "Hamlet" she left the theatre heartsick and discouraged. To-night she was leaving it alert and triumphant.

"Anne has been touched by the finger of Genius," smiled Miss Southard, as she marshaled her charges to their automobile.

"How did you know?" asked Anne, but in spite of her smiling lips her brown eyes were full of tears.

"My dear, living with Everett has taught me the signs," said his sister simply.

"I should like to play Ophelia to Mr. Southard's Hamlet," said Anne dreamily.

"Perhaps you will have the chance to do so some day. Everett thinks you would be a more convincing Ophelia than the young woman you saw in the part to-night," encouraged Miss Southard.

Anne looked so delighted at those words that Miriam and Grace exchanged swift glances. It was evident that the genuine love of her profession lay deep within the soul of their friend.

"We will go for a short drive, then come back for Everett," planned Miss Southard. "He has promised to hurry to-night—then we will have a nice little supper at home." Their hostess and her brother had agreed that there should be no after-the-theatre suppers at any of the so-called fashionable restaurants for their young guests. "I am sure their mothers would not approve of it," Miss Southard had said, "and I feel that I am responsible for them every moment they are here."

The party at home was an informal affair in which there were many cooks, but no broth spoiled. To see Mr. Southard earnestly engaged in making a Welsh rarebit, an accomplishment in which he claimed to be highly proficient, one would never have suspected him of being able to thrill vast audiences by his slightest word or gesture.

"I can't believe that only two hours ago you were 'Hamlet,'" laughed Grace. "You look anything but tragic now."

"He looked every bit as tragic just a moment ago. I saw a distinct Hamlet-like expression creep into his face," stated Miriam boldly.

"You have sharp eyes," smiled Mr. Southard. "I happened to remember that I had forgotten what goes into this rarebit next. I could feel myself growing cold with despair. Then the inspiration came and now it will be ready in two minutes."

The rarebit was voted a success. After decorating the actor with a bit of blue ribbon on which Miriam painstakingly printed "first premium" with a lead pencil, he was escorted to the head of the table and congratulated roundly upon being able not only to act but to cook.

The next morning every one confessed to being a trifle sleepy, but appeared at breakfast at the usual time. After breakfast Mr. Southard carried Anne off to met Mr. Forest, while Miss Southard, Miriam and Grace decided to go for a drive through Central Park. It was a clear, cold, sparkling day with just enough snow to make it seem like real Thanksgiving weather.

"Too bad Anne can't be with us," said Grace regretfully.

"Everett will take her for a drive before bringing her home," replied Miss Southard.

Shortly after their return to the house Mr. Southard and Anne returned from their drive. Anne's eyes were sparkling and her cheeks rosy as she ran up the steps.

"Anne must have heard good news!" exclaimed Grace, running from her post at one of the drawing room windows into the hall, Miriam at her heels.

"The deed is done, girls," laughed Anne. "Behold in me the future star of the Forest Stock Company. It doesn't sound much like Rosalind, does it? and it means awfully hard work, but I'll earn enough money next summer to almost finish paying my way through college."

"Hurrah!" cried Grace. "We won't allow you to become lonesome. We will come and visit you during vacation."

"That ought to reconcile me to having to work all summer," smiled Anne. "I shall be selfish and manage to have some of you girls with me all the time."

"How do you like Mr. Forest?" asked Miriam.

"Ever so much," returned Anne. "Like most successful men, he is quiet and unassuming. Mr. Southard and he did almost all the talking. I spoke when I was spoken to and did as I was bid."

"Good little Anne," jeered Miriam. "As a reward of merit we will take you shopping this afternoon."

"How would you like to go to the opera to-night?" asked Mr. Southard. "'Madame Butterfly' is to be sung."

"Better than anything else, now that I've seen 'Hamlet'!" exclaimed Grace, with shining eyes. Miriam and Anne both expressed an eager desire to hear Puccini's exquisite opera, and Miss Southard called two of her friends on the telephone, inviting them to join the box party. The same evening gowns had to do duty for the opera as well as for "Hamlet," but this did not detract one whit from their pleasant anticipations. "The people who saw us at the theatre the other night won't see us at the opera," argued Grace. The three girls were in Grace's room holding a consultation on the subject of what to wear.

"That is if they saw us at all," laughed Miriam. "Elfreda says Oakdale isn't down on the map, you know."

"That reminds me, what excuse did you make to Miss Southard about Elfreda not coming with us, Anne?" asked Grace.

"I merely said she had changed her mind about coming."

"Did you mention that she changed it violently?" slyly put in Miriam.

"I did not," was the smiling assertion. "I don't like to think about it, let alone mention it."

"Do you suppose she'll improve the opportunity and tell Anne's private affairs all over college?" questioned Miriam.

"I don't know," said Grace briefly. "Let us put her out of our minds for now. It won't do any good to worry about what she may or may not do. When we go back to Overton we shall know."

That night the girls listened to the wonderful voice of the

Jessie Graham Flower

prima donna whose name has become synonymous with that of "Chu Chu San," the little Japanese maid. Anne wondered as she drank in the music whether this beautiful young prima donna had ever had any scruples about appearing before the public. Miriam was thinking that David would be bitterly disappointed when he knew that Anne was going back to the stage during vacation. While, though she would not have confessed it for worlds, the throbbing undercurrent of heart break that ran through the music was filling Grace with unmistakable homesickness. She wanted her mother and she wanted her badly. What would she not give to feel her mother's dear arms around her. When the curtain shut out the still form of the Japanese girl and the prima donna received her usual ovation, the tears that stood in Grace's eyes were not alone a tribute to the singer and the tragic death of Chu Chu San.

* * * * *

On Saturday morning the girls went on another shopping expedition, and in the afternoon attended a recital given by a celebrated pianist. After the recital, instead of going home, Miss Southard surprised her guests by taking them over to the theatre where her brother was playing. Mr. Southard had arranged that they should be admitted to his dressing room. It was the same theatre in which Anne had played the previous winter and several of the stage hands recognized her and bowed respectfully to her as she passed through to the actor's dressing room. They found him still in costume. He never changed to street clothing on matinee days.

"You are respectfully and cordially invited to eat dinner in my dressing room," announced Mr. Southard the moment they were fairly inside the door. "I have ordered dinner for six o'clock."

Eating dinner in a dressing room was an innovation as far as Grace and Miriam were concerned, but to Anne it was nothing new. It had been in the usual order of things during her brief engagement in "As You Like It." As it was after five o'clock when they arrived it seemed only a little while until a waiter appeared with table linen and silver, which Mr. Southard ordered arranged on the table that had been brought in for the occasion. Then the dinner was served and eaten with much gayety and laughter. After dinner, a pleasant hour of conversation followed, and later on the visitors were introduced to the various members of the company. Unlike many professionals who have achieved greatness, Mr. Southard was thoroughly democratic, and displayed none of the snobbish tactics with his company which so often humiliate and embitter the lesser lights of a theatrical company.

At eight o'clock they said good-bye to the actor. Through the courtesy of Mr. Forest they were to witness a play in which a wonderful little girl of fifteen who had taken New York by storm was to appear. After the play they were to pick up Mr. Southard at his theatre and go home together. That night another jolly little supper was held in the Southards' dining room, then three sleepy young women fairly tumbled into their beds, completely tired out by their eventful day.

As the return to Overton was to be made on the noon train, the Southard household rose in good season on Sunday morning. Breakfast was rather a quiet meal, for the shadow of saying good-bye hung over the little house party.

"When shall we see you again, I wonder?" sighed Miss Southard regretfully. "You are going home for Christmas, I suppose."

"Oh, yes," replied Grace quickly. "I wish you might spend it with us, but I suppose it would be out of the question. You must come to Oakdale next summer. We can't entertain you with plays and recitals, but we can get up boating and gypsy parties. The boys will be home, then, and we can arrange to have plenty of good times. Will you come?"

"With pleasure if all is well with us at that time," promised Mr. Southard, and his sister.

When the last good-byes had been said and the girls were comfortably settled for the afternoon's ride that lay before them they were forced to admit that they were just a little tired.

"We have had a perfectly wonderful holiday," asserted Grace, "and the Southards are the most hospitable people in the world, but it seems as though I'd never make up my lost sleep. I shall become a rabid advocate of the half-past ten o'clock rule for the next week at least. I wonder how the boys spent Thanksgiving. Of course they went to the football game. I'll warrant Hippy ate too much."

"I wish Jessica and Nora could have been with us," remarked Anne. "Miss Southard wrote them, too, but they couldn't come. Did you see Nora's telegram?"

"Yes," replied Grace. "It said a letter would follow. I suppose she'll explain in that. Well, it's back to college again for us. I wonder if Elfreda has moved."

"We shall know in due season," returned Miriam grimly. "I have visions of the appearance of my hapless room, if she has vacated it. I expect to see my best beloved belongings scattered to the four corners or else piled in a heap in the middle of the floor."

"Perhaps she has thought it over and come to the conclusion

that there are worse roommates than you," suggested Anne hopefully.

The early winter darkness was falling when the three girls hurried up the stairs at Wayne Hall as fast as the weight of their suit cases would permit. Miriam's door was closed. She knocked on it, at first softly, then with more force. Hearing no sound from within she turned the knob, flung open the door and stepped inside. Striking a match, she lighted the gas and looked about her. The room was in perfect order, but no vestige of Elfreda's belongings met her eye. The stout girl had kept her word.

Jessie Graham Flower

CHAPTER XVII

CHRISTMAS PLANS

The month of December seemed interminably long to Grace Harlowe. Since her visit to the Southards the longing to be at home remained with her. She hung a little calendar at the head of her bed and every night marked off one day with an air of triumph. During the three weeks that followed their trip to New York, Overton had not been the most congenial spot in the world for Grace or Anne. 19—was a very large class, and considered itself extremely democratic; nevertheless, the story of Anne's theatrical career was bandied about among the freshmen and passed on to the sophomores, until the truth of it was lost in the haze of fiction that surrounded it.

A certain percentage of the class who knew Everett Southard's standing in the theatrical world and understood that Anne must have the highest ability to be able to play in his company treated the young girl with the deference due an artist. Then there were a number of young women who, though fond of attending the theatre, looked askance at the clever men and women whose business it was to amuse them. They approved of the theatre, but for them the foot-lights divided the two worlds, and they wished no trespass-sing of the stage folks on their territory. Quite their opposite were the girls who were desperately stage struck and cherished secret designs on the stage. They were extremely friendly for the sake of plying Anne with questions about her art. At first Anne's position among her classmates was rather difficult to define. After the ball which Elfreda had set in motion had rolled itself to a standstill for want of more gossip to keep it going, Grace saw with secret trepidation that despite the loyalty of a few, Anne had lost caste at Overton.

"History is repeating itself," she remarked gloomily to Miriam, as together the two left the library one afternoon and set out for a short walk before dinner. "Anne told me last night that the girls in her elocution class are very distant since she came back from New York. It's Elfreda's fault, too. How could she deliberately try to make it hard for a girl like Anne?"

A slow flush mounted to Miriam's forehead. She gave Grace a peculiar look.

Grace, interpreting the look, exclaimed contritely: "Forgive me, Miriam. I wasn't thinking of you when I spoke."

"I know it," replied Miriam. "It seems as though I can never do enough for Anne to make up for behaving so contemptibly toward her in high school."

"Anne had forgotten all that, ages ago," comforted Grace. "Don't think about it again."

"I'd like to find an opportunity for a serious talk with Elfreda," returned Miriam. "I think I could bring her to her senses. She keeps strictly away from me. She knows that I wish to talk with her, too. I wonder how she likes rooming with Virginia, or rather how Virginia likes rooming with her."

"She is furious with both Anne and me," declared Grace. "She won't look at either of us. It seems a pity, too. She can be awfully nice when she chooses, and I had begun to feel as though she belonged with us. Here we are on the threshold of 'Peace on Earth, Good Will Toward Men,' and are at odds with at least five different girls. Miss Alden doesn't like us because Mabel Ashe does. Miss Gaines disapproves of us on general principles. Miss Wicks and Miss Hampton dislike me for defending Elfreda's rights. Elfreda thinks us disloyal and deceitful. And it isn't mid-year yet. We are not what you might call social successes, are we?" she concluded most bitterly.

"Still we have made some staunch friends like Ruth and Mabel and Frances. Then there are the girls at Morton House, and Constance Fuller, and I think the freshmen at Wayne Hall are friendly."

"Perhaps they are," sighed Grace. "I hope I'm not growing pessimistic, but I can't help feeling that the girls in our own class are not as friendly as the upper class girls have been. I supposed it would be just the opposite."

Miriam was on the point of saying that she wished she had been wise enough to refuse to room with Elfreda. Then she bit her lip and remained silent.

"I'm glad I've kept up in all my work," Grace said after they had walked some distance in silence. "Mother will be glad and so will Father. I've done my level best not to disappoint them, at least." She sighed, then said abruptly, "Have you bought all your presents yet?"

"I bought some of them in New York. I shopped as long as my money held out. Almost all the things were for the girls here. I'll have to buy my home presents in Oakdale."

"That is just about my case," remarked Grace. "I sent Eleanor's almost two weeks ago, and Mabel Allison's last week. And I gave Miss Southard hers and her brother's with strict injunctions not to open them until Christmas."

"So did I," laughed Miriam. "I forgot to mention it to you at the time. I hope I haven't left out any one. I shall have to ask Mother for more money, too."

The few intervening days before Christmas seemed all too short to the students who were going home for their Christmas vacations. Interest in study declined rapidly. Those girls who usually made brilliant recitations distinguished themselves by just scraping through, while those who were inclined to totter on the ragged edge unhesitatingly confessed themselves to be unprepared. One had, of course, to decide just what to pack, whether to take the morning or evening train and whether it would be worth while to take one's books home on the chance of studying a little during vacation. These were weighty problems to solve satisfactorily, and coupled with the constant, "Have I forgotten any one's present?" were sufficient to drive all idea of study to the winds.

In spite of the mischief Elfreda had endeavored to make, Grace found that she had calls enough to pay to fill in every unoccupied moment before going home.

Late in the afternoon of the day before leaving Overton, she started out alone to pay two calls, going first to Morton House to say good-bye to Gertrude Wells and Arline Thayer. Gertrude was in and welcomed her with enthusiasm, but, to her disappointment, Arline was out. She spent a pleasant half hour with 19—'s president, then, looking out at the rapidly gathering twilight, said with a start: "I didn't know it was so late. I must go down to Ruth Denton's before dinner."

"Perhaps you'll meet Arline there," suggested Gertrude. "She was going there, too. She and Ruth are great friends. She was greatly disappointed to learn that Ruth has been invited somewhere else for Christmas. She had set her heart on taking her home with her. Considering the fact that Arline's father has so much money, she is an awfully nice little girl. She isn't in the least snobbish or overbearing."

"I like her immensely," agreed Grace. "Do you know whether Ruth accepted the invitation, Gertrude?" she asked suddenly.

"Arline said she thought Ruth wanted to go with her, but was too loyal to the other girl to even intimate any such thing," replied Gertrude.

Five minutes later the two students had exchanged good-byes and Grace was on her way to Ruth's with Gertrude's words ringing in her ears. Several weeks ago she had invited Ruth to go with her to Oakdale for the holidays. At first Ruth had demurred, then accepted with shy gratitude. The three Oakdale girls had become greatly attached to Ruth, and Anne, in particular, had looked forward to taking her home with them. Grace had purposely forestalled Anne in inviting Ruth, because she had decided in her mind that her facilities for entertaining were greater than Anne's. She had managed so adroitly, however, that Anne had never even dreamed of her real motive in inviting the lonely little girl. Now, there was Arline Thayer's invitation to be considered. Grace suspected that Ruth secretly worshipped dainty little Arline. She would have died rather than admit to the girls who had been so good to her that she could find it in her heart to care more for another Overton girl than for them. "I'm sorry, of course," Grace murmured to herself as she hurried along through the shadows, "but I'm going to make her accept Arline's invitation. She can go home with us at some other time."

She rang the bell at the dingy old house where Ruth lived, was admitted by the tired-faced landlady and ran upstairs two at a time. Ruth's door stood partly open. Grace heard Arline Thayer say regretfully, "You are sure you can't go, Ruth?"

Then she heard Ruth say, very quietly: "I am quite sure I can't. I promised Grace first."

Without waiting to hear more, Grace walked briskly into the room, saying decisively, "Of course she can go, Arline."

"Why, Grace Harlowe, where did you come from?" exclaimed Arline, her blue eyes opening wide with surprise.

"From downstairs," laughed Grace. "Just in time, too, to make Ruth change her mind. Now, Ruth, tell us the truth, the whole truth, and nothing but the truth. Wouldn't you rather go to New York City with Arline than to Oakdale with us?"

Ruth flushed. "That isn't a fair question," she protested. "It isn't because I care more about going to New York than Oakdale. It is—" she hesitated.

"Because you care more for Arline than for us," finished Grace calmly. "I understand the situation, I think. Your friendship for Arline is growing to be the same as mine for Anne. Naturally, you'd rather be with her than with any one else. Now, Arline, I'll leave her in your hands. We wouldn't have her go to Oakdale with us if she begged on her knees to do so," concluded Grace.

"Grace Harlowe, you're a dear!" exclaimed Arline, catching Grace's hand in both of her warm little palms. "I just love you. Next to Ruth, I think you are the nicest girl at Overton. Thank you a thousand times for being so nice over Ruth.

Now, you simply must go," she announced, turning to Ruth.

"I will," answered Ruth happily. "You don't blame me for saying so?" she asked, looking pleadingly at Grace.

"Not after having just given my official consent," retorted Grace. "Your penalty for deserting us is that you must come to see us at Wayne Hall to-morrow. We have rich gifts for you. Now I must go. Are you going my way home?"

"No," answered Arline. "I'm sorry, but Ruth and I are going to cook our own supper. I've been asked to help. We are going to have a regular feast. Won't you stay and help eat it? Ruth doesn't care who I invite," she added saucily.

"Please stay, Grace," begged Ruth.

Grace shook her head. "Not to-night. Invite me some evening after the holidays. Good-bye, Arline." She extended her hand, but Arline put both arms around Grace's neck, kissing her warmly. "I hope I can do something for you some day," she whispered. After the usual good wishes for a Merry Christmas had been exchanged, Grace emerged from the house, filled with that sense of warmth and elation that comes from having made others happy. She smiled to herself as her mother's face rose before her. It was only a matter of hours now until she would see her. She could almost hear her father's voice and feel his hand on her shoulder in the old caressing way. Smiling to herself Grace walked rapidly on toward Wayne Hall, so rapidly, in fact, that she ran squarely against a tall girl, who, coming from the opposite direction, had apparently been traveling at the same rate of speed. The collision occurred directly under the arc light. The tall girl gave a smothered exclamation and would have rushed on, but Grace put forth a detaining hand, saying: "Stop a moment, Elfreda. I wish to say something to you."

"I don't wish to hear anything you have to say," sneered Elfreda. "Take your hand off my arm. You can't fool me twice. I know What a hypocrite you are."

Grace's hand dropped to her side. "I beg pardon," she said formally. "I am sorry you have such a bad opinion of me. I was about to say that Anne, Miriam and I join in wishing you a Merry Christmas."

"You can keep your good wishes," snapped Elfreda. "I don't want them." With that she turned on her heel and walked angrily away from Grace and reconciliation.

Jessie Graham Flower

CHAPTER XVIII

BASKETBALL RUMORS

After the holidays a great interchanging of visits began at Overton that drove away, for the time being, the terrifying shadows of the all too rapidly approaching mid-year examinations. Almost every girl had brought back with her some treasure that she insisted her friends must see, or some delicious goody they must taste. It was all very delightful, but extremely demoralizing as far as study was concerned.

Santa Claus had been particularly kind to Anne, Grace and Miriam, as Miriam's muff and scarf of Russian sable, Grace's camera, and Anne's diamond ring (a present from the Southards) testified. Then there were the less expensive but equally valued remembrances in the way of embroidered sofa pillows, center pieces, and collar and cuff sets, every stitch of which had been taken by the patient fingers of their girl friends.

Miriam and Grace, while at home, had been given permission to raid the preserve closet and had brought back an assortment of jellies, preserved fruits and pickles, tucking them in every available space their trunks and suit cases contained, regardless of the risk of breaking glass.

The evening after their arrival they had picked out a number of the choicest goodies in their stock and accompanied by Anne had called on Ruth Denton. They found her wrapped in the folds of a blue eiderdown bathrobe, Arline's Christmas present to her. There were slippers to go with it, she declared, proudly thrusting forth a felt-incased foot for their inspection. A most mysterious thing had happened, however. The night before she had gone on her vacation two large boxes had been delivered to her by a messenger. One of them contained a beautiful navy blue cloth suit, the other a dark blue velvet hat. On a plain card were written the words, "'Take the goods the gods provide.' I Wish you a Merry Christmas."

"Have you the card?" Grace asked, after the first exclamations regarding the mysterious boxes had subsided.

Ruth opened the top drawer of her bureau and took out a card. Then going to her wardrobe she displayed the blue suit on its hanger, then took the new hat from the shelf. "Here they are," she said.

The three girls praised the suit and hat so warmly that a flush of pure pleasure in her clothes rose to Ruth's face. Grace, however, examined the inside of the coat and the lining of the hat with the utmost care. Every telltale mark had been removed. Even the boxes themselves were plain. The giver had evidently wished his or her identity to remain a mystery. The writing on the card was not particularly distinctive. There was only one thing of which Grace made mental note. The s's were unfinished and the a's were not closed at the top. This in itself amounted to little, and Grace decided that as far as she was concerned the mystery would have to remain unsolved. So she said nothing about this unimportant discovery, and handed Ruth's treasures back to her without comment.

"I thought Arline might have sent it," declared Ruth, "but she swears solemnly she knows nothing of it, and has given me her word that she had nothing whatever to do with it."

"You'll find out some day if you have patience," declared Miriam. "Sooner or later good deeds like that are sure to come to light."

"I wish I knew," sighed Ruth, "but if I had known, then I couldn't have accepted them, you see."

"Evidently the person who sent them was aware of that," reflected Anne. "Therefore, it is some one who knows all about Ruth Denton's pride."

The flush on Ruth's face deepened. "I can't help it," she said. "I don't like to feel dependent on any one."

On the way to Wayne Hall, the mysterious presents formed the main subject for discussion.

"We ought to have Elfreda's opinion," laughed Miriam. "She would find a clue. Don't you remember what she said about Ruth's pride the first time we took her to call on Ruth?"

"Yes," replied Grace absently. Then the full force of Miriam's words dawning on her she looked at her friend in a startled way. "I know who sent Ruth those presents. It was Elfreda herself. I'm sure of it. She knew Ruth to be too proud to accept clothes, so she sent them anonymously. Now I know why those 'a's' and 's's' looked so familiar. That's Elfreda's writing. I know she did it. She just had to be nice in spite of herself," concluded Grace.

"But why do you think it was Elfreda?" persisted Miriam.

"It was what you said that put me on the right track," replied Grace. "I believe she made up her mind that day to send Ruth the suit and hat."

"If she did send them, there is still hope that she will come back to us," said Anne.

It was agreed among the three girls that not even Ruth should be told of their suspicions, and that if any possible opportunity arose to conciliate Elfreda it should be promptly seized.

During the short space of time that elapsed before the dreaded examination week swooped down upon them, the three friends were too busy preparing for the coming ordeal to give much thought to the discovery they had made. Elfreda avoided them so persistently that there seemed small chance of getting within speaking distance. It was a week of painful suspense, broken only by brief outbursts of jubilation when some particularly formidable examination, that everyone had worried over, seemingly to the point of gray hairs, turned out better than had been expected.

In the campus houses wholesale permission to burn midnight oil had been granted. Lights shone until late hours and flushed faces bent earnestly over text books as though trying to absorb their contents verbatim. On Friday, the strain, that had been lessening imperceptibly with each succeeding examination, snapped, and Overton began to think about many things that had no bearing on examinations.

"I'm almost dead!" exclaimed Grace, coming into her room on Friday afternoon and dropping into the Morris chair near the window.

"I'm tired, too," returned Anne, who had come in just ahead

of her, and was engaged in putting her freshly laundered clothing in the two drawers of the chiffonier that belonged to her.

"Thank goodness, we have four whole days of rest between terms at any rate," sighed Grace. "I'm going to skate and be out of doors as much as I can. I must make a few calls, too. I'm going to give a dinner at Vinton's, too. I'll invite Mabel, Frances, Gertrude Wells, Arline Thayer, Ruth, of course. That makes five," counted Grace on her fingers. "Oh, yes, Constance Fuller, six, you two girls, and myself. That makes nine. I told Mother about it when I was at home and she gave me the money for it. I'll have it Tuesday night. The new term begins Wednesday. To-morrow I'll go calling and deliver my invitations in the morning. There's a trial basketball game to-morrow afternoon."

"When will there be a real game?" asked Anne. "I haven't heard you mention basketball for ages."

"Christmas and examinations put a damper on it, but now all the girls are anxious to play and we have challenged the sophomores to play against us the second Saturday afternoon in February. I am going to play right guard, and Miriam is to play left forward. A Miss Martin is our center, and two freshmen I don't know very well are to play the left guard and right forward. We have a good team. Miss Martin is a wonder. You can see us practice if you wish, Anne."

"Perhaps I will," returned Anne. "Who is on the sophomore team?"

"I don't know," answered Grace. "I don't have much to say to the sophomores. Most of them appear to dislike me, consequently I shall greatly enjoy vanquishing them at basketball."

At the dinner table that night a discussion concerning Saturday's practice game arose, to which Grace and Miriam listened quietly without taking part.

"I suppose I ought to go to this practice game, to see what the freshmen team can do. I think we can make them look sick and sorry before we are through with them," drawled Virginia Gaines.

Grace and Miriam exchanged lightning glances. This was the first intimation they had received that Virginia intended to play on the sophomore team. Miriam frowned. She was thinking of the time when she had been Grace's enemy on the basketball field and off. The recollection was not pleasant. It was very unfortunate that they had to oppose Virginia. Miriam determined to look out for herself and Grace, too, on the day of the game. Involuntarily her face hardened with resolve. She set her lips firmly, then glancing in the direction of Virginia she saw Elfreda, who sat next to the sophomore at the table, eyeing her intently. There was a disagreeable smile on the stout girl's face as she leaned toward Virginia and made a low-toned remark. Miss Gaines looked toward Miriam, smiled maliciously, and shrugged her shoulders.

"That's a danger signal," decided Miriam. "She does mean mischief. I'll speak to Grace about it as soon as we go upstairs." But before they left the dining room the door bell rang. The maid admitted Gertrude Wells and Arline Thayer, and in the pleasure of seeing them, Miriam's resolve to warn Grace was quite forgotten.

The practice game ended in an overwhelming advantage for Grace's team. The other team behaved good-naturedly over their defeat and challenged the winners to play again the following Saturday. They promptly accepted the challenge, and, when the second practice game was played, again came off victorious.

Grace's old basketball ardor had returned threefold and every available moment found her in the gymnasium hard at work. The other members of the teams had imbibed considerable of her enthusiasm. Miss Martin, the center, laughingly said Grace was a human whirlwind and simply made the rest of the team play to keep up with her. Miriam's playing also evoked considerable praise. The first Saturday in February marked the last game with the Number Two team. It turned out to be quite an event and the gallery of the gymnasium was crowded with a mixed representation of classes. Virginia Gaines and Elfreda sat in the first row, and as the play proceeded Virginia watched the skilful tactics of Miriam and Grace with anything but enthusiasm. Elfreda, narrowly watching her companion, read apprehension in Virginia's face, although she made light of the playing of the freshmen team and predicted an easy victory for the sophomores. Scarcely knowing why she did so, Elfreda had doggedly insisted that if the sophomores hoped to beat that freshman team, they would have to play exceptionally well. Whereupon an argument arose regarding the respective merits of the two teams that lasted all the way to Wayne Hall, and ended in the two girls not speaking to each other again that night.

"Did you see Elfreda in the gallery this afternoon?" asked Anne, as she and Grace left the gymnasium and set out for Wayne Hall. Anne had waited in the dressing room until Grace finished dressing.

"I did not see any one," laughed Grace. "I was far too busy. I am surprised to learn that she came to the game."

"She was there, in the third row balcony," replied Anne. "She sat with Virginia Gaines, who looked ferocious enough to bite."

"I wish something would happen to make Elfreda see that we are her friends," sighed Grace.

"She will see, some day," predicted Anne. "Sooner or later she will realize her mistake and come back to us."

CHAPTER XIX

A GAME WORTH SEEING

The second Saturday in February dawned anything but encouragingly. The night before a blizzard had set in, and at one o'clock Saturday afternoon the temperature had dropped almost to zero. The wind howled and shrieked dismally, and to venture out meant to nurse frozen ears as a result of facing the blast. But neither wind nor weather frightened the enthusiastic basketball fans. With knitted and fur caps pulled down over their ears they gallantly braved the storm. Even the majority of the faculty were in the front seats that had been reserved for them and by two o'clock every available inch of space in the gallery was filled.

The sophomore colors of blue and gold mingled with the red and white of the freshmen colors in the decorations that were displayed lavishly about the gymnasium. The faculty, too, wore the colors of their respective favorites, while the president of the college held two immense bouquets, one of red, the other of yellow roses, showing that he at least was impartial. On each side of the gallery a group of girls stood ready to lead their respective classes in the basketball choruses that are sung solely with the object of urging the teams on to deeds of glory. These choruses had been written hurriedly by loyal fans who had more enthusiasm than ability as verse writers, and fitted to popular airs. The fact that they possessed neither rhythm nor style troubled no one. The main idea was to make a great deal of noise in singing them, and nothing else counted.

The freshmen and sophomore substitutes were the first to emerge from their dressing rooms on either side of the gymnasium, dressed in their respective gymnasium suits of black and blue, the sleeves and sailor collars of which were ornamented with their colors. They were greeted with a gratifying burst of song from both sides which lasted until they took their places, eager and alert, ready to make good if the opportunity presented itself. After a brief interval the dressing room doors opened again and the real teams appeared. This time the burst of song became so jubilantly noisy that the president of the college half rose in his seat as though to signal for order, then, apparently changing his mind, settled himself in his chair, smiling broadly. Immediately the song ended the referee's whistle blew and the great game began.

From the moment the ball was put in play it was plain to the spectators that this was to be a game worth seeing. The sophomores, with Virginia Gaines as center, adopted whirl-wind tactics from the start and the freshmen did little more than defend themselves during the first half, which came to an end without either side scoring. That the freshmen could hold their own was evident, and when the whistle blew for the second half the freshmen in the gallery applauded their team with renewed vigor.

During the brief intermission Grace and Miriam had clasped hands and vowed to outplay the sophomores in the second half or perish in the attempt. The three other members had thereupon insisted on being included in the vow, and when the five girls trotted to their respective positions at the sound of the referee's whistle, it was with a determination to stoutly contest every inch of the ground. Luck seemed against them, however, for the sophomores scored through the clever playing of Virginia Gaines. The freshmen then set their teeth and resolved to die rather than allow the enemy to score again. Then Miriam secured the ball and dodging and ducking this way and that she passed the ball to another player who made the basket and the score was tied. This put the sophomores not only on the anxious seat, but also on their mettle, and try as they might the freshmen found themselves unable to pile up their score.

The end of the second half crept nearer and the score still remained tied. Grace, who was becoming more and more apprehensive as the minutes passed, stood anxiously watching the ball, which was being played perilously near their opponents' goal. Catching the eyes of Miriam, who stood nearest it, Grace made a desperate little upward motion. Miriam understood and redoubled her efforts to secure the ball, which she finally did by springing straight up into the air and intercepting it on its way to the basket. A shout went up from the freshmen which grew to a roar. Miriam had thrown the ball unerringly to Grace, who caught it, and facing quickly toward the freshman goal, balanced herself on her toes preparatory to tossing her prize into the basket.

"She'll never make it," groaned a freshman. But her remark was lost in the clamor.

With one quick, comprehensive glance, Grace measured the distance, then with a long, swift overhand toss she sent the ball curving through the air. It dropped squarely into the basket, bounded up in the air, then dropped gently into place.

For the next few minutes pandemonium reigned in the gymnasium. The happy freshmen burst into song and drummed on the floor in expression of their glee. The freshmen team had outplayed that of the sophomores. Only once before in the history of the college had such a thing occurred. To Grace Harlowe and Miriam Nesbit was given the principal credit for this latest victory. Grace's goal toss had been a record-breaker. Never had a freshman been known to make such a toss.

Now that the excitement was over, Grace felt suddenly weak in the knees. She started for a seat at the side of the gymnasium, but before she reached it there was a rush from the freshman class. Her classmates lifted her to their shoulders and began parading about the gymnasium floor, singing:

"Nineteen—is looking sad,
Tra la la, Tra la la,
I wonder what has made her mad,
Tra la la, Tra la la,
Her coaching was in vain,
The freshman team has won again,
Little sophomores, run away,
Come again some other day."

Then there followed a song that brought a shout of laughter from hundreds of throats, and one in which the sophomores did not join:

Backward, turn backward, O ball in your flight,
Why did you drop in the basket so tight?
Sadly the sophomores are rueing the day
They asked the freshmen in their yard to play,
Sophomore banners are hung at half mast,
Sophomore tears they are falling so fast,
Sophomore faces are turned toward the wall,
Sophomore pride has had a hard fall.

Grace had been seized and carried around and around the gymnasium on the shoulders of her exulting classmates, who sang lustily as they marched, then gently deposited her in the dressing room. Miriam also had received that honor. When the two girls left the dressing room twenty minutes later, they were taken charge of by a delegation of admiring freshmen and informed that there would be a dinner given that night at Vinton's in honor of them.

An air of deep gloom pervaded the sophomore dressing room, however. Virginia Gaines dressed in gloomy silence. One or two of her team ventured to speak to her. She answered so shortly that they did not trouble her further, but went out talking among themselves as soon as they had changed their gymnasium suits for street clothing. Outside Elfreda waited impatiently. "I thought you were never coming," grumbled the stout girl. Then the unpleasant side of her disposition, which she had tried to eliminate during her brief friendship with the Oakdale girls, came to the surface and she said maliciously: "I thought you said they couldn't play, Virginia. Funny, wasn't it, that you had such a poor idea of their playing? It was the best game I ever saw, but all the star playing was on the freshman side."

Virginia's face grew dark. "Stop trying to be sarcastic," she stormed. "I won't stand it. Do you hear me?"

"Yes, I hear you. I'm not deaf," returned Elfreda dryly. "As for standing it, you don't have to. Good-bye." Turning sharply about she set off in the opposite direction, her hands in her pockets, a look of intense disgust on her round face. "That's the end of that," she muttered. "I'll move to-morrow. This time it will have to be out of Wayne Hall, unless—." Then she shook her head almost sadly: "Not there," she added. "She wouldn't have me for a roommate."

CHAPTER XX

GRACE OVERHEARS SOMETHING INTERESTING

After the famous basketball game a marked change was noticeable in the attitude of the freshman class toward the Oakdale girls. Grace and Miriam received numerous invitations to dinners and spreads, in which Anne was frequently included. Then the girls at Wayne Hall gave a play in which Anne enacted the role of heroine, stage manager, prompter, and producer, besides doing all the coaching. After that her star was also in the ascendant and the little slights and coolnesses that had been noticeable after Elfreda's ill-timed gossip had done its work, died a natural death.

The stout girl had lost no time in leaving Virginia. The evening after her quarrel with the sophomore she had moved her belongings into the hall the moment she reached her room, then gone downstairs and demanded another room. As it happened, a freshman whose cousin lived at Morton House had invited her to share her room. She had departed that very afternoon and Mrs. Elwood offered Elfreda the now vacant half of her room. Emma Dean, the tall, near-sighted freshman, occupied the other half. There was a single room in the house of Mrs. Elwood's sister, but Elfreda had refused to consider it. Despite the fact that there were now four young women at Wayne Hall with whom she was not on speaking terms, she could not bring herself to leave the house. In her inmost heart she knew that it was because she did not wish to leave the three girls she had repudiated, but not for worlds would she have acknowledged this to be the case.

Several times she had been on the point of throwing her pride to the winds and apologizing to Grace, Miriam and Anne for her childish behavior. Then she would scoff at her own weakness and go doggedly on. Her new roommate, Emma Dean, was a cheery sort of girl who lived every day as it came and refused to borrow trouble. She never criticized other girls, nor did she gossip, and she was extremely thoughtful of the comfort of her roommate. After several days of dubious speculation the stout girl decided she liked Emma, and Emma decided that Elfreda was rather an agreeable disappointment.

There were two young women, however, who had suddenly appeared to take a great interest in Elfreda. Alberta Wicks and Mary Hampton had met Elfreda in Vinton's late one afternoon, and had made distinctly friendly overtures to her. At any other time she would have passed them by in disdain, but on that particular occasion, feeling gloomy and down-cast, she decided to forget her grievance against them. Then, too, she did not know them to be the girls who had sent her the anonymous letter. Grace had never told her the truth of the affair, so she played unsuspectingly into their hands. They had invited her to have ice cream with them, and she had insisted that they be her guests at dinner. After that they had invited her to Stuart Hall to dinner and she had entertained them at Wayne Hall one evening, greatly to the surprise of Grace, who suddenly remembered that, after all, Elfreda was not so much to blame as she did not know the truth. But why should these two girls accept the hospitality of the very girl they had tried to drive away from Overton? It was a puzzle that Grace could not solve. She discussed it with Anne and Miriam but they could throw no light on the mystery.

The coming of the Easter vacation gave the three girls more pleasant matters of which to think. This time Ruth Denton accompanied them to Oakdale as Grace's guest, while Miriam invited Arline Thayer also, as a surprise to Ruth. When Arline serenely joined them at the station the morning of their departure, Ruth could hardly believe the evidence of her own eyes.

The two weeks in Oakdale flew by on wings. With the boys and the other members of the Phi Sigma Tau at home, too, there were more things to do and places to go than could possibly be squeezed into that brief space of time. Arline Thayer, who was a joyous, irrepressible spirit, announced with conviction that Oakdale was even nicer than New York. She and Nora became sworn friends and the joint guardians of Hippy, who declared that he never would have believed there were two such relentless tyrants in the world, if he had not seen them face to face.

Mrs. Gray, who had been in Florida during the Christmas holidays, had returned in time to welcome her adopted children home. She was especially delighted to see Anne and would scarcely allow the quiet little girl out of her sight. She had been greatly disappointed because Anne had refused to accept from her the money for her college education, but secretly exulted in Anne's independence and smiled to herself when she thought of a certain clause in her will that had amply provided for her adopted daughter's future welfare.

Altogether it was a vacation long to be remembered, and the

four originals separated with the glad thought that the next time they met it would be months instead of weeks before their little company would again set their faces in opposite directions.

The night after their return to Overton, Grace, after having made a conscientious effort to study, threw down her history in despair. "I know a great deal more about the history of Oakdale than I do about the history of Rome," she sighed.

"I wish I had never heard of trigonometry," returned Anne, shutting her book with a snap. "I can't think of anything except the good time we've had. Home has completely upset my student mind." She rose, laid down her book and walked listlessly toward the window. It had been an unusually warm day for early spring and the night air had that suspicion of dampness in it that betokens rain. "It will rain before morning," she declared. "There isn't a star in sight and the moon has gone behind a cloud."

Grace joined Anne at the window. The two girls stood peering out into the darkness of the spring night. "I feel as though I'd like to go out and walk miles and miles to-night," declared Grace.

"So do I," agreed Anne. Then glancing back at the clock, she remarked, "It's twenty minutes past ten. Too late for us to go now. We can go to-morrow night, can't we?"

Grace nodded. "We'll get our work done early, or, better still, we can go walking early in the evening and study when we come back. I wish you'd remind me that I must call on Mabel Ashe this week. In fact, all three of us ought to go over to Holland House."

The next day, however, Anne remembered regretfully that

she had promised to help a troubled freshman through the mazes of an especially trying trigonometry lesson, while Miriam had a theme to write which she had neglected until the last minute, and had to rush through on record time.

"You're a set of irresponsible young things who don't know your own mind from one minute to the next," laughed Grace. "As I can't very well go walking alone, I'll make my call on Mabel."

Directly after dinner she set out for Holland House and Mabel's delighted: "I'm so glad you came, Grace. Where have you been keeping yourself?" sounded very sweet to Grace, who adored Mabel and outside of her own particular chums liked her better than any other girl she knew at home or in college. The two young women were deep in conversation when a rap sounded at the door. Mabel opened it, looked inquiringly at the girl who stood outside and exclaimed contritely: "Oh, Helen, I'm so sorry I forgot all about you. I'll get ready this minute. Come in. Miss Harlowe, this is Miss Burton. Grace, I wonder if you will mind making a call to-night. I promised Helen I'd take her down to Wellington House and introduce her to a junior friend of mine who plays golf. Helen is a golf fiend."

"So am I," laughed Grace. "I brought my golf bag to Overton, but didn't play much in the fall. I'm going to try it, though, as soon as the ground is in shape."

"How nice!" exclaimed Helen Burton, with a friendly smile that lighted up her rather plain face and brought the dimples to her cheeks. "We can have some nice times together. You had better come with us now."

"Thank you, I shall be pleased to go," replied Grace politely. "I have never been in Wellington House. It is an upper class

Jessie Graham Flower

house, isn't it?"

"Yes," replied Mabel. "It is given up entirely to juniors and seniors. It is the oldest house on the campus, and very difficult to get into. Personally, I like Holland House better. I had an opportunity to get into Wellington House last fall, but refused it." Grace noted that Mabel frowned slightly and set her lips as though determined to shut out an unpleasant memory.

To reach Wellington House was merely a matter of crossing one end of the campus. Grace looked about her curiously as they were ushered into the long, old-fashioned hall that extended almost to the back of the house. They entered the parlor at one side of the hall and sat down while Mabel excused herself and ran upstairs after Leona Rowe, the junior she had come to see. She had hardly disappeared before a flaxen head was poked in the door and a surprised voice said: "For goodness sake, Helen Burton, when did you rain down? You are just the one I want to see. What do you think of to-morrow's German? I can't translate it. It's frightfully hard. Come up and help me, dearest."

The ingratiating emphasis she placed on the word "dearest" caused both Grace and Helen to laugh.

"All right, I will for just two minutes. Want to come upstairs, Miss Harlowe?"

Grace smilingly shook her head. "I'll stay here in case Mabel comes back."

"Thank you," returned Helen. "Miss Harlowe, this is Miss Redmond."

The two girls exchanged friendly nods. Then the

flaxen-haired girl led the way, followed by Helen Burton, and Grace settled herself in the depths of a big chair to await their return. As she sat idly wondering what the subject of her next theme should be, the sound of voices reached her ears, proceeding from the back parlor that adjoined the room in which Grace sat. Two girls had entered the other room, but the heavy portieres which hung in the dividing arch, hid them from view. The voices, however, Grace recognized with a start as belonging to Beatrice Alden, the disagreeable junior, and Alberta Wicks of the sophomore class.

"I'll be glad when my sophomore year is over," grumbled Alberta Wicks. "Mary and I have asked for a room here. I hope we get it. If we do we will be able, at least, to eat our meals without the eternal accompaniment of Miss Harlowe's and Miss Nesbit's doings. Ever since that basketball game, Stuart Hall has talked of nothing else."

"Are there many freshmen at Stuart Hall?" asked Beatrice Alden.

"Too many to suit me," was the emphatic answer.

"If you are so down on freshmen in general, how in the world do you manage to endure that dreadful Miss Briggs?"

"J. Elfreda is a joke," replied Alberta. "Nevertheless, she is a very useful joke. In the first place, she has plenty of money to spend, and we see to it that she spends a good share of it on us. Then, too, we can borrow money of her. She is a great convenience. The funny part of it is she doesn't know about that letter we wrote. For once that priggish Miss Harlowe did manage to hold her tongue to some purpose."

"Suppose she does find out?"

"She can't prove that we wrote the note," was the quick retort. "When Miss Harlowe tried to pin us to it that day at Stuart Hall I merely said that a number of sophomores felt justified in sending the note. Of course, she drew her own conclusions, but conclusions are far from proof, you know. She would hardly dare circulate any reports concerning it. We aren't going to bother with J. Elfreda much longer at any rate. It's getting too near warm weather to risk being bored to death. Mary expects a check from home soon, and I've written Mother for some extra money, so we won't need hers. Besides, I don't wish to let our acquaintance lap over into my junior year. She's frightfully ill bred, and I'm going to begin to be more careful about my associates next year."

"What a frightful snob you are, Bert," said Beatrice rather disgustedly.

"Well, you are my first cousin, you know," retorted Alberta significantly. "I never considered you particularly democratic."

"I'm not deceitful, at any rate," reminded Beatrice. "If I dislike a girl I take no pains to conceal it, and I am certainly not a grafter."

"Neither am I, Beatrice Alden, and the fact of your being my cousin doesn't give you the right to insult me. I intended to tell you about a stunt we had planned for Friday night, but since you seem to be so conscientious about Miss Briggs, I shan't tell you anything."

Then a silence fell that was broken the next instant by the violent slam of the front door. Grace rose to her feet, took a step forward, paused irresolutely, then pushing apart the heavy curtains walked into the other room. Beatrice Alden stood unconcernedly running through the leaves of a magazine she had picked up from the table.

"Miss Alden!"

The senior turned quickly, looking inquiringly, then sternly, at Grace. "How long have you been here?" she said abruptly.

"I heard part of the conversation," replied Grace coldly. "When you began talking I recognized your voices, then I heard my name mentioned, and true to the old adage about listeners I heard no good of myself. When I heard Miss Briggs's name spoken I decided that under the circumstances I was justified in listening further, as I intended at any rate to announce my presence and just what I heard as soon as you two had finished speaking. Miss Wicks's sudden departure prevented me from carrying out my intention as far as she was concerned. I shall, however, notify her at the earliest opportunity." Grace paused, looking squarely at the older girl.

Beatrice Alden's expression of intense displeasure gave way to one of reluctant admiration with dislike struggling in the background. "You are extremely frank in your statements, Miss Harlowe," she said sarcastically.

"There is no reason why I should not be," returned Grace composedly. "Miss Wicks and Miss Hampton, for reasons best known to themselves, chose to make Miss Briggs the victim of an unwomanly practical joke on the very day of her arrival at Overton. I think you are in possession of the story. Miss Briggs's method of retaliation was unwise, I will admit, but Miss Wicks and Miss Hampton had no right to try to drive her from Overton on account of it. In her distress over a certain anonymous letter she received, Miss Briggs came to me, and I, suspecting the source from which the letter came, tried as best I could to straighten out the tangle, without allowing Miss Briggs to know who was at fault.

"Since then, unfortunately, a misunderstanding has arisen between us. I have now no influence whatever with Miss Briggs, and she has played directly into the hands of the only two enemies she has in college. All along I have been certain that Miss Wicks and Miss Hampton meant mischief. What I have heard to-day confirms it. Miss Alden, you are Miss Wicks's cousin. I heard her say so. As a true Overton girl, will you not use your influence with her in persuading her to abandon whatever plan she and Miss Hampton have made to annoy Miss Briggs?"

Beatrice Alden eyed Grace reflectively but said nothing.

Grace looked pleadingly at the irresponsive junior. For a moment tense silence reigned. Then Beatrice Alden shook her head.

"I'm sorry, Miss Harlowe," she said soberly. All trace of hauteur had disappeared. "But you know how angry Alberta was when she left here. She wouldn't listen to me. I doubt if she speaks to me again this year. She has a frightful temper and holds the slightest grudge for ages. She will carry out her plan now, merely to show me how utterly she disregards my disapproval."

"I'm sorry, too," smiled Grace ruefully. "I shall try to see Miss Briggs, but she is utterly unapproachable."

The two girls looked into each other's eyes. Then they both laughed. Beatrice Alden stretched out her hand impulsively. "We're both in an evil case, aren't we?" she laughed.

Grace met the hand half way. "But we are of the same mind, aren't we?" she asked.

"Yes," replied Beatrice simply. She hesitated, looked rather confused, then added: "I used to think I disliked you, Miss Harlowe, but I find my feelings toward you are quite the opposite. I hope we shall some day be friends."

"I hope so, too," agreed Grace earnestly. "We have a mutual friend, you know, in Mabel Ashe, although yours and Mabel's friendship began long before I came to Overton." A shadow crossed Beatrice's face. Grace noted it and interpreted it correctly. "You are very fond of Mabel, are you not, Miss Alden?" she asked.

"Very," was the short answer.

"Anne Pierson is the dearest girl friend I have in the world," declared wily Grace. "Then two Oakdale girls who are studying in an eastern conservatory of music come next, and after that Miriam Nesbit. There are also three other girls, members of a high school sorority to which I belong, and a girl in Denver, who have very strong claims on my affection. I have a number of dearest friends, you see. Some time I should like to tell you more of them."

Beatrice had brightened visibly as Grace talked. She now felt assured that this attractive freshman with her clear grey eyes and straightforward manner would never attempt to monopolize Mabel's entire attention.

At this moment Mabel's voice was heard at the head of the stairs. She descended, followed by Leona Rowe and Helen Burton.

"Why, hello, Bee!" cried Mabel. "I asked for you upstairs, but was told you were out."

"So I was," smiled Beatrice, "but I'm here now. What is

your pleasure?"

"Come over to Holland House and have tea and cakes and candy, if there's any left in the box of Huyler's that came last night. Every girl in the house sampled it. You know what that means."

"I'll go for my hat and coat," returned Beatrice brightly. "See you in a minute." She ran lightly up the stairs, smiling to herself. Helen and Leona rushed out in the hall to interview a girl who had just come in. Finding themselves alone for the moment Mabel turned to Grace with a solemnly inquiring air, "How did you do it?" she asked in a low tone.

"I'll tell you some other time," replied Grace. "It was a surprise to me, but the chance just happened to come and I took advantage of it."

The return of the three young women cut off further opportunity for explanation, but as Grace walked back to Holland House, one arm linked in that of Mabel Ashe, while Beatrice Alden, heretofore frigid and unapproachable, walked at the other side of the popular junior, she could not help wishing a certain other tangle might be as easily straightened.

CHAPTER XXI

AN UNHEEDED WARNING

The next day found Grace rather at a loss how to proceed in the case of Elfreda. From what she had overheard it was evident that Alberta Wicks and Mary Hampton had decided to make Elfreda the victim of some well-laid plot of their own. What the nature of it was Grace had not the remotest idea. To approach Elfreda was embarrassing to say the least. To warn her against the two mischievous sophomores without being able to state anything more definite than what she had overheard at Wellington House was infinitely more embarrassing.

"What time had I best try to see her?" Grace asked herself. She had come from Overton Hall with Anne and Miriam late that afternoon and the three girls had lingered on the steps of Wayne Hall, reluctant to go indoors. Spring was getting ready to fulfill all sorts of tender promises she had made to her children. The buds on the trees were bursting into tiny new green leaves. The crocuses were in bloom in the yards along College Street, and the grass on the campus was growing greener every hour. The roads, too, were obligingly drying, so that adventurous walkers might visit their favorite haunts in the country surrounding Overton without running the risk of wading in the mud.

Jessie Graham Flower

There was Guest House, the famous colonial tea shop that had been built and used as an inn during the Revolution. In this quaint historic place ample refreshment was to be found. There one could satisfy one's appetite with dainty little sandwiches, muffins and jam, tea cakes and tea, fresh milk or buttermilk.

There was also Hunter's Rock that overhung the river, and whose smooth, flat surface made an ideal spot for picnickers. It was five miles from Overton, but extremely popular with all four classes, and from early spring until late fall, it was occupied on Saturday by various gay gipsy parties from the college. Then there were canoes for the venturesome, and staid old rowboats for the cautious, to be hired at a nominal sum, while girlish figures dotted the golf course and the tennis courts. Girls strolled about the campus in the early evenings, or gathered in groups on the steps of the campus houses. It was the time of year when spring creeps into one's blood, making one forget everything except the blueness of the sky, the softness of the air and the lure of green things growing.

"I must go into the house," sighed Miriam Nesbit. "I have that appalling trigonometry lesson for to-morrow to prepare from beginning to end. I haven't looked at it yet."

"I peeped at it yesterday," said Anne. "It's the worst one we've had, so far."

"The end is not yet," reminded Grace.

"Well it will be in sight before long. Our freshman year is almost over, didn't you know it, children!" queried Miriam laughingly.

"It has seemed long in some respects and short in others,"

reflected Grace. "I think—" Grace paused. A tall, rather stout girl came hurriedly up the walk. She stalked up the steps and into the house without looking to the right or left. Even in that fleeting moment Grace noted that she seemed rather excited and that she carried in her hand an open letter. "I wonder if now would be a good time to tackle her," speculated Grace. Then deciding that, after all, there was nothing to be gained without making a venture, Grace walked resolutely to the door. "I'll see you later, girls," was her only remark as she passed inside.

Once outside Elfreda's door, Grace did not feel quite so confident. Summoning all her courage, however, she knocked. An impatient voice called, "Come in," and Grace accepted the rather ungracious invitation to enter. J. Elfreda sat facing the window intent upon the letter Grace had seen in her hand. She turned sharply as the door closed, then catching sight of Grace, sprang to her feet, her face clouded with anger. "How dare you come in here?" she stormed.

"You said 'Come in,' Elfreda," returned Grace quietly.

"Yes, but not to you," raged Elfreda. "Never to you. Leave my room instantly and don't come back again."

"I won't trouble you long," returned Grace. "I came to put you on your guard against two young women who are about to make mischief for you. I am very sorry I did not tell you long ago that Miss Wicks and Miss Hampton were the originators of the anonymous letter which caused you so much unhappiness. I suspected as much at the time, and accused them of writing it. They neither affirmed nor denied their part in the affair, although they admitted that certain members of the sophomore class wrote the letter. I threatened to take up the matter with the sophomore class if the two young women persisted in making you unhappy, and this threat evidently influenced them to drop their crusade against you.

"To a certain extent I feel responsible for what has followed, for if I had told you this before you would hardly have afterward become friendly with them. However, I can do this much. From a conversation I overheard the other day I am convinced that Miss Wicks and Miss Hampton intend to play a practical joke on you on Friday night. I am afraid that it will not be of the tame variety either, and may cause you trouble. These two girls do not like you, Elfreda, and they have not forgiven you nor never will."

"You are awfully anxious to make me think that no one but you and your friends ever liked me, aren't you?" sneered Elfreda. "Well, just let me tell you something. Those girls may have their faults, but they aren't stingy and selfish, at all events. This letter here is an invitation to—, well, I shan't tell you what it is, but it's far from being a practical joke, I can assure you."

Grace looked doubtfully at Elfreda, who stood very erect, her head held high with offended dignity. Perhaps, after all, she had been too hasty. Perhaps the two sophomores really intended playing some harmless trick. Then the words, "We are not going to bother with J. Elfreda much longer," returned with a force that left Grace no longer in uncertainty.

"Elfreda," she said earnestly, "I wish you would listen to me for once. Miss Wicks and Miss Hampton are not your friends. If you accept their invitation for Friday night you will be sorry. Take my advice, and steer clear of them."

"Please mind your own business and get out of my room," commanded Elfreda fiercely.

Casting one steady, reproachful look at the angry girl, Grace left the room in silence. Once outside her own door she clenched her hands and fought back her rising emotion. Tears of humiliation stood in her gray eyes, then winking them back bravely, she drew a long breath and opened her door. Anne, who in the meantime had come upstairs, turned expectantly. "What luck?" she questioned.

"None," returned Grace shortly. "She ordered me out of her room."

At this juncture Miriam Nesbit joined them. "What's the latest on the bulletin board?" she inquired, smiling mischievously.

"Don't laugh, Miriam," rebuked Grace. "Things are serious. Elfreda has some sort of engagement for Friday night with those two girls. She almost told me what it was, then changed her mind and invited me to mind my own business and leave her room. I'm going to try to find out something about Friday night and see that she gets fair play. After that I shall never trouble myself about her," concluded Grace, her voice trembling slightly.

"Don't feel so hurt at Elfreda's rudeness, Grace," soothed Miriam. "She doesn't mean half she says. She'll be sorry some day."

"I wish 'some day' was before Friday," replied Grace mournfully. "I wonder who else is to take part in this affair?"

"Watch Miss Wicks and Miss Hampton," advised Anne quietly.

"That's sound advice," agreed Grace. "I appoint you and Miriam as secret service agents. You must unearth the enemy's plans for Friday night."

"What will you do if we should happen to stumble upon them?" asked Miriam curiously.

"I don't know, yet," said Grace slowly. "It will depend entirely on what they are. Since we can't prevent Elfreda from going to her fate, we may be obliged to go along with her. If I were to ask you girls to drop everything and follow me on Friday night, would you do it?"

Anne and Miriam nodded.

"Then that's settled," was her relieved comment. "I am going to take two other girls into our confidence. I shall tell Mabel Ashe and Frances Marlton. They will come to the rescue if I need them. Besides they are juniors, and if I am not mistaken, upper class support may be very desirable before we are through with this affair."

"And all this anxiety over J. Elfreda," smiled Miriam. "But to tell you the truth, girls, I shall be only too glad to fare forth in the cause of Elfreda. I thought her a terrible cross when she first came, but now I am positively lonesome without her, and I don't care how soon she comes back."

CHAPTER XXII

TURNING THE TABLES

For the next two days the three girls bent their efforts toward discovering the plot on foot against Elfreda, but to little purpose. So far, Grace had refrained from imparting her vague knowledge of what impended to Mabel and Frances. Her naturally self-reliant nature would not allow her to depend on others. She preferred to solve her own problems and fight her own battles if necessary. Whatever the two sophomores had planned was a secret indeed. By neither word nor sign did they betray themselves, and by Thursday evening Grace was beginning to show signs of anxiety.

"I haven't been able to find out a thing," she declared dispiritedly to Anne. "I suspect one other girl, but I'm not sure about her. Anne, do you think Virginia Gaines is in this affair, too?"

"Hardly," replied Anne. "She and Elfreda are not friendly, and Elfreda could not be coaxed to go where she is likely to see Miss Gaines."

"But suppose Virginia Gaines kept strictly in the background, yet helped to play the trick," persisted Grace.

"Of course she could easily do that," admitted Anne. "But what makes you think she would?"

"Just this," replied Grace. "I saw her in conversation to-day with Mary Hampton. They were standing outside Science Hall. They didn't see me until I was within a few feet of them. Then they said good-bye in a hurry, and rushed off in opposite directions. Now, what would you naturally infer from that?"

"It does look suspicious," agreed Anne.

"That is what causes me to believe Virginia Gaines to be one of the prime movers in this affair," was the quiet answer. "They are all very clever. Too clever, by far, for me."

A knock at the door caused Grace to start slightly. "Come in!" she called, then exclaimed in surprise as the door opened: "Why, Miriam, where did you go? You disappeared the moment dinner was over."

"I had to go to the library," replied Miriam quickly. "Do you know whether the girls on both sides of us are out?"

Grace nodded. "What's the matter, Miriam?" she asked curiously. "What has happened? You look as mysterious as the Three Fates themselves."

"I've made a discovery," announced Miriam, taking a book from under her arm and opening it. "I found something in this book that you ought to see. I was in one of the alcoves to-night looking for a book that I have been trying to lay hands on for a week. It has been out every time. To-night I found it and inside the leaves I found this." She handed Grace a folded paper.

Grace unfolded it wonderingly and began to read aloud:

"Dear Virginia:

"We decided that the haunted house plan would be quite likely to subdue a certain obstreperous individual. We have already invited her to a moonlight party at Hunter's Rock, as you know. Once she is there we will see to the rest. Sorry you can't be with us, but that would give the whole plan away. A little meditation in spookland will do our friend good, and this time if she is wise she will keep her troubles to herself. Of course, if any one should see her going home in the wee small hours of the morning it might be unpleasant for her, but then, we can't trouble ourselves over that.

"Yours, hastily,

"Bert."

Grace stared first at Anne, then Miriam, in incredulous, shocked surprise.

"What a cruel girl!" she exclaimed. "Poor Elfreda!"

"Of course, the writer meant Elfreda," agreed Miriam. "'Bert,' I suppose, stands for Alberta. In the first place, what haunted house does she mean?"

"I don't know," answered Grace, knitting her brows. "Wait a minute! I'll go down and ask Mrs. Elwood."

Within five minutes she had returned, bristling with information. "I found out the whole story," she declared. "It is an old white house not far from Hunter's Rock. Two brothers once lived there, and one disappeared. It was rumored that he had been killed by his older brother, and that the spirit of the murdered man haunted the place so persistently that the other brother left there and never came back. They say a white figure, carrying a lighted candle, walks moaning through the rooms."

"How dreadful!" shivered Anne. "It is bad enough to think of those girls coaxing Elfreda to go there. I believe they intend to persuade her to go there, then leave her, too."

"We might show Elfreda this note," reflected Miriam. "No; on second thought I should say we'd better make up a crowd and follow the others to Hunter's Rock. Of course, we won't stay there. Those girls are breaking rules by going there at night. We shall be breaking rules, too, but in a good cause."

A long conversation ensued that would have aroused consternation in the breast of a number of sophomores, had they been privileged to hear it. When the last detail had been arranged, Grace leaned back in her chair and smiled. "I think everything will go beautifully," she said, "and several people are going to be surprised. Miriam, will you see Mabel Ashe, Constance Fuller and Frances Marlton in the morning? Anne, will you look out for Arline Thayer and Ruth? That will leave Leona Rowe and Helen Burton for me, and, oh, yes, I'll have a talk with Emma Dean."

To all appearances, Friday dawned as prosaically as had all the other days of that week, but in the breasts of a number of the students of Overton stirred an excitement that deepened as the day wore on. As is frequently the case, the object of it all went calmly on her way, taking a smug satisfaction in the thought that she was the only freshman invited to the select gathering of sophomores who were to brave the censure of the dean, and picnic by moonlight at Hunter's Rock. For almost the first time since her arrival at college Elfreda felt her own popularity. Despite her native shrewdness, she was particularly susceptible to flattery. To be the idol of the college had been one of her most secret and hitherto hopeless desires. Now, in the sophomore class she had found girls who really appreciated her, and who were ready to say pleasant things to her rather than lecture her. She was glad, now, that she had dropped Grace and her friends in time, and resolved next year that she would put the width of the campus between herself and Wayne Hall.

As she slipped on her long blue serge coat that night—the air was chilly, though the day had been warm—a flush of triumph mounted to her cheeks. Then glancing at the clock she hurriedly adjusted her hat. Her appointment was for half-past seven. Alberta said the party was to be in honor of her and she must not keep her friends waiting. She looked sharply about her to see who was in sight. She had been pledged to secrecy. Alberta had said they would return before half-past ten, so there would be no need of asking Mrs. Elwood to leave the door unlocked for her. Then she walked briskly down the steps and up the street.

Fifteen minutes before she left the house, three dark figures had marched out single file down the street. Two blocks from the house they had been met by a delegation of dark figures, and without a word being spoken, the little party had taken a side street that led to Overton Drive, a public highway that wound straight through the town out into the country. The company had proceeded in absolute silence, and finally leaving the road had turned into the fields and plodded steadily on. It was the new of the moon and the landscape was shrouded in heavy shadows. On and still on the silent procession had traveled, and when their eyes, now accustomed to the darkness, had espied the outlines of a tumble-down, one-story house that stood out against the blackness of the night a halt had been made and each dark figure had taken from under her arm a bundle. Then the faint rustle of paper accompanied by an occasional giggle or a smothered exclamation had been heard, and last but most remarkable, the dark figures had given place to a company of sheeted ghosts who had glided over the fields with true ghost-like mien and disappeared in a little grove just off the highway.

In the meantime, Elfreda had been received with acclamation by the treacherous sophomores, who vied with each other as to who should be her escort. There were nine girls, and each of them also bore a bundle, which contained not sheets, but the eatables for the picnic. This procession also set out in silence, which was broken as soon as the town was left behind. Alberta, who walked with her arm linked in Elfreda's, began to relate the story of the haunted house.

"Do you suppose for one minute that that house is really haunted?" said Elfreda sceptically.

"No one knows," was the disquieting reply. "People have seen strange sights there."

"What sights?" demanded Elfreda.

"They say the murdered brother walks through the house and moans," replied Alberta, shuddering slightly.

"That's nonsense," said Elfreda bravely. Nevertheless, the idea was not pleasant to contemplate. "I don't believe in ghosts," she added.

"I dare you to go into the room where the man was murdered," laughed Mary Hampton.

"I'm not afraid," persisted Elfreda.

"Prove it, then," taunted Mary.

"All right, I will," retorted Elfreda defiantly. "Show me the room when we get there and I'll go into it."

"I don't think we ought to go near that old house at night," protested a sophomore. "We'd get into all sorts of trouble as it is, if the faculty knew we were out."

"Now, don't begin preaching," snapped Alberta Wicks. "If you are dissatisfied, go home."

"I wish I'd stayed at home," growled the other sophomore wrathfully.

While this conversation was being carried on, the party was rapidly nearing the haunted house. They halted directly in front of it, and Mary Hampton said, "Now, Miss Briggs, make good your promise."

Elfreda walked boldly up to the house, although she felt her courage oozing rapidly.

"I'll go inside with you, and show you the room. It's that little room off the hall," volunteered Alberta.

The outside door stood wide open. Elfreda peered fearfully down the little hall, then stepped resolutely into the little room at one side of it. A door slammed. There was the sound of a key turning in a lock, a rush of scurrying feet; then silence. Across the field fled the dark figures, nor did they stop until they had crossed the highway and entered the little grove that led to Hunter's Rock.

Suddenly a piercing scream rang out. It was followed by a succession of wild cries, and with one accord the terror-stricken conspirators made for the highway. But at every step a white figure rose in the path filling the air with weird, mournful wails. Fright lent speed to sophomore feet, and without daring to look behind, eight badly scared girls ran steadily along the road to Overton, intent only on putting distance between themselves and the terrifying apparitions that had sprung up before them. If they had stopped to deliberate for even five seconds they would, in all probability, have stood their ground, but the silent, ghostly figures that had bobbed up as by magic, coupled with the tale of the haunted house which Alberta had related, was a little too much for even vaunted sophomore courage.

A death-like stillness followed the ignominious flight of the plotters. Then from behind a tree stepped a white figure and a cautious voice called softly: "Come on, girls. They have gone. We must hurry and let Elfreda out of that awful house." At this command a ripple of subdued laughter rose from all sides and the ghosts began to appear from their nearby hiding places.

"Wasn't it funny?" laughed a tall ghost with the voice of Frances Marlton.

"I know several sophomores who will walk softly for the rest of this year at least," predicted another ghost, ending with the giggle that endeared Mabel Ashe to all her friends.

"These masks are frightfully warm," complained a diminutive spectre. A quick movement of her hand and the mask was removed, showing the rosy face of Arline Thayer.

"Keep your mask on, Arline," warned Gertrude. "Even in this secluded spot some one may be watching you."

The party proceeded with as little noise as possible to the

haunted house. Pausing at the front door a brief council was held. Then removing their masks and the sheets that enveloped them, Grace and Miriam resolutely entered the hall and went straight to the locked door, behind which Elfreda was a prisoner. The key had been left in the lock. It turned with a grating sound. Slipping her hand in the pocket of her sweater, Grace produced a tiny electric flashlight which she turned on the room. In one corner, seated on the floor, her back against the wall and her feet straight in front of her, sat Elfreda. She eyed the flashing light defiantly, then saw who was behind it and said grimly: "I might have known it. If I had taken your advice I wouldn't be here now."

"Oh, Elfreda!" exclaimed Grace. "I'm so glad you are not frightened. It was a cruel trick, but, thank goodness, we found out about it in time."

Elfreda rose and walked deliberately up to Grace and Miriam. "I'm sorry for everything," she said huskily. "I've been a ridiculous simpleton, and I don't deserve to have friends. Will you forgive me, girls? I'd like to start all over again."

"Of course we will. That was a direct, manly speech, Elfreda," laughed Miriam, but there were tears in her own eyes which no one saw in the darkness. She realized that in spite of her childish behavior she was fond of the stout girl and was glad that peace had been declared.

"Let us forget all about it, shake hands and go home," proposed Grace, "or we may find ourselves locked out."

The two girls shook hands with Elfreda, and all around again for good luck, then linking an arm in each of hers they conducted the rescued prisoner to where the rest of the party awaited them. During their absence the ghosts had doffed their spectral garments and the instant the three joined them the order to march was given. Once fairly in Overton, conversation was permitted, and on the same corner where they had met, the rescuers parted, after much talk and laughter.

"Come into my room and have tea to-night, Elfreda," invited Miriam, as they entered the house. "I have a pound of your favorite cakes."

"I'd like to come to stay," said Elfreda wistfully. "But I've been too hateful for you ever to want me for a roommate again."

"It's rather late for you to move now," replied Miriam slowly. "But I'd love to have you with me next year."

"Would you, honestly?" asked Elfreda, opening her eyes in astonishment.

"Honestly," repeated Miriam, smiling.

"I'll think about it," returned Elfreda, flushing deeply.

"But there is nothing to think about," protested Miriam. "I wouldn't ask you if I did not care for you."

"That isn't it," said Elfreda in a low tone. "It isn't you. It's I. Don't you understand? You are letting me off too easily. I don't deserve to have you be so nice to me."

"We wish you to forget about what has happened, Elfreda," said Grace earnestly. "Everyone is likely to make mistakes. We are not here to judge, we are here to help one another. That is one of the ways of cultivating true college spirit."

"I'll tell you one thing," returned Elfreda, her eyes shining, "whether I cultivate college spirit or not, I'm going to try to cultivate common sense. Then, at least, I'll know enough to treat my best friends civilly."

CHAPTER XXIII

VIRGINIA CHANGES HER MIND

What the vanquished sophomores thought of the trick that had been played on them was a matter for speculation. Once back in Overton, the truth of the situation had dawned upon them. Their common sense told them that real ghosts, if there were any, never congregated in companies the size of the one that had risen to haunt them the previous night. Obviously some one had overheard their plan to picnic at Hunter's Rock and treated them to an unwelcome surprise. It did not occur to any one of them until they had returned to their respective houses that they had left J. Elfreda locked in the haunted abode of the two brothers. Then consternation reigned in each sophomore breast.

Directly after chapel the next morning, eight young women were to be seen in an anxious group just outside the chapel. Several freshmen and two or three juniors glanced appraisingly at them, then passed on.

"Did you notice the way that Miss Wells looked at me this morning?" muttered Mary Hampton to her satellites.

"Never mind a little thing like that," snapped Alberta Wicks. "The question is, where is J. Elfreda? If she is still shut up in that house we might as well go home now instead of waiting to be sent there."

"Nonsense, Bert," scoffed one of the sophomores. "You are nervous. We may not be found out."

"Found out! J. Elfreda will be raging. She'll go straight to the dean, the minute she is free. Oh, why didn't we think to run back and let her out in spite of those ridiculous white figures?"

"What made you lock her in there, then, if you were afraid she'd tell?" asked one of the others rather sarcastically.

"Yes, that's what I say!" exclaimed a second. "This affair has been very silly from start to finish. I'm ashamed of myself for having been drawn into it, and in future you may count me out of any more such stunts."

"You girls don't understand," declared Alberta Wicks angrily. "We only meant to even an old score with the Briggs person. We were going to call for her on the way home, and tell her that we had evened our score. She wouldn't have breathed it to a soul. She knew that we'd make life miserable for her next year if she did. She wouldn't tell a little thing like that, but to leave her there all night. That really was dreadful. Mary and I are in for it. That's certain."

"If I'm not mistaken, there goes Miss Briggs now!" exclaimed a girl who had been idly watching the students as they passed out of the chapel.

"Where? Where?" questioned Mary and Alberta together.

The sophomore pointed.

"Yes; it is J. Elfreda," almost wailed Alberta Wicks. "I'm going straight back to Stuart Hall and pack my trunk. Come on, Mary."

"Better wait a little," dryly advised the sophomore who had announced her disapproval of the night's escapade. "You may be sorry if you don't."

"Good-bye, girls," said Alberta abruptly. "If I hear anything, I'll report to you at once. Now that J. Elfreda is among us, we'd better steer clear of one another for a while at least."

She hurried away, followed by Mary Hampton.

"That was my first, and if I get safely out of this, will be my last offense," said another sophomore firmly. "All those who agree with me say 'aye.'" Five "ayes" were spoken simultaneously.

In the meantime, Grace was trying vainly to make up her mind what to do. Should she go directly to the two mischievous sophomores, revealing the identity of the ghosts, or should she leave them in a quandary as to the outcome of their unwomanly trick? One thing had been decided upon definitely by Grace and her friends. They would tell no tales. Grace could not help thinking that a little anxiety would be the just due of the plotters, and with this idea in mind determined to do nothing for a time, at least, toward putting them at their ease.

But there was one person who had not been asked to remain silent concerning the ghost party, and that person was Elfreda. Grace had forgotten to tell her that the night's happenings were to be kept a secret and when late that afternoon she espied Alberta Wicks and Mary Hampton walking in the direction of Stuart Hall she pursued them with the air of an avenger. Before they realized her presence she had begun a furious arraignment of their treachery. "You ought to be sent home for it," she concluded savagely, "and if Grace Harlowe wasn't—"

"Grace Harlowe!" exclaimed Alberta, turning pale. "Do you mean to tell me that it was she who planned that ghost party?"

"I shall tell you nothing," retorted Elfreda. "I'm sorry I said even that much. I want you to understand, though, that if you ever try to play a trick on me again, I'll see that you are punished for it if I have to go down on my knees to the whole faculty to get them to give you what you deserve. Just remember that, and mind your own business, strictly, from now on."

Turning on her heel, the stout girl marched off, leaving the two girls in a state of complete perturbation.

"Had we better go and see Miss Harlowe?" asked Mary Hampton, rather unsteadily.

"The question is, do we care to come back here next year?" returned Alberta grimly.

"I'd like to come back," said Mary in a low voice. "Wouldn't you?"

"I don't know," was the perverse answer. "I don't wish to humble myself to any one. I'm going to take a chance on her keeping quiet about last night. I have an idea she is not a telltale. If worse comes to worst, there are other colleges, you know, Mary."

"I thought, perhaps, if we were to go to Miss Harlowe, we

might straighten out matters and be friends," said Mary rather hesitatingly. "Those girls have nice times together, and they are the cleverest crowd in the freshman class. I'm tired of being at sword's points with people."

"Then go over to them, by all means," sneered Alberta. "Don't trouble yourself about your old friends. They don't count."

"You know I didn't mean that, Bert," said Mary reproachfully. "I won't go near them if you feel so bitter about last night."

It was several minutes before Mary succeeded in conciliating her sulky friend. By that time the tiny sprouts of good fellowship that had vainly tried to poke their heads up into the light had been hopelessly blighted by the chilling reception they met with, and Mary had again been won over to Alberta's side.

Saturday evening Arline Thayer entertained the ghost party at Martell's, and Elfreda, to her utter astonishment, was made the guest of honor. During the progress of the dinner, Alberta Wicks, Mary Hampton and two other sophomores dropped in for ice cream. By their furtive glances and earnest conversation it was apparent that they strongly suspected the identity of the avenging specters. Elfreda's presence, too, confirmed their suspicions.

In a spirit of pure mischief Mabel Ashe pulled a leaf from her note book. Borrowing a pencil, she made an interesting little sketch of two frightened young women fleeing before a band of sheeted specters. Underneath she wrote: "It is sometimes difficult to lay ghosts. Walk warily if you wish to remain unhaunted." This she sent to Alberta Wicks by the waitress. It was passed from hand to hand, and resulted in four young women leaving Martell's without finishing their ice cream.

"You spoiled their taste for ice cream, Mabel," laughed Frances Marlton, glancing at the now vacant table. "I imagine they are shaking in their shoes."

"They did not think that the juniors had taken a hand in things," remarked Constance Fuller.

"Hardly," laughed Helen Burton. "Did you see their faces when they read that note?"

"It's really too bad to frighten them so," said Leona Rowe.

"I don't agree with you, Leona," said Mabel Ashe firmly. Her charming face had grown grave. "I think that Miss Wicks and Miss Hampton both ought to be sent home. If you will look back a little you will recollect that these two girls were far from being a credit to their class during their freshman year. I don't like to say unkind things about an Overton girl, but those two young women were distinctly trying freshmen, and as far as I can see haven't imbibed an iota of college spirit. Last night's trick, however, was completely overstepping the bounds. If Miss Briggs had been a timid, nervous girl, matters might have resulted quite differently. Then it would have been our duty to report the mischief makers. I am not sure that we are doing right in withholding what we now know from the faculty, but I am willing to give these girls the benefit of the doubt and remain silent."

"That is my opinion of the matter, too," agreed Grace. "It is only a matter of a few days until we shall all have to say good-bye until fall. During vacation certain girls will have plenty of time to think things over, and then they may see matters in an entirely different light. I shouldn't like to think that almost my last act before going home to my mother was to give some girl a dismissal from Overton to take home to hers."

A brief silence followed Grace's remark. The little speech about her mother had turned the thoughts of the girls homeward. Suddenly Mabel Ashe rose from her chair. "Here's to our mothers, girls. Let's dedicate our best efforts to them, and resolve never to lessen their pride in us with failures."

When Elfreda, Miriam, Anne and Grace ran up the steps of Wayne Hall at a little before ten o'clock they were laughing and talking so happily they failed to notice Virginia Gaines, who had been walking directly ahead of them. She had come from Stuart Hall, where, impatient to learn just what had happened the night before, she had gone to see Mary and Alberta. Finding them out she managed to learn the news from the very girl who had declared herself sorry for her part in the escapade. This particular sophomore, now that the reaction had set in, was loud in her denunciation of the trick and congratulated Virginia on not being one of those intimately concerned in it.

But Virginia, now conscience-stricken, had little to say.

She still lingered in the hall as the quartette entered, but they passed her on their way upstairs without speaking and she finally went to her room wishing, regretfully, that she had been less ready to quarrel with the girls who bade fair to lead their class both in scholarship and popularity. It was fully a week afterward when a thoroughly humbled and repentant Virginia, after making sure that Anne was out, knocked one afternoon at Grace's door.

"How do you do, Miss Gaines," said Grace civilly, but

without warmth. "Won't you come in?"

Virginia entered, but refused the chair Grace offered her. "No, thank you, I'll stand," she replied. Then in a halting fashion she said: "Miss Harlowe, I—am—awfully sorry for—for being so hateful all this year." She stopped, biting her lip, which quivered suspiciously.

Grace stared at her caller in amazement. Could it be possible that insolent Virginia Gaines was meekly apologizing to her. Then, thoughtful of the other girl's feelings, she smiled and stretched out her hand: "Don't say anything further about it, Miss Gaines. I hope we shall be friends. One can't have too many, you know, and college is the best place in the world for us to find ourselves. Come in to-night and have tea and cakes with us after lessons. That is the highest proof of hospitality I can offer at present."

"I will," promised Virginia. Then impulsively she caught one of Grace's hands in hers. "You're the dearest girl," she said, "and I'll try to be worthy of your friendship. Please tell the girls I'm sorry. I'll tell them myself to-night." With that she fairly ran from the room, and going to her own shed tears of real contrition. Later, it took all Grace's reasoning powers to put Elfreda in a state of mind that verged even slightly on charitable, but after much coaxing she promised to behave with becoming graciousness toward Virginia.

Over the tea and cakes the clouds gradually dispersed, and when Virginia went to her room that night, after declaring that she had had a perfectly lovely time, Grace took from her writing case the note that Miriam had found, and tore it into small pieces. She needed no evidence against Virginia.

CHAPTER XXIV

SAYING GOOD-BYE TO THEIR FRESHMAN YEAR

The few intervening days that lay between commencement and home were filled with plenty of pleasant excitement. There were calls to make, farewell spreads and merry-makings to attend, and momentous questions concerning what to leave behind and what to take home to be decided. The majority of the girls at Wayne Hall had asked for their old rooms for the next year. Two sophomores had succeeded in getting into Wellington House. One poor little freshman, having studied too hard, had brought on a nervous affection and was obliged to give up her course at Overton for a year at least. There was also one other sophomore whose mother was coming to the town of Overton to live and keep house for her daughter in a bungalow not far from the college.

It now lacked only two days until the end of the spring term, and what to pack and when to pack it were the burning questions of the hour.

"There will be room for four more freshmen here next year," remarked Grace, as she appeared from her closet, her arms piled high with skirts and gowns. Depositing them on the floor, she dropped wearily into a chair. "I don't believe I can ever make all those things go into that trunk. I have all my clothes that I brought here last fall, and another lot that I brought back at Christmas, and still some others that I acquired at Easter. If I had had a particle of forethought I would have taken home a few things each trip. Don't dare to leave the house until this trunk is packed, Anne, for I shall need you to help me sit on it. If our combined weight isn't enough, we'll invite Elfreda and Miriam in to the sitting. I am perfectly willing to perform the same kind offices for them. Oh, dear, I hate to begin. I'm wild to go home, but I can't help feeling sad to think my freshman joys are over. It seems to me that the two most important years in college are one's freshman and senior years.

"Being a freshman is like beginning a garden. One plants what one considers the best seeds, and when the little green shoots come up, it's terribly hard to make them live at all. It is only by constant care that they are made to thrive and all sorts of storms are likely to rise out of a clear sky and blight them. Some of the seeds one thought would surely grow the fastest are total disappointments, while others that one just planted to fill in, fairly astonish one by their growth, but if at the end of the freshman year the garden looks green and well cared for, it's safe to say it will keep on growing through the sophomore and junior years and bloom at the end of four years. That's the peculiarity about college gardens. One has to begin to plant the very first day of the freshman year to be sure of flowers when the four years are over.

"In the sophomore year the hardest task is keeping the weeds out, and during the junior and senior years the difficulty will be to keep the ground in the highest state of cultivation. It will be easier to neglect one's garden, then, because one will have grown so used to the things one has planted that one will forget to tend them and put off stirring up the soil around them and watering them. I'm going to think a little each day while I'm home this summer about my garden and keep it fresh and green."

Grace laid the gown she had been folding in the trunk and looked earnestly at Anne as she finished her long speech.

"What a nice idea!" exclaimed Anne warmly. "I think I shall have to begin gardening, too.'

"Your garden has always been in a flourishing condition from the first," laughed Grace. "The chief trouble with mine seems to be the number of strange weeds that spring up— nettles that I never planted, but that sting just as sharply, nevertheless. It hurts me to go home with the knowledge that there are two girls here who don't like me. I know I ought not to care, for I have nothing to regret as far as my own conduct is concerned, but still I'd like to leave Overton for the summer without one shadow in my path."

"Perhaps, when certain girls come back in the fall they will be on their good behavior."

"Perhaps," repeated Grace sceptically.

The entrance into the room of Elfreda and Miriam, who had been out shopping, brought the little heart talk to an abrupt close.

"We've a new kind of cakes," exulted Miriam. "They are three stories high and each story is a different color. They have icing half an inch thick and an English walnut on top. All for the small sum of five cents, too."

"We bought a dozen," declared Elfreda, "and now I'm going out to buy ice cream. This packing business calls for plenty of refreshment to keep one's energy up to the mark. I've thought of a lovely plan to lighten my labors."

"What is it?" asked Grace. "Your plans are always startlingly original if not very practical."

"This is practical," announced the stout girl. "I'm going to give away my clothes; that is, the most of them. I found a poor woman the other day who does scrubbing for the college who needs them. I found out where she lives and I'm going to bundle them all together and send them to her. I don't wish her to know where they came from. I'll just write a card, and—"

The three broadly smiling faces of her friends caused her to stop short and regard them suspiciously. "What's the matter?" she said in an offended tone.

Grace ran over and slipped her arm about the stout girl's shoulders. "You are the one who sent Ruth her lovely clothes last Christmas. Don't try to deny it. I was sure of it then."

"Oh, see here," expostulated Elfreda, jerking herself away, her face crimson. "I—you—"

"Confess," threatened Miriam, seizing the little brass tea kettle and brandishing it over Elfreda's head.

"I won't," defied Elfreda, laughing a little in spite of her efforts to appear offended.

"One, two," counted Miriam, grasping the kettle firmly.

"All right, I did," confessed Elfreda nonchalantly. "What are you going to do about it?"

"Present you with your Christmas gifts now," smiled Miriam. "You wouldn't look at us last Christmas, so we've been saving our gifts ever since. Wait a minute, girls, until I go for mine."

As she darted from the room, Grace said softly: "We hoped that you would understand about Thanksgiving and that everything would be all right by Christmas, so we planned our little remembrances for you just the same. Then, when—when we didn't see you before going home for the holidays, Anne suggested that we put them away, because we all hoped that you'd be friends with us again some day." Rummaging in the tray of her trunk she produced a long, flat package which she offered to Elfreda. Anne, who, at Grace's first words, had stepped to the chiffonier, took out a beribboned bundle, and stood holding it toward the stout girl. Another moment and Miriam had returned bearing her offering. "I wish you a merry June," declared Miriam with an infectious giggle that was echoed by the others. Then Elfreda opened the package from Miriam, which contained a Japanese silk kimono similar to one of her own that her roommate had greatly admired. Grace's package contained a pair of long white gloves, and Anne had remembered her with a book she had once heard the stout girl express a desire to own.

"You had no business to do it," muttered Elfreda. Then gathering up her presents she made a dash for the door and with a muffled, "I'll be back soon," was gone. It was several minutes before she reappeared with red eyes, but smiling lips. Then a long talk ensued, during which time the art of trunk-packing languished. It was renewed with vigor that evening and continued spasmodically for the next two days. In the campus houses the real packing dragged along in most instances until within two hours of the time when the trunks were to be called for. Then a wholesale scramble began, to make up for lost minutes. One of the most frequent and painful sights during those last two days was that of a wrathful expressman, glaring in impotent rage while an enterprising damsel opened her trunk on the front porch to take out or put in one or several of her various possessions which, until that moment, had been completely forgotten.

The night before leaving Overton the four girls paid a visit to Ruth Denton. The plucky little freshman had refused an invitation to spend the summer with Arline Thayer, but had accepted a position in Overton with a dress-maker. The last two weeks of her vacation she had promised to spend with Arline at the sea-shore.

Their last morning at Overton dawned fair and sunshiny. Grace, who had risen early, stood at the window, looking out at the glory of the sparkling June day.

The campus was a vast green velvet carpet and the pale green of the trees had not yet changed to that darker, dustier shade that belongs only to summer. Back among the trees Overton Hall rose gray and majestic. Grace's heart swelled with pride as she gazed at the stately old building surrounded by its silent, leafy guard. "Overton, my Alma Mater," she said softly. "May I be always worthy to be your child."

"What are you mooning over?" asked Anne, who had slipped into her kimono and joined Grace at the window.

"I'm rhapsodizing," smiled Grace, her eyes very bright. "I love Overton, don't you, Anne?"

Anne nodded. "I'm glad we didn't go to Wellesley or Vassar, or even Smith. I'd rather be here."

"So would I," sighed Grace. "Next to home there is no place like Overton. I almost wish I were coming back here next fall as a freshman."

"But it's against the law of progress to wish one's self back," smiled Anne, "and being a sophomore surely has its rainbow side."

"And it rests with us to find it," replied Grace softly, placing her hand on her friend's shoulder.

A little later, laden with bags and suit cases, the three Oakdale girls, accompanied by Elfreda, walked out of Wayne Hall as freshmen for the last time.

"When next we see this house it will be as sophomores," observed Elfreda. "I'm glad we are all going home on the same train. Do you remember the day I met you? I thought I owned the earth then. But I have found out that there are other people to consider besides myself. That is what being a freshman at Overton has taught me."

"That's a very good thing for all of us to remember," remarked Grace. "I'm going to try to practise it next year."

"You won't have to try very hard," returned Elfreda dryly. "How much time have we?"

"Almost an hour," replied Miriam, looking at her watch.

"Then we've time to stop at Vinton's for a farewell sundae. It's our last freshman treat. Come on, everybody," invited the stout girl.

"No more sundaes here until next fall," lamented Miriam, as they sat waiting for their order. "I shall miss Vinton's. There is nothing in Oakdale quite like it."

"And I shall miss you girls," declared Elfreda bluntly.

"Why don't you pay us a visit, then?" suggested Miriam. "We expect to be at home part of the time this summer."

"Perhaps I will," reflected Elfreda. "But you must write to me at any rate."

At the station groups of happy-faced girls stood waiting for the train.

"We are going to have plenty of company," observed Anne. "Do you remember how forlorn we felt when we were cast away on this station platform last fall? We won't feel so strange next September."

"We shall feel very important instead," laughed Miriam. "It will be our turn to escort bewildered freshmen to their boarding places."

"Yes, and we'll see that they don't stray, too," retorted Elfreda grimly.

"Or mistake the Register for the registrar," smiled Grace.

What befell Grace and her friends during their sophomore year is set forth fully in "Grace Harlowe's Second Year at Overton College." How they lived up to their girlish ideals, finding the "rainbow side" of their sophomore year, is a story that no admirer of Grace Harlowe can afford to miss.

The End

Jessie Graham Flower

Choose from Thousands of 1stWorldLibrary Classics By

A. M. Barnard
Ada Leverson
Adolphus William Ward
Aesop
Agatha Christie
Alexander Aaronsohn
Alexander Kielland
Alexandre Dumas
Alfred Gatty
Alfred Ollivant
Alice Duer Miller
Alice Turner Curtis
Alice Dunbar
Allen Chapman
Alleyne Ireland
Ambrose Bierce
Amelia E. Barr
Amory H. Bradford
Andrew Lang
Andrew McFarland Davis
Andy Adams
Angela Brazil
Anna Alice Chapin
Anna Sewell
Annie Besant
Annie Hamilton Donnell
Annie Payson Call
Annie Roe Carr
Annonaymous
Anton Chekhov
Archibald Lee Fletcher
Arnold Bennett
Arthur C. Benson
Arthur Conan Doyle
Arthur M. Winfield
Arthur Ransome
Arthur Schnitzler
Arthur Train
Atticus
B.H. Baden-Powell
B. M. Bower
B. C. Chatterjee
Baroness Emmuska Orczy
Baroness Orczy
Basil King
Bayard Taylor
Ben Macomber
Bertha Muzzy Bower
Bjornstjerne Bjornson

Booth Tarkington
Boyd Cable
Bram Stoker
C. Collodi
C. E. Orr
C. M. Ingleby
Carolyn Wells
Catherine Parr Traill
Charles A. Eastman
Charles Amory Beach
Charles Dickens
Charles Dudley Warner
Charles Farrar Browne
Charles Ives
Charles Kingsley
Charles Klein
Charles Hanson Towne
Charles Lathrop Pack
Charles Romyn Dake
Charles Whibley
Charles Willing Beale
Charlotte M. Braeme
Charlotte M. Yonge
Charlotte Perkins Stetson
Clair W. Hayes
Clarence Day Jr.
Clarence E. Mulford
Clemence Housman
Confucius
Coningsby Dawson
Cornelis DeWitt Wilcox
Cyril Burleigh
D. H. Lawrence
Daniel Defoe
David Garnett
Dinah Craik
Don Carlos Janes
Donald Keyhoe
Dorothy Kilner
Dougan Clark
Douglas Fairbanks
E. Nesbit
E. P. Roe
E. Phillips Oppenheim
E. S. Brooks
Earl Barnes
Edgar Rice Burroughs
Edith Van Dyne
Edith Wharton

Edward Everett Hale
Edward J. O'Biren
Edward S. Ellis
Edwin L. Arnold
Eleanor Atkins
Eleanor Hallowell Abbott
Eliot Gregory
Elizabeth Gaskell
Elizabeth McCracken
Elizabeth Von Arnim
Ellem Key
Emerson Hough
Emilie F. Carlen
Emily Bronte
Emily Dickinson
Enid Bagnold
Enilor Macartney Lane
Erasmus W. Jones
Ernie Howard Pie
Ethel May Dell
Ethel Turner
Ethel Watts Mumford
Eugene Sue
Eugenie Foa
Eugene Wood
Eustace Hale Ball
Evelyn Everett-green
Everard Cotes
F. H. Cheley
F. J. Cross
F. Marion Crawford
Fannie E. Newberry
Federick Austin Ogg
Ferdinand Ossendowski
Fergus Hume
Florence A. Kilpatrick
Fremont B. Deering
Francis Bacon
Francis Darwin
Frances Hodgson Burnett
Frances Parkinson Keyes
Frank Gee Patchin
Frank Harris
Frank Jewett Mather
Frank L. Packard
Frank V. Webster
Frederic Stewart Isham
Frederick Trevor Hill
Frederick Winslow Taylor

Friedrich Kerst	Hayden Carruth	James Branch Cabell
Friedrich Nietzsche	Helent Hunt Jackson	James DeMille
Fyodor Dostoyevsky	Helen Nicolay	James Joyce
G.A. Henty	Hendrik Conscience	James Lane Allen
G.K. Chesterton	Hendy David Thoreau	James Lane Allen
Gabrielle E. Jackson	Henri Barbusse	James Oliver Curwood
Garrett P. Serviss	Henrik Ibsen	James Oppenheim
Gaston Leroux	Henry Adams	James Otis
George A. Warren	Henry Ford	James R. Driscoll
George Ade	Henry Frost	Jane Abbott
Geroge Bernard Shaw	Henry James	Jane Austen
George Cary Eggleston	Henry Jones Ford	Jane L. Stewart
George Durston	Henry Seton Merriman	Janet Aldridge
George Ebers	Henry W Longfellow	Jens Peter Jacobsen
George Eliot	Herbert A. Giles	Jerome K. Jerome
George Gissing	Herbert Carter	Jessie Graham Flower
George MacDonald	Herbert N. Casson	John Buchan
George Meredith	Herman Hesse	John Burroughs
George Orwell	Hildegard G. Frey	John Cournos
George Sylvester Viereck	Homer	John F. Kennedy
George Tucker	Honore De Balzac	John Gay
George W. Cable	Horace B. Day	John Glasworthy
George Wharton James	Horace Walpole	John Habberton
Gertrude Atherton	Horatio Alger Jr.	John Joy Bell
Gordon Casserly	Howard Pyle	John Kendrick Bangs
Grace E. King	Howard R. Garis	John Milton
Grace Gallatin	Hugh Lofting	John Philip Sousa
Grace Greenwood	Hugh Walpole	John Taintor Foote
Grant Allen	Humphry Ward	Jonas Lauritz Idemil Lie
Guillermo A. Sherwell	Ian Maclaren	Jonathan Swift
Gulielma Zollinger	Inez Haynes Gillmore	Joseph A. Altsheler
Gustav Flaubert	Irving Bacheller	Joseph Carey
H. A. Cody	Isabel Cecilia Williams	Joseph Conrad
H. B. Irving	Isabel Hornibrook	Joseph E. Badger Jr
H. C. Bailey	Israel Abrahams	Joseph Hergesheimer
H. G. Wells	Ivan Turgenev	Joseph Jacobs
H. H. Munro	J. G.Austin	Jules Vernes
H. Irving Hancock	J. Henri Fabre	Julian Hawthrone
H. R. Naylor	J. M. Barrie	Julie A Lippmann
H. Rider Haggard	J. M. Walsh	Justin Huntly McCarthy
H. W. C. Davis	J. Macdonald Oxley	Kakuzo Okakura
Haldeman Julius	J. R. Miller	Karle Wilson Baker
Hall Caine	J. S. Fletcher	Kate Chopin
Hamilton Wright Mabie	J. S. Knowles	Kenneth Grahame
Hans Christian Andersen	J. Storer Clouston	Kenneth McGaffey
Harold Avery	J. W. Duffield	Kate Langley Bosher
Harold McGrath	Jack London	Kate Langley Bosher
Harriet Beecher Stowe	Jacob Abbott	Katherine Cecil Thurston
Harry Castlemon	James Allen	Katherine Stokes
Harry Coghill	James Andrews	L. A. Abbot
Harry Houidini	James Baldwin	L. T. Meade

L. Frank Baum
Latta Griswold
Laura Dent Crane
Laura Lee Hope
Laurence Housman
Lawrence Beasley
Leo Tolstoy
Leonid Andreyev
Lewis Carroll
Lewis Sperry Chafer
Lilian Bell
Lloyd Osbourne
Louis Hughes
Louis Joseph Vance
Louis Tracy
Louisa May Alcott
Lucy Fitch Perkins
Lucy Maud Montgomery
Luther Benson
Lydia Miller Middleton
Lyndon Orr
M. Corvus
M. H. Adams
Margaret E. Sangster
Margret Howth
Margaret Vandercook
Margaret W. Hungerford
Margret Penrose
Maria Edgeworth
Maria Thompson Daviess
Mariano Azuela
Marion Polk Angellotti
Mark Overton
Mark Twain
Mary Austin
Mary Catherine Crowley
Mary Cole
Mary Hastings Bradley
Mary Roberts Rinehart
Mary Rowlandson
M. Wollstonecraft Shelley
Maud Lindsay
Max Beerbohm
Myra Kelly
Nathaniel Hawthrone
Nicolo Machiavelli
O. F. Walton
Oscar Wilde
Owen Johnson
P.G. Wodehouse
Paul and Mabel Thorne

Paul G. Tomlinson
Paul Severing
Percy Brebner
Percy Keese Fitzhugh
Peter B. Kyne
Plato
Quincy Allen
R. Derby Holmes
R. L. Stevenson
R. S. Ball
Rabindranath Tagore
Rahul Alvares
Ralph Bonehill
Ralph Henry Barbour
Ralph Victor
Ralph Waldo Emmerson
Rene Descartes
Ray Cummings
Rex Beach
Rex E. Beach
Richard Harding Davis
Richard Jefferies
Richard Le Gallienne
Robert Barr
Robert Frost
Robert Gordon Anderson
Robert L. Drake
Robert Lansing
Robert Lynd
Robert Michael Ballantyne
Robert W. Chambers
Rosa Nouchette Carey
Rudyard Kipling
Saint Augustine
Samuel B. Allison
Samuel Hopkins Adams
Sarah Bernhardt
Sarah C. Hallowell
Selma Lagerlof
Sherwood Anderson
Sigmund Freud
Standish O'Grady
Stanley Weyman
Stella Benson
Stella M. Francis
Stephen Crane
Stewart Edward White
Stijn Streuvels
Swami Abhedananda
Swami Parmananda
T. S. Ackland

T. S. Arthur
The Princess Der Ling
Thomas A. Janvier
Thomas A Kempis
Thomas Anderton
Thomas Bailey Aldrich
Thomas Bulfinch
Thomas De Quincey
Thomas Dixon
Thomas H. Huxley
Thomas Hardy
Thomas More
Thornton W. Burgess
U. S. Grant
Upton Sinclair
Valentine Williams
Various Authors
Vaughan Kester
Victor Appleton
Victor G. Durham
Victoria Cross
Virginia Woolf
Wadsworth Camp
Walter Camp
Walter Scott
Washington Irving
Wilbur Lawton
Wilkie Collins
Willa Cather
Willard F. Baker
William Dean Howells
William le Queux
W. Makepeace Thackeray
William W. Walter
William Shakespeare
Winston Churchill
Yei Theodora Ozaki
Yogi Ramacharaka
Young E. Allison
Zane Grey

NIGHT'S MELODY

NIGHT'S MELODY
AN MMMM PHANTOM OF THE OPERA RETELLING

MONSTERS & MAYHEM

DRAKE LAMARQUE

* * *

Content note:

This book contains sharing/multiple partners, mentions of dead parents, violence, stabbing and murder (not between the main characters), BDSM scenes and drama queens.

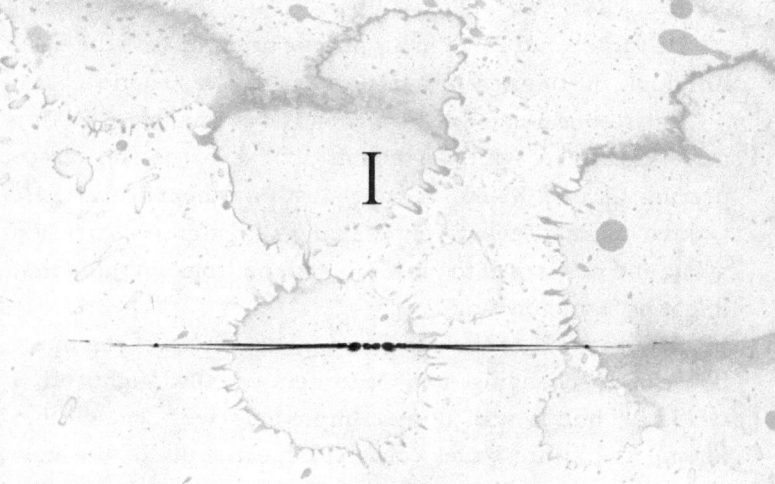

I

Paris, 1884
The Opera La Rêve

Matthieu

CHANGES, everything changes. That was the one constant in Matthieu's life. Changes. Changing clothing from practice leotards to stage costume, and then changes of stage costume. Every show had multiple scene changes which meant there were changes, and oftentimes the character Matthieu played changed as well.

The myriad changes ran through Matthieu's mind as he went through the new choreography with the rest of the ballet corps, cursing himself silently when he landed from a jeté just off the beat instead of on it.

He looked up to see his mother watching, one eyebrow raised. Of course she'd seen his mistake. She never missed errors in her dancers. He had to concentrate harder.

He turned and saw Christophe, *he* never missed the beat. Although, outside of rehearsal he wasn't quite so perfect.

Christophe Daaé, his best friend, was changing, getting more distracted with daydreams than ever before, disappearing at odd hours. It tugged at Matthieu's heart. He wanted to know what was drawing Christophe's attention away, and he wanted to protect his friend from anything that might be troubling him.

On top of all of that, the very management of the opera house was changing too. Matthieu tried to fight off a headache but it was utterly impossible with his mother forcing the entire ballet corps to repeat drills of the new choreography until they satisfied her expectations. She expected perfection so that's what they had to be.

Madame Giry had been the head of the ballet corps since before Matthieu's birth, and she was exacting in her training. They were, Matthieu knew, the best ballet corps in any opera in all of France, and probably the world, due to her diligence, but that didn't ease any of the pain in his ankles, calves and toes.

Nor did it do anything to assuage his headache.

Madame Giry struck the floor with her ever-present walking stick and the ballet corps, as well trained as any hunting dogs, came to an instant cessation of movement, heads turned towards their teacher.

"All right, that's enough!" She waved a hand in the air, a gesture which meant 'there's nothing more I can do with you,' and they were dismissed. "Back and in costume for the dress rehearsal at 2.30 sharp!"

The new managers were meant to be arriving some time that afternoon. Matthieu hoped they would see some of the dress rehearsal and be impressed, but more than that, he hoped the dreaded Opera Ghost wouldn't make things difficult.

The Ghost was thought to be a legend outside of the theatre, but those who performed and worked inside it knew better. The Ghost was very real, and he didn't like change.

Matthieu was intrigued by the stories of the Opera Ghost, although he feared it, he was also deeply curious about who it was, who it had been. Was it truly a ghost? Was it someone alive who enjoyed terrorising the performers?

If they had a disastrous dress rehearsal the gala might be in danger, and if the gala failed the new managers might well decide it was all too much trouble and shut the theatre altogether.

Then what would they all do?

Matthieu

MATTHIEU'S HEADACHE WAS WORSE.

The rehearsal for Hannibal was an utter disaster.

First Piangi, the lead tenor tripped on his own feet and crashed into the papier mâché elephant, tearing a huge hole in the side of the prop.

Then the diva, an incredible singer named Carlotta, decided that she wasn't being given the appropriate amount of attention and stormed off to pout in her dressing room. The stage manager had to leave to beg her to return.

Absolutely all the performers were on edge due to the impending visit of the new managers and their patron.

The ballet corps, who were always superstitious, nudged each other and whispered.

"A bad dress rehearsal means a good performance, right?"

"Absolutely."

A blonde girl called Elise leaned on Matthieu's shoulder. Her hair colour was so like his they could have been siblings, although there was no relation there as far as he knew. "We did alright though, didn't we?"

"I thought so," Matthieu said. "No one's twisted an ankle, anyway."

"Don't even say something like that!" Christophe exclaimed, and smacked Matthieu on the shoulder with the flat of his palm. "You'll jinx us all."

"Sorry, sorry," Matthieu said. "But they're right, a bad rehearsal means a good show."

They nodded at each other, reassured, and then stood to attention when Madame Giry thumped her cane on the boards.

"Focus, all of you."

Matthieu sighed and fiddled with his costume, the tiny bolero-style jacket wasn't sitting quite right. The outfits they had for this portion of the show were scandalously minimal. Boleros and soft pants that only reached to their knees. The girls had leotards and skirts made of nothing but strings. He had to admit that Christophe made the outfit look absolutely wonderful though.

They began the dance again, Madame Giry keeping time with the thump of her cane and shouting at any whose turnout was suffering or who's hands weren't held at exactly the right angle.

There was a bustle of noise at the front of the theatre, and the doors opened to let in a small group of men in fine suits.

The director called everyone to attention as the men approached the stage and silence fell over the assembled cast.

The departing theatre owner led the way. He was a dour man by the name of Carlisle who had been relatively absent in his management of things. Matthieu wouldn't be sad to see him go.

He led the other three men up to the stage. He waved to the conductor.

"Just a moment's time, if you please," he said.

"Of course," the conductor said. He said it graciously, as if he was doing them a large favour, although the orchestra had been sitting idle.

Carlisle stepped up on stage with the other men, and just at that moment Carlotta returned in her most fabulous costume from the opera, ready to be presented.

"Thank you for your attention," Carlisle said. "I wish to introduce you to the new managers of the Opera La Rêve. This is Monsieur Richard Firmin and Monsieur Giles André. Please welcome them as warmly as you once welcomed me."

There was polite applause from the assembled dancers and chorus singers. Carlotta stepped forward with a simpering smile and held out a hand to the new managers.

Carlisle hesitated just one moment too long before he cleared his throat. "May I present Madame Carlotta, our preeminent diva. And here is Señor Piangi, our star tenor."

Both managers took Carlotta's fingers and kissed the back of her gloved hand in turn. Piangi bustled forward, limping slightly, and shook both of their hands.

"An honour, truly," André said. He beamed at both of them, and turned as if he were about to introduce the third man who stood with them, but Firmin spoke again.

"You have a magnificent talent," Firmin said. His hand

found Carlotta's again. "I saw you perform last winter and I was in tears. Please, if it's not too much of an imposition might you consider-"

Carlisle cut him off. "I must leave, I sail for London within the hour. Thank you all, and it was nice knowing you."

Before anyone could say anything else, Carlisle turned on his heel and strode down the stage steps and up the aisle towards the front of the theatre.

Matthieu tried to catch Christophe's eye, wishing to share a moment of delight that Carlisle was gone. But Christophe was utterly distracted, watching the new managers and their mysterious friend with rapt attention.

Carlotta cleared her throat and everyone's attention refocused on her, as if Carlisle was utterly forgotten already.

"I beg your pardon, messieurs but I believe you were about to ask something?" Carlotta said, pitching her voice to ensure all attention remained on her.

"Ah, yes, if it's not too much of an imposition on your rehearsal, might we hear the aria from act two? I would very much appreciate it." Firmin smiled a little too ingratiatingly for Matthieu's taste but Carlotte seemed to be lapping it up.

"Of course," Carlotta said. She gestured at the conductor, who stifled a sigh, picked up his baton and tapped it. The orchestra soon began the introduction to the aria, and Carlotta swanned in a circle about the stage, pushing the chorus and other performers back so that she would have a nice open space to perform.

The managers retreated to the stalls with their mysterious friend and sat in the front row, expectant smiles on their faces.

Carlotta took a deep breath and began to sing. It was Matthieu's opinion that Carlotta sang far too much in her nose, producing an unpleasant tone, but it was an opinion that he had only shared with Christophe, and bound him to the utmost secrecy. An opinion like that could get him removed from the ballet, regardless of who his mother was. Carlotta required an awful lot of praise.

She was an excellent performer, drawing attention and moving gracefully, but Matthieu got bored after a few bars, and started doing some small stretches in place, to ensure his muscles stayed warm.

There was a sudden scream - one of the ballet girls - and the rolled up backdrop for act three fell from the rafters, directly onto Carlotta. She had no warning at all, so wrapped up was she in her aria.

One moment she was singing to the new managers, the next she was flat on her face, half crushed by the heavy piece of stage furniture.

"The Phantom did it!" Elise screamed, and was instantly hushed.

Matthieu expected Carlotta to start screaming for someone to save her, but she stayed quite still, which was far more chilling.

Matthieu and two other male chorus members went to lift the huge roll of painted paper off her with the help of the stage hands, and it became clear that Carlotta was seriously injured.

A stretcher was produced from somewhere and two of the handymen who worked at odd jobs around the theatre carried her off to the nearby hospital for examination. She didn't stir throughout the entire procedure.

The mysterious man who hadn't been introduced left with the stretcher, although it wasn't clear if he was planning to help or simply wanted to remove himself from the entire scene.

After a long moment's silence, Firmin climbed up onto

the stage again and clapped his hands twice, as if trying to clear the air. "Well, that was a rather unfortunate accident, to be sure."

Madame Giry glanced at him, then sighed, rolling her eyes expressively to the heavens. "Buquet?" she called.

Joseph Buquet was the head stagehand, and seemed as old as the building himself, although he was very spry and strong. Matthieu disliked him, as he was fond of telling ghost stories and further scaring the ballet corps.

"It wasn't an accident, monsieur." Buquet emerged from the wings, looking ashamed, something clutched in his hand. "I saw movement up in the flies, but I was too slow to stop what happened." He held out a shorn off piece of rope. "Sabotage."

"Who would do such a thing?" Firmin asked. He had gone quite pale, and Matthieu felt for him.

"The Opera Ghost!" one of the ballet girls, Edith, exclaimed. Three others joined her, insisting it was so.

Madame Giry glared at the entire ballet corps until they quieted down, and then strode over to Firmin.

"Did Monsieur Carlisle not tell you of the Opera Ghost?" she demanded.

Matthieu would forever be in awe about how his mother made everything she said sound like a personal failing of the other person.

Firmin shook his head and looked back at André, who had joined him on stage. "He did mention something, but I don't understand," André said. "You can't be serious. It's a fairy story surely."

"You think so, monsieur?" Madame Giry turned away. She gestured upwards. "Just make sure you leave box five open for his use, and make sure to pay his monthly fee."

"Monthly fee?" André and Firmin were astounded.

The stage manager stepped up as Madame Giry moved off. "What do you wish to do about the Gala, monsieurs? It is only hours away and the tickets are all sold."

"Is there an understudy?" Firmin asked, his voice strained.

"Not for La Carlotta," the conductor said. He sighed, shook his head. Matthieu knew what he was reacting to - another Manager who didn't understand the arts or the precise art of casting.

"Is there no one who could fill in? Who knows the part?" Firmin looked around at the assembled actors. His expression was quite confounded.

"We can't refund everyone," André said. "The cost is astronomical. There must be an option." He fiddled with the hem of his jacket. "I must say this is not how I expected today to go."

Firmin patted André on the shoulder, a placating and familiar sort of gesture.

Madame Giry turned back, her skirts swirling. She extended one hand towards Christophe and beckoned him forth.

Matthieu's instinct was to grab onto Christophe to hold him back, but he schooled himself, and put his hands behind his back. Christophe went towards Madame Giry, his eyes fixed on the floorboards, his shoulders hunched and his expression rather nervous.

"It is rather unconventional, but you might let Christophe sing for you. He has been taught by a master." Madame Giry positioned Christophe in front of her and tapped the base of his spine. He instantly uncurved his shoulders and stood up straight. He didn't lift his chin though.

Firmin looked him up and down, scepticism written across his face which softened slightly as he took Christophe in. "Well. I suppose I do like some of the things they've been doing with the unusual casting of the comic operettas up in Montmartre."

André by contrast looked absolutely delighted. "What a wonderful way to introduce ourselves to the audience, by making a statement! Shaking up the traditional opera regime, if you will." He stepped a little closer to Christophe and lowered his voice to a softer tone. "What's your name, my lad?"

Christophe lifted his chin then and met the gaze of the manager with his beautiful hazel-brown eyes. "Christophe Daaé, monsieur."

"And who is this master, who has taught you to sing?"

Matthieu leaned forward, he wished to know the answer to this question as well.

Christophe looked down again, long eyelashes laying on his cheekbones. "I don't know his name, monsieur."

"And can you reach the high notes? Carlotta's role is of course, for a soprano..."

Christophe nodded. "I have been practising range, my master is pleased with the quality and reach of my falsetto."

"How very peculiar," André said. "I absolutely love it. Go on, Richard, let us try it out."

Firmin huffed. "Well, none of this matters if we don't like the way you sing, how about it?" He turned to the conductor, who waved his baton and started the orchestra playing.

The managers stepped back, giving Christophe the stage, and he cleared his throat. Before he began to sing, he looked at Matthieu, his expression beseeching.

Did Christophe want to be rescued, or reassured?

Matthieu smiled and nodded, hoping that reassurance was the correct response. It seemed to be. Christophe squared his shoulders, lifted his chest and began to sing.

2
MATTHIEU

———————————————

S ome hours later, after the uproarious ovations had finally, finally died down and the gala-goers had returned to their homes, Matthieu found Christophe in Carlotta's changing room. Matthieu pushed the door open and saw Christophe fussing with a lace dressing gown that Matthieu recognised as one of Madame Giry's hand-me-downs. She must have given it to Christophe for the occasion.

"Good evening," Christophe said. His voice gentle as a dove's wing, a high contrast to the fine pure notes he'd been belting out earlier.

Christophe had a lithe form, masculine with powerful dancer's thighs, and well-defined muscles, but Matthieu had always admired his grace. Every movement of Christophe's was fine art. There was something delicate in the way he approached everything he did and it never failed to entrance Matthieu. He had learned to turn his head slightly away when they were dancing together on stage, lest he lose his focus on his own dance and trip.

Christophe had his hair loose, he'd worn it out on the stage, over the hastily adjusted lead character dress that

Carlotta was meant to have worn. Instead, Christophe had fully embraced his new role and become something other than a man, something that wasn't a woman either, something in between. Something more beautiful that transcended gender and set the theatre audience alight.

His hair fell in loose waves now, caressing his shoulders, and Matthieu's hand itched to pick up his comb and groom it, as he had a thousand times before.

They had started caring for each other as children, looking after one another... both of them fatherless, without siblings, Christophe motherless as well. They'd met soon after Christophe's father had passed away, leaving him an orphan, at the Paris ballet conservatory.

As they had grown older, Matthieu's feelings had grown into something more than simple friendliness for Christophe. He instead harboured a fiery yearning, something that compelled him for more reasons to touch Christophe, to hug him, to sit close and lean in to listen to him. Christophe always had strange fancies or dreams to share, and excuses were easy to find to indulge him.

Matthieu approached him now, picking up the wide-toothed wooden comb, but he froze before he could offer to brush his hair. Christophe had lifted his hand to brush something off his shoulder, and Matthieu saw he had rings of abrasions around both his wrists.

"Christophe! What are these?" Matthieu exclaimed. Christophe started, as easy to frighten as a wild rabbit, and with similarly large, endearing eyes.

"Matthieu, mon dieu!"

Sinking down onto the spare chair, Matthieu took both of Christophe's hands in his own and examined the marks. Each was a narrow ring, a bracelet around each delicate forearm, and the abrasions looked almost like...

"Are these rope marks?" Matthieu asked.

Christophe snatched his hands back and pulled the frilled sleeves of the dressing gown down to cover the marks. His cheeks were pink under the remaining stage makeup, and he refused to meet Matthieu's eyes.

"It's nothing."

"It isn't nothing."

Christophe shook his head and continued to look determinedly away.

"Please, Chris," Matthieu said. "You know you can tell me anything. I don't like it that you're keeping secrets from me. At least tell me, if you won't talk about the marks, how did you learn to sing so beautifully as you did tonight? My mother mentioned a tutor in passing when you missed a dance rehearsal the other day, but I've never seen a stranger coming into the theatre, and now... these marks...I'm afraid for you, Chris."

Christophe looked around, as if half-expecting Madame Giry to pop out from behind the rail of costumes and scold them. But the door was closed and they were alone in the room.

"You must promise not to tell anyone." Christophe's hand landed on Matthieu's where he was resting it on the dressing table. His eyes were wide, his pupils huge in the dim light of the gaslamp.

"I promise," Matthieu said. "You know I'd never betray you, Chris."

"I know Matty," Christophe nodded. He reached a tentative hand out and took Matthieu's. His hand was quite cold and Matthieu resisted the urge to wrap both his hands around it to warm it up. Christophe took a breath and began. "Before we met, when I was young, my father told me lots of stories. Mother died when I was so young, so I often worried I would lose him too. So he often told me that when he died, and was in heaven, he would send the Angel of Music to guide me." Matthieu's heart sank. Christophe was given to romances, fanciful stories that he would make up and start to believe in. It always led to disappointment and it was always worse when it concerned Christophe's beloved, late father. "Well it's true. Father is dead, Matty, and I have been visited by the angel."

"You have?" Matthieu tried his best to keep his voice level but he was sure the concern he felt coloured his tone.

"He is always listening when I sing, and he gives me tutelage. Some of his methods may sound rather strange, but... well, you have seen the results of his lessons, Matty. You have heard how well he has trained me."

Matthieu nodded. "You sounded wonderful, Chris, but I don't quite understand. Is he a real angel? Have you seen him? Or have you been dreaming about him, only?" Matthieu's heart thumped with fear.

Christophe shook his head, causing his curls to shift prettily from shoulder to clavicle. He still wore a jewelled comb on one side of his head, holding a sweep of hair to the side. Matthieu ached to gently pull it from his tresses, brush his hair to the side and kiss Christophe's neck until he calmed and stilled. To gentle him like a pet rabbit.

"Nothing like. I hear his voice. I've heard it in my bedchamber, or in the changing room. In here, tonight. All around me."

"But Chris," Matthieu shook his head. "What your father told you, it was beautiful but it was just a story, it wasn't something that could really happen."

Christophe looked at Matthieu with wide, hurt eyes and Matthieu bit his tongue and tried to entice Christophe to speak more. He had to be more careful about it.

"Have you... have you only heard him?"

Christophe softened again. "Well, several times he has requested I put on a blindfold, and when I do, he comes into the room with me. He touches me, and then the lessons are more intense, and far more useful."

Matthieu sat back, one hand to his chest, the other now clutching Christophe's fingers. His blood chilled with fear, and something else as well. Who was this man Christophe was letting into the room? Touching him? Who was heard in various parts of the opera house?

And could it be the Opera Ghost?

"What..." he hardly dared to ask, but he knew he had to. "What does he do when you are together and you are blindfolded?"

"Lessons," Christophe said, as if it were plainly obvious. "He trains my voice and my body, and through his instructions, I am made better. He has perfect pitch, and his ear catches every note. He improves me, Matt, just as I always dreamed he would."

"Where does he touch you? These marks on your wrists-" Matthieu pressed.

Christophe's expression closed off. It wasn't something Matthieu had often seen, and it struck him to be the one to have provoked it.

"It's part of his training methods, I'm sure you would get the wrong idea. You don't understand and you don't wish to. All that matters is that thanks to his training I have been given the chance to star in an opera, and I adored it."

"No, please..." Matthieu looked away and saw his own face in the mirror beside Christophe's. His blue eyes were wide, concern writ large over his features. Christophe turned back, met his eyes in the mirror. He was pleading, silently willing him to accept his words and not be worried. Matthieu knew Christophe so well they barely needed words at all, and Christophe was excelling, that much was true. The gala had been an undisputed triumph, and it had been so close to being cancelled. Christophe had always dreamed of being a star.

Matthieu sighed, and turned back to Christophe.

"If you're happy, then I'm happy, too, Chris. I just want to be sure that you're safe as well."

Christophe smiled wide, threw his arms around Matthieu and hugged him with abandon. Christophe felt his breath catch as Christophe's body pressed against his. He wrapped his arms around him in return, half pulling him into his lap and allowing himself a moment to bury his nose in Christophe's beautiful hair. A terrible, indulgent moment.

"I'm so glad you understand," he said. "Sometimes it does frighten me, it's true, but I trust him, and he really has done as I dreamed. I want to be so much "

Matthieu looked up suddenly, sensing an unseen presence in the room. He clutched Christophe closer to him and looked all around, but the room was quite empty.

Their reflections were the only ones in the mirror.

Raoul

RAOUL DE CHAGNY had been delayed long enough. He was used to getting what he wanted, and when he knew what he, or rather, who he wanted was in an adjacent room, it tried his patience. He must act.

He excused himself from the exuberantly triumphant celebrations of Richard Firmin and Giles André and made his way backstage. The gala was long since over, although the celebratory champagne was flowing in the entrance hall for any who would stay.

On any other night, Raoul would be happy to imbibe and entertain a chorus girl or boy (he wasn't fussy), but tonight wasn't like any other night. The man who had taken the stage in the role that was always played by a woman, and sung so beautifully, was Christophe and he longed to be reunited with him.

He navigated the back passages of the old theatre and found the door marked *Carlotta Giudicelli*, and knocked.

One of the dancers from the ballet corps opened the door and eyed him suspiciously. He was still wearing his costume, and it was marvellously good at showing off the young man's shapely form. He had blond hair slicked back for dancing and piercing blue eyes.

For a moment, Raoul couldn't remember why he was there. The blue eyes struck something deep inside him and his mouth went quite dry. He *wanted*... No, he wanted Christophe. He cleared his throat.

"Please forgive my intrusion," Raoul said. He removed his top hat and proffered a fine bunch of flowers. "I wished to give my regards to the diva of tonight's performance, if that's all right."

The blond dancer glanced behind him and then nodded, holding the door wider.

Christophe sat at the mirror, removing the stage make up but his eyes met Raoul's in the mirror with an expression of confusion.

Raoul wanted him to remember. He cleared his throat and began to tell one of the old stories they used to share as children, long ago.

"There was a young man from the depths of the black forest. He made a trip to the edge of the forest, with a plan to learn what the stars were, for he had only ever seen them through the branches of the trees."

The dancer made a confused and irritated noise, but Christophe looked intrigued.

"Those words, I remember that story. It used to make me cry..."

"Yes, and then I would lend you my handkerchief, pull faces and make jokes until you smiled again." Raoul couldn't hide his grin. He crossed his eyes and stuck out his tongue for good measure.

Christophe's confusion cleared and he leapt to his feet. "Raoul?!"

Raoul laughed out loud and held his arms out. Christophe ran into them with his own musical laugh, and they embraced as old friends. Christophe pulled back, studying his face.

"Matt, this is Raoul, he and I used to play together as children."

But the dancer had gone, and Christophe was speaking to no one. He shook his head. "It's so good to see you, Raoul, you look wonderful, oh I've missed you so much."

"You're the wonderful one." Raoul pressed the bouquet into Christophe's hands. "A standing ovation wasn't enough to pay tribute to you. You are a star, a true diva."

"Thank you!" Christophe seemed utterly delighted, taking the flowers and inhaling the scent of them, smiling wide. "These are just beautiful."

Raoul's blood was high, he was bubbly from champagne

and from the success of the evening. The gala being a success was a reassurance that he hadn't invested money in a failing institution, but all of that hardly registered against the thumping of his heart.

Christophe, *his* Christophe! The boy he had sworn to marry, and here they were, reunited as adults.

"You're beautiful, and I have missed you and I'm so glad to be back with you," Raoul said. "Now, you must come to dinner, we have so much to talk about. So many things to share and reminisce over."

Christophe's smile widened and then faded abruptly. "I can't," he said.

"I don't understand," Raoul said. "Are you betrothed to someone? Do you have a serious suitor courting you?"

"No, no suitors."

"Then there's nothing stopping you." Raoul laughed a little. "I have a coach outside, I just need to call it. Let me buy you dinner, I have missed you for so many years now, and I wish to learn everything about your life now."

"We weren't more than eight when you knew me," Christophe said. He swiped at his face, his eyes misty all of a sudden. "Now I am twenty, and you must be twenty-one."

"Indeed, and free of college, finally," Raoul said. "But I never forgot you, Christophe, although I couldn't find you anywhere."

"I must stay in, the angel of music-" Christophe said.

"I remember that story too," Raoul cut him off. "Your father's stories of the angel of music were inspiring. You have truly been blessed by the angel, none could doubt that who heard you sing tonight. Come we shall have chocolate gateau, isn't that your favourite still?"

"It is, but Raoul, I don't know... he's very strict."

"Please, get dressed and we can go. I'll go and call the coach right now and get my cloak from the cloakroom."

"Well, perhaps a quick supper..." Christophe softened and shrugged off the charmingly lacy dressing gown, revealing a bare chest which made Raoul's breath catch. Christophe had grown up into a truly gorgeous specimen. Raoul hoped tonight would start a wonderful courtship, and that soon he could truly call Christophe his own.

"Quick as a wink," Raoul said. He added a wink, because he could never stop himself flirting with a beautiful person. Then he turned and hurried to collect his things and call for his coach.

Behind him, the door banged closed with a certain finality.

Christophe

CHRISTOPHE'S HEAD WAS SPINNING. Which wasn't exactly an unusual occurrence, but this time it was due to events in the real world, and not simply things he had imagined.

The last few hours had passed in a bubbly high, the culmination of his fondest dreams. He had been given an opportunity to sing, and it had been so easy to do well. It had been so easy to impress the new managers of the opera, and earn a place on stage.

Aside from the initial reaction there was no apparent concern about the usual gender of the character, Christophe had earned the role simply from skill. The skill he'd honed with the assistance of his beloved angel.

He did, briefly, worry about how Carlotta was faring in hospital, but it was hard to hold onto anything like worry while butterflies were swirling in his stomach.

The performance had been a fantasy, with the audience so warm and responsive to Christophe's acting and his voice. Heavenly.

And then! Sharing his secret with his best friend in all the world! Certainly, Matthieu had been concerned at what Christophe had said, but he had accepted it. That was the important thing.

And as if all that wasn't enough, fate and the stars had brought Chrisophe his oldest friend. Long lost to a distant preparatory school, and presumed gone forever, since Christophe's father had died and Christophe had gone to a dancing conservatory and then the opera to pursue a career in performance.

Raoul! Dear Raoul, who told stories, and brought treats and who remembered Philbin Daaé, which was perhaps the most important thing. Raoul would remember things that Christophe might have forgotten.

There wasn't a day that went by that Christophe didn't think of his father, mourn his loss, and long to talk to someone who understood.

Matthieu was an excellent and beloved friend, but he had never known his own father, and they'd met after Philbin had already died. He didn't know what it was to have a father, let alone lose one.

Christophe hurried to remove the last of his stage make up and get dressed, but he was stopped in his tracks by a familiar voice.

"Bravo, bravo. You did well tonight, my best student."

Christophe flushed under the praise and sank into his chair, robe half falling off him.

"Thank you, Master." The voice seemed to come from everywhere and nowhere at all. Angels could do that of course, and Christophe didn't bother to look for the source of the sound.

The voice didn't reply immediately, but that was normal. Sometimes the angel came and went, and sometimes they had an entire conversation. Christophe, elated from the success of the evening, decided to be bold and try to get the angel's attention.

"If I excelled, it is all because of you and your divine teachings, my master," he said. "It was you that made me what I am. I am forever in your debt."

"Flattering..." the angel sounded intrigued. His voice lowered to something seductive and almost purring. "Perhaps I should reward you for such words, for your performance and for your sweetness."

"Oh, please! Please, I should love a reward." Christophe wished suddenly that he was in his bedchamber and not the changing room. He wanted to blindfold himself, to be ready for the angel.

As if the angel knew what he was thinking, the response came swiftly. "Tonight you shall see me, my darling. Look into the mirror, and know me."

Christophe blinked, seeing his own wide eyes staring back at him. But as he leaned in, pushing aside the make up pots and power puffs to get closer, the reflection rippled. Magic.

Magic like Christophe had always known was real.

He reached a hand up to touch the silvery surface and it swung backwards, revealing a tunnel behind the wall. There was a shape there, that of a man in a long black opera cloak.

Christophe's angel.

Raoul's knock on the changing room door was utterly unheeded, as Christophe climbed across the table and slipped into the tunnel. The mirror swung neatly shut behind him just as Raoul opened the changing room door.

Eric

ERIC FELT the world slotting into the correct position, and he sent praise to the stars he almost never saw.

Eric couldn't have been more happy, or more annoyed with how the evening had gone.

Christophe had looked like an angel on the stage, radiant in the prima donna's costume. His voice had been transcendent as well, seemingly reaching notes high and low without effort, simply beauty, taking the performance back to its purest form, stripping away the affectation and ego that Carlotta simply couldn't leave behind.

No, Christophe had been exactly the protégé that Erik had wanted. His purpose on this earth. His project of the last six months, and yes, perhaps, his obsession.

But then the mood had been utterly destroyed by Christophe entertaining first the dancer and then the blasted Vicomte de Chagny in his dressing room.

The foolish, fashionable and predictably handsome man who had been blessed with the dice roll of fate to money and a title. Never having to want for anything and with no idea of the privilege of his position.

Eric wanted to take him in his hands and break him down, show him the true meaning of power, and have him beg for Eric's forgiveness. Make him beg for Eric's attention.

Eric had listened closely to the reunion, and silently cursed the stars. Of all the people to turn up, it had to be someone who clearly wanted to steal his Christophe from him.

Thankfully, Christophe wasn't so easily swayed, and with just the right words, he was Eric's again. Eric took a large risk in showing Christophe the hidden tunnel, but the time was right. The Vicomte would be an alluring distraction, and Eric had to make his own bold move to keep Christophe.

Christophe followed Eric down the damp tunnel as obedient as a lamb or a pet rabbit, trusting and sweet. Eric knew he couldn't show his masked face until they were deep in his inner sanctum, where hopefully, Christophe would be distracted enough by what he had down there to not wish to ask questions.

Eric couldn't deny his own apprehension. He wanted this evening to go as beautifully as possible, for it to answer the yearning he felt for companionship. But he knew he could very easily scare off Christophe forever. In fact, he expected that their connection would be fleeting. He had always scared off the people he wanted, and what other outcome was there available, for a monster?

Or... Or he could simply keep Christophe down here with him, forever.

That was also an option to consider.

He had enjoyed the performance, and of course he would like to see his student excel again on the stage. But there was a definite temptation to chain him to the bed and keep him. Keep him as a true pet.

But he was getting ahead of himself. If he stayed silent for too long, Christophe would start to fret.

"Not much further now, my pet," Eric said. "Just one more flight of stairs and we will be in my residence." He chanced a glance over his shoulder to see Christophe's reaction. He looked bewildered, perhaps a little afraid but he was still following him. Still trusting him.

How tempting it was to take him now, to do everything he had dreamed of doing... but no. He had to be careful with this one.

He pushed open the door at the bottom of the hallway and paused. The path around the lake was narrow, and Christophe might fall. He took up one of the candles from the sconce in one hand, and offered the other to Christophe.

He stepped into the light and took Eric's gloved hand without question, eyes wide as he gazed at the walls of the subterranean cavern and the glassy surface of the lake.

"I had no idea there was anything like this under the opera house," he breathed. His voice lowered, reverent.

"Step carefully and hold tight to my hand, the path is uneven," Eric said. He turned and led the way, walking with one hand behind him, careful to not to walk too fast and make him stumble.

They wended their way towards the area that Eric had made into his home, and Christophe seemed to find some courage.

"Who are you?" He asked. His grip on Eric's hand remained steady, but Eric wondered if he would let go, and flee back up the stairs if he didn't like the answer. Of course, the door had already closed, and it needed a key to unlock again.

"I am your Angel of Music," Eric said. He flushed a little, under his mask. It was an unfitting name in many ways, but it was true that he loved music and he loved to see his protégé excel. It was also the safest answer by far.

"Are you also…" Christophe's question faltered. Eric didn't respond, no sense in answering a question which hadn't been answered.

They were stepping up the shallow stairs into the light of Eric's home. He saw it as if for the first time. A wide platform overlooking the lake, and a series of rooms behind, not really visible from this vantage point.

Finally, Christophe completed the question. "Are you the opera ghost?"

Eric sighed, set the candle into a candelabra and turned back to Christophe, pushing the hood back so that he could see the porcelain mask that Eric had to wear.

"I am called many things, my pet. To you, I am an angel, and I prefer that to a great deal of the other names."

He watched Christophe's face as he took in the mask.

There was wonder, certainly, his pupils blowing wide with the strangeness of it all.

Fear, perhaps because Eric hadn't denied he was the so-called 'Opera Ghost', but curiosity, too. A desire to know more, to understand.

Eric's heart sped up again and he felt the pull to show Christophe more of himself. To throw him down on the bed, bind him tightly and make him his for certain. They had already played such games before, but briefly, in stolen moments where Eric always had an ear on the noises outside of the room, frightened that they might be interrupted.

But now they were alone for certain.

Now he could do just as he liked with his precious songbird.

Christophe

CHRISTOPHE'S HEART was a wild bird, fluttering its wings against his ribcage, demanding to be let out, to escape. A small voice in the back of his head told him that he knew how to get out of there, he just had to turn back, run fleet-footed along the path and make his way back to the world of the living.

A far larger part of himself wanted to stay, to learn more, to truly get to know his Angel of Music, to know everything there was to know.

Why did he wear that mask?

Why did he live here, below the streets of Paris like a demon, removed from the world above?

What did he intend to do with Christophe?

Christophe remained.

The man, the Angel... the Phantom... looked at Christophe with an intensity that probably should have been frightening. He thought briefly of the tender way that Matthieu looked at him, a stark contrast although no more or less desirous.

This was the hunger of the predator who had caught his prey and intended to devour it.

Christophe didn't run. He knew there was power in being the cornered one. He had all of this man's attention on him. He was desired. He was *wanted* in a way he had never been before.

Heat flashed through him and down to his nethers, a stiffening of interest.

He wanted more.

He took a small step towards his Angel. "Are we going to do some more training?"

Christophe's cheeks burned at his own brazenness, but he revelled in it. The way the man's eyes (one brown, one blue, curious) heated still further behind the mask, the way his shoulders straightened and he inhaled, his chest puffing up. He wanted to be in control.

Christophe wasn't innocent.

He had been tumbled before after a night out at a drinking hall, or a particularly raucous show party. He knew that usually singing training had nothing to do with being blindfolded and bound, teased by rough hands until he was screaming his pleasure into his pillow. But by some magic that Christophe didn't begin to understand, it really did work.

Perhaps it was the screaming? Perhaps it was the knowledge of his own body and what he was capable of? It didn't matter because the Angel's method worked, and Christophe craved more.

The Angel nodded once. "Is that what you desire?" His voice was rough, needy. The growl of the wolf before it closes its teeth on the rabbit's throat. Christophe almost swooned.

"Yes. You've brought me here for a reason, haven't you?"

Feeling more bold and brazen than he had ever expected to be, Christophe lifted a hand and pressed it onto the angel's chest. He was warm, under his suit, just a man, after all. But his heart was pounding almost as much as Christophe's.

"I did."

"Then show me what that reason is." He lifted his hand again, going to touch the mask, with the intent to remove it. Surely they didn't need to pretend any more?

The Angel's hand flew up and caught Christophe's wrist. "You ask so prettily, my songbird. I am more than happy to oblige."

In an instant, Christophe was spun around, hands pulled behind his back, the Angel's other hand on his throat.

"You will call me Master, and you will do as I say, won't you, pet?"

Christophe was leaking into his underthings, he was so aroused his knees buckled. This was what he wanted, there was no doubt of it. "Yes, Master."

The Angel tightened his grip on Christophe's throat. "Then remove your clothes and get on your knees on the bench over there." He moved his hand from Christophe's throat to his jaw, forcing him to look in the direction of a bench. It was the seat of a piano, a fine looking grand piano in a cavern under the opera house.

Christophe wondered if this was all a particularly real dream, but the Angel let go of him and he stumbled towards the piano. He shed all his clothes before turning so his back was to the piano. He knelt on the bench, on instinct, he put his hands behind his back, offering the angel his submission as was correct for his role as prey.

The Angel, his Master, had removed his cloak and jacket and hung them both on a coat rack which stood incongruously next to a desk stacked with papers, quills and ink pots.

He turned to see Christophe's pose and moaned softly. "What a good little pet." He shrugged off his waistcoat, pulled off his gloves and rolled up the sleeves of his shirt. "Wait there, don't move." His Master opened an old, battered chest which sat at the foot of a magnificent bed, and withdrew something that clanked and rattled.

Christophe's eyes widened as he saw the shiny shackles in his Master's hand. He had bound him before, but only with silk scarves or soft ropes. It hadn't stopped Christophe from marking himself with them, he loved to tug against the bindings and feel that he couldn't escape. Shackles were a different affair. They were heavy, unrelenting and far more... permanent.

But the fear simply added to how exciting and arousing it all was.

He lifted his chin and watched as the Angel moved between him and the piano. He closed his eyes, savouring the feel of the cold metal on his wrists. The clank of them closing around his arms, and then the way he was tugged gently as his master locked each shackle with a padlock.

"How does that feel, my pet?" The Angel leaned in and kissed Christophe's shoulder. Lips far more tender than the bite of cold metal.

"It feels..." Christophe tried to think of the perfect word. "Divine, master."

"Does it now?" There was the rustle of something else, and the Angel tied something silky around Christophe's eyes. Christophe couldn't help but whine as his sight was taken away.

"I want to see you, Master."

The only response was the tightening of the blindfold around Christophe's head.

"My precious songbird, my pet," his Master said. "You will learn of my hungers tonight."

Christophe was thrilled to hear those words. It was as if the Angel had seen into his mind, had divined that Christophe wanted the attention of the prey. To be the perfect *thing* that the wolf wanted to devour.

"Yes, Master. I welcome it."

The Angel, his Master, pressed against his back and his hands moved over Christophe's chest. His fingers were long and his touch light, feathering teasing touches over his clavicle, his nipples, never staying long enough in any one place for any sort of satisfaction.

Christophe's breath wouldn't stay steady, catching every time his Master touched somewhere new. He felt utterly on edge, ready for something that wasn't starting.

"Remember your breathing exercises," the Angel murmured, his voice low, paternal almost. He cared for Christophe so much.

Yes, the breathing exercises. Focus on the diaphragm and breathing from the bottom of it, not high in the chest. In a moment, Christophe had mastered it, and although his Master was still teasing him, he was able to maintain his focus.

"You may be as loud as you wish this evening, pet. I want to hear every single utterance. And if you're very good, then you will feel what it's like to be filled up by your angel."

Christophe rocked his hips and moaned, letting it fall loudly from his lips. "I want to be good for you, Master. I want to feel you..."

"Mmm, I think you will."

Without warning the Angel bit into the flesh of his shoulder, hard and sharp, and Christophe cried out, bucked. The sharp pain faded and he realised he was hotter, more aroused than before.

"That's it," the Angel murmured. He peppered soft kisses over the area that he'd bitten, soothing Christophe. "Let the pain become pleasure. It is far sweeter this way, you'll see."

"I do see." Christophe bucked his hips into the air and found he was panting again. *Breathing exercises.* "Please, might I have some more, Master?"

The Angel laughed, a threateningly low sound, and in a

moment his teeth were on Christophe's neck. Christophe moaned, as the Angel sucked hard, surely enough to bruise.

The next moment, Christophe was aloft, held tight in strong arms, and being carried. He felt like he was being moved to the dinner table, perhaps, and it was hardly a surprise when he was placed on a hard surface. The Angel fiddled with the padlocks on the shackles, undid the chains and pulled Christophe's arms up over his head, fastening them again to something solid. If it was indeed a table, or even the piano, perhaps Christophe had been chained to one of the legs, spread out like a ritual sacrifice, naked and wanting.

He moaned, needy and knowing he had to express that if he wanted more attention, for the Angel to move faster and get on with the devouring.

"I want more!" he exclaimed.

His Master laughed out loud, harsh and delighted at the same time. "It is not for you to demand, my pet." A cool hand pressed to Christophe's sternum and he went still.

"I know what is best for you, do I not?"

"You do." Christophe swallowed, berated himself for questioning his master. "I'm sorry Master, I was impatient."

"You were," his Master agreed. "But it is flattering that you want me so much. I shall punish you, but then you will have all of me."

Punishment? Christophe hardly knew what to expect from a promise like that. In an instant he was whining again. Something cold and hard was being screwed onto his nipple. It pinched, and it made him even harder. It was a curious feeling, the screw going tighter and tighter and winding him up more and more. He tugged against the shackles, trying to get away for the first time in the evening.

Then when it felt like it couldn't possibly get any tighter

without damaging him, the angel stopped, and did the same to the other nipple. Christophe was making all sorts of noises, moans and whines and something very high pitched and embarrassingly needy.

The angel tightened the clamp on his second nippled and then there was another surprise. Something cool and metal around Christophe's neck. A collar? It felt soft inside, perhaps it was lined with satin, or velvet? Christophe's over-stimulated mind could hardly keep track of all the sensations.

There was the *snick* of a lock and a tugging on the collar and Christophe realised that his Master had locked the collar on him.

He truly belonged to him now, and although there was still a flutter of fear, he felt mostly bliss. The Angel knew him, knew how to make him the best he could be. Who better to give himself over to than him?

Something nudged at his knees until they were bent, hitched up, and Christophe hoped and hoped that soon his aching cock would get some attention.

"You're doing very well, pet." It was the first time in what felt like aeons that the Angel had spoken. Christophe was so focused on the metal on his nipples, and the sensation of being bound and owned, that time seemed to have slowed. Each breath felt like a week or longer. His body responded to the words of praise though. He felt he had flushed from his hairline to his toes.

"Thank you, Master."

"I'm going to open you up now." This, at least, was familiar territory. With fingers and sometimes with tongue, the Angel had teased him open before. It hadn't happened too often, but every time it had, Christophe had orgasmed with the power of the sun. He let his knees fall to the sides, opening himself up more fully as his Master probed into him with a finger slick with some sort of oil.

He worked quickly, if a little roughly, and Christophe was glad of it. He wanted more than anything to feel filled by his Master, and this felt like an annoying requirement that had to be passed before he got what he wanted.

"Please Master," he moaned. "Please, I need more."

The fingers withdrew, and there was a rustling of fabric, Christophe could barely hear it over his own needy panting. Then his legs were being lifted and he felt something warm, far larger than a finger, pressing against him. He bucked his hips, trying to urge him inside.

The Angel thrust his hips and Christophe was filled.

He was thick and large, larger than Christophe had taken before.

It almost felt like being split open, the harsh sting of it combining with a delicious fullness that he craved as soon as he knew it. He groaned, rolling his hips to encourage more.

His Master didn't disappoint. In an instant, he was withdrawing and thrusting inside again, setting a fast pace that had Christophe crying out with pleasure. His hand touched the metal things on Christophe's nipples, tugged at them both at once - was there a chain connecting them? - and then his mouth was on Christophe's, swallowing his moans and biting his lips, his tongue.

Christophe's wildest dreams had never been this dirty, had never involved the incredible blending of pain with desire, of fear and devotion. But he saw that this had been what he craved all along. His Master knew him and his Master was giving him what he needed. He knew him better than Christophe knew himself, and Christophe thanked him for it.

3

ERIC

When he was spent, and Christophe had come all over his own stomach and the lid of the grand piano, Eric pulled out. Christophe was breathing shallowly, a moaning, melted mess of a man. It was a sight more perfectly exquisite than Eric could have believed, and his chest ached with it. Satisfaction, longing, desire, affection and possessiveness all filled his body and made him feel like he might burst.

He knew he didn't deserve this. Knew it couldn't possibly last, someone like Christophe was destined for greatness, and Eric was destined to stay below the surface of the ground. A monster who lashed out and hurt people. Who controlled the theatre with an iron fist, full of vengeance.

Christophe whimpered softly, and he realised he had been staring instead of taking care of his gorgeous pet.

He carefully removed the shackles and the nipple clamps, but left the collar and the blindfold in place. He lifted Christophe off his piano and carried him to the bed, cleaned him up with a damp cloth and told him how pretty he was, how perfect.

"There's no one as precious as you, my lovebird, my perfect cherub," he murmured. "I am so pleased with you, so proud of you."

Christophe was mostly asleep, as soon as he'd touched the softness of the bed he had relaxed utterly, limbs long and loose, trusting him utterly.

Eric tucked him in, and sang him a lullaby that he remembered from his own ruined childhood. When his breathing evened out and he was sure his pet was asleep, Eric ensured the blankets were covering him, stroked his cheek and backed away.

He had done it. He had held back enough of his wild hunger to not absolutely terrify Christophe. He had taken him, true, but he hadn't tortured him.

Eric knew he couldn't sleep after that experience. He was full of emotion and inspiration. Inspiration must be captured. Perhaps he could write a love song?

He pulled on a pair of soft trousers and a Japanese silk kimono.

He extinguished the candles that lit his residence, aside from the ones around his desk, and sat down to write.

Matthieu

MATTHIEU TURNED OVER IN BED. He had a very narrow bed in the cheap apartments that Madame Giry and most of the ballet corps lived in, as a kind of subsidised dormitory. It was a fine arrangement, two to a room, which allowed the dancers to spend all hours together, discussing choreography, stretching out their sore limbs. Or, on certain occasions, letting loose with wine, cheese and fresh bread from the bakery on the ground floor.

The apartments were only a block away from the Opera La Rêve, which was convenient for rehearsals and the late nights of performances.

Matthieu frowned, looking at the other side of the small room, where Christophe's bed sat, pristine. It hadn't been touched since he had made it the morning before.

Matthieu's hackles instantly went up. Had Christophe stayed out all night with the Vicomte? He must have. They were looking very friendly with each other when he'd slipped out of the changing rooms, sharing in-jokes or stories or something that Matthieu couldn't understand. There was some history there, something from before he knew Christophe.

Matthieu washed up quickly and changed from pyjamas to street clothes, pulled on his boots and made his way out into the street. He wasn't exactly sure where to look for Christophe, he had absolutely no idea where the Vicomte lived, but perhaps someone at the Opera would know. His feet slapped the cobbled streets as he dodged around other people on their early morning business. The boulangeries and coffee shops were already doing a busy trade, and there were many of the familiar locals Matthieu was used to seeing. He nodded at Monsieur Lyon who worked as superintendent of the apartment block. He was sitting at a table just outside the café door and sipping his morning espresso, reading the paper and slowly eating an almond croissant, as he always was at this time of day. He raised a hand and said good morning, but Matthieu hurried on.

Matthieu couldn't spare time for pleasantries. He had to know that Christophe was safe.

It was a bright morning, although the clouds gathering to the west felt ominous, as if there was bad weather on the way. There was an autumnal chill in the wind that reinforced that notion. Matthieu wondered if he shouldn't have picked up his jacket and scarf, but he didn't want to waste time.

The Opera La Rêve was never busy first thing in the morning but in Matthieu's experience there was usually *someone* around. He moved quickly up the steps to the main entrance and tried the heavy door. It opened without complaint.

Inside he found both of the new managers in the entranceway, both dressed for a day's work in well fitted suits, and both frowning at pieces of paper.

Richard Firmin, whose suit was a fine mahogany brown if somewhat plain, held his letter at arm's length and squinted at it, as if he were perhaps having trouble with his eyes. Giles André by contrast, wore a charcoal suit with a bright crimson pocket square and held his letter up, a few inches from his face, as if he could better understand if from that distance.

They both looked at Matthieu as the door closed behind him.

"Good morning?" Firmin ventured.

Matthieu bobbed a quick curtsey, forgetting for a moment that he wasn't one of the girls in the corps de ballet.

"Good morning, messieurs. I am Matthieu Giry, from the ballet chorus."

André nodded, recognition blooming on his face as he lowered the piece of paper. "Of course, welcome my dear. Surely it is too early for a rehearsal, though?"

"Indeed it is. I'm looking for Christophe," Matthieu said. "I wonder if you might have seen him?"

"So are we," Firmin said. His face was drawn with worry. "Seems he vanished from his dressing room last night."

"Vanished?" Matthieu's hand flew to his chest. That was far worse than what he'd been imagining Christophe might be up to. "I thought he was with the Vicomte."

"The Vicomte was quite beside himself and took it upon himself to search."

The door opened forcefully and banged against the wall, the Vicomte himself strode in as if summoned.

He looked rumpled, he obviously was still in his suit from the night before, and there were bags under his eyes. Despite these conditions, his beauty was unmarred.

"Has he turned up?" he demanded of the managers, quite ignoring Matthieu.

André shook his head mournfully. "I take it you had no luck, either."

"Nothing, until this note was delivered to my valet. I must say I certainly don't appreciate the tone of it, messieurs. I thought our relationship was above this." He shook a folded piece of paper at the managers. André snatched it off him.

"We didn't send this, monsieur."

"Well, if you didn't, who did?" The Vicomte looked furious. Matthieu tried not to note how much more attractive it seemed to make him. He told his heart quite firmly to cease fluttering. It was Christophe he loved, not the Vicomte who had barely said two words to him.

"It's the same sort of paper." André held it out to Firmin who took it, sniffed it and then handed it back to the Vicomte with the air of deepest seriousness.

The Vicomte looked perplexed. "Why did you smell it?"

"I don't understand," Matthieu said. "Do any of the notes mention Christophe?"

All three of them looked at him as they'd forgotten he was there.

Matthieu rolled his eyes. "None of you know anything?"

"Pardonnez moi," the Vicomte said. "We have not been formally introduced. I am Raoul de Chagny." He extended a hand and gave a soft smile, polite, but a little smouldering at the same time.

Matthieu nodded, shook his hand. The touch of the Vicomte's warm hand sent tingles up his arm that set his heart beating faster. The Vicomte tugged him closer ever so slightly and Matthieu cleared his throat, trying not to be seduced by the way he was looking at him.

"I know who you are. I'm Matthieu Giry, I'm in the corps de ballet and Christophe is my best friend. Please. I'm anxious to find him."

Raoul offered Matthieu the note he had brought and Matthieu unfolded it, reading aloud.

Do not pursue Christophe Daaé. I'm sure it is new to you, that there are some things that money cannot purchase. But rest assured, Christophe's talent is more valuable than whatever tumble you had planned.

His career is of the utmost importance, do not interfere with his new opportunities and cease calling on him forthwith

~ O. G.

Matthieu's blood ran cold at the sign off, and then flashed hot with indignation that Raoul might indeed be intending to court Christophe. And how intensely strange that of all the things the ghost might have to communicate, it was telling the Vicomte to cease his suit.

"Who is O.G?" Raoul said. "And why does he care what I do?"

"It's the Phantom," Matthieu said. "The O.G. stands for Opera Ghost."

André laughed, an air of nervousness colouring the sound. "There's no such thing as phantoms or ghosts."

"How would you care to explain these notes?" Firmin shook his pieces of paper. "He wants us to put Christophe in the lead role, and for us to leave box five for him to view every performance. Who else would make such demands of us, but a madman who is haunting the theatre?"

"One shouldn't talk of the Phantom in such terms," Madame Giry walked in from a side door. She barely glanced at Matthieu. He seized the distraction her arrival afforded and snatched the notes off both managers. Each note's handwriting was identical and each signed 'O.G.'

"Excuse me for interrupting," Madame Giry said. Her tone indicated she had no remorse at all. "Christophe Daaé has returned, messieurs."

Raoul's sigh of relief set a small bit of comfort in Matthieu's heart. He clearly did care for Chistophe, at the very least.

"Where is he? I would like to see him," Raoul asked.

Madame Giry shook her head. "He needs to rest, he is very worn out. Please calm yourself, he will be well enough to sing in the next performance."

Matthieu chewed his lip. He had a good idea of where his mother would have put a worn out Christophe, there were old rooms in the attic of the opera and dancers often used them to rest in between rehearsals. But he didn't want to slip out and miss any of the extraordinary discussion either, so he stayed put.

"I also have this note for you," Madame Giry said. The

managers groaned in unison. Fìrmin rolled his eyes and ran a hand through his hair and Andrè slumped his shoulders. Apparently unruffled by this reaction, she unfolded it and read it out.

"*Christophe Daaé has been returned. I am adamant that his career should be of the utmost priority to you all.*

With that in mind, he is the obvious choice for the lead in tonight's performance. Carlotta regrettably, will not be returning to the Opera La Rêve after she passed away in the night."

Matthieu gasped at this. There was precious little love he had for Carlotta, and she certainly disdained the chorus, but he had known her for years. She was as much a fixture of the theatre as his mother.

"Our diva, dead?" Andrè breathed.

"We're ruined, Andrè..." Fìrmin tugged on his own hair. "Some adventurous casting worked for us last night, and perhaps now and then, but we need an established star if we wish to stay open."

"Shall I continue?" Madame Giry raised one perfectly arched eyebrow.

Fìrmin gestured for her to go on and then went back to raking his fingers through his hair.

"*Retain Christophe in the lead role for the season, leave box five empty for my exclusive use and if you leave my salary within as well, we shall avoid any unpleasantness between us.*

I look forward to our continued partnership and the success of the business going forth.

~ O.G."

FÌRMIN AND ANDRÈ GROANED AGAIN.

"Thank you, I suppose," André said. He took the note from Madame Giry and then retrieved the ones Matthieu was holding and turned to go, beckoning Firmin. "We shall have to discuss how we handle this going forward."

"If I may, messieurs," Madame Giry said. They turned back to look at her without question or irritation. The power his mother held was truly impressive, Matthieu reflected once again. "I would recommend you not defy the Phantom. He has been here longer than you have, and he has terrible powers."

They nodded, then bustled off. Madame Giry gave Matthieu a look, flicked her eyes upwards and then back at him. He nodded slightly, she was telling him that Christophe was in fact in the attic rooms as he had suspected.

Raoul surged forward and took Madame Giry's hand. "Please, was Christophe unharmed?"

Madame Giry's eyes slid to the side, something she almost never did.

"He is well enough," she said. Matthieu's blood ran cold all over again. He didn't wait to hear more, he took the grand staircase two steps at a time and hurried upwards through the theatre to find Christophe.

Christophe

A FEW HOURS EARLIER...

Christophe had fallen asleep so soundly after the lesson with the angel of music that when he awoke it was almost as if from death.

He was temporarily confused by the darkness, but then he remembered the blindfold, and lifted his hand to remove it.

There wasn't a lot of light in the cavern, but it still made Christophe wince a little. The room was just as pretty as he remembered. High soaring ceilings carved out of a natural tunnel, candlelight flickering and reflecting on a lake, and a series of terraced platforms which served as a residence for the angel. The bed was set towards the wall, a short level down from a platform with a lot of musical instruments set up.

The room wasn't quiet. The Angel was working at an organ, playing something that Christophe had never heard before. Then he stopped, scribbled something and played it again, slightly differently.

Christophe smiled. The Angel, *his* Angel, was composing music!

Could it be that their evening together, the training which had turned into a glorious consummation of their connection, had inspired him?

Christophe certainly felt inspired. He was sure he had reached a new high note when he had screamed his pleasure the night before. His entire body felt alive, every inch of him aware of the softness of the sheets, the coolness of the air and the ghosting echoes of the angel's touch.

Christophe sat up and looked around for something to cover his nakedness with. There was a Japanese kimono nearby, the silk a pale sky blue and decorated with pink blossoms. He pulled it around himself as he stood, smiling a little as he felt the gentle pressure of the collar still around his neck. He would love to see what the Angel was writing... Perhaps he could even surprise him?

The organ was set up in such a way that it faced away from the bed, and the Angel sat with his back to Christophe. Perfect for a playful surprise, and perhaps they could have sex again? His body trembled at the thought.

As he got closer, he was surprised to see that his Angel appeared to truly be just a man. He had felt his hands, of course, but he had wondered if perhaps he only had a physical form some of the time, or that there was something magical and mystical about him.

But he was a man in a white shirt, sweat beading on the back of his neck. His long black hair looked shiny, slicked back from his face. Christophe longed to see that face.

His hands were long fingered, beautiful pianist's fingers. Christophe watched from mere feet away as those hands pulled back from the keyboard of the organ, crumpled up a piece of paper and tossed it aside, before plunging back to the keys. A dramatic but somehow charming piece of music emerging from the movement.

Christophe summoned up his excitement and his courage and put his hand on the Angel's shoulder.

The response was instant, the Angel whirled to face him, one hand gripping Christophe's wrist and the other up at his face, trying to conceal it.The grip he had on Christophe's hand was powerful, crushing, as if he could grind Christophe's bones together in just a moment.

The Angel shouted, howled in anger, cursing, and Christophe's feet gave out. He fell back, his wrist still vice-gripped by the Angel, who turned away, grabbed up a white mask and held it to his face.

But Christophe had seen. His face was horrifying and bizarre. Was it scarred? Deformed? Mutated somehow? Or was he not actually a man after all, but a monster?

His skull seemed to be closer to the skin than other people's, the cheekbone and brow so clearly delineated and impossible to ignore. His eyes were sunken deep into sockets, and shadowed with black as dark as night. On the left side of his face, terrible lines that cobwebbed out, raised and shiny as scars. A ragged scar cut through his temple and through his ear which didn't seem to have grown correctly.

His left eye was a pale blue, and his right a blazing brown.

It was hard to breathe.

"Christophe! You fool! Why did you do that? Are you happy, now that you have seen?! Now you know that your Angel is truly a monster? A demon coughed up from the bowels of Hell?!"

He let go of Christophe's arm, or rather, tossed it aside to turn himself away, still cursing softly.

Christophe cowered, pressing himself to the bookshelf behind him. He watched with horror as the man curled in on himself, his shoulders hunching and his head bending down to his chest.

Christophe hardly knew what to expect. Was he fighting some terrible anger, the desire to lash out and hurt Christophe? He was capable of violence after all, Christophe knew that. Was this the moment where the Angel's apparent affection for him wore out and now he would feel the cold steel of a blade? Or hands around his throat, squeezing the life out of him?

Christophe's heart thrummed, half in his mouth, as he waited, frozen in place for the violence that would surely come.

But no blows fell, no daggers appeared. After a few long seconds, Christophe processed what he was seeing.

The Angel was on his knees, cradling his face in his hands, his back a curve that shook with tension.

Christophe realised it wasn't rage that was wracking the man's body, but sadness. He was sobbing.

Christophe's fear evaporated and was replaced instantly with concern for him, and an overwhelming desire to care for him, to comfort him.

He got to his knees, and crawled towards the Angel, placing a gentle hand on his shoulder. The Angel flinched away from him and Christophe cleared his throat.

"There, there," he said, pitching his voice soft and soothing. "It's alright. It's going to be alright, Angel."

This time when he touched the Angel again, he didn't shake Christophe off. He relaxed under his hand and slowly, slowly straightened his back. He set the mask back into place and turned to look at Christophe with wonderment.

"You're not afraid?"

Christophe didn't believe in lying to people he cared about. "I am a little."

The Angel nodded but didn't look pleased exactly. "Thank you for not lying to me."

Christophe reached a hand up to cup the unmasked side of the Angel's face. Angel? Demon? Or Phantom? It didn't matter.

The Angel leaned into his touch, closing his eyes and almost smiling. "You're my Master, my Angel of Music. I could never lie to you."

"Please. You must call me Eric, that's my true name."

"Eric," Christophe said. He smiled and rubbed his thumb over the ridges of Eric's face. "What happened to you, to make you look like this?"

Eric shook his head. "I was born strange looking, and I was attacked..." he inhaled and swallowed back a sob. "It's not a pleasant story."

"You don't have to tell me now," Christophe said. "I would like to hear it but only when you are ready. I want to know all that there is to know about you."

"You are..." When Eric spoke his voice was raw, almost shaking with emotion. Christophe swallowed, wondering what he was about to say. Then the Angel, Eric, opened his eyes and glanced at a clock on the wall. "We must get you back, before you're missed."

— ⸎ ● ⸎ —

Christophe

CHRISTOPHE WOKE AGAIN in one of the beds in the attic. The door had creaked, and let Matthieu in. Christophe smiled and sat up, one hand going to his throat and feeling a wash of disappointment when he remembered the Angel had removed the collar before returning him to the theatre proper. He missed the feel of it around his neck.

But he also still felt shaken from what had happened between them. The reveal of his true visage, and the unbridled anger he had displayed had frightened Christophe badly. He knew he had seemed utterly exhausted and upset when he had come across Madame Giry. The Angel had brought him back via a staircase that let out into the hallway near the rehearsal rooms, and

Madame Giry had been there to put her arms around Christophe and give him a moment's reassurance before she sent him to bed.

He wasn't sure how he looked now.

Matthieu looked handsome and familiar, dressed casually. His golden blond hair pulled back from his face, and his blue eyes wide and concerned. He had a subtle dusting of freckles over the bridge of his nose and cheeks, and even from across the room, the sight of them warmed Christophe's heart.

He crossed the room and sat on the bed, immediately wrapping Christophe in his arms. "Chris, I was so worried. I thought you'd spent the night with the vicomte and I'd never see you again."

Christophe hugged his dearest friend close to him, burying his face in the warmth of Matthieu's neck and smiling when he heard his words.

"Oh my darling, that will never happen. Whatever the future holds you will always be in my life."

Matthieu breathed out audibly, and squeezed Christophe close against him. "What do you need, Chris?"

"Just this," Christophe said. He pressed his cheek against Matthieu's shoulder and inhaled the familiar scent of his neck. He felt infinitely comforted already, grounded. Matthieu's sensible nature and constant presence linked Christophe to the real world, the one above ground. The fear that Christophe had felt earlier began to fade out.

Matthieu hummed. Then with infinite care and gentle hands, he moved them both so that Matthieu was lying propped against the pillows with Christphe laying half on top of him, safely entwined in his arms.

"You're safe, Chris. My sweetest friend. You can sleep again, if you wish."

Christophe closed his eyes and smiled, feeling sleep take him, safe in the warm, strong arms of his beloved Matthieu.

WITH THE NEWS of Carlotta's death spreading through Paris, the Opera La Rêve closed for a week, in her honour. During this time, the new managers settled into their roles, moved their things into their offices and gave the entire cast and crew three days of rest.

On the fourth day, Christophe and Matthieu returned to rehearsals. Hannibal had been scrapped after the gala, and now they were rehearsing a relatively new opera, Carmen, that Firmin had a penchant for after seeing it performed in Venice.

Carlotta had no understudy, but an alternative had been sourced from an opera house in Lyon and she arrived by train on the first day of rehearsals.

Christophe, if he was disappointed in not being cast in Carlotta's place, did not show it, and instead dedicated himself to learning the new choreography.

Matthieu kept a close eye on Christophe, and noted with dread that he would often disappear for a few hours each day, and return looking flushed and happy, if somewhat tired.

The Vicomte and Christophe went on two dates to dinner at fine restaurants, and it was generally understood within the theatre gossip circles that the Vicomte was formally courting Christophe.

Such a thing would perhaps be called a scandal in the society circles Raoul de Chagny usually frequented, but it was nothing like as shocking to those in the performing arts.

Eric, in the underbelly of the Opera house, became more

and more annoyed. Christophe had received a great number of positive reviews, but even still, the managers looked for a more seasoned replacement to his perfect angel.

Christophe

THE REHEARSALS WERE GOING WELL. Christophe was pleased with the progress the ballet corps had made, and none could deny that Esmerelda, the soprano they had lured away from the Lyon Opera, was up to the task of lead role.

But there was the problem of the accidents.

Esmerelda had fallen down the stairs which Buquet had constructed to represent a bridge in Seville.

It appeared that one of the stairs had been rigged to fall away when stood on, something that Buquet swore wasn't the case when he built it.

Esmerelda had got up again briskly and dusted off her skirts and continued the rehearsal, a reaction which had stunned the assembled cast. Carlotta would never have been so blasé or pragmatic.

The stair was investigated and a small trigger contraption found underneath it, which Christophe guessed had been constructed by the Phantom.

During a practice one of the ballet girls, Eloise, made a snide comment about Christophe's turnout. One hour later she slipped on a flat piece of floor and twisted her ankle.

When Madame Giry asked Eloise how she had fallen she said that something had startled her from the stalls of the theatre. When the rows of seats were investigated there was nothing to be found.

"The Phantom of the Opera," Elise, one of the ballet girls, whispered.

Christophe trembled. He simultaneously wanted to see more of Eric, but he didn't want this. Eric hurting people or causing accidents simply because he was fond of Christophe. Eric certainly had to be the Phantom of the opera, but Christophe held this belief alongside the assurance that at the same time he was the Angel of Music, sent from heaven by Christophe's father.

There was simply confusion around how he acted, and how others understood what he was there for.

The week was up quickly, and the opera opened to a huge line of patrons, eager to see who would be singing the lead.

Christophe's role was in the chorus as usual, and as he and Matthieu got dressed side by side, he had a sense of foreboding over how Eric would react to Esmerelda's performance. She was truly a wonderful singer, but Christophe had found a single red rose tied with a black ribbon on his makeup station, and it had sent a chill through his body.

Just as he was trying to decide how to articulate these fears to Matthieu, there was a knock at the changing room door and Raoul came in.

Christophe's fear dulled some at the sight of his handsome face and bright eyes.

"Raoul!"

"I came to wish you luck," Raoul said. He handed Christophe a large bouquet of mixed hothouse flowers, all colours of the rainbow and pleasantly scented. He then turned to Matthieu and handed him a smaller version of the same arrangement. Matthieu blushed, and lost his words altogether, which was highly unusual. It set Christophe's heart fluttering with hope.

"Thank you, these are beautiful!"

"The show is completely sold out," Raoul said. His smile was bright. "I'll be seated in box five with the managers, to watch."

"But box five is the Phantom's box!" Matthieu had evidently found his voice again and as he spoke there was genuine alarm in his tone.

Raoul smiled, shrugged one shoulder. Christophe lost all thoughts except for how dashing he looked in his tuxedo, with a pristine white wool scarf to top it off.

"I have no choice, monsieur. There are no seats left in the house except for box five. I'm sure it will be fine."

Christophe abruptly recalled the anger Eric had displayed and set the flowers aside to take one of Raoul's hands. "Please be careful."

"Yes," Matthieu added. "Be careful."

"Of course I will." Raoul's smile was bright, he leaned in and placed a warm kiss on Cristophe's cheek. "Have fun out there, both of you." He looked at Matthieu, hesitated as if he wished to give him a kiss too. The two of them stared at each other for one heated moment.

Then Raoul shook his head, waved goodbye and was gone. Matthieu and Christophe looked at their flowers and giggled as if they were nine years old again.

"He's very handsome," Matthieu said. "You're so lucky, Chris."

"I think..." Christophe tried to puzzle out his thoughts. "I think he likes me, because we were childhood friends... sweethearts maybe.

"Do you like him?"

"I do, very much. He knows me, and he would make a fine companion don't you think? I do so long to be adored."

"Well, he certainly adores you, Chris, anyone can see that."

"But... I think he likes you as well. You two certainly had a moment together." Christophe nudged Matthieu with his elbow.

"I don't know about that." Matthieu giggled again and shook his head. "He will choose you, even if he did notice me."

"I don't understand why anyone has to choose," Christophe said. "Sometimes I feel as if I have enough love in my heart for several people to share equally."

It was a shocking thing to say, and as soon as he'd said it, Christophe covered his mouth with one hand. "I didn't mean..." he mumbled, but he was thankfully interrupted. Madame Giry struck her cane to the floor in the hallway, and they were all in a hurry to stage.

Christophe

CARMEN WAS a fun opera to perform, so much passion in the movements, so much colour in the costumes. Matthieu genuinely enjoyed performing on any occasion but he felt a real thrill as they got through the first part of the first act with no mistakes or hitches.

It was during Carmen's song about the nature of love, however, that there was a frightening interruption.

The lights of the chandelier which hung over the audience

flickered on and then off again. A hauntingly cruel laugh that echoed throughout the teatre, even drowning out the impressive volume of Esmerelda's belt.

The sound sent a chill up Matthieu's spine. He feared there was about to be another terrible accident, due to Esmerelda taking the stage when the Phantom had insisted the role was Christophe's.

The audience murmured, moved about, looking for the source of the voice.

In a moment, the voice returned, echoing over the theatre.

"I am very disappointed in the new managers," the voice boomed. Matthieu's dance partner, Edith, clung to him so hard her nails dug into his skin even through his loose white costume shirt.

"The Phantom of the Opera!" Edith cried.

"I was explicit in my desires. Christophe in the lead role, and not some ridiculous understudy. And box five to be left for my use!"

Matthieu looked up at box five, and saw the managers and Raoul looking about themselves, trying to see where the voice was coming from.

"My demands have been ignored. Christophe has been relegated to a non-singing role, his talent wasted. I am furious. I have no choice but to show you how serious I am."

There was a horrible *snap* from somewhere in the rafters, high up in the theatre. Matthieu's eyes flicked to the ceiling above the audience and saw a shadow moving in the crosswalks that the lighting staff used.

The chandelier shuddered.

Matthieu shook his head. He couldn't possibly mean to bring down the chandelier, not in a full house... not while they were still on stage. Only a madman would do such a thing... But the Phantom had killed before. Matthieu had no reason to expect that this would be too far an action. But he hoped that it wasn't true all the same. He kept his eyes on the chandelier.

"You would do well to remember that I do not make threats lightly." The Phantom said.

"Get out of the stalls! Now! Run!" The conductor had turned towards the audience, and was gesturing wildly. He must have seen the same thing Matthieu had.

"Clear the stage!" Matthieu cried. He put a firm arm around Edith and whisked her and the rest of the chorus into the wings, making sure that Christophe was among them.

They were just in time.

With another *snap* that reverberated through the theatre, the chandelier swayed, and fell.

The chandelier crashed to the ground, and shards of glass sprayed the stage and all around.

4

MATTHIEU

There were screams and panic from all over the theatre. Matthieu, from the safety of the wings, peeked back out and caught a glimpse of the shadow, disappearing into a hidden door in the theatre ceiling. The Phantom was up there.

The Phantom had caused this destruction and he was about to run free.

He had to do something.

Backstage was a panicked confusion of people. Raoul the Vicomte appeared, put his arm around Christophe and led him away. So, Matthieu knew that Christophe was safe, Raoul as well, he noted, with a little bit of confused satisfaction. He wasn't sure exactly why he cared that Raoul was safe, but he was.

Matthieu was free to pursue the Phantom.

He battled his way through the panicking throng of dancers and singers and made his way to the back wall of the stage, and then took the ladder up to the flies. He was grateful for his costume as he climbed. Tight black trousers and a loose shirt were easy enough to climb a ladder in, especially compared to some of the other costumes he'd had to wear in his time.

As he climbed the ladder, doubt began to set in. Who was he to confront the Phantom? A chorus dancer, and unarmed at that. But his curiosity and the adrenaline running through his veins spurred him on.

Once up in the flies he dared not look down, he didn't wish to see the destruction that the chandelier had caused. He was sure there would be deaths, and many injured. That wasn't his concern right then.

Grateful for his ballet training which gave him fine balance, he made his quick way across the flies and to the place he had seen the Phantom open a door in the ceiling.

He ran his fingertips over the wooden wall, searching and finally discovering the panel. He pushed against it and it lifted. Matthieu wasted no time, he climbed inside.

His feet hit solid flooring and found himself in a tunnel which ran within the walls. He climbed down to the pathway. It went in both directions, and he had absolutely no idea which way was correct.

He sniffed, decided on going right for no particular reason, and started walking. The pathway was solid wood, built into the walls and slowly descending. Once it reached what Matthieu guessed might be ground level, the floor became brick and mortar, and the damp set in.

He had no idea how long he walked, but eventually he found himself at a door. He tried the handle and found it locked. He huffed and looked back. He didn't want to have to walk all the way back up and have wasted all this time for nothing.

He tried knocking on the door. "Let me in!"

The silence that greeted his demand felt sentient.

Pregnant with possibility.

Someone was there, on the other side. He was absolutely sure of it. He couldn't hear breathing, but he was sure he sensed someone there.

He leaned forward and pressed his forehead to the door, trying to work out what it was he wanted to say, to get from this. He cleared his throat and just started to talk.

"I know you are obsessed with Christophe. I just want to know that he's safe, that you're not hurting him. I..." Matthieu took a quick breath and sighed it out. What did he have to lose? Talking to a door which might not even have someone on the other side. "I love him, I always have. He's the most precious thing in the world to me, and I've never told him. I want you to know that if you do hurt him, if you have nefarious plans for him, I will hunt you down and kill you with my own hands."

More silence. It stretched out so long Matthieu wondered if he had imagined the presence earlier, and had been talking to a door and nothing else.

Then came the distinctive *snick* of a lock being opened.

Matthieu straightened up. He took a quick, steadying breath and opened the door.

He walked through. In an instant there were arms around him, the Phantom must have hidden behind the door.

Matthieu struggled, tried to get free, but the Phantom had incredible strength, he held him tight as if his arms were bands of steel. Matthieu's body flushed warm with the proximity of such a strong man, he felt unaccountably aroused at being held like that.

"Calm yourself," the voice said. "If you are good, I will show you my torture chamber."

"Why would I want to see something like that?" Matthieu went still though, and stopped fighting. The voice was so beautiful, hypnotic and undeniably enticing.

"Because it will calm you, relax you. You will see that what I share with Christophe is nothing to fear, my pretty dancer."

Pretty dancer, such simple words and yet they reverberated through Matthieu in a way he had never before experienced. Heat flooded his chest and torso, then gathered in his crotch.

He cleared his throat. "I don't fear you."

The Phantom laughed, soft and low. "Do not lie to me, dancer, or we shall get nowhere at all. You chased me, didn't you? I expect you wish to receive answers."

Mathieu relaxed further, resisting the urge to lay his head back on the man's shoulder, but only just. "I did. I do."

"Then come this way." The Phantom said it as if he were leading and Matthieu was following when in reality, he propelled Matthieu from behind, walking him through what had appeared to be a recess in the wall but actually concealed a small room. The room had a series of rings attached to the far wall, from which hung chains and shackles. There was a mirror set into the ceiling, and a rack set into the near wall, which held a variety of wicked looking knives, whips and a cane.

How could such a thing exist in the theatre? Who had built it in? The Phantom?

Matthieu shivered in the Phantom's grasp. "This really is a torture chamber," he said.

"Of course. I have many enemies." The Phantom gripped his hips and spun him around. For the first time, Matthieu saw the Phantom of the Opera up close. He was tall, and his shoulders broad. He wore a fine porcelain mask over most of the left half of his face, it covered his nose and ended just at the corner of his mouth. His hair was long and dark, worn slicked back. His eyes blazed, one blue and one brown, and seemed to see directly into Matthieu's soul, revealing his utmost secrets as if reading a book.

Although he had said the most important secret out loud, without prompting. The one about loving Christophe.

The Phantom looked him over, and smiled softly. "You really are very beautiful, with your blond hair, like that of an angel." He tugged gently on a lock of Matthieu's hair.

Matthieu could think of absolutely no response to that. The man's voice lulled him somehow, made him feel he could trust him. He was just a man, after all, not a ghost or a monster. He was dangerous, to be sure, but a man all the same.

"Let me show you a little of what I do, then you will understand," he said.

Matthieu's mind whirled. There was no reason in the world to trust this man, save one. He had just caused massive destruction in the theatre, he had killed Carlotta, and heavens only knew how many others. He was happy to be thought of as a vengeful ghost, although Matthieu could plainly see that he was a flesh and blood man. He was something of a tutor to Christophe, who called him an angel. And that was the reason Matthieu had to trust him.

Because Christophe did.

He felt absolutely wild, on the edge of a terrible precipice, and he half expected to die in this room, but still he nodded his head.

"I want to understand you. You and Christophe. Yes, show me," his mouth said, with barely any input from his mind.

It was all the Phantom had needed.

In an instant Matthieu's back was to the cold stone wall and the Phantom was chaining him to it with a pair of shackles. Matthieu's heart raced and he wondered what had compelled him to agree to this.

Eric

ERIC STEPPED BACK and admired the way the dancer looked with his arms up, his fingers curling over his head as he relaxed into the chains.

There was something about him that Eric found difficult to ignore. Even on the night Christophe had sung, Eric's eyes had been tugged away now and then, to watch as Matthieu moved across the stage. He was beautiful, and the grace and precision that he performed with was distracting. He had a charisma to him on stage that drew attention, even as he was supposed to be blending into the background.

He had definitely caught Eric's eye, even if he was eclipsed by Christophe.

And now here he was. He had sought Eric out, he wanted to understand. He had consented.

Eric licked his lips and considered. He had seen the way Christophe looked at Matthieu, he had heard Matthieu's admission of love through the door, and Eric had overheard more than one whispered conversation as he kept watch over Christophe. He knew the depth of desire.

He didn't wish to frighten Matthieu away entirely, and he didn't wish to betray what he had with Christophe. But at the same time, having Matthieu on his side would be a valuable move in the larger game of chess.

He had enough control over Christophe already, he would make him understand.

But in the mean-time, how to torture Matthieu, to make him want this, want Eric as well as Christophe, without scaring him away?

Matthieu was tugging against the chains and trying to pretend that he wasn't aroused by what was happening. Eric had felt it, when he held Matthieu's wrists, the boy yearned to be controlled.

He would take it slowly. Use his own desire against him.

He moved closer to Matthieu and slowly trailed one finger up his chest, then his throat, smiling when Matthieu tilted his head to the side, exposing more of his next to Eric.

Yes. The dancer wanted it badly. He needed this, to be controlled, and protected, just as much as Christophe did. He was like a cat, pretending to be independent, but also desperate for affection.

He closed his fingers around Matthieu's throat and squeezed for just a moment before he let go and ran both of his hands down Matthieu's chest and stomach, feeling the taut muscles. His own body responded to the feel of Matthieu under his fingers and the way the dancer's breath caught as he touched him.

He moved both his hands down, teasingly close to the swelling area in Matthieu's crotch, but skidded his hands to the sides, caressing his hips and then down his powerfully muscular thighs.

Eric wished suddenly for some of his inventions. He had a particularly nasty little cage that could fit around a man's private parts and prevent him from reaching climax. He imagined how he could fit around Matthieu's parts and leave him needy for days...

He swallowed his own moan and mentally shook himself. He had to focus on Matthieu.

He scratched Matthieu's thighs, curling his nails to make an impression through Matthieu's trousers.

Matthieu made a soft noise, a whine. He wanted more.

"How does it feel?" he asked, keeping his voice low. "Tell me."

Matthieu squirmed, trying to get away from Eric's hands but pressing into them at the same time. "Teasing..." Matthieu said.

"Indeed," Eric said. "You're catching on."

"I expected more pain..."

Eric smiled. "Do you wish to feel pain? I can give you pain that transcends into incredible pleasure."

Matthieu was flushed, his breath coming fast and his chest heaving. He wanted more, he wanted so much it was plain on his face, and from the way his blush had spread over his ears and down his neck.

"I don't..." Matthieu blinked, looking at Eric with a pleading look. Eric wished to strip him naked, blindfold him and play with him for hours and hours. But he didn't have the time. He had to find Christophe and ensure he wasn't utterly terrified.

Matthieu was a delightful distraction, but that was exactly what he was... a distraction.

Eric nodded. "Perhaps another time." He moved his hands over him again, teasing, tugging at his nipples through his shirt, pinching at the muscles on his arms and legs just to startle him, squeezing his throat again just to hear him moan.

"I have trained Christophe to sing better, through my strange methods. I could train you as well, if you would consent to being mine. My pet."

Matthieu was panting hard. Eric reached up to adjust the shackles. These were a special invention of his own, a clock-work lock that would tick down and spring open after a certain amount of time, once the button was activated. He was pressed bodily against Matthieu's heaving body now, and the desire between the two of them couldn't be denied. Matthieu's hips bucked, seeking friction from Eric's own hardness through their clothing.

Eric shoved his own thigh hard against Matthieu, giving him something to rut against, which he did, with a longing series of moans that ignited all sorts of desires in Eric. Desires he had to ignore, for the moment.

"You will be free in a while," Eric murmured. Matthieu's face was close, he was shorter than Eric but not by much, not enough that he couldn't push up on his toes and kiss Eric full on the mouth.

That was a surprise, and Eric stilled for just a moment before he gave him and kissed him back. Pushing his lips hard against Matthieu's and nipping his lower lip before he stepped back, and adjusted his suit.

"If you take the door to the left, you will find yourself in familiar surroundings," Eric said. "The other doors will be locked."

Matthieu whined loudly. "Please... please, more..." he said. The begging made Eric smile, and he turned on his heel. He felt powerful, heady with the feeling of control over such a beautiful specimen.

"Perhaps another night," Eric said. "A bîentot, kitten."

And he took the door that led to a staircase to the roof. He ensured the door locked behind him, and tried to banish the image of the struggling, aroused Matthieu from his mind's eye. It was a difficult task, to be sure.

Christophe

CHRISTOPHE WAS IN SHOCK, perhaps, or simply overwhelmed. One moment he had been dancing on stage and then he had heard Eric's voice, full of irritation and retribution.

Then, disaster.

Esmerelda, the replacement soprano, had been at the front of the stage when the chandelier fell, and Christophe hadn't seen what had become of her. Matthieu had shouted, hustled him and the rest of the chorus off the stage and then Raoul had appeared, put a warm arm around Christophe and led him to safety. Away from the crowd, away from the cacophony, and up to the roof of the theatre.

It was quiet up there, and surprisingly cold after the heat of the press of bodies. Christophe wrapped his arms around himself.

Raoul roamed the roof, looking behind the gargoyles as if he thought someone might be hiding there. Perhaps they were. Eric always seemed to know exactly where to find Christophe.

Christophe felt a shiver rack his body and bend forward, crouching, until it passed.

In a moment, Raoul was beside him, draping his tuxedo jacket over Christophe's shoulders, pulling him up into a warm, steadying embrace.

"I have to get you out of here," Raoul said. Christophe pressed his ear to Raoul's chest and heard the unwavering rhythm of his heart. He closed his eyes and wished for sanctuary, as if Raoul's arms were the interior of the Notre Dame.

"I can't leave," Christophe said. "He'll never let me go."

He felt the way Raoul's body stiffened at those words. The

way his arms tightened around him. When he met Christophe's gaze again his eyes were blazing with intensity. "Christophe, I want to protect you, and the only way I can do that is outside of this theatre."

"But..." Christophe tried to make sense of the jumble of emotions in his chest. "I love it here, I love to perform, and he has made me what I am. My dream has always been that I want to be a star, up on the stage where everyone can see me. He has taught me how to achieve that goal, how to reach it, and he has improved my performance."

"Perhaps he has," Raoul said. He pulled back, hands on Christophe's shoulders and forced him to look him in the eye. "But he is willing to kill, we have already seen evidence of that, he hurts people who scorn you. His obsession with you is dangerous; he is dangerous."

Christophe swallowed against the sudden, painful lump in his throat. It was true, he knew it was, and yet... "But perhaps. Perhaps I am obsessed with him as well."

Raoul frowned, and his eyebrows drew together. "Christophe I don't understand. I thought I had made my intentions clear to you."

Christophe's heart rose in his throat and joy overwhelmed everything else.

"Raoul, please be plain. I'm so confused, everything's changing so fast and I am at sea here. Please, I need something steady."

Raoul nodded, loosened his hold on his shoulders and let his hands move slowly down his arms until he held Christophe's hands in his own.

"Christophe, I love you. I have loved you since we were children, and seeing you again up on that stage, it all came back to me." Raoul's expression was nothing but open, he was speaking directly from his heart, Christophe had no doubt of that. "If you would accept me, I would be your devoted servant for the rest of time. Please let me take you into my home, to love you and adore you, and protect you."

Christophe closed his eyes as tears of joy flowed out. Raoul made it sound so achievable, so simple. He had the solution to all the confusion and pain, and it was simply him. To be with him. And Christophe couldn't deny he longed for that too.

Christophe leaned in and kissed Raoul on the mouth.

So different from the kisses he had shared with Eric, this kiss was about surety, about steadfast devotion and a tenderness that made Christophe's breath catch. Raoul would do everything in his power to care for Christophe, that's what he learned through kissing him and he believed it, utterly. Raoul was nothing if not sincere in his actions.

Christophe wrapped his arms around Raoul's neck and deepened the kiss. Raoul responded with an arm around his waist and a soft noise of happiness that Christophe wanted to hear again.

Christophe had no idea for how long they kissed. They broke here and there to take a breath, to look deep into each other's eyes and confirm that yes, yes, they wanted this, they wanted more. Then they would plunge into each other and kiss again, each time as delightful as if it were the first time.

At some point Christophe's knees buckled, and Raoul sank to the ground, pulling him into his lap so that they could continue. The familiar heat pooled in Christophe's lower abdomen, and for a while he ignored it, until he realised that although he wished to lose himself utterly in Raoul and his promises of a comfortable future, part of him was still longing for something else.

Reluctantly, Chirstophe pulled back, shuffled a little off

Raoul's lap so that his hardness was no longer pressing against his rear.

He took a moment to catch his breath, giving Raoul an appreciative look over, before he cleared his throat and attempted to speak.

"Raoul," he started.

Raoul took one of Christophe's hands and rubbed his thumb over the back of it. "That warmed you up a little," he said, laughing.

Christophe, charmed, nodded and ducked his head.

"Indeed. I must be honest with you Raoul, and it may not make a lot of sense, but I will try to express it as best I can."

Raoul's bright expression faded a little, and Christophe hated himself for it. He hurried to explain.

"I do love you, Raoul. As you said, all my affection from when we were children has returned, tenfold or more since we were reunited. I love you, and I very much want to believe in the future you have promised. But I cannot let go of my Angel so easily. The things we have done together, the way he has inspired my voice, and my performance cannot be discarded."

"But he's a murderer, Christophe," Raoul said. "He means harm."

"I know it is hard to understand, I know how strange it is, how it must sound," Christophe said. He squeezed Raoul's fingers and then let go, reaching up to loosen his hair from its ribbon and relieve a little of the tension headache he was rapidly developing. "I am afraid of him, some of the time, and I don't fully understand what he wants. But I do understand something about who he is."

There was a soft creaking noise nearby on the roof, Christophe suspected that meant Eric had joined them, unseen. Raoul turned his head instantly towards the sound, alert as a hunting dog. Christophe took his hand again and gently guided his attention back.

"I cannot let go of what the Angel and I share," Christophe said. "He is in my heart, and yet you are in my heart too, and..." he faltered, examining the truth of what he said even as he spoke it. "Matthieu as well. I couldn't abandon him, he is my dearest friend and perhaps, perhaps I would like something more with him as well."

Raoul's expression wasn't one of hurt, which was a relief, but it was full of confusion. "What are you saying, Christophe?"

"Perhaps there is some way forward," Christophe said. "I was speaking with Matthieu and I told him that it feels like I have enough love in my heart for more than one partner. I still believe that, with every part of me."

Raoul blinked. He opened his mouth and closed it again. He looked away, out over the city lights, and then chuckled a little. He turned back to Christophe.

"That sounds very avant garde, Christophe."

"Christophe..."

Christophe heard Eric echo his name, as faint as a whisper. Christophe was pleased his intuition had been correct.

"I know. It's a lot to ask of anyone," Christophe said.

"I'm sure there are ways it can be done," Raoul said. He tilted his head, and Christophe realised he was truly considering it, not just humouring Christophe but thinking it through. "Matthieu has certainly aroused my interest, I have to admit. But you are asking a lot for me to include the Phantom in this possible relationship."

"It is a lot," Christophe raised his voice a little, urging Eric to hear and to understand. To not make it harder. "But I would ask the same of each of you. To understand that my heart holds you all, and that it would pain me to lose one of you. I would... it would give me so much pleasure if you would all look at each other with love as well."

"I... he is a murderer, Christophe." Raoul shook his head. "What if he turns on you?"

"That will never happen."

Christophe gasped as Eric emerged from the shadows, far closer than he had imagined he was lurking.

Raoul spun, went to his knees and put himself bodily between Eric and Christophe. Eric chuckled. He looked less composed than Christophe might have expected. Perhaps a little flushed under his mask, and when Christophe dragged his eyes over his body he saw a telltale bulge in his trousers.

Curious indeed.

"I will not let you hurt him." Raoul said. He patted at his hip as if looking for a sword which wasn't there.

"I have no intention of hurting Christophe, and I can assure you I would never turn on my precious pet." He raised his hands to show they were empty, to show that he wasn't a threat at that moment.

Christophe's heart swelled at Eric's words. The hope that all of them could somehow be together flared right in his chest.

"Why are you wearing a mask?" Raoul demanded. "Who are you?"

"I am..." Eric gestured into the air. "No one to be trifled with. You are a fashion-obsessed fool, drenched in your wealth, but I can see that your passion is pure. You truly are devoted to Christophe and I admire that. What Christophe speaks of... I would not be opposed to sharing in some capacity."

"You wouldn't?" Christophe smiled, and put a hand on Raoul's waist. "Please, Raoul. I know it's a lot to ask. But if you could consider it."

"I have just had a rather interesting encounter with your young Matthieu," Eric said. He met Christophe's eyes with a fiery blaze that Christophe recognised from their time in the bed. That explained his dishevelled appearance and arousal then. "I believe that he would enjoy such an arrangement as well, although we will have to wait to hear from him. I left him in a slight predicament."

"If you have hurt him then I will-" Raoul blustered. Eric held up a hand and Raoul went quiet.

"He is unhurt. Although he may be feeling rather unfulfilled."

Christophe stifled a laugh, fairly certain he knew the kind of treatment Eric may have given Matthieu.

"It will be hard for you to understand," Eric continued. "Until you see for yourself. I am not averse to sharing my pet and his heart with other men, but I do insist that I be in control of anything that happens between us. I am not one to submit to the will of another."

Raoul moved to rise, but Eric's hand swiftly took hold of his hair, fisting in his loose flowing dark hair and holding him in place. He didn't say anything, but watched Eric with narrowed eyes, his hand opening and closing at his side.

"I see you are not one to submit to another easily either, it sets you apart from both Christophe and Matthieu. But I can see that you yearn to be controlled, to be shown a strong will to let go and submit to. You would find such freedom if you agreed, and I do like a challenge. "

Eric smiled under his mask and his eyes flicked to Christophe. "Come here my pet. Show him how to behave correctly for your Master."

Eagerly, and not a little aroused by seeing Eric hold Raoul in place, Christophe crawled to Eric's feet and knelt there, hands behind his back and knees slightly splayed. This was a position Eric liked for Christophe to adopt when he was blindfolded and waiting.

Christophe could feel Raoul's eyes on him, and he smiled, hoping that he was pleasing his Master.

"Like this, Master?" he asked.

"Indeed. Raoul, how does Christophe look to you?"

Raoul breathed out heavily and he cleared his throat. His voice, when he spoke, cracked with desire. "Like your pet."

"Yes, and does he look upset about it?"

"No." Christophe felt Raoul's hand on his ankle and his breath caught.

"Perhaps I should make you my assistant for some of the time," Eric mused. Christophe turned to look at Raoul just as Eric tugged sharply on his hair and he hissed. Eric let go of him. "But not until after I have broken you, I think."

"Broken?" Raoul's voice sounded cracked. Eric stepped back, letting them both see him as he removed his long hooded cloak and let it pool on the ground behind him. He pulled something from his pocket, something black and leather.

"Stand, Raoul, face me as I know you wish to. Let us settle this."

Raoul

Oh, how Raoul yearned for his sword.

He cursed himself for leaving it in the box in his hurry to

get to Christophe's side. However, even without his sword, he was a fairly capable fighter. He got to his feet and walked towards the Phantom, fists raised a fighting stance.

His body was flushed with desire, something about the way that Christophe knelt, open and willing and eager, combined with the way he himself had felt while the Phantom held him. It was confusingly attractive, and the confusion irritated him. He wished to put the Phantom in his place, to regain control over the situation.

The Phantom smiled wider. "You think Christophe would like it if you fought me?" he asked, his tone mocking. "After all the sweet words he said?"

Raoul hesitated. That was true enough. Christophe had asked him to tolerate this man, to agree to share him. His fists dropped to his sides. He didn't wish to lose Christophe because of his temper.

"That's it, that's a good boy," the Phantom crooned. The hairs on the back of Raoul's neck prickled up and he tried not to visibly tremble. There was something intoxicating in the sound of the phantom's voice. "Show us both how willing you are, how you wish to please Christophe, which will mean me as well. You can impress me with your dedication to him."

Raoul blinked. Well, that was an easy enough way to impress. "I am devoted to Christophe."

"Then show us," the Phantom said. "Show your devotion. Put your hands behind your back, go to your knees and expose your throat to me."

Raoul glanced behind him at Christophe, who was nodding his encouragement, a pleased smile lighting his features. Features which had been so afraid and confused before. This seemed like a simple enough task, given how the day had gone before.

It seemed easy, but Raoul found it surprisingly difficult. It felt like he was giving something up as he complied, but Raoul knew that some things worth fighting for were worth any kind of difficulty. He adored Christophe, he wanted Christophe, and he would do anything to have him. Including this.

He sank to his knees before the Phantom, wiped his palms on his trousers, and then clasped his hands behind his back.

Looking up at him and exposing his neck was the hardest part. He had seen the Phantom pull what looked like a belt out of his pocket.

What if he intended to strangle Raoul right then and there and take Christophe for his own?

His mind feared it, but his heart doubted such a thing. The Phantom seemed as if he truly loved Christophe, which meant he wouldn't harm Raoul in front of him. Such a thing would lose Christophe's trust forever, especially if he had been watching the way that they had kissed.

He looked up, his heart racing and his breath the same and met the eyes of the Phantom. Something in his warm, approving expression filled Raoul with heat. Perhaps this submitting thing wasn't as hard as he had thought?

"That's a good boy." He was being spoken to as if he were a dog, and although he felt like he ought to hate it, the praise sent more heat through him. Was it possible that he wanted to please the Phantom as much as Christophe did?

Raoul took a deep, shuddering breath in and tilted his head up further, exposing the skin of his throat as requested.

The Phantom hummed in approval and leaned in, fastening something around Raoul's neck. A leather collar, just as one might put on a dog. The Phantom fiddled at the back of Raoul's neck for a moment, and there was the *snick* of something locking, which set Raoul's heart skipping. Then, gentle hands caressed the base of his skull, petted his hair, and dragged down his cheek and jaw. Raoul was just beginning to relax into it, to enjoy the tender affection when a hand gripped his jaw and forced him to look the Phantom in the eye once more. He clipped something to the collar around Raoul's neck.

Raoul realised it was a leash.

The leash played out between them and the Phantom smiled, approval mixed with what could have been affection. "Such a good boy. As obedient as a puppy who wishes to please his Master. What do you think, Christophe?"

Behind him, Christophe's voice was hoarse with something undeniably carnal. "He looks so good in a collar, Master."

"Come here and reward him for being so obedient, my pet."

With a rustle of fabric Christophe moved swiftly alongside Raoul. He looked up at the Phantom and they seemed to share some silent communication. The Phantom moved to the side, although he kept hold of the leash he didn't tug on it. Christophe moved in front of Raoul and kissed him deeply, one hand in his hair, the other winding around his shoulders.

Something in Raoul wished to reach out, to take Christophe in his arms, but a larger part of him understood the meaning of the collar and leash and didn't wish to fight it. He was under his Master's control now, and that meant he didn't act unless he was told to. He wanted to impress his Master, and by acting in this way, he was proving his devotion to Christophe.

He enjoyed the kiss very much and moaned his delight into Christophe's mouth.

Christophe broke away, far too soon for Raoul's liking. Raoul could feel the pleasant ache in his groin which demanded release.

He looked up at his master with a pleading expression.

"What is it that you'd like, pup?" The Phantom asked. "You went so pliant as soon as you were collared, you haven't even spoken. You are allowed to speak now."

Raoul was surprised at the truth of his Master's words. He hadn't realised he had been quiet. He dedicated he'd think about what that meant another time. He'd been asked a question, and he had to answer it.

"I should like release, Master, if you please."

"That's very nice asking. But...I don't think so," the Phantom said. "The two of you have been through a lot tonight and I am pleased with your display of obedience and devotion, pup. But it is now time for the two of you to go back to your lives. Find your beds, rest and dream of me. We will talk soon, with Matthieu."

Raoul couldn't hold back the needy whine at the Phantom's words, but there was very little in him which wanted to disobey. He nodded.

Christophe, beside him, nodded as well, and tilted his head up. "Please might I have a kiss, Master?"

The phantom's face softened immeasurably and he leaned in to kiss Christophe. Raoul was surprised at how absent the sensation of jealousy was. He wanted Christophe to be happy, and of course, he was when he was being kissed by their Master.

The Phantom broke the kiss, unclipped the leash from Raoul's collar and pocketed it. He tilted his head and nodded. "I will leave you with your collar on, I think. It is very fetching on you, and it will keep you somewhat focused on the conversation we have had tonight. Do not forget, puppy, that your obedience to me shows your devotion to Christophe and your willingness to make him happy. If you continue to behave, then I will give you all the pleasure you can imagine. All three of you."

Raoul opened his mouth although he hardly knew what he intended to say. The Phantom picked up his cloak, swirled it around his shoulders and vanished into the shadows of the rooftop.

In the sudden silence, Christophe's hand was a welcome reassurance.

They helped each other up. Christophe wrapped Raoul's white opera scarf around his neck to conceal the dog collar, and the two of them made their way down the stairs and back into the theatre.

"You have a lot to think about," Christophe said, kissing Raoul on the cheek. "Go and think, you know where to find me."

It actually felt slightly difficult to speak, as if the Phantom had hypnotised him, or as if the act of submitting wasn't quite done although his Master was gone. He still wore the collar and it was as if the command was linked to it somehow.

With effort, Raoul managed to fight through the curious instinct to stay quiet.

"I love you Christophe, and I think I do understand some of it all, now. Good night. I'll see you soon."

He left the theatre and went to his waiting carriage.

5

RAOUL

The next day, the Opera La Rêve was closed and construction began.

Over the next few days, Raoul made sure to provide a large sum of money to the managers to ensure the theatre wouldn't have to be closed for too long. The builders, painters and a whole group of chandlers worked long hours to get things back to the way they were.

Raoul had also sent money and flowers to the families of all those who had died in the theatre disaster, and had every intention of sending more. He had a certain feeling of guilt over the way he had behaved on meeting the man responsible for such a tragedy, and he wanted to ensure that they were all taken care of in their grief.

Three days after the chandelier fell, Raoul dropped in on the managers.

Firmin and André had their hands full dealing with the newspapers and gossip magazines over the deaths at the opera house, and the disappearance of Esmerelda. Not a soul had seen her since the chandelier fell, and Raoul very much hoped she had simply fled back to Lyon and was lying low.

Raoul had put on a fine suit for his visit to the theatre, but by necessity had to add a scarf over the top to hide the leather collar that was locked onto his neck. He had tried to remove it once he was alone in his chambers, but there was a locking mechanism built into it which simply wouldn't budge.

He felt conflicted about this.

He considered taking a pair of shears to the thing, slipping a blade between the collar and his skin, but he hadn't quite wished to go so far. He stood before a looking glass and pulled his hair back in one hand, regarding the way the leather collar sat on his throat. It was almost becoming.

He remembered, so clearly, the guidance the Phantom had given him. His obedience would show his devotion to Christophe. Raoul did love Christophe, so he did want to show his devotion. He also feared what the Phantom may do to Christophe if he was angered. The collar then, could well be a test of his loyalty. Of his determination to win Christophe, to be with him. If he left it on and went about his day, perhaps the Phantom would reward him. Perhaps the Phantom would let him have Christophe, even if it was just for a short time. His mind rebelled against the submission. He was accustomed to getting what he wanted without having to earn it with peculiar games he didn't understand. But Christophe... Christophe was devoted to the Phantom, and Raoul was devoted to Christophe. Therefore, Raoul was also devoted to the Phantom.

So it was, that although the weather was unseasonably warm, he was wearing a blue checked scarf in addition to his three piece suit.

"Aren't you warm?" Fìrmin asked, glancing up from various telegrams and other correspondence. His eyes lingered on the woollen scarf.

"Not at all," Raoul lied. He hoped his flushed cheeks weren't giving him away. "I'm rather chilly."

"If you say so," Firmin said. "What are we going to do about this Phantom fellow?"

Raoul bit his lip, that wasn't at all what he'd come to talk to them about.

"If there was some way to find out who he is, perhaps then we could oust him. He does seem exceptionally fond of young Christophe." André and Firmin both eyed Raoul significantly.

"I have no idea who he is or why he's so fixated on Christophe," Raoul said. He felt his cheeks flushing under their scrutiny, as if they could somehow sense Raoul's experience on the roof and were waiting for him to explain. "I have no experience in this kind of thing."

"No, neither do we," Firmin said. He sighed. "When we decided to invest our time and parts of our fortunes in this place, we hardly expected jealous and violent ghosts."

Raoul, eager to leave the subject of the Phantom as quickly as possible, brought up the idea he had been toying with instead.

"I wished to talk to both of you about the reopening of the theatre. It's only right and necessary that we should stay closed for some time to allow for the rebuilding and to honour those who died."

"Two weeks, perhaps, if the builders can work fast enough," André said. "We simply cannot afford a full month, although perhaps that would be more sensible."

"It would allow the news of our disaster to fade from the newspapers, and the public's eye," Firmin added.

"I had an idea about that, which I wanted to run past you," Raoul said. "In order to wash away the dreadful news, how about we reopen with a magnificent masquerade ball?

They're all the rage, and it will give people pleasant associations with the place."

The managers looked at each other.

André frowned. "I'm not sure it's quite the message we wish to send..."

"However, it would be a nice gesture for those who had tickets for the nights we've had to close," Fìrmin said. "And anyone who had tickets for That Night, as well."

"Indeed," Raoul said. "And a celebration for the cast as well, they have all had a terrible shock. Let's dance it away, with fine music and wine."

Fìrmin grinned wide and clapped a hand on André's shoulder. "It would be a fine outing for those masks we bought in Florence, don't you think?"

André smiled a little. He regarded Fìrmin. "Well, if you really think it's a good idea, I suppose it would be fun."

"Excellent," Raoul said. "I shall start the planning, expect messages from me as I need decisions made and so on. For now we can plan for Friday before reopening."

⟶ ⟶ ● ⟵ ⟵

Matthieu

MATTHIEU WATCHED Christophe stretch his leg out on the barre and brooded.

While the theatre was being refurbished, rehearsals weren't allowed to be held within its walls. Madame Giry had arranged the use of a nearby ballet studio for them to rehearse in, instead. The ballet girls were working on their part of the choreography, which left Matthieu, Christophe and the rest of the male dancers to stay warm and ready for the next section of choreography.

Although they shared a room, and had exchanged pleasantries since the chandelier had fallen, Christophe and Matthieu hadn't *really* talked.

Matthieu had wanted to confide in Christophe immediately when he escaped the Phantom's 'torture chamber', but he hadn't come home for hours, and Matthieu had fallen asleep after relieving himself of sexual tension.

The day after that Madame Giry had insisted that Matthieu go with her to tour the nearby rehearsal spaces, and help her select the best option. Which was, in a lot of ways, laughable, as Madame Giry knew what she wanted, and had no trouble making decisions, but she also could not be denied. She had insisted Matthieu go with her, so he went.

And then the rehearsals had started, and there never seemed to be a good time. Madame Giry drilled them hard, and they were both exhausted by the time they had dinner and went back to their apartment.

So, Matthieu watched Christophe stretch, and tried to imagine how handsome he would look bound to the wall as Matthieu had been, and what exactly the Phantom did with him next. It was a poor thing to imagine, as his practice gear left little to the imagination as it was, and his arousal had to be quelled the second he felt it.

He distracted himself by trying to interpret Christophe's mood. He seemed elated, in some respects, but utterly subdued at the same time. He was diligent in his practice as ever, graceful and elegant, but Matthieu could see his heart wasn't in it. He was lost in a dream, some deep train of thought, that Matthieu was slightly worried about interrupting with his own account of what he'd done with the Phantom. Or more accurately, what the Phantom had done with him.

There was a knock at the studio door and Madame Giry crossed the room to answer it. Her chin high and her brows arched with annoyance that someone might dare to interrupt her work.

Raoul de Chagny walked in. Christophe immediately perked up and a bright smile flooded his face with light. He brought his leg down from the barre and hurried to Raoul's side. The pianist had ceased playing, and the ballet girls were giggling and clustering together, no doubt charmed simply by the vicomte's presence.

Matthieu folded his arms, and tried not to feel the same way. It was a losing battle, he couldn't deny he desired the handsome vicomte.

<hr />

Christophe

CHRISTOPHE COULDN'T HELP HIMSELF. He had replayed their kisses on the rooftop over and over in his mind. He was tentatively optimistic about an arrangement between the two of them and Eric, and Matthieu too if he ever managed to find a moment to talk to him.

Raoul gave him a quick, warm smile, and then turned his attention to the ballet mistress, all politeness and formality.

"I am sorry to interrupt your rehearsal Madame Giry; I simply wished to let you all know some good news."

He paused, and the room seemed to hold its breath as Madame Giry considered, and then inclined her head to encourage him to go on.

"There is to be a grand masquerade ball to reopen the theatre, and you are all invited to attend." Raoul spread his arms wide, as if giving benediction.

There was a round of applause and appreciative outbursts from the entire ensemble, Matthieu and his mother excluded.

Christophe gripped Raoul's arm and kissed his cheek. "How wonderful, Raoul, what a lovely idea!"

Raoul smiled, his cheeks going slightly pink. Christophe smiled back, reflecting the joy he felt into Raoul's eyes.

"I shall send the details to Madame Giry to pass on," he said. He turned to Christophe and kissed him chastely on the mouth. "I do not wish to detain you from your rehearsal any longer."

Raoul had barely turned to leave when another knock sounded at the door to the studio and a messenger stepped in with a folded piece of paper. He stepped in and handed it to Christophe.

"I..." Christophe said, opening it to quickly scan the contents. His heart started to pound and for a moment he wondered if he was dreaming, or something similar. He turned to the one person he knew would always tell him the truth. "Madame Giry, you should see this. It seems I am invited to play the lead role of Carmen..."

Raoul attended as Madame Giry read the letter and nodded once. She folded it and handed it back to Christophe. "We shall not keep you from your calling, Christophe. I'm sure the Opera Ghost will be pleased to see you in the lead."

Christophe's heart fluttered with excitement. Another

chance to sing on stage? And to wear a fabulous dress as well? Eric would be overjoyed, Madame Giry was right.

All in all, Christophe was ecstatic.

The other dancers tittered and jostled each other, for although they were still afraid of the Phantom, they had also paid attention to his apparent affection for Christophe. Christophe bowed to Madame Giry and went to change into his street clothes.

He was out on the street before he realised he hadn't said goodbye to Matthieu, and resolved instead to stay awake long enough to have a proper conversation with him that night. Raoul was waiting with his carriage.

"Here, I'll give you a ride to the rehearsal space."

The conductor and the singing chorus had chosen a nearby playhouse to rehearse in during the day before the shows went on in the evening, and Raoul's carriage driver was directed to it. Christophe felt like he was made of impatient butterflies, unable to sit still. He sat opposite Raoul, who seemed content to watch him and not speak.

He regarded Raoul and his scarf in the mild afternoon, and remembered.

"Are you still wearing...?" He gestured to his own throat.

Raoul's expression was both irritated and somewhat embarrassed. "Yes. He didn't unlock it., so I can't remove it."

"Might I see it?" Christophe asked. He moved across the carriage to squeeze in beside Raoul as he sighed, and unwound the scarf.

"May I touch?" Christophe had never been able to resist touching the things which fascinated him.

Raoul's cheeks pinked. "I don't... I'm not sure if he would... is it appropriate for you to?"

Christophe saw then the sweet uncertain young man Raoul had once been. Far more shy, stumbling over his words and afraid of saying something that might upset Christophe. It made Christophe see a little of what Eric had been trying to achieve with the collar. If Raoul was less certain of himself, he would think before attacking Eric again. That had to be a good thing.

Christophe smiled and reached slowly up to brush his fingers over the black leather of the collar, humming in his throat when Raoul's eyes fluttered shut.

"You like it?"

"I don't like it," Raoul said, stiffly. "I am stuck with it."

Christophe felt the old spirit of mischief flare up inside him, perhaps it was spurred by the flash of the old Raoul?

He hooked two fingers through the ring at the front of the collar and tugged. Raoul made the softest of moans as he was pulled forward, and Christophe rewarded him with a kiss.

This probably would anger Eric, Christophe being so free with Raoul when Eric couldn't possibly see. He dropped his hand from the collar and sat back. "Thank you. I shouldn't have done that, I think. But I enjoyed it."

"As did I." Raoul took one of Christophe's hands and looked deep into his eyes. "I am devoted to you Christophe, you are in my heart."

Christophe blushed hard, and threw himself into Raoul's arms.

Matthieu

MATTHIEU GOT BACK from rehearsal exhausted. He opened the door and found Christophe sitting on the end of Matthieu's bed, looking bright and excited. It was the expression that Matthieu had long come to associate with an exciting new plan or scheme based on some fancy or whim of Christophe's. It was the look that had them running through the streets of Paris in the small hours of the morning to sneak into a bar for a glass of absinthe, or else to find the latest open cafe where they might find a slice of cake, or the first bakery open for the freshest possible croissant.

It was also the look which Matthieu could never say no to.

"Matthieu!" Christophe jumped to his feet and wrapped his arms around Matthieu. "I'm so happy."

"I'm glad," Matthieu said. "I'm pleased for you to get the role of Carmen. Do you know what the costuming will be like?"

"I shall be playing Carmen as the fiery woman that she is," Christophe said. He pulled back from Matthieu and lifted an arm, stuck out his chin and stomped his foot. "Like a true Spanish firebrand, yes?"

Matthieu laughed. "Yes, you will be perfect."

Christophe went serious all of a sudden and tugged Matthieu to the bed. "But I must talk to you, my darling friend."

Matthieu's mouth went dry and he nodded. "I have something to talk to you about as well."

Christophe blinked and his eyelashes fluttered. "You go first, Matty. I think I have an inkling…"

Matthieu cleared his throat and began the story of how he had pursued the Phantom on the night of the chandelier crash, and what had happened between them. He was quite pink when he finished describing the incident, and realised he was absently rubbing his wrist, remembering the feel of the shackle around it. Christophe, far from being upset or angry, looked absolutely delighted. Matthieu noticed he didn't seem surprised either, perhaps he had heard something from the Phantom?

Christophe clasped Matthieu's hands and leaned closer. "That's perfect, Matty!"

"It is?" Matthieu was relieved and somewhat confused. "Isn't he... isn't he the same as your angel?"

"Yes," Cristophe said. "I don't exactly understand it, but he is the one who has been training me. And well, something happened between us and with Raoul as well. I want to speak to you, because I am very much in love with both of them, but you are my dearest, closest friend, and I love you too."

Matthieu's heart drummed and he squeezed Christophe's hands. He loved him? Matthieu had been dreaming of hearing those words, but to hear them compounded with two other men was less than a perfect dream.

Matthieu blinked. "Three of you? I don't understand," he said.

"Yes." Christophe leaned closer. "I know it's unusual, and terribly bohemian, but don't you see? I have so much love inside me. I feel it could work, and Raoul has certainly noticed you, and now you've told me about what you did with Eric-"

"Eric?" Matthieu felt a sinking horror and gently took his hands back from Christophe to rub his own arm.

"Eric is his actual name," Christophe said. "Not Phantom or Angel. Now that you've had an encounter with him, which you didn't seem to hate, judging from your body's reaction."

Matthieu crossed his legs. hiding the fading swelling there.

"Now that you know him in a sense, you are free to join us! And all of us together can share in our loves."

Matthieu nodded, his mind feeling full of grey noise and

very little else. This hadn't been what he expected, although... although he was hard pressed to say what he had expected? Perhaps for Christophe to be angry and yell at him.

To feel guilty and humiliated.

This was so unexpected. He felt a shifting in his stomach, an uncertainty that made him question what he had wanted to come out of this conversation. What did he want in the long run? Christophe, of course, but stability with him. A nice little flat just their own, with flowers in the window boxes and kissing every night. What Christophe was offering was nothing like that.

"I'm not sure," he said finally. Christophe's face fell piteously and Matthieu's heart twisted. "I'm sorry, Christophe. It's a lot to ask, I ... I need some time to think about it."

Christophe nodded and breathed out heavily. "I think I understand."

"I am sorry," Matthieu said.

"No, it's a lot, it is. I'm sorry for, for assuming that you would be interested."

Matthieu bit his tongue, winced at the sudden pain and grabbed one of Christophe's wrists.

"I have been in love with you for so long, Christophe. For years. I had no idea you would ever feel the same way, but this isn't how I imagined it ever being. I, I might be interested, but I need to weigh the options."

Christophe looked mollified. He had always needed to be noticed, to be loved, Matthieu knew. It was simply in his nature. If someone disliked him, or was mean to him, Christophe would mope for days.

Christophe inhaled again and nodded. "All right. Thank you for telling me that. Perhaps it's simply a matter of time."

"Perhaps it is," Matthieu said.

6

MATTHIEU

The day of the Masquerade ball was a flurry of errands for Matthieu and Christophe. They hadn't talked seriously about relationships, instead keeping conversation over the last few days shallow, focused on rehearsals and excited planning for the Masquerade. The Masquerade absorbed a lot of time. They had to pick their costumes, then take them to the tailors to ensure the perfect fit. The Vicomte had graciously offered to pay for whatever the cast of the opera needed for the event, and they both enjoyed indulging in more expensive options.

On the day of the Masquerade, they picked up their costumes from the tailor's, stopped for lunch, then went back to the dorm, helping the others get into their costumes. The entire chorus was in a fluster, people were running through the halls in various stages of dress.

"Who took my hairbrush?"

"Does anyone have a spare pair of stockings? Mine have all chosen tonight to fall apart..."

"Pastries in my room if anyone's hungry!"

"The heel just broke off my shoe, does anyone have any glue?"

"You can't be a cat! *I'm* being a cat!"

Matthieu was in demand for his hairstyling skills, so he spent a good couple of hours in the afternoon fixing the hair of Elise and the other girls. Christophe and two of the others set up a makeup station in one of the bathrooms, and there was much bustle and outcry over whose turn was next and how long a turn should take.

Finally, after a few scuffles, Matthieu was done with other people's hair and was pulling on his costume. He had chosen an outfit to evoke the Greek god Apollo, although he wasn't usually quite so confident in his own appearance, Christophe had encouraged him.

The costume consisted of a short white tunic, draped like a toga, with a wide golden leather belt that laced in the back. There was a fine golden cloak that fastened on the left and draped over the right shoulder. His favourite part of it was a leafy headband which supported a head-piece that resembled a halo, a large golden ring with small spikes emanating out of it to resemble the sun. The tailors had adjusted it all to fit him just right, the tunic showing off his shoulders and arms, and a fair bit of his decolletage. The tunic dropped to his mid thighs, which was a little scandalous off the stage, but well, what were Masquerades for if not a chance to be someone you wished to be?

He had requested a dusting of golden glitter over his cheeks, and Christope had rather gone overboard with it, putting more into his hair and outlining his eyes in heavy kohl. Matthieu had to admit the effect was good though, and it suited his costume excellently.

Christophe, for his part, had been terribly torn over two

possible costumes for the night and had finally settled not on the songbird, but the rabbit.

"Perhaps I should have been the bird after all," Christophe said. He pulled on the full petticoat that went under his rabbit dress.

"No, remember? We decided it was too obvious," Matthieu said.

"It was," Christophe sighed and turned to take his grey dress down from the hook on the wall. "And this one is lovely, but it's not quite as impressive as yours."

"I think it will be very impressive once you have it on."

Christophe slipped the grey dress over his head and then turned, waiting for Matthieu to fasten it in the back. Matthieu moved closer to him, trying his best not to touch Christophe's smooth skin as he laced the dress up.

The dress was a work of art.

The bodice was simple, and fitted to his waist perfectly to create a charming hourglass effect. The skirt was full, and hung down to his knees, puffing out pleasantly over the petticoats. Christophe had some fine silver boots laced to his knees underneath it.

The dress was trimmed all over with soft grey fur, and there was a panel of white velvet up the front to imitate the soft white underbelly of a rabbit. Matthieu's favourite part was the fluffy tail set at the base of Christophe's bodice. It was very charming, and Matthieu couldn't resist ruffling the fur of it as he finished lacing him in.

Christophe's hair was gathered up the way a woman's would be, and he set the mask on top of the piled curls, a silver mask with tall rabbit ears sticking straight up. His makeup was relatively natural, but he had whitened around his eyes to make them look larger and dusted some pink blush on his nose. It was frankly, adorable.

Matthieu stood side by side with him looking in the mirror and they smiled at each other.

"We look wonderful, don't we?" Christophe asked.

"I think we really do," Matthieu said.

"I like to look like this," Christophe said. "I think women's clothes simply suit me, don't you agree?"

Matthieu nodded. "I think you're right. You've never exactly been the most masculine person around, after all. You should wear what you like best."

Christophe turned and kissed Matthieu on the cheek. "Handsome man." Then he turned, picked up a fan and flounced out to the waiting carriage. Matthieu took a moment to gather himself up before hurrying after him.

Raoul

RAOUL, since he was more or less hosting the Masquerade at the theatre, got there early to ensure the set up was going well, and the servants had everything they needed to make the ball a success.

He changed into his costume at the theatre. He had chosen a suit of armour, made cleverly from shiny silver satin which looked rather like plate metal. He had a bright red tabard that went over the torso, and it had a golden lion emblazoned on it. The tailor had told him it was meant to represent Sir Lancelot of the round table. Raoul rather liked that association. The romantic knight errant who won the heart of the lady...

He adjusted the costume as he looked in the mirror. It was a becoming costume, he was pleased to note. His tall frame and strong shoulders filled out the armour, and his hair seemed to suit it as well, something mediaeval about the way it fell on his shoulders.

He was pleased that the armour had a high collar that stood up, concealing the leather collar that remained around his neck. He had stopped resenting it altogether, and now saw it as a symbol of his devotion. He still didn't want it to be common knowledge that he wore it though.

And if, once night had fallen and he was alone in his room, he tugged on the collar with one hand and stroked himself to completion with the other, thinking variously of kisses with Christophe and the way the Phantom had commanded him to his knees, well. No one needed to know about that.

He looked good, the preparations were done. He had to admit that he was nervous. He knew he would see Christophe and Matthieu tonight, and dance with each of them. But would their Master come to the ball as well?

He wasn't sure, he expected that he wouldn't be able to resist such an event. A chance to make a splash with all these people present. A chance to walk unnoticed amongst a crowd all wearing masks, a chance to fit in.

Was that why Raoul had wanted to make it a masked ball? He hadn't considered it in depth when the idea had occurred to him. He'd just thought of it and decided to do it. Now his stomach was all butterflies and his skin seemed to tingle.

He shook himself out of his reverie. It was almost time for the guests to arrive. He set his silver mask into place on his face, strapped his sword to his hip and went out to start the evening.

Christophe

THE CROWD WAS large enough that Christophe found the masks to be rather confounding. He had chosen not to wear his own mask on his face, but very few of the other guests had made that same choice. He walked in with Matthieu, and soon took hold of his arm, not wishing to get lost in the beautiful sea of strangers. Several people complimented him on his choice of costume, and said they were looking forward to hearing him sing again.

Christophe enjoyed the attention and smiled warmly at them.

Matthieu left him with Elise (dressed as a butterfly), to find them drinks. Elise lingered for a while before running off after one of the other ballet girls.

After another ten minutes elapsed and the music started for dancing, Christophe realised he was quite alone. Matthieu hadn't returned, which probably meant he'd been distracted somehow. Perhaps Eric was in the crowd somewhere and was talking to Matthieu?

Or Raoul, maybe?

Christophe longed to find one or all of them. It was miserable being alone when all you wanted to do was belong to someone.

As he pushed through the crowd he felt a swirl of unexpected emotions. There was something frightening about not recognising anyone, and not knowing where the objects of his ardour were, but at the same time he found it rather freeing. Christophe was at liberty to dance with who he chose, or to drink, or to behave however he chose, and that was a heady sensation.

He went into the crowd, wondering if he would be able to recognise Raoul.

Matthieu

MATTHIEU WAS on his way to find drinks when the musicians started to play. Immediately, someone asked Matthieu to dance. He turned to regard the man, who was wearing a very impressive and rather startling red costume with a skull face mask. He had a huge red hat with a red feather pluming out from it, and a heavy looking red cloak over the ensemble, even red leather gloves. Matthieu felt rather underdressed beside him.

The mask was undoubtedly frightening, but something in the man's voice wasn't at all as he asked Matthieu to dance, by name.

Matthieu nodded, and they went onto the dance floor.

The man took Matthieu in his arms and pulled him close. Closer than was polite, but when Matthieu went to pull back, his grip was firm and Matthieu recognised it instantly.

He was dancing with the Phantom. With Eric. His breath sped up.

"This is a very becoming look for you, dancer. Lion-like, perhaps I should call you kitten?" Eric's voice was low, as seductive as it had been when they had been alone in the hidden chamber.

Matthieu felt more than underdressed, he felt naked suddenly, unmasked and revealed to the man holding him. *Kitten?* Why did that word take his breath away?

He cleared his throat. "I'm not sure how to answer that, monsieur."

"You could say yes," Eric said. He had his hand in the small of Matthieu's back, subtle shifts of pressure indicating the direction they were about to turn. He whirled Matthieu around the floor, and Matthieu was grateful for his years of dance practice. All the long hours conditioning his body now allowed him to pay no attention to the steps or the movement, his body knew what to do. He could focus instead on trying to see the eyes under the dark sockets of the skull mask. His heart was racing.

"You wish for me to say yes to torture? To watching you torture my best friend? To share between the three...no, four of us like some..." Matthieu couldn't complete his thought. Eric had removed his hand from Matthieu's back to twirl him, their clasped hands held high. It was rather impressive, the skill and grace with which Eric performed the twirl, given the height of Matthieu's headpiece and the heaviness of the other's costume. Matthieu wondered where Eric had learned to dance so well.

"Your body is so beautiful, your finest instrument," Eric said, once they were chest to chest again. "I could help you make it do things you can't even imagine."

Matthieu flushed under the simple golden eye mask he had on. "I'm sure you could."

"I know I could. You have heard Christophe sing. You know what I'm capable of."

Matthieu did know. He thought instantly of those killed and injured by the falling chandelier. What would happen to him if he refused the Phantom?

He knew that Eric cared about Christophe, though. Would Christophe's affection protect Matthieu from the Phantom's rage?

And how long would that protection last? How long would any of this last?

As they moved over the floor he allowed himself to consider what would happen if he didn't refuse. Eric seemed content to let him be silent for a time. Let him mull his options.

"How did you enjoy my torture chamber?" He asked, finally.

Matthieu's cheeks were red again in an instant, remembering. "It was an unusual experience."

"Unusual indeed." Eric nodded, pulled Matthieu even closer to murmur in his ear. "If I was given another opportunity, I would chain you up and make you watch as I give Christophe pleasure which makes him scream. I would give you that same pleasure, bind your body with ropes that press on all the best pressure points, unlocking ecstasy that you have never known, and would never know otherwise. I have trained with masters, I can increase your flexibility and your control. Let me teach you, my pretty kitten, and you will not regret it."

Matthieu's mouth was too dry to respond immediately. He could so clearly imagine the things that Eric said, as if his voice were putting vivid pictures directly into his mind's eye.

"I-I..." Matthieu stuttered. Eric's hand slid from holding Matthieu's, to encircling his wrist. In an instant he had pulled it behind Matthieu's back. He took the other one and pinned them both in the small of Matthieu's back.

"This costume you have chosen is debauched, showing off so much of your legs, your body, you want to be seen, to be worshipped, to be used," Eric whispered. "I should bind you right here, throw you over my shoulder and have my way with you."

Matthieu shuddered although it wasn't an unpleasant feeling at all. Eric's threat was incredibly arousing.

Their feet were still moving. Unless anyone looked closely in the close press of dancers, they might not notice anything untoward happening. His body was responding with heat and desire and he knew he wouldn't be able to say no. He wanted this, wanted everything the Phantom promised him, and he wanted Christophe as well.

But if he said yes now, would Eric do what he said? Would he bind Matthieu on the spot and drag him from the party? Surely not. Not in front of so many people.

But the idea was thrilling in ways that Matthieu couldn't deny.

"I will be your student," he whispered. "On a trial basis, once I have spoken to the others, only."

"That's a good kitten." The Phantom released his wrists, drew his hands back to a normal dance hold, and while Matthieu gripped his shoulder and his waist, he withdrew something from a pocket in his trousers. Matthieu saw the glint of gold before it was fastened around his left wrist. A thick cuff bracelet, hinged, with a tiny locking mechanism which clicked shut.

"What are you-" Matthieu heart thrummed. Was this it? A binding already?

"You're mine now, for the moment at least," Eric said. "Enjoy your evening."

He ran a firm hand down Matthieu's chest and belly, reached under the skirt of the tunic and stroked his semi-hard length and then let go of him entirely. Matthieu gasped for air, looked around at the swirling mass of masked faces and put the back of his hand to his forehead. Air. He needed air. Or a stiff drink. Perhaps a stiff... something else.

* * *

Raoul

RAOUL CAUGHT sight of Christophe as he made his way across the floor. Raoul set his glass of wine down and walked towards him. He was dressed very fetchingly in a dress that made him look like a rabbit.

It wasn't a surprise to Raoul, that Christophe had worn a dress. Even as a child he had always adored pretty things and never seemed to care if people thought it strange. He would wear what he liked, and the world could deal with it.

Raoul admired that about him.

He intercepted Christophe and took his hand. "You make a very beautiful bunny."

Christophe's eyes roamed up and down over Raoul's costume and then settled on his face, the picture of confusion. "A knight?"

"It's me, Raoul," Raoul said. Christophe's face broke into a wide smile.

"I'm so pleased to see you, I can't recognise anyone."

"I suppose it is rather the point of a Masquerade, but I'd

rather you weren't feeling confused." Raoul pulled his own mask off and slipped it into his pocket. "Is that better?

"Much." Christophe pulled back to strike a pose, showing off the tail on the dress and winking coquettishly over his shoulder. "How do I look?"

"Divine," Raoul said. "Absolutely gorgeous, sweetheart."

"Let's dance," Christophe said. He held his hand out to Raoul who kissed the back of it, and then led him onto the dance floor.

"Anything you wish for, you shall have," Raoul said. He took Christophe in his arms and they began to dance. Raoul lost himself in Christophe's huge eyes and was content. The world fell away and all that existed was the delicate man in his arms.

"This suits you," Christophe said, after a time. "The shining armour, it fits your personality."

"I daresay the rabbit suits you as well, but I don't think you're as timid as a rabbit," Raoul said.

"Rabbits aren't only timid," Christophe said. "They are important in a lot of myths and stories. Did you know that the Japanese see a rabbit on the moon, not a man?"

"I didn't," Raoul said.

"Lots of people say that rabbits are lucky, or that they inspire creativity," Christophe continued, then broke into a giggle. "I don't exactly know *why* I was so drawn to it, I just love them."

Raoul leaned in and planted a soft kiss on Christophe's tinted lips. "I like it, you've convinced me."

Christophe laughed again, and Raoul thought that perhaps there was nothing he wouldn't do to hear that sound for the rest of his life.

Christophe's hand wandered on Raoul's shoulder, tugging his costume aside and dipping a finger underneath to touch the leather collar. Raoul couldn't suppress the way his body shivered at the reminder.

"I like you. And I have spoken with Matthieu, he is... considering. I am so excited at the prospect." Christophe tugged on the collar with one finger and giggled at the way Raoul's eyes fluttered. He let go of the collar and wrapped his arms tight around Raoul's shoulders. "I want to know everything Eric has planned for us."

Raoul licked his lips, adjusted his hold on Cristophe's waist and smiled when his fingers found the soft fur. "I'd do anything for you, Christophe. You know that, don't you? You have my heart, and I'd follow you anywhere."

He had tried to say it in a lighthearted way, wrapped up in the moment and the costumes, but it sounded far too sincere. Christophe's mirth melted and he nodded, matching Raoul's intensity.

"I know, my love."

"I want to be with you always, forever," Raoul said. He reached a hand up and caressed Christophe's face.

"I wish for that, too. And I know I am asking so much from you, but I truly do believe it will be of benefit to all of us, if we could all be together." He leaned in and kissed the corner of Raoul's mouth, a teasing gesture that left him wanting more.

"I trust you." Raoul pressed his hand against Christophe's lower back and held him tight. Whatever was in store, Raoul would stay by Christophe's side.

"Meet me in half an hour," Christophe said. His expression was mischievous. It set Raoul's heart thundering as in the final moments of a hunt. "Somewhere private, hmm. Perhaps... the changing room you visited me in on the night we were reunited?"

"And what will we do there?" Raoul asked, his voice low.

Christophe giggled, kissed his cheek and pulled out of his arm. "Meet me there to find out." On impulse he added one of his favourite commands from the Angel. "And blindfold yourself."

Christophe

CHRISTOPHE DUCKED into the crowd of dancers, joyful and giggling at his own forwardness. He wasn't even sure where he was going, or why he wanted to tease Raoul in such a way.

He reflected that perhaps it was simply because he had that collar on, and Christophe knew the power of such things, of knowing that someone desires you, and wished to pass it on to his beloved. Or possibly, he was just high on the excitement of the party.

Through the crowd he pushed, pausing to compliment a young man in a stunning blue sequined peacock outfit who was dancing with a tall man all in an black pirate costume.

He spun with the music, feeling free and wild, and someone caught his elbow. Laughing, high on the evening and on his own plans, he turned to face the stranger.

He wore an Italian-inspired opera costume, bright red with a plumed hat and cloak, but his mask was that of a skull. Christophe caught his breath, it was like seeing the face of death in the middle of a festival.

He put a hand to his chest.

"It seems I've caught a rabbit," the voice said, softly, drawing him closer.

Christophe relaxed. There was no one else that could be. "Eric? Is that you, under there?"

"I wasn't invited," Eric said. "But the ball was happening in my house, so it seemed only correct that I would be here, don't you think?"

Christophe pressed himself against Eric's chest and relaxed, putting his arms around him. He felt rather than heard Eric's soft sigh of happiness.

"I'm glad to see you, Master."

Eric's hand stroked down Christophe's back, soothing and warm, a possessive gesture that one would give a beloved pet. Christophe closed his eyes, revelling in it.

"You're too sweet to me," Eric said. "Your devotion will be rewarded, my darling."

Christophe shivered pleasantly, imagining chains and immense pleasure.

"Tell me how your evening has gone." It wasn't a question, it was a command, and Christophe answered it readily.

"I danced with Raoul," he said. "I teased him. You would be proud of me, I think. Another thing I've learned from you."

"You did? Tell me more, my sweet."

So Christophe explained how he had toyed with the collar, and promised to meet Raoul in a secret place, at a secret time. Eric clutched Christophe just a little tighter. "That is deliciously wicked of you, Bunny."

"Bunny?" Christophe grinned and leaned up to peck a kiss on the cheekbone of the skull mask. "Perhaps I ought to join you, and we can torment him together. He doesn't bend to my will the way you and Matthieu do."

"Have you seen Matthieu? His costume is very handsome I thought," Christophe said.

"I have. We have spoken. He has submitted to my will, for the moment," Eric said. Christophe trembled, feeling a swelling between his legs and glad for the voluminous skirts that hid any such stirrings.

"That's … that's wonderful."

Eric stroked his hand down Christophe's back once more and then played with the fluffy tail of the dress.

"You have given me an idea with this tail," he said. "But we would need to go somewhere more private for what I wish to do."

"I can take you somewhere private," Christophe didn't hesitate. "Come, there are plenty of alcoves…" He trailed off, realising that if anyone knew about dark places to hide, it would be Eric.

He took him by the arm and led him off the dance floor. They crossed the theatre's entranceway and went into the deserted ticket booth.

Once they were inside, Eric spun Christophe so he was facing the wall, and then pressed him against it. "Spread your legs, Bunny. Palms to the wall and don't move."

Christophe did as he was asked, gladly. He moved his legs apart, a good couple of feet thanks to his dancer's flexibility, and leaned his chest and cheek against the wall. His hands moved up to lay flat on either side of his head. It was a very vulnerable position, made even more so when Eric flipped the skirts and petticoats up to expose Christophe's legs and ass. He wore delicate silk undergarments and he was pleased beyond measure to hear the way Eric murmured his appreciation.

"What kind of man are you, Christophe?" he asked, one gloved hand stroking over the curve of his cheek and then squeezing hard.

Christophe didn't think he expected a response, but it was

something he had long ago decided about himself, although never spoken aloud.

"I'm not sure I am a man," he said. His cheeks flushed as Eric drew the silk panties down to his thighs and gently spread his cheeks open. "I don't think I'm a woman either. I'm both, but neither. Some days I'm definitely more of a woman, like today. But some days I'm definitely more of a man. I don't know how to explain it beyond that, I simply dress how I feel, and I feel…" he trailed off, utterly distracted as Eric probed a finger between his cheeks.

"How do you feel, bunny?"

"I feel wanted, and hot all over," Christophe said. His heart had started to race, explaining how he felt about his own gender to his angel, but he knew he needn't have been afraid. The Angel loved him, and would accept him no matter what. He knew that. He expected that Raoul and Matthieu would be the same as well, but it was still frightening to say such a new and strange thing out loud.

Eric seemed unconcerned, in fact. He pulled back, taking a moment to pull out a pot of oil from his pocket. Christophe was panting, looking over his shoulder. He whined when Eric went to pull off one of red leather gloves.

"Leave it on, Master," Christophe said. His voice was far breathier.

Eric hummed his approval. He still had his mask on, his entire costume, and Christophe stood with his ass exposed like a common whore. He thought he might come simply from the feel of the oiled glove slipping inside him and the thought of what he must look like. If someone were to walk in on them now… he moaned loudly.

"That's it, Bunny. My precious, beautiful girl," Eric crooned. Christophe gasped and bucked, so close they really could come from Eric's words.

"Oh stars in heaven, that's good," they breathed. They had never expected to feel so fulfilled, so wonderfully whole simply from someone calling them a girl.

"You may not orgasm until I say so," Eric said. "And in fact I might command you to hold it for some time tonight, but you're a good girl, aren't you? You'll do that for me?"

Christophe closed their eyes and nodded, swallowing another moan as Eric's finger curled into the sweet spot and teased it. Enjoyment flooded them and they had to work hard to hold it in as Eric had commanded.

"That's it, you're such a well-behaved little pet."

Eric's other hand rustled, pulling something else out of a pocket, but Christophe couldn't bring themself to open their eyes and look. Their entire being was focused on the finger gently pushing in and out of the tight ring, every movement of the leather another thrill of need.

Then the finger gently withdrew, and Christophe whimpered, his body rebelling against staying still, and he moved back, trying to chase the touch. Their skirts had fallen back down during this and Eric tutted his tongue.

"Bunny, hold your skirts up for me. Display yourself so that I can work, and don't move your chest from the wall."

Christophe flushed but did as they were told, flipping the skirts up with both hands, and feeling the cool draft on their exposed cheeks once again. It was all too much. They wanted to rut against the wall like a rabbit in heat, but they wanted to obey their master even more.

"That's it. Good girl." Eric's praise was the reward they needed. The urge to orgasm didn't fade, exactly, but it was less urgent, it was something Christophe could master, could control if it meant pleasing their master.

"This might be a little cold." That was all the warning

they had before something cold and hard, metal? Glass? Pushed inside their waiting hole.

It was unyielding, forcing Christophe open and stretching them until they felt full and complete. They moaned and whined, unheeding of how loud they were being or how lascivious it must sound.

Eric didn't say anything, simply pushed until the plug was in place, and then slapped their ass, making them jolt. "How does it feel, bunny?"

Christophe let out a heavy sigh. "I feel so full."

"Mm. It will keep you ready to be used," Eric said. "And I have one more thing, to stop you from orgasming until I say you're ready."

He slipped his hands around their waist, stroked their cock, eliciting another moan from Christophe, and clipped something hard and metal around it. It felt like a ring, which slipped under their balls as well. Christophe gasped again, body practically vibrating with the need to release under Eric's hand

He pulled their panties back into place, gentle leather-gloved fingers smoothing the fabric down, slipping around Christophe's hardness, and over the plug. He was filled and teased and ready for more, but Eric moved back.

"You may let your skirts down, now," Eric said. "You've done marvellously well. I must go and meet Raoul now."

Christophe dropped their skirts and turned, eyes wide and panting. "But-"

"You go and find Matthieu, my pet. We can all gather soon. Go and dance with him, enjoy yourself and I'll take care of Raoul. I will find you soon."

Eric

ERIC MADE his way to the assigned meeting place with some difficulty. It was all very well to tease and torment his pet, but it had a physical effect on him as well. He yearned for release, and he was determined to get it. His most challenging pet would provide that release.

He was a few minutes late, he was always indulgent with Christophe, and he had no regrets about that at all.

He pushed into the changing room to find Raoul, fully dressed in a handsome knight costume, his eyes covered by the black silk blindfold that Christophe had so often used in their encounters. Smiling, he closed the door behind him and locked it.

Raoul's head whipped towards the sound. "Christophe?"

Eric didn't reply, instead he removed his hat and cloak, his gloves (now delightfully soiled) and even his mask, taking a small risk which he hoped would pay off. He moved closer.

"Is that you?" Raoul fidgeted, shifting his feet. He lifted his hands as if to take off the blindfold and Eric caught him by both wrists. Raoul's breath caught.

He didn't think he could precisely emulate Christophe's sweet voice, but he wasn't quite ready for Raoul to rebel either. He threaded his fingers through Raoul's and spread them to the side. Raoul let this happen, pliant and eager. Eric could see how much he needed to be dominated, to give over his decisions and his actions to someone else. He had a dominant streak in him for certain, but he would also love giving himself over. It was clear from the way his breath caught, the way he moaned ever so softly. And Eric had seen the blustering way that Raoul dove into action, it wasn't always in his best interests to do so. A little control could go a long way for Raoul.

He leaned in and kissed Raoul as gently as he thought Christophe might.

Raoul relaxed instantly, and moaned softly into the kiss. Eric nipped his lower lip and kissed him again, slipping his grip to Raoul's wrists and pulled them gently but inexorably behind his back.

Raoul fought this a little, but Eric sensed it was simply instinct, not a true desire to escape. He pinned both hands with one of his own, and reached in his pocket for another toy. He had in part, chosen this costume because of the potential it had to conceal many items, and he was glad of it. The evening had required many of his gadgets and private collection.

He pulled out one of the heavier items he had been carrying around. A pair of handcuffs very like the ones the gendarme used.

"What's that sound?" Raoul asked. His chest moved quickly, betraying how fast his breathing was.

Eric didn't reply, simply tightened his grip on Raoul's wrists.

It would be easier to turn Raoul around, or to command him to turn, but he didn't wish to reveal himself until he had the vicomte restrained. He had a very real sword strapped to his hip, and Eric didn't wish to feel the steel of it.

So, he slipped the cuffs behind Raoul's back and locked them in place.

Raoul whined softly, a far more needy sound than Eric

expected to hear from him so soon. It simply confirmed his suspicions that he needed this, needed Eric. He would be better for it, Eric only had to convince him of it. To show him.

Eric tested the locks briefly, ensured they were secure, and let go of him. He stroked a hand up Raoul's cheek and smiled, admiring how handsome he was. Christophe certainly attracted excellent specimens to their side.

Eric licked his lips and grinned, any nervousness he felt over revealing his identity subsumed in the dark delight of frightening someone so rich, so powerful. He slipped a finger up under the blindfold and tugged it free, watching with fascination as Raoul blinked in the sudden light, then looked at Eric with surprise, disbelief and horror. The way Eric's face looked was a source of terrible shame, but it had its uses as well. If he had to frighten Raoul into obedience then so be it.

"Good evening, Monsieur le Vicomte," Eric said. He used the deep, purring tone that he knew would lull the listener, soothe him.

"You," Raoul said. He struggled then, properly, against the metal cuffs holding him. "Let me go!"

"You let me bind you," Eric said. He stroked a hand up Raoul's chest, pressing his fingers into him to feel the muscles there. "You wanted this. You waited with your eyes covered and hoped for this to occur."

"I was waiting for Christophe!" Raoul took a deep breath and mastered himself, an impressive feat, Eric had to admit. This man had so many reserves of strength and confidence, a benefit to the privilege he'd been raised in, perhaps. He lifted his chin and glared at Eric. "What have you done with him?"

"Christophe is perfectly safe," Eric said. "I would never hurt my beloved pet."

"Then where?"

"Dancing with Matthieu, I would assume." Eric stroked

his hand down Raoul's front again, and was rewarded with trembling. He didn't touch the visible bulge under his silver trousers. His other hand he lifted to tug aside the high collar of the costume to find the leather collar. "Well well, I see you didn't remove my collar."

Raoul flushed and bit his lip. "I considered it."

"But you didn't. You could have, I'm sure, with a sharp enough blade. You chose to keep it on."

Raoul couldn't meet his eyes, so Eric gripped his jaw and forced his face up to look in his eyes. Raoul swallowed, the movement of his throat an entire performance in itself. Every moment Eric showed his mastery, Raoul responded with desire.

Eric's demand was touched with mockery.

"Tell me why you didn't, Sir Knight."

"I am devoted to Christophe, and this is the symbol of that devotion."

Eric smiled, leaned in and kissed him hard, demanding access to his mouth with an impatient tongue. Raoul tried to take control of the kiss, but it was a battle he was destined to lose and they both knew it. His shoulders moved, fighting against the metal cuffs. Eric didn't give in. He slipped his hand to the base of Raoul's skull to hold him in place, his other hand moving down to stroke his hardness.

Raoul gave in all at once. His shoulders relaxed, he moaned, loosened his jaw to give Eric more access and pressed against his hand, desperate for more.

Eric broke the kiss and let go of his cock. Raoul whined, leaning in to chase his lips, utterly heedless of Eric's deformity, all sense of self preservation or righteous anger gone the moment his cock was touched.

Eric hooked his fingers in the back of the collar and held him back. Raoul whimpered.

"So needy all of a sudden. Do you want more, Sir Knight?" Eric murmured, glorying in the desperate way Raoul was bucking his hips to get more friction from his hand. "You must ask for what you want."

Raoul stilled, his cheeks aflame. He met Eric's eyes briefly and then looked down, shy suddenly. He was truly delightful, Eric thought. His arrogance was still present even as he was utterly debasing himself. He couldn't bring himself to say it, so Eric leaned in, tugged on the collar and stilled his hand to hold him in place.

"Raoul, you are a man who has grown up with everything he ever desired. Isn't that right?" He paused, and Raoul nodded. "But you can't have what you want right now, unless I give it to you. Do you understand?" Again, Raoul nodded, but this time it was accompanied by a soft, yearning moan.

"I need you to understand, I will give it to you, if you behave. If you're a good dog, and do as you're told, and that includes speaking when I ask you. You are devoted to Christophe, but you are also devoted to me. I put the collar on your neck, and I locked it there. It shows your willingness to be utterly controlled, and I know how much you yearn for that. To have your privilege stripped away. You want that, don't you? Answer me now."

The silence stretched between them, and Raoul's jaw worked as he fought his own will. Eric's own arousal was still unabated, and it was beginning to ache. He let go of Raoul's length to fist himself through his costume trousers. Raoul caught sight of the movement and moaned again.

"You see the effect you have on me? I can give you so much, Raoul. You simply have to give me your will. You have done it before, up on the roof of this very building. You did it just now, while we kissed. I know you want to, you just have to say it out loud and I will serve you as your Master."

Raoul swallowed again, cleared his throat and admitted it. "Yes, I do want that. I have to admit I'm afraid of wanting it, of what it means, but I want to give you my will."

"Good boy. You're such a good boy." Eric gave himself another firm stroke, not enough, by far, but enough to alleviate a little of the ache. "Now, beg me to bring you to orgasm."

Raoul's eyes fluttered shut and his face was bright pink, but to his credit he did it.

"Please, please bring me to orgasm," he said. He sounded a little resentful, but he'd said the words. This one would take longer to break entirely, and Eric relished the challenge.

He let go of the Vicomte's collar and used both hands to pull his trousers down, shove the embroidered tabard aside, and then shoved his own costume trousers down as well. He took hold of the collar again, and took both of their lengths in his other hand. Both of them moaned softly at the slickness of the precum, the way the velvet skin chafed.

"You may come, my dog, my knight," Eric said. "Show me how well you can obey my command."

It didn't take long at all. Raoul's body, if not his mind, was responding to Eric's ministrations, and soon he was jerking his hips to come. Raoul groaned, and swore softly, and Eric came a moment after, slicking his cock and Raoul's softening one with Raoul's spending. It was a delicious release.

"That's a good boy," Eric said. "You've impressed me, this evening. It wasn't easy for you, and I very much appreciate that you did it."

Raoul sighed. Eric let go of his collar and pressed his shoulder, pulling him into lean on his chest. Raoul gasped against his neck and moaned again.

Eric slipped his other arm around him to pull the trousers back up. "How do you feel now, my puppy?"

Raoul took a deep breath and sighed, blissful. "Free."

Eric's grin was so wide it hurt his twisted cheek.

How he *loved* to be right.

"That's right. There's freedom for you in submission."

He pushed Raoul back into a straightened position and spun him. He wanted to keep him chained, to continue the training with a long stretch of restraint, but he had a stuffed full Christophe to check on, and Matthieu, who had given him permission as well.

Another time.

"We must get you back to your ball," Eric said. He unlocked the cuffs and took them back to replace in one of his pockets. "I'm sure you've been missed."

Raoul turned back, his expression open and vulnerable. "What ... this encounter, what does this mean?"

"It means that you're mine, along with Christophe and Matthieu." Eric shrugged, and turned away to replace his mask and hat. "You will hear from me soon."

7

RAOUL

I t wasn't as if Raoul could simply pull himself back together after an encounter like that.

But the Phantom had reminded him he had a host duty to perform. His guests may not have missed him in the last maybe half hour, but that would only last so long. The Phantom himself had vanished almost the moment he had his mask and hat back on.

Raoul tugged on his costume, trying to get it to sit flat. He was uncomfortably sticky in his underthings, but there wasn't a lot he could do about that. He had just had a very personal encounter with the Phantom of the Opera, and he had definitely enjoyed it. The things the man had said were shocking to be sure, but they also rang true in a way he certainly couldn't deny. There was a freedom in being bound, and in giving himself to another. He could let go of the need for action and decision, and simply be.

He had never dreamed that was a thing that he needed in his life.

And from such a man?

The Phantom's true face was truly frightening, but at the

same time, it wasn't that which scared Raoul. The way a person looked didn't determine who they truly were, after all. It was what they did that told you who they were. The Phantom had killed and injured people seemingly without remorse, and that was far more frightening than a disfigurement. He had been startled, but the shock had largely worn off, replaced with sinful pleasure and fulfilment.

Was the Phantom a man or a monster? And when he could do such things with his hands, and his voice, did Raoul even really care?

He ran his fingers through his hair and made his way down to the ballroom once more, searching the crowd for a pair of rabbit ears.

The dance floor was less packed than it had been. There were clusters of people by the tea and coffee table, helping themselves to the pastries and chocolates he had ordered in for a light supper. There were also more than one couple leaving the floor, presumably to go home or to find an alcove... Raoul's cheeks flushed, a large part of him still unable to believe in what he had just done.

Then his eye caught sight of Christophe, his arms around Matthieu, gliding across the floor as if they were born to it. Faces close together, whispering intently.

Raoul tried to make his way to them, but was waylaid by people giving him their compliments for a fine evening. He had to physically pull away from the managers, who were both very drunk and very handsy.

"So handsome, monsieur le Vicomte," Fìrmin said, squeezing Raoul's bicep.

"I'm so sorry about him, Raoul," Andrė said, slinging an arm around his shoulder. "Too many glasses of champagne and he forgets we're as good as married."

"I could never forget that!" Fìrmin's grasp on Raoul

slipped as he tugged himself away. Firmin turned to André and cupped his face in both hands, squeezing it so that his lips bulged out. "But there are *so many* handsome people here tonight."

"Indeed," Raoul took the opportunity to escape and giving them a smile. "I'm glad you're having fun."

He made his way across the floor. Christophe and Matthieu spotted him coming and broke apart. Christophe had a terribly mischievous look on his face, knowing. Matthieu looked somewhat overwhelmed, his eyes wide and full of wonder.

Christophe took one of his hands, and Matthieu the other. "How was it?" Christophe asked.

Raoul felt his cheeks flame again and shook his head. "I cannot begin to describe it, although I was somewhat disappointed that *you* weren't there. I still had... a satisfying time."

"More than satisfying, I'd wager sweetheart." Christophe went up on his toes and kissed Raoul's cheek. "I have something to tell the both of you. I'm not sure if it will be a surprise or not, but..." he looked down and Matthieu slipped his arm around his waist.

"Chris, you can tell us anything you know. It certainly can't be more shocking than... certain other things you've asked of us, and haven't we agreed to those?" Matthieu said.

"Indeed." Raoul led them both to the side of the dance floor, out of the crowd. "Please, Christophe, you can trust us."

Christophe raised his chin and looked first at Raoul and then at Matthieu. "I'm not a man, really. But I'm not a woman either. It sort of fluctuates."

Matthieu smiled and nodded. "I wondered if there was something like that going on."

"You did?" Christophe looked surprised, and then squeezed Raoul's hand. "And you, my love?"

Raoul thought what they'd said through and shook his head. It didn't make any difference to him at all. "I don't mind what you are, or how you identify yourself, my dear. I simply love *you*."

"How should we refer to you then?" Matthieu asked. "Is it correct still to say you're a he?"

"I think..." Christophe tilted his head to the side. "I think if you use my name, and then whatever pronouns you like? Eric called me a girl earlier, and I liked that, but perhaps if you simply leave gender out of it that might be the most correct."

Raoul leaned in and kissed Christophe's cheek. Matthieu did the same on the other side. Christophe closed their eyes and beamed.

"Your wish is our command," Raoul said, softly. Matthieu nodded his agreement.

"Absolutely."

"You are so angelic, the both of you." Christophe slipped their arms around both their necks and pulled them in, kissing them each in turn before letting go again. "And I have a need that needs fulfilling. Come, let's find Eric."

"Is Eric the Phantom?" Raoul whispered to Matthieu, who nodded.

Christophe took them each by the hand and pulled them into the waning crowd. Eric's red plumed hat was easy enough to spot, and Christophe laughed, tugging them both along in their wake.

Someone in a green brocade suit and a silvery mask that looked like the moon turned to their companion and said rather loudly. "That new soprano is ridiculous. A man wearing a dress? Who does he think he's fooling?"

Christophe blinked, faltered, and slowly kept walking but their expression was stricken.

Raoul however, would not let a comment like that slide.

He dropped Christophe's hand and turned to face the moon-faced stranger.

"How dare you speak of Christophe in that way?"

The crowd around them went silent and still, dancers halting to form a loose ring, interested to see what might happen next.

The moon-faced person scoffed. "Ah, I see he has ensnared the Vicomte. How many lovers are there now? A dozen? I heard he was having it off with most of the corps de ballet, I suppose you will at least be able to pay for his new fancies and fripperies."

Raoul put his hand on the hilt of his sword and stepped closer. "If you do not cease your insults and leave, then I cannot be held responsible for my actions."

"You would not challenge me over the simple truth. The chorus dancer is nothing but a whore, and you have been sucked in -"

Raoul went to draw his sword at the same moment Christophe grabbed his arm.

"It's not worth it, Raoul," Christophe said.

In the same instant a blade sunk into the moon-faced person's back and he crumpled to the ground, his mask falling aside as the people around him gasped.

Eric, the Phantom of the Opera, stood behind him, holding a bloody dagger.

The surrounding crowd began to scream.

"The Phantom of the Opera!"

Raoul on instinct, pulled Christophe and Matthieu behind him. "Everyone please stay calm!" Raoul shouted, although there was little effect.

People fled the dance floor screaming. Eric stood up straighter and shouted. His voice was extra sonorous, filling the room and able to be heard even over the screams and upset.

"Christophe Daaé is under my protection! If you don't wish to meet an untimely death like this fool, then you will hold your tongue!" His voice changed as he spoke, and all of it different to how Raoul remembered it, his voice became manic and hoarse, lifted in an impassioned scream.

"Hide!" Christophe hissed over Raoul's shoulder. For a moment Raoul thought they meant that Raoul should hide. Instead Eric looked over the three of them. Nodded, and retreated to the shadows and was gone.

The ball ended in a panic. The managers fought against the crowd and arrived at Raoul's side as he watched Eric disappear. The pool of blood around the moon-faced person was steadily growing and he hadn't moved at all.

The gendarme arrived quickly, and bustled Raoul and his companions off the floor to examine the body. Although there was hardly any need for an investigation with so many eyewitnesses.

Madame Giry escorted Christophe and Matthieu away to the Manager's office, assuring Raoul that she would make them both chamomile tea to calm down. Raoul gave the officers what information he could, but they seemed at a loss for what to do next.

Firmin, who had quite sobered up, put forward a suggestion.

"Perhaps we should try and trap him," he said. "Lure him out with Christophe's performance, and seal the doors. He is likely to go for box five after all."

The gendarme officer in charge nodded, his expression serious. "I'm sure we can spare the men to carry out such a plan."

Raoul was torn. He couldn't condone murder, and he had

seen it done right in front of him. But Eric had such a connection to Christophe, and... well, to himself and Matthieu as well, it felt like betrayal to agree to such a plan. He dithered, which wasn't something he had ever done before.

André patted him on the shoulder. "You've had quite a shock, my boy. Perhaps we should call it a night, and confer tomorrow?"

Raoul nodded, grateful for the excuse and thanked them both before heading up the stairs to their office.

<hr />

Christophe

CHRISTOPHE WAS adamant that they should immediately find Eric. They were tearful, upset, and clutching at their chest, but at the same time, they weren't at all capable of sitting still. The plug that Eric had so playfully put in place wouldn't allow it. It teased Christophe and was utterly distracting. They knew that what Eric had done was terrible, frightening and awful.

But it didn't mean that Christophe wanted him any less.

It made them think that perhaps they were a terrible person, cold and unfeeling for those they didn't know personally, but if so, well. So be it. They needed to see him.

Matthieu sighed and begged for them to sit. Christophe ignored him.

Madame Giry was outside the door, waiting for Raoul or the managers to let her know what had happened.

"Please, Chrissy," Matthieu tugged on their hand. "Just sit and wait."

"I can't sit! I have to see Eric!" Christophe said.

There was the sound of speaking outside the door and then it opened to let Raoul in. He looked drawn, paler than usual. "Are you both all right?"

"I'm all right," Matthieu said, "although it was horrible to witness. Chris won't sit down."

Christophe rushed across the room, pressed themself to Raoul's chest and blinked up at him, hoping their doe eyes would soften Raoul's steely resolve. They feared that Raoul's mind would have turned against Eric again, ruining all their plans.

"Please, Raoul, there's simply been a misunderstanding."

"I don't see how this was a misunderstanding, Chris." Raoul placed his hands gently on Christophe's upper arms and rubbed his thumbs over his bare skin. It felt divine and went a small way towards calming Christophe down. "That man insulted you and the next moment he was dead."

"But, perhaps Eric simply doesn't understand," Christophe said. "Who knows how long he's been living down there, in the caves. He's been away from society, he doesn't see people unless they're in the theatre. I don't think he realises it's not the civilised way to go about things. Or perhaps he's not sure how to control such impulses and he does them without thinking?"

Matthieu sighed and got up. "I think he knew exactly what he was doing. But the real question is what do we do next?"

Raoul

RAOUL SWALLOWED. He knew how this news would be taken, but he had to share it all the same. "The managers wish to trap him, probably to kill him."

"We can't let that happen!" Christophe said. They shook their head. "No. I won't allow it. He has given me so much. I know he did some terrible things, but I'm sure with time and love, he would change. He isn't a monster, not at heart."

"It does seem that he's not entirely evil," Matthieu said slowly. His hand moved to a fine golden cuff Raoul hadn't noticed before. It made Raoul think of the collar locked around his neck. They had all in their ways, agreed to belong to the Phantom. And that meant dealing with the fall out of his actions.

Perhaps if they were to all go to him and cement that connection, it might ease some of the Phantom's less than desirable urges? Or perhaps it would simply heighten them?

What was the right course of action?

"Perhaps there is some way to help him," Raoul said. "If as you say, he doesn't understand, or has urges he doesn't know how to school. Perhaps there is some way that we can assist him to understand better."

"I'm sure that playing with me has improved his control," Christophe said. They frowned then. "Although his attachment does seem to have made him more deadly as well... but that's because he seeks to protect me, he cares so deeply. I think we should go to him. To talk and to see what we can do to help."

Matthieu caught Raoul's eye and between them an understanding passed. They were both of them devoted to

Christophe, and through them, to the Phantom. They had to listen to Chiristophe at this moment. Raoul cleared his throat.

"Christophe, do you know how to find him?"

Christophe's sudden bright smile was almost enough to alleviate Raoul's worries, it was so bright.

"Through the mirror, in my changing room," Christophe said. They were decisive, standing up and nodding. "There's a passageway. I'm sure I remember how to get there."

"Then we must use it, and go to him," Raoul said. Knowing the next action to take filled him with sureness and he felt energised once again. "Right this instant."

Matthieu

MATTHIEU WAS AFRAID, but he wasn't nearly as afraid as he had been the first time he'd climbed into a tunnel to pursue the Phantom.

This time, he had friends with him.

This time, he knew the Phantom's name.

This time, he had already agreed to belong to him.

The golden cuff was so comfortable that he had all but forgotten he was wearing it, although every now and then the gleam caught his eye and he examined it. There were curious engravings on it, which Matthieu wanted to understand, but now certainly wasn't the time for that.

The three of them had stepped through the hidden door

of the mirror, and it felt like they were making their way down into the depths of the underworld.

Christophe led the way, deciding between branching tunnels with surety and confidence. Matthieu was glad of that, sure that the other paths led to traps and torture chambers like the one he had been caught in. Although the idea was no doubt exciting, there wasn't time for it.

Finally, they came to a still lake, and on the water just where the steps ended was a small boat, a Venetian-style gondola. It was lit by a lantern which hung on a stick at the back of the boat.

"I think he means for us to take this, I haven't seen it here before," Christophe said. They stepped into it fearlessly, Raoul holding their hand to steady them. Once Christophe was seated at the front of the boat, Raoul turned to hand Matthieu in as well. He accepted the assistance, leaning on Raoul's steady arm to get in and then settling in the centre of the boat. Raoul took up the paddle and stepped into the back of the boat. However he needn't have worried because as soon as he was in it the gondola started to move of its own accord, sailing them across the water and directly towards a darkened platform. The first part of the Phantom's lair seemed to be stagelike, a series of platforms looking over the lake and arched over by a high cavern ceiling.

As they approached, Matthieu could hear music, something playing on a gramophone perhaps. There were a few candelabras lit, but it gave precious little light. Matthieu imagined him lurking in the shadows waiting for them, a blade in his hand. The darkness could be disguising all manner of things; insects, bats, horrors beyond imagining. Matthieu shivered.

"Is this where he lives?" Matthieu asked. Christophe glanced back and nodded.

"Romantic isn't it?"

"A little damp," Raoul said. Matthieu couldn't tell if he meant it as a quip or a true observation.

Matthieu's own heart was thumping. He was flooded with doubts now that they were down in the belly of the beast. What were they thinking? The Phantom had just stabbed someone to death because they'd said some rude things. How long would it be before he lost interest in them and the tables would turn?

He'd been so angry, maybe he would be angry that they'd come down now?

But Christophe was beside themself, and Matthieu knew they'd have had to do something to set their mind at ease.

Maybe Christophe was right, and they could change Eric?

Matthieu had to set aside his own fears and simply deal with whatever came next. Matthieu's heart thudded as they reached the dock and Raoul secured the boat to the mooring pole with a heavy rope.

Raoul would protect them all if something went wrong. Matthieu was sure of that. He felt better, knowing that Raoul was there. He was strong and handsome and good-hearted. He knew that Christophe could be led astray, fooled by their own dreaming heart, but Raoul was more down to Earth and he had experienced so many things.

Matthieu hoped that his faith in Raoul wasn't going to be undermined.

─ ──►─ ◆ ──◄── ─

Christophe

CHRISTOPHE COULD HARDLY CONTAIN THEMSELF. The events of the night had been too much, so much anxiety and longing, such shock. But they knew they were taking the right course of action.

Raoul got out of the boat first and offered his hand for Christophe to take. They looked around the seemingly deserted platform which served as Eric's home. He wasn't at the organ or the piano.

Christophe cleared their throat and called out. "Angel? We're here. Please, don't hide from us. We wish to talk, and possibly more."

The creak of a door opening. A door? In the cavern? Christophe's mind dismissed this new befuddlement and focused on the important thing. Eric emerged from a room, costume discarded. Dressed instead in a plain white shirt and black suit pants, his porcelain mask back on his face. He was drying his hands on a towel as if he'd just washed up.

"Greetings, my dears," Eric said. He seemed perfectly calm and composed, taking the role of the magnanimous host as if he had been expecting just such a visit.

Christophe went right to him and took the proffered arm, leaning up to kiss him on the cheek.

Eric smiled, the expression in his eyes softening behind the mask, and nodded at Raoul and Christophe.

"Welcome. Come through, the both of you, it must be time to show you my special room."

Matthieu cleared his throat. "Is it like the other room you showed me?"

"Something like." Eric turned and guided Christophe to the room behind one of the many doors. It was a strange sort of room, not like anything Christophe had seen before. There was little by way of recognisable furniture, although there was one long bench sitting out from the wall and a wooden X in one corner.

In between contraptions and strange-looking furniture were erotic paintings of men and women bound with ropes, their private parts on display in between the bindings, expressions of ecstasy on their faces.

The ceiling was crisscrossed with low wooden rafters, and one wall had shelves built into part of it. The shelves held not books or trinkets, but coils of rope, and small devices made of metal and leather. There were more plugs, like the one that Christophe had almost forgotten about, they had adjusted to it so well. Christophe's cock stood to attention once more, straining against the metal ring that Eric had placed there.

Christophe whimpered, and Eric turned to smile, his gaze sharp. "Not much longer now, my pet. But I do need you all out of these costumes, fetching as they are. Then we can get started."

Christophe wanted to get started very badly. They turned to Matthieu. "Will you unlace me, darling Matty?"

Matthieu, whose eyes had gone wide and round, looking around with an almost frightened look, nodded and went to unlace the back of Christophe's dress. Christophe hummed, turning to kiss Matthieu softly and ease his worry.

Raoul stepped forward and looked Eric in the eye. "I do think we need to discuss some issues before things progress any further," he said.

Eric had moved to the shelves and busied himself choosing hanks of rope, but he paused and looked back at Raoul.

"Perhaps you wish to challenge me, *again,* monsieur le Vicomte," he said. "I will win, just as I have every other time you have tried. But if you wish to try again I am ready for you."

"After what you just did up there," Raoul's hand went to the sword on his hip. "Perhaps I should."

"You have come to my house," Eric said. He uncoiled one of the ropes and set the others aside. "You have brought your self-righteous energy to the fore again. Is it possible you have so quickly forgotten the words you said to me, mere hours ago?"

Raoul drew his sword, but his expression of determination faltered. "Things have changed in that time, you killed someone in cold blood! In front of dozens of witnesses!"

Eric advanced, his posture casual, apparently utterly unconcerned about the sharp steel Raoul wielded.

"He was unforgivably rude about my pet."

Matthieu had stopped unlacing Christophe's gown and had slipped his arms around their waist instead. Christophe longed to intervene between Eric and Raoul, but Matthieu's grip tightened around them, holding them in place.

"No, Chris this is something they need to work out between them. Let it play out." Christophe whined, but stopped trying to pull away. The words Matthieu said rang true. "Raoul is too proud to give himself over easily, and I don't believe Eric would ever take the submissive role. And we do need to speak of what he did."

"You toss people aside, you end their lives as if they mean nothing!" Raoul said.

Eric shrugged one shoulder, letting the rope play out between his hands, so he was holding large loops, ready to ensnare. "They do mean nothing."

Raoul growled and feinted with his sword, Eric easily dodged the thrust, Christophe could see he had never meant it to land. It was a challenge.

"What if one day one of us stops meaning something to you?" Raoul demanded. His voice was raising. Behind Christophe, Matthieu gasped. Raoul advanced, jabbing with each question he shouted. He was undeniably handsome when he was angry. Christophe took one of Matthieu's hands and brought it to their chest.

Raoul was relentless. "What if you decide you don't care for Christophe or Matthieu any longer? What happens on that day? Will you toss them aside?"

Eric had backed up under the onslaught. Raoul's questions truly seemed to be affecting him. He shook his head vehemently.

"No. That day will never come."

"Never? And what is that worth, the promise of a murderer? Of a ghost?" Raoul's passion was evident in his heightened colour, and the cracking of his voice. He was in pain and afraid.

Eric saw it too.

In a movement too quick to be seen, Eric tossed a loop of rope and pulled it tight around Raoul's sword arm. Raoul gasped, for a moment the two of them simply stared at each other, Raoul's sword and Eric's rope between them, connecting them. Eric leaned into it, letting the sword press into his chest.

"It is worth everything. I mean what I say. Do you understand me, Raoul? I would shed my own blood before I harmed Christophe. I would never abandon them, or you. Even if Matthieu only agreed to a trial period, he is still worth everything to me. You as well, if you would stop with this foolish fighting and give in as I know you desire. I am dedicated to you three, and to protecting you."

Raoul deepened his lunge, pressing the point of his sword to Eric's chest until Christophe could see a red drop of blood blossoming in the linen of his shirt. Chistophe didn't dare to breathe.

All their hopes and dreams were balanced on the point of Raoul's sword.

Raoul made a soft whimper, as if it were his own body he was harming, and then dropped the sword. His head fell forward, and Eric moved in, his eyes never leaving Raoul's face. His hand slipped around Raoul's shoulders. The words they exchanged next were so soft that Christophe couldn't make them out, but they began to breathe again.

Matthieu's hand smoothed circles over Christophe's chest. Christophe pulled away just enough to let the dress fall to the floor, leaving them in petticoats and underthings. They pulled Matthieu's hand back to their chest and wrapped themself in his other arm. Matthieu pressed against Christophe from behind and Christophe could feel his hardness pressing through the petticoats.

"Matthieu..." Christophe whispered.

Both them had their eyes on Eric and Raoul though. Eric pulled Raoul's arms behind him and made quick work of securing them there with rope. He pulled the costume tabard off, and undid the front fastenings of Raoul's costume, pulling it open to reveal his muscular pectorals.

Raoul moaned softly, and they could clearly see the movement of his chest as he panted. He thrashed his shoulders, once, twice, and then went still as Eric drew the rope forward and wrapped him in it, making a clever design with knots and loops that utterly encircled Raoul's chest, and secured his arms at several points. He tugged the last knot tight and then kissed Raoul on the mouth.

Despite his fighting, Raoul returned the kiss as a man starved, and Christophe moaned as if he could feel the passion on his own lips.

Eric picked up Raoul's leather leash and clipped it to the loop on his collar. He lifted his arm, and secured the other end of the leash to a hook on the rafter above them. It wasn't tight enough to pose a danger such as hanging, although the visual was there. It certainly stopped Raoul from moving about the room. The leash hung not quite taut, and Raoul tipped his head back to look at the fastening, and then closed his eyes. Christophe recognised that he was giving himself over to the wonderful floating feeling of devoted submission that they knew so well.

Eric checked each knot, and Christophe rocked their hips, grinding their ass shamelessly on Matthieu's hardness. They drew one of his hands into their mouth and nibbled on his fingers, the other hand palming themself through their petticoats.

Eric, satisfied, looked up from his work and over at Christophe and Matthieu.

"Now, Christophe, you are to assist me in stripping and binding the gorgeous Matthieu."

Christophe moaned, delighted, they released his fingers from their teeth then turned in Matthieu's arms to start their task.

Matthieu

Matthieu was loath to let go of Christophe.

Finally having them in his arms, he wanted beyond

reason to keep them as close as possible, but watching Eric with Raoul had been intoxicatingly hot. Part of him was desperate to know what would happen next, and what precisely the binding Eric had in mind for him was.

Eric was utterly in his element, at ease moving around the torture room, and finally pausing beside Christophe with some ropes in his hand.

Christophe lifted the sunshine headdress off Matthieu first, and then made quick work of the rest of the brief costume. Matthieu stepped out of it and tossed his hair back, straightening his shoulders. He was proud of his body and not at all embarrassed about being utterly naked in front of people.

Eric's hand found the golden cuff he had locked onto Matthieu earlier in the evening and turned Matthieu's wrist so his hand was palm up.

"Look at this," he said, to Christophe. "You can learn the secret so you may use it, my dear."

"Secret?" Christophe asked. They watched carefully. The engravings Matthieu had barely had time to examine were revealed to conceal small latches and buttons. With a quick series of movements, Eric revealed the true secret of the cuff. The middle part of the cuff unfurled and a short golden chain unwound from the bracelet. Christophe caught on immediately and grabbed Matthieu's other hand, bringing beside the other. Eric looped the chain around his bare wrist and secured the bead at the end of the chain in the channel on the first cuff. Matthieu tugged on it and the chain held fast and sure.

"That's wonderful," Christophe said. They kissed Eric on the bare cheek. "You are such a genius, Master. Inventing things like this and then making them, you are so talented."

Eric's gaze was focused on Matthieu though. "How does it feel, Kitten?"

"Secure," Matthieu said. He swallowed, knowing Eric wanted to hear more. "Good... good as it felt last time."

"Good Kitten, answering for me so well."

"Kitten? That's a perfect name for Matty." Christophe kissed Matthieu this time, on the mouth, and Matthieu returned it happily.

"Indeed. Matthieu is the kitten and Raoul is my puppy." Matthieu spared a glance to Raoul, and could plainly see how aroused he was, from his exposed position, his eyes focused on the three of them. "Now, how to make best use of the kitten's flexibility?"

He put his hand on Matthieu's back and in an instant Matthieu was bent at the waist, his bound wrists on the floor. A moment later he was pulled upright by the hair.

"Over by the puppy, I think." Eric mused.

He was tugged towards Raoul by a laughing Christophe, and given a brief moment to kiss Raoul before Eric was pulling him back.

"No stealing kisses," he said, sharply. He slapped his palm across Matthieu's bare ass, making him jolt. The sensation was more surprise than pain, and Matthieu found he liked the way the smarting smack made his skin warm.

Eric took hold of Matthieu's bracelet from behind him and pressed with three fingers in specific spots, releasing the chain. He then pressed Matthieu's back to bend him forward once more. "Wrap your arms around your legs, Kitten. Christophe, help him balance if he needs it."

Matthieu did as he was asked, folding himself neatly in half with his feet in first position, and wrapping his arms around his thighs just above the knees. It wasn't a difficult stretch to get into but would certainly tell on him over time.

Eric crouched and started to wind the ropes around him. He reattached the chains so that Matthieu' wrists were linked and then secured his upper arms to his thighs, winding several times around each point to make it strong and secure.

Then he moved down to tie Matthieu's ankles as well, looping the ropes several times around both legs and then winding the ropes around in between them before knotting. It was almost a cushioning effect, to ensure Matthieu's ankle bones didn't rub together.

It could have been the blood rushing to his head, or the simple fact of being tied in such an exposed position, but Matthieu felt his worries and fears evaporate entirely. He was at Eric's mercy now, whatever happened. There was freedom in that, he didn't have to worry about what to do next.

"Oh, Angel," Christophe said. Their hands were braced on Matthieu's hips, thumbs rubbing circles on his skin. "The things one could do with him in this position..."

"Indeed." Eric said. He ran his hands over the ropes, checking each knot and slipping his finger under them here and there. "Puppy will get the first turn."

Matthieu groaned loud enough for all of them to hear.

Raoul responded instantly. "Please, Master, I should like that very much."

"But we must secure them, first," Eric said.

Matthieu was manoeuvred into position, and there was rustling as Raoul's hardness was freed and then pressed tantalisingly against Matthieu's hole. "Christophe, use this oil and get Matthieu ready for being used," Eric said.

In a moment, Christophe's long and slender fingers were teasing at Matthieu in the most stimulating way. Matthieu moaned again, tried to shift to get more, but he had no movement at all in this position.

Eric slipped a thick leather belt around Matthieu's waist,

threading it through his folded body, and then tugged on it, securing it firmly behind Raoul. Matthieu wished he could see how they looked, how the leather was secured on Raoul. Perhaps it hooked to the back of his collar somehow?

Matthieu felt like a pony, hitched up to a cart. But with the tease of Raoul's thick cock, pressing against him meant he didn't mind it at all.

Christophe teased him open, making Matthieu pant and whine. "Please," he said. He barely knew who he was pleading with. He only knew... "I need more."

"In just a moment." Christophe's hands withdrew. From Matthieu's position he could see his own legs, Raoul's legs, and the shadows Christophe and Eric moving.

Matthieu whined louder still, trying to rock his hips, which quickly showed him he would overbalance.

"Now, Matthieu cannot stay in that position for too long," Eric said. "But I want Christophe bound before the two of you start to enjoy one another."

Matthieu moaned, his own arousal trapped in the fold of his body, and his hole felt like it was gaping and empty, ready to be filled.

This truly was torture, if torture of a rather thrilling sort. His heart raced with anticipation and he hoped that Eric would move quickly.

Behind him, Raoul moaned softly, yearning. It sounded as if he was just as eager to get to the fucking as Matthieu was.

* * *

Christophe

CHRISTOPHE FELT INTOXICATED, soaring on heavenly wings as they watched Eric bind first Raoul and then Matthieu. And in such ingenious ways. Christophe thought they recognised the pattern of the rope binding on Raoul from one of the paintings on the wall.

They had also very much enjoyed the way Eric used him as a prop or tool, to assist with binding and teasing, and at his word that now it was Christophe's turn, he felt his arousal surge even higher. If it weren't for the ring encircling their cock they would certainly have already spent themself.

Eric pulled them close, and stripped them of the last of their costume. He left the ring and the plug in place, although he didn't seem to be able to resist tapping the plug and rolling the ring a little, simply to have Christophe whine with need.

"Where did you learn all this, Master?" Christophe asked.

He wound ropes around Christophe's body quickly, his hands touching and teasing as he knotted.

"A Japanese master, I was lucky enough to visit with him while he was in Paris," Eric replied. "Bondage has been an art form for centuries in the east."

Christophe's arms were bound in front of his chest, hands clasped as if praying, and the ropes secured them in place, looping around his biceps and tying in back. It all happened quicker than Christophe could keep track of, he was in such a dreamy, floaty state, able only to move where directed by Eric and to moan.

"I'm going to fuck you," Eric murmured in Christophe's ear.

"Yes, please, Master, I need you."

"This way." Eric moved Christophe to the nearby bench and laid him down on it. His head tipped off the end so he could see, upside down, Raoul and Matthieu's delicious predicament. Christophe spread his legs and Eric hitched them up, bending his knees, and tying each ankle to the corner of the bench. It was rather comfortable, all things considered, and Christophe groaned his approval. They must look utterly debauched, spread open, bound up and wanting.

They felt extra desirable since they had shared their gender feelings with the others, and had been accepted. They were wanted, needed and sexy even though they weren't what they others had thought they were. Not one of their loves had rejected them.

"Just one moment and I'll be back with you, Bunny," Eric said. He stroked his hands up Christophe's thighs, then moved away to the other two. "You may come from fucking Matthieu," Eric said, his voice stern. "And Matthieu, I would like to see you come multiple times. Is that a thing you are capable of?" He stroked a hand over Matthieu's thigh and up his hip, like petting a thoroughbred stallion. "I believe it is, your body is incredible."

"I can try, sir," Matthieu said, his voice muffled and a little strained.

Eric reached between them and guided Raoul inside of Matthieu. The responding moans of pleasure from the two of them were divine. He tightened the leather strap so there was no danger of Matthieu slipping off.

Christophe writhed in pleasure, the idea of seeing them fuck, and of Matthieu orgasming multiple times almost sending them over the edge again.

Eric returned to Christophe and finally, finally, stripped off his own clothes. With lithe movements he slipped onto the bench, threading his legs under Christophe's so that his knees tented Eric's powerful thighs.

Christophe lifted his head to drink in the sight of Eric,

mask off, pushing inside of him. There was no horror in his twisted visage any more. When Christophe looked at him they saw only the object of their desire and affection. Perhaps even love.

They dropped their head back down when Eric started to twist the plug, pushing it gently in and then drawing it slowly out of him. Christophe closed their eyes, enjoying this exquisite tease that would lead into the release they so desperately needed. But then they realised if they kept their eyes closed they would only hear the moans from Raoul and Matthieu, and not see them enjoying each other.

They forced their eyes open, moaning as Eric inserted a very oily finger, slicking his already stretched hole. Raoul's face was one of concentration, his eyes focused on Matthieu as his hips thrusted in and out relentlessly. Matthieu, bent in half, was making noises Christophe had never heard from his mouth before, high and needy, almost keening. He sounded close to completion, and Christophe hoped silently that he would be able to do as Eric commanded and come multiple times.

Then Christophe's concentration vanished as Eric pushed inside him, filling him utterly, making him realise how little the plug had done for him. Eric's hand stroked up their belly, over the ropes that held their arms in place, and closed on their metal collar.

"You're so ready for me, aren't you, Bunny?" Eric murmured. It was only then that Christophe understood just how much this had all affected Eric himself. His voice was chocolatey rich, and there was an edge of urgency there, he had hidden it while he was commanding them all. He had kept his own desire at bay, but now he was loosing it all on Christophe. Christophe hadn't thought they'd be able to feel more affection and desire but seeing how Eric had held himself back increased it all over again.

"Yes, I'm soaking, Master! Please remove the ring, Please!"

"Of course." With an oiled hand, Eric unclipped the mechanism and discarded the ring. Christophe's cock immediately felt engorged to the point of pain and they writhed under him. Christophe loved the sting and ache of it as Eric moved his hips.

He thrust once, deep and hard, then adjusted his angle to hit the spot inside which had Christophe keening, almost matching Matthieu's noises.

Eric

NEVER IN HIS wildest dreams had Eric allowed himself to imagine such a scene. It was a transcendent experience.

He exalted in his skill: he had convinced three beautiful people to be his and he had allowed himself to be truly experimental in his treatment of them, and they were all about to orgasm from his experiments. He hadn't even felt the need to go terribly cruel with it, he had so many people and limbs to account for, the urge to hurt, to truly frighten into submission had faded. He had instead carefully observed what they all needed, and found a way to supply it to them.

Matthieu needed challenging in his position, and to be filled gloriously. He also needed to be reassured with his freedom taken away, and to be pleasured.

Raoul needed to be mastered, and to be rewarded for giving in.

He looked down over Christophe, his beautiful pet, neither man nor woman but somehow both at once. So incredibly precious. They needed him right now, to exert his force and control for certain, but they also needed him to praise and adore as well.

He closed his hand over Christophe's throat, constricting their breath for just a moment, as it always sent their voice into greater heights after.

For a few incredible seconds, the only sounds in the room were harsh breaths, moans and the slapping of skin on skin. The most perfect symphony he had ever heard. The melody of Matthieu's high-pitched moans and Christophe's counterpoint, even higher and more pure. Raoul, who seemed to go almost entirely non-verbal when he was being dominated, but a relentless man of action nonetheless. His constant thrusts into Matthieu constituting a steady rhythm section.

Eric didn't bother to hold himself back anymore. He had done enough of that already simply getting them all into position and ensuring they were getting what they needed.

Instead, he wrapped his hand around Christophe's cock and started to pump it as he got himself off, using Christophe's hole to pleasure himself.

"Come for me, angels," Eric said. He hardly expected to be heard, but Christophe responded instantly, bucking into his hand and then squeezing him so beautifully that he came almost in the same instant, filling them utterly.

Raoul made a pained noise and arched his back, and Matthieu responded with a breathless cry. Raoul's hips moved twice more and Matthieu's cry was repeated. Incredible. Eric had known that his body would be capable of great things, and a small part of his mind was already at work inventing some sort of machine that would milk Matthieu's cock and have him orgasming over and over. He had already orgasmed, after all, with no one touching his cock, Eric imagined what he could do with assistance.

An idea worth pursuing later.

He had to take care of his pets immediately. Play the rescuer now, after being the captor. Turning from villain to hero, a switch he could never do outside of sexual play.

He reached behind to untie Christophe's ankles and pulled out slowly.

Christophe whimpered as if he were being horribly deprived, so Eric retrieved the plug and pushed it back in, trapping his own seed inside. Christophe stilled instantly, smiling contented as a cat.

Eric tugged them more fully onto the bench so their head was supported and then went to free the other two. Matthieu first. He carefully undid the leather sling.

He picked up a small knife he had on hand in the room and swiftly cut the ropes, and unlocked Matthieu's bracelet. Instead of pulling him upright, he tugged him down to the floor. Better to let him recover there than fall over. Once he was in a comfortable enough position, Eric turned to Raoul.

He used the knife to cut those ropes as well, unclipping the leash from the hook in the ceiling last. Raoul's eyes were a little glazed, his demeanour utterly pliant, and Eric could see he would have to be very gentle with all three of them all for the rest of the night. They needed him to care for them, to show he was capable of it, after his rash blade at the ball.

The torture room wasn't a room of comfort, he would have to move them to something softer.

"Raoul, you were a very good dog," Eric said. His voice was clear, to ensure that Raoul understood utterly, heard him through his haze. "I need you to do one more thing. Pick up

Christophe, and carry them through to the bed in the next room. The next door to the left after you exit this one. Can you do that for me?"

Raoul nodded and smiled slightly. Eric tugged once on the leash to get him to move, and then let go of it. "Off you go, do it now."

Obediently as if he had been trained for years and not mere hours, Raoul went to Christophe, scooped them gently in his arms, and carried them out.

Eric bent and lifted Matthieu in his arms. Matthieu would no doubt need a massage for his sore muscles, but for the moment, warmth and comfort would do. Eric carried Matthieu into the room, and set him down next to Christophe. Raoul had done exactly as he was told and was now standing next to the bed looking uncertain. Eric paused to rub his back. This room was a bedroom that Eric seldom used. Furnished with a large comfortable bed and multiple blankets, an old but comfortable armchair, sideboard, a trunk of clothes and a shelf of books, Eric had never been sure if he would actually get to use this room for a pet, let alone three of them.

"You get in next to the others, Pup." Eric said. "Make sure everyone's warm and comfy, yourself included."

Raoul again, obeyed instantly. It all proved Eric's theory that he had needed this badly. Eric spared a moment to cut the ropes that held Christophe and set them aside. He picked up a bottle of wine from the sideboard and poured some into a glass, giving each of them a sip or two before he slipped into the bed as well, behind Matthieu. Christophe nestled into Raoul's arms, already mostly asleep. Matthieu stretched his limbs to their full extent, reaching arms up over his head, then curled them against his chest. He pressed back against Eric, demanding wordlessly to be cuddled.

Once again, Eric marvelled at how wonderful it all was. How utterly beyond his wildest imaginings. He pulled the coverlet up over their shoulders and slipped his arms around Matthieu, holding him tight against his chest. Matthieu's hand closed over Eric's forearm, warm and reassuring. This tiny gesture was almost enough to make Eric choke up, but he had to stay focused and provide the care his pets needed.

"I am immensely proud of you all," he said. "You all outshone my expectations, and I am very, very pleased. I am beyond impressed with each of you. Go to sleep now, I'm sure you need it." He was rewarded by sleepy smiles from all of them.

He started to sing a soft lullaby, and watched as they each drifted to sleep in turn. Christophe, then Matthieu. It took Raoul a little longer to relax, he seemed content to watch Christophe breathe, and then finally, he dared to glance at Eric. Eric was pleased to see his expression was more relaxed, less glassy, and he gave Eric the smallest of smiles, before he fell asleep as well. Perhaps he had needed the reassurance that Eric would take care of them all, guard them against the night. Eric silently swore that he would do everything in his power to protect them, to keep them and make them as happy as they were now, if not more so.

Eric soon fell asleep as well, contented beyond his wildest hopes, although his sharp mind was fast at work, planning for the future.

8
MATTHIEU

Matthieu was the first to wake, mostly because his muscles were demanding a good stretch. He was in the middle of the bed, Christophe on one side and Eric on the other. Eric's arm was over his waist, and his legs were tangled with Christophe's. Raoul had Christophe in a tight embrace, and they looked utterly serene.

Matthieu needed to move though. So, he gently withdrew Eric's arm from his waist and shimmied down under the covers, squirming awkwardly until he emerged at the bottom of the bed.

After a quick look around, he found a trunk overflowing with clothes and pulled on some loose trousers and a shirt and tied his hair back with a ribbon.

He left the room and went into the main area - the platform overlooking the lake.

He was surprised that he felt so calm after the events of the night before. It had been so very much, so intense. All four of them giving in to basest desires, and with a man who had killed someone only hours before. But his mind didn't seem to want to dwell on any of it, so he didn't. He let it be, and concentrated on his body instead. As Eric had said, it was his greatest tool. He remembered Eric's words of praise, and a smile came to his face as he began to move.

He spent the next twenty minutes using the back of a chair as a barre to stretch out his leg muscles and go through some basic exercises, warming his body until it wasn't aching any longer. He noticed he had better extension on some of the stretches, but wasn't ready to assume that one session with Eric had already improved him.

In this time, Eric had emerged from the bedroom. He was wearing a loose white shirt and black pants. He nodded at Matthieu, then busied himself in the back of the cave.

Raoul and Christophe came out together, dressed as Matthieu was in clothes from the trunk.

Eric bustled over, looking decidedly not Phantom-like in a worn out yellow apron with a patch pocket on the front of it, and a tray laden with hot toast and cups of coffee.

He set it on a table and gestured them all over to the dining table near the room he'd been cooking in. "Come along, you'll have to eat before rehearsals."

It was bizarre, a strange situation no doubt, but Matthieu's mouth watered at the smell of melting butter and fresh coffee. He hurried over to sit at one of the rickety chairs.

So they began their strange breakfast. Christophe, at least, seemed utterly at ease and not at all concerned. Raoul gave Matthieu a warm smile but his eyes kept scanning the cavern and he didn't seem as relaxed.

Eric, for his part, was playing the gracious host, ensuring everyone had milk and sugar if they wanted it, and got up to bring back another batch of toast. It was all such normal behaviour and Matthieu tried to reconcile this with the Opera

Ghost, or the sexual Master of the night before. He seemed to want to look after them, which was reassuring. But how had he come to be here?

Finally Raoul cleared his throat. "So, I have to ask. What happens next?"

"Next?" Eric blinked. "Christophe and Matthieu must go to rehearsals for *Carmen*, and I have some correspondence to catch up on. Some instructions for the new managers."

Matthieu snorted, sure that the managers would certainly be displeased about such correspondence.

"Rehearsals," Christophe said. "Yes, so I can appear as Carmen."

"What about the person you stabbed?" Matthieu asked.

"A society idiot, I'm sure he won't be missed." Eric sniffed and put another piece of buttered toast on Matthieu's plate. He blinked at the toast and then up at Raoul, who looked about as uncertain as Matthieu felt.

"Perhaps," Raoul said, slowly. As if trying to soothe a wild animal. "Perhaps you could try to refrain from killing people?"

Eric frowned, and looked around the table. Matthieu nodded encouragingly. "It might be a good idea."

Christophe looked pained, their face open and full of compassion as they took one of Eric's hands. "It does rather make you frightening."

"That is the entire point," Eric said. "I need people to fear me, or they'd hunt me down and kill me. So, I learned to harness my rage."

"Perhaps when you feel like your anger is taking over, you could find me, or one of us?" Christophe's fingers rubbed at Eric's hand. "You could play with us, train us, use the energy of your anger in a better way?"

Eric's visage showed the deep love he had for Christophe. His vaguely annoyed expression melted into clear affection.

"I can't... is that something you would volunteer for?"

Christophe nodded immediately. "Of course, Master."

Eric looked at the other two and Raoul cleared his throat, his gaze suddenly firmly focused on his plate of toast. "I expect I would as well, it's an act of kindness, if it is protecting innocent lives."

Matthieu considered the trial period that he had agreed to, and thought back over his experience of the night before. He couldn't possibly walk away and never experience anything like that again. He wanted more already, even now. And perhaps, if this would offer Eric a way to move on from murdering and hurting it was for the greater good? Help Eric to be more of a man and less of a monster.

"Yes," Matthieu said. "I would also volunteer. It's better than you lashing out at others. And... well, it's very fun, as well."

Eric's eyebrows knitted together, although Matthieu could only see half of his face under the mask.

"I don't understand."

For a moment no one said anything. Matthieu looked at Christophe with desperation. Christophe nodded once.

"You've never been shown kindness in your life, have you?" Christophe said. They shuffled closer and rubbed Eric's upper arm with one hand. "You don't recognise it when it's offered. We all had a transcendent time last night, and I'm sure we'd all be happy to experience it again."

"My life..." Eric sat down in the last chair and took both of Christophe's hands in his. "I have been beaten, laughed at, run from and tormented. I have had to maintain a murderous behaviour simply to be able to live as well I can, as miserable as it is, down here."

"Well, that's changed now," Matthieu put in. "If you agree to this, I'm sure we can make things better for you."

Eric didn't say anything for a long time. He stared deep into Christophe's eyes, and then to Matthieu. Raoul, finally, looked up and met Eric's gaze again. He nodded slightly, and by the set to his jaw, Matthieu could see that he agreed absolutely.

"I will do everything in my power to abide by this agreement," Eric said solemnly. "I cherish the trust you have all placed in me, and I will do my best to honour it and serve you in return."

<hr />

ERIC ESCORTED them all back up to the theatre and they parted ways.

Christophe and Matthieu went to wash up and change for practice. Matthieu into dancing clothes, and Christophe into loose fitting gear they could move in as they began their vocal warmups.

Raoul went to check in with the managers and ensure that things were as good as they could be. He told them he had escorted a distraught Christophe and Matthieu to his own townhouse to ease their nerves, but that they were both now well-rested and ready for practice.

The gendarme had of course been unable to find the culprit, since he had all but vanished into the walls of the theatre itself.

The failure of the gendarme and the lack of knowledge that they had might have been expected to stay confidential. However, theatre and society gossip moves quickly and somehow the mystery was immediately known to all who had been at the event, been nearby, or indeed, simply heard of it.

The news spread across Paris faster than the morning rain. The general gossip was that the Opera Ghost had struck again and there was precious little anyone could do to prevent this happening again.

To Firmin's great relief, rather than damage the theatre's reputation, the news seemed to instead have created more excitement for opening night.

He went to his partner with the box office takings for the morning annotated on a long piece of paper.

André, who was in the midst of writing letters to the paper to plead their case, looked up.

"You wouldn't believe the ticket sales," Firmin said. He shook the piece of paper, making it impossible to read.

"Should I keep writing letters?" André asked. He held out his hand to read the sum at the bottom of Firmin's piece of paper. "Perhaps not?"

"We might make more money if we put the Opera Ghost himself on stage," Firmin said. Only half joking.

"Don't be ridiculous."

"How are the rehearsals going? Did you get a chance to look in?" Firmin ventured, leaning against the desk as André set aside his pen and stretched out his neck.

"I did not." André grimaced and shook his head. "The conductor and director wanted a closed rehearsal this morn-ing. I was pleased to see Christophe this morning though, he looked rather radiant, which I didn't expect."

"I'm sure the vicomte's hospitality is most soothing," Firmin ventured. "Right, well. I was going to get some lunch at that new little bistro, would you have time to join me?"

"I expect so." André smiled, and got up to pull on his

jacket. "Perhaps a little champagne to celebrate those ticket sales, and the infamous and profitable Opera La Rêve?"

Christophe

CHRISTOPHE'S WEEK passed in a blur. The rehearsals for Carmen were at once tremendously fun and terribly taxing. Getting a nice, clear falsetto that rang out pretty and true every single time wasn't the easiest task they'd ever set themself to achieve, but with Eric's coaching and the guidance of the conductor and director, they were pleased with their ability to carry the opera.

Piangi was struggling with performing opposite them, though.

He was a man trained in the finest opera schools in Rome, and very much of the old school, so he didn't entirely approve of Christophe's casting. Although even he had to admit that the sopranos were in danger, should they try to perform in Christophe's stead.

He was grudging and held himself stiffly when he had to interact with Christophe. To make it somewhat easier on him, Christophe had taken to wearing their hair in a more feminine style, arranging it in a partial pile atop their head, and tying the ribbons higher up. Their decision to also wear a soft, flowing robe over their loose trousers and shirt was perhaps not helping as much as they hoped it would.

Christophe had known that not everyone would be as accepting of who they were as their lovers had been, but it was still unpleasant to experience it. Especially when being given such a role was a dream come true. Christophe wished for it to be only enjoyable, and now it wasn't.

It came to a head on Wednesday afternoon. He rolled his eyes and scoffed when Christophe struck a pose. Christophe folded their arms over their stomach.

"For your sake, señor," Madame Giry said, stepping forward from the wings. "I should hold back your contempt. I believe we are all aware of the Opera Ghost's affection for and protection of young Christophe."

Christophe shook their head. "No, there's no need-"

Madame Giry held up a hand and Christophe instantly went silent.

"Señor Piangi, it is for your own safety that I remind you of this."

Piangi looked into Madame Giry's eyes and his expression of contempt vanished, replaced with a sort of stoic seriousness. He nodded. "Of course, madame."

There was an unnatural quiet on the stage, and Christophe felt rather horribly alone, until he caught Matthieu's eye. Matthieu was dressed in his dance practice outfit, golden cuff visible on his forearm, and he winked at Christophe, and flashed his gorgeous, bright, infectious smile. Christophe knew what he was saying. *You've got so much talent that Piangi is jealous. Do your best, and make us proud.*

The conductor tapped his baton on the music stand and got them back into practice, but Christophe was heartened by Matthieu's message.

Over the week, Eric's 'borrowed' Matthieu, Raoul and Christophe, one at a time, every second evening or so. He also sent messages of corrections to staging, costume and performance that he sent down to the managers and the conductor, which always caused a squabble and delayed rehearsals. It all made the week go quickly.

Suddenly, it was the day of the show.

Christophe

OPENING night had never felt like this to Christophe before. They had never been in the starring role before, of course, but more than that, they had never felt so confident in their own abilities.

They were in the diva's changing room, fixing their hair to curl just so on their temple, when there was a knock on the door and Raoul let himself in. He had a large bouquet of red roses in one hand.

Christophe turned and beamed. "Raoul! I've missed you." They flew from their chair and into his arms.

Raoul smiled just as wide and kissed them passionately on the mouth. "My darling, you look wonderful." He handed them the flowers and looked them up and down.

"Thank you."

Christophe was already dressed in their act one Carmen dress, a red dress with a low cut bodice and a voluminous skirt with black petticoats, dripping with lace. They did a quick spin to show off and set the flowers down on the table.

"But I had rather hoped you wouldn't be in your costume yet," Raoul said.

A prickle of excitement flooded Christophe's veins. "You didn't? Why-ever not?"

"Our Master gave me instructions," Raoul said. His smile was mischievous now. He reached into his trouser pocket and produced a hank of slim red rope.

Christophe whimpered and licked their lips, tasting lipstick.

"Well then, just let me..." the costume thankfully, had hooks and eyes in front which made it easier to remove and fasten than lacings. Christophe slipped off the dress and petticoats, and stood before Raoul in just their drawers.

Raoul moved close in and kissed them, pushing their lips open and lashing their tongues together. Christophe whimpered, wanting more, wanting him so badly it made their knees weak.

Raoul pulled back from the kiss and got to work then, tying the rope around their torso into a pretty web that hugged tight without cutting into the skin.

The rope even passed between their legs and put a subtle but impossible to ignore pressure on Christophe. Raoul ran his fingers here and there, slipping his fingers between rope and skin just as Eric was fond of doing.

Christophe was breathing hard. Raoul hummed to himself.

"Yes, good level of tightness," he said.

"Is there... a science to it, then?" Christophe asked, trying to think of absolutely anything except their own hardness.

"If it's too tight it can cut off blood flow, or damage the nerves, apparently," Raoul said. He looked up, smiled and kissed Christophe again. "But this is a good snug fit. Will you let me help you back into your dress?"

Christophe nodded, turned to pick it up and caught sight

of themself in the mirror. The rope harness was beautiful, accentuating their slim torso and the curve of their hip bone.

They were unbelievably aroused now, and it was with trembling hands that they lifted their dress. Raoul, whose hands were still steady, ended up doing most of the work in dressing Christophe again.

"Master says that he has a surprise for you tonight, uh, in addition to this one." Raoul ran his hands over the fitted bodice of the dress, and Christophe felt the ropes press against his skin underneath. The dress held it all close to his skin, and in some ways, alleviated the immediate arousal from the ropes.

"I hope he realises that I shall be challenged to sing my best with ropes chafing me," Christophe said. Their voice was breathy and their cheeks flushed red.

"I have faith in your abilities. Besides, if you impress him, I'm sure the rewards will be great," Raoul said. He kissed Christophe again. "I love you, dearest, enjoy yourself. I must get to my seat."

Christophe wondered, briefly, if Eric intended to view the performance from box five, alongside Raoul. But they had to focus and get themselves ready to be on stage. They'd already warmed up their voice, but there were always more breathing exercises they could do.

Christophe

CHRISTOPHE'S NERVES flared up quick as a flame to paper, as they waited beside the stage. The chorus carried the opening number, and then it was Christophe's cue to run in and introduce the audience to fiery Carmen.

They fixed their eyes on Matthieu and tried to forget their own fears. Matthieu looked so good on stage, so confident and so graceful in all his movements. He could be a principal dancer, if he ever left the opera for a proper ballet company. That thought set Christophe's nerves on edge, they didn't want Matthieu to ever leave their side.

Christophe wrapped their arms around themself. Matthieu had never expressed a desire to be a star. He seemed happy enough in the chorus, working with all the others to make a perfect company to accentuate the performance of the singers.

Christophe heard the music change and shook their head. Once again they'd gotten lost in dreams when they ought to be concentrating. They took a deep breath and centred their thoughts.

They became aware of the ropes under their costume all over again. Time had almost made them ignorable, certainly while Christophe had been musing. Now they brought Christophe back to their own body and grounded them. It was as if Eric himself was holding them tight.

The reminder of him, and of Raoul doing his bidding, filled Christophe with blissful happiness.

Eric, Raoul and Matthieu all believed in Christophe. They knew they couldn't let any of their lovers down. They would perform at the very best they were capable of, and show not just the managers, but the entirety of Paris itself, that they were a deserving diva, even if they weren't the usual sort.

When the musical cues played, Christophe tossed their hair, gripped the skirts of their dress with one hand and bounded onto stage, giving themself over to the character of a woman with nothing to lose. A woman everyone wanted. A woman who causes all sorts of trouble and laughs while she does it.

The performance was stellar, even Christophe could tell.

The energy from the audience was vibrant, bouying all on stage up to greater heights. The notes were never so high and so powerful in rehearsals, the jokes had never been as funny as they were on stage. Christophe felt at the top of the world, swanning about the stage and utterly embodying Carmen.

It was intoxicating. Every minute that passed was truly the performance that Christophe had dreamed of.

The acts flew by, at intermission Christophe changed into another dress, and smiled in the mirror at the way the ropes held their body tight.

It was in the final act that things started to go awry.

The part of José, the main love interest of the piece, was played by Piangi. The part Escamillo, the dashing toreador, by the next best tenor in the chorus. However Piangi missed a cue, and when José came back on stage finally, he was wearing a hooded cloak. The cloak had been part of his costume during the smuggling sequence, but he wasn't supposed to be wearing it now, in the Seville Square.

He moved lighter on his feet than Piangi had, and when he sang, Christophe's heart fluttered with recognition.

Eric! Eric was on stage with them.

They felt their performance ascend even further to transcend anything they'd ever sung before, urged on by Eric's tenor, and then by the touch of his hand.

He knew the choreography, from all his hours watching the rehearsals, and Christophe was glad of it, thinking of nothing but the performance.

They circled each other on stage, singing to the rafters, and the world seemed to drop away.

That is until a scream punctured the bubble of their duet and the orchestra stopped playing with a discordant mess of noise.

"Piangi!"

Christophe looked to the source of the scream, just off-stage in the shadow of the wings, Elise, the ballet dancer, was pointing at a limp form on the floor.

"The Phantom of the Opera!" another of the chorus shouted.

The conductor leaned forward, peering with narrowed eyes as if he could somehow see through the cloak to see the identity of the man playing José.

"What did you do?" Christophe hissed. Eric wrapped his arm around Christophe and leaned close.

"I was watching but I couldn't help myself. I couldn't bear watching him paw all over you when I know he doesn't respect you. You are mine and not his."

Christophe's heart thumped hard and they looked around, hoping for guidance. The performance was in tatters.

A shout from the audience. "Who's that on stage?"

"Is it him?"

"Is it the Phantom in that cloak?"

"He has Christophe!"

"Pull the curtain!"

Eric tugged Christophe off stage, towards the back. The opposite side to where Elise had found Piangi's body.

A shot rang out, desperately loud over the panic. Something punched a hole in the painted backdrop close to Christophe.

"Those careless fools, they'll hit you in their madness," Eric said. He wrapped his cloak around them both and led them to a trapdoor in the furthermost corner of the wings. "Quick, come down here."

He opened the door and gestured for Christophe to jump down first. Christophe lowered themself into the space and hurried in, not sure exactly where they were headed, except that it would be safe if they were with Eric.

9

MATTHIEU

Matthieu despaired. The heartless killing of Piangi in the middle of the performance was apparently the tipping point for the patrons and population of the theatre. While the Phantom had been an interesting story, a notorious point of difference for the Opera La Rêve, this had stirred the audience into true anger.

The theatre managers were shouting, calling in the gendarme. The head officer led a huge troupe, and directed them to search every corner of the place to winnow him out and shoot on sight.

The members of the chorus were in a panic as well, rushing here and there, trading stories which got more outlandish with each telling - although they had a significant place to start from with Piangi's body stabbed on the floor-boards and slowly bleeding his last.

Heartsick, Matthieu looked first for Christophe, but they and Eric seemed to have vanished entirely. No doubt another secret door or similar.

Instead, Matthieu made his way to the boxes, to try and

find Raoul. Raoul met him halfway, his face pale and his eyes wide.

"What happened, Matty?"

Matthieu shrugged, feeling hopeless "I can only guess. Eric saw Christophe sing, was overcome and took Piangi's place on stage."

"I thought there was a difference in the quality of the singing," Raoul mused.

Matthieu rolled his eyes and took Raoul by the hand. "The quality of the singing is the *last* thing we should be worrying about right now."

Raoul snapped to attention and he nodded. Matthieu noticed he had a white silk scarf wrapped around his neck, presumably to hide the collar that Eric had locked on him.

But again, that was not the thing to be distracted by.

"We need to find them," Matthieu said.

"Of course. They'll have gone below, I presume," Raoul said. "There's a passageway nearby, the one he uses to get to Box five."

Matthieu bit his lip. "Do you know where it is? I've never used this one."

Over the last week he had learned the position of two more of the doors Eric used to get around, but neither of them were over this side of the theatre. Raoul shook his head.

"Best we use one of the tried and true ones, perhaps. The changing room?"

Matthieu tugged on Raoul's hand, already heading that way. "Between the two of us hopefully we can-"

Madame Giry blocked the way to the dressing room. Her expression was exceptionally stern and uncompromising. Her cane planted on the floor before her, both hands stacked on the handle. Matthieu's heart sank.

"Matthieu," she said. "Unhand the Vicomte and come home at once."

Matthieu had learned that contradicting his mother generally was the worst possible course of action. But this wasn't an ordinary night, and it hadn't been an ordinary week. Matthieu knew that she had noticed the golden cuff bracelet that Matthieu had been wearing since the Masquerade. She had raised an eyebrow but said nothing of it, asked nothing.

"Mother, I can't. I have to find Christophe, immediately, and... and the Phantom as well. Raoul is part of that as well."

Madame Giry's expression softened somewhat as she looked between the two of them.

"Madame, please," Raoul said. He stepped forward so his shoulder brushed Matthieu's. "It does seem as if you understand more than most about the Phantom, and his circumstances. Is there anything you can tell us that might help?"

Madame Giry shook her head slightly but Matthieu dropped Raoul's hand to move forward and take one of his mother's. "Mother, if there's any way you can assist? We know so little of him, but we want to help. We want to stop the violence and the madness, if it's at all possible."

Madame Giry looked deep into Matthieu's eyes, surprised at his forthrightness, perhaps. But the expression turned into understanding. She slipped her hand up his wrist to reverently touch the golden cuff.

"I see. I see what you've been doing. If it will help, then... I know very little, honestly. But I don't think he has ever had anything but fear and hatred from others. Why else would he choose to live as he does?"

"He loves music so much," Matthieu said. "He can hear it here."

"And there was a space for him to carve out," Madame

Giry nodded. "Christophe, I think, has the sort of pure soul who can accept and love without prejudice. He is capable of seeing with eyes unclouded by hate. If the two of you can also do that, if you can show him that you all love him, accept him, perhaps he will feel he can belong."

Matthieu breathed out hard and nodded.

There was a low rumble of noise from the door that led to the theatre proper and Madame Giry gripped Matthieu's wrist. "The mob is forming. They will not be satisfied until he is dead."

"Mob?" Raoul sounded surprised.

"One 'accident' too many," Madame Giry said. "Piangi was beloved, for a long time, and the crew and cast of the theatre do not enjoy living in fear. They have been pushed too far now."

Raoul ducked past to look through the door. He came back, pale. "We must hurry."

"Mother, I-" Matthieu started. Madame Giry shook her head.

"As the Vicomte said, you must hurry. I will do what I can to buy you time, but you must not be found with him! And make sure Christophe shows them that he hasn't been harmed, if you can."

Matthieu leaned in to kiss his mother on the cheek and then he resumed hurrying to Christophe's changing room. Raoul was close behind.

Eric

ERIC HAD TAKEN Christophe without thinking.

In fact, thinking seemed to have rather deserted him for the evening. Instinct had taken over his entire being.

He had acted without consideration when he dispatched of Piangi, he simply had known that he should be the one on stage with Christophe. Touching their waist beneath that exquisite red dress. Feeling the ropes he had given to Raoul with careful instructions.

When he made the plan he'd thought he would have been able to be patient for the entire performance, only taking what was his after the final curtain call.

But his impulses took control as he watched Christophe flirt and flounce across the stage. As he heard the dulcet tones of Christophe's voice reaching the upper registers that Eric himself had trained them to.

His impulses were all of fierce possession and desire.

He had moved without knowing he did it, strode through the back passageways and to the stage wings, where it had been terribly simple to knife Piangi and take the outermost pieces of his costume.

Then Eric had been on stage, his own singing voice heard for once by ears other than his own. His strong tenor filled the opera house. Now blending with Christophe's soprano, now acting in counterpoint, a hedonistic experience of pure beauty that Eric would hold in his heart forever.

It had been a wonderfully heady sensation, knowing that the audience heard and saw him, although he had taken care to hide his face and the mask from the crowd. He had never wanted to be seen before, but in that moment it was akin to touching the face of God.

But in his haste he had neglected to properly conceal the

dead body. Rash, impulsive and ultimately foolish. The dream he had briefly enjoyed had finished, and he had to face the end of everything.

Here they were, rushing down one of his hidden staircases to his lair, Christophe panting and afraid behind him. He'd kept his hand clamped around their wrist, terrified that he'd pushed them too far, that Christophe would finally see him for the monster he was. That if he let go, Christophe would flee.

His thoughts had returned to him, and they were all of fear. What had he done? How far could he push his angel or his other pets before they rebelled against him and left him alone again.

Horrified, he felt tears well up at the idea of losing them.

He tore off his mask and threw it down in the entrance of the tunnel before arriving in the back of his living space. He growled in frustration, yanking off the costume pieces and discarding those as well before finally, finally making himself face the cowering Christophe.

"Well?" he demanded. Christophe flinched back from him, hand flying to their chest and eyes round. The damage was well and truly done. Eric decided to get it over with quickly. "Well, now do you see what a monster I am? The full extent of my depravity and the danger I am to you?"

Christophe took a breath and shook their head.

Eric hadn't expected that response. The part of him which loathed himself wanted to be punished by Christophe's words. Needed to see the fear in their eyes, so it would know it was correct, he was a monster.

So, he advanced with three steps, looming over Christophe who cringed back as perfectly as if they had rehearsed it.

"You can't pretend you don't fear me," Eric said. His voice

was strained, more growl than tenor now. "I can see it in your face, in your body language. You are just like the others, you fear and then you hate, and then you abandon!"

His voice cracked on the final word and he brought his fist to his mouth, biting on his own scarred knuckle to try and gather himself again.

Christophe was crying, tears running freely down their face. Eric's heart twisted to see it, the last thing he ever wanted was to frighten Christophe and here he was doing it on purpose.

"Yes, tears, tears and screams, those are the sounds I should hear."

Eric turned away, swallowing back his own sob, and went to his piano. There was music partially composed on it. He hardly knew what he'd been thinking - writing something of his own? There was no way that anyone would ever put on an opera written by a monster. He lashed out, scattering the papers then leaning his weight on the keys of the piano, making a strange discordant noise.

He kicked the pieces of his composition away, tore his stolen jacket off and threw it across the room. In the back of his head he knew he was acting irrationally, being destructive for no good reason, but the larger part of him roared.

That part of him knew that destruction was all he deserved. A monster like him didn't deserve love or pleasure, didn't deserve three attentive pets to care for. He turned to the nearest candelabra and hauled it over so it smashed onto the ground, candles rolling everywhere. He roared his frustration out loud, revelling in letting the monster take control.

He turned back, half considering lashing out at Christophe next, but they had covered their face with both hands and were sobbing so pathetically the monster went quiet.

The energy drained out of him abruptly and he sank to his knees, resting his arm on the piano bench and his head on his arm. It was all utterly hopeless.

He could no sooner hurt Christophe than he could restrain his own evil impulses.

He heard footsteps and sighed. Probably the theatre managers and the gendarme, come to kill him. Make him pay for his crimes.

So let them come.

* * *

Christophe

CHRISTOPHE SANK TO THEIR KNEES, buried their face in their hands and sobbed.

Their mind was a confusion of emotions: fear, yes and pain. Pain that Eric thought this was the only course of action he could take. Those years of neglect and isolation had convinced him so completely that he was in fact a monster. Christophe cried for him, and for themself, dragged into such a bizarre and complex situation, and for their father, as well.

The idea of Eric had always been tied up with the stories a beloved father told of the Angel of Music. They had wanted so desperately for a link to their father, to what they had lost, they had cleaved to Eric, to his teachings and his guidance, and not given it a second thought.

They looked deep inside their own heart in a confused

whirl, trying to understand what was real and what was made up. Were any of these feelings real?

Had they attached themself to Eric out of a misguided need for a father figure?

Perhaps, in the first instance. Christophe had to admit that they had been willing to fool themself just at first.

But perhaps in the time that had passed since, those feelings had changed.

Or had they? Christophe wiped his eyes on the back of his costume sleeve and immediately regretted it. The stiff lace wasn't absorbent or soothing.

Had their feelings for Eric, for their Angel, their Master, been true, or had they simply wished them to be? Were they playing another part, like Carmen or...

No. They shook this idea off. They knew they weren't acting when it came to how they were around Eric. They wanted to be with him, yearned to be.

That had to be real.

Christophe had felt it after all. Had seen the looks of adoration, and the willingness to push themselves past what was ordinary or acceptable.

So, what they had to do now was convince Eric that it was true. Eric was just as confused as Christophe, they could see that. He was a wreck.

Christophe sniffed, ignored the tears rolling down their face and went over to where Eric was slumped. They hesitated a split second before putting their hand on his shoulder.

Eric's body startled slightly but there was no other reaction. His sobs were soft and unabated, the broken crying of a man who has given up on everything.

Christophe sank to their knees and wrapped their arms around him. "Eric, it's all right."

Steps sounded nearby, someone approaching?

Christophe looked up, peering into the darkness towards the sound and saw two figures. Relief washed over them when they saw it was Raoul and Matthieu. But they knew Eric wasn't ready to talk to anyone yet, so they waved and then gestured for the two newcomers to stay put.

"Eric, please," Christophe said. "I'm here with you, and I'm not going."

Eric shifted, pulled away from Christophe's grasp and half turned to look at them. "You should leave. You will leave, it's inevitable."

"I won't."

"Why are you lying about this? No one wants me, a monster, a disfigured thing. You fear me, you all fear me!"

Christophe took a deep breath, they thought they understood what Eric needed to hear now. "I do fear you." Christophe said. "You frightened me badly just before." Eric made a strangled noise, regret and pain at what he'd done. Christophe continued talking. "But I know you didn't mean all that. You don't want me to go, you're just afraid of me leaving so you're trying to scare me off before it happens."

Eric looked away, past Christophe's shoulder at Raoul and Matthieu, nearby. "You should all go, have a good life. Leave me here to the mercy of the mob."

"Well, we're not going to." Christophe took hold of Eric's chin and forced him to look at them directly. "Eric. We need you. Do you think any of us can see so clearly what we need the way you can? You have a gift, you can see what people need and you give it to them, you've made us all better in some way, and I at least, am hungry for more."

"I am too," Matthieu said. He moved closer, Raoul by his side. Christophe let go of Eric's chin but threaded their fingers through his and squeezed. "I've been in love with Christophe for as long as I can remember, but I was never brave enough to say anything, to do anything about it. You have opened up the door for our affection, I might never have done anything without you."

"The door is open now." Eric gestured dismissively. "You don't need me any longer."

"I need you," Raoul said. "You show me the importance of restraint. I have always been impulsive, taking action and not thinking of the consequences. I'd have whisked Christophe away on that first night and perhaps they never would have performed again, if it had been up to me."

Christophe made an indignant noise, and Raoul responded with an apologetic look. "I'm sorry, Chris, but I might have. And then I expect after a whirlwind romance of a few weeks we would have tired of each other and been full of regrets. That's how it always is."

Christophe's full heart ached. "Raoul..."

"It's better with you," Raoul said. He came closer still, crouched on the far side of Eric. Eric turned to him and peered into his eyes. "You saw my recklessness and took me in hand. And I fought you, and I'll probably fight you again, but it feels so right, and so good every time you conquer me."

Christophe's body flooded with heat, hearing Raoul talk in that manner. Matthieu knelt beside Christophe and slipped an arm around them.

"We must leave," Matthieu said. "The mob... my mother said she can hold it off for a time, but she won't be able to do much for long. Please, Eric. We need you."

Eric

Eric couldn't understand why they were saying such things. Christophe, Raoul and Matthieu had each other now, they didn't need him. They would be so much better off without him, he knew that. He would never be able to control himself.

The monster inside him would always win.

It always had before.

And now a mob would come and put an end to his misery forever. It was as it should be, the correct ending to his story.

He had enjoyed a perfect night and morning with three of them, it was more than he deserved to have. More than he could have dreamed of.

With an effort, he stood, pulled away from Chrisophe's pawing and turned away from all of them. How could he convince them to leave?

He would have to show them the monster again. He cleared his throat, focused on the rageful monster within and found... it wouldn't respond.

Growling with frustration, he brought both hands to his forehead and tugged on his hair. He just had to focus on the things which had angered him before. Someone touching Christophe on stage, someone insulting Christophe.

He urged his anger to overtake him. But this was something he had never attempted before, and he didn't seem to have the skill for it. The rage had always come unbidden, and he had no idea now how to provoke it.

The flame of rage kindled slightly, but stayed small. He strode across the room, deliberately knocking candlesticks over. Maybe he could set the place aflame, and then they'd see how he deserved to be left alone. His tears were running freely down his face. He lifted the trunk of clothes, second hand, stolen from audience members and theatre staff alike. It was heavy, but Eric was strong. He tipped it on its side with a mighty effort and let all the things he'd collected spill out. His ears rang from the effort. He pushed the trunk over and it fell with a crash.

"Eric!"

He didn't look around to see which of them called. He went to the bed and tore the bedclothes off it, ripping the sheets in his hands. He had no idea why he was doing any of it, but he didn't have any other clue what to do.

Christophe appeared beside him, put a hand on his arm, their voice was soft and tender far too soft for Eric's ears. "Eric, will you please listen?"

He shook them off. "You need to go," he growled. "The mob will be here soon. Protect yourself."

Firm hands caught him by the waist and turned him around. Eric was so surprised he was speechless. Raoul stood tall, holding him firmly in place. His eyes blazed as he stared Eric down.

"You are acting like a child," Raoul said. "Why aren't you listening to us?"

Eric hesitated. His first instinct was to shake Raoul off, to tell him to leave all over again. But his second instinct responded to the way Raoul was looking at him. He demanded attention. Eric had never submitted to anyone in his life, and he wasn't about to start, but he had to admit that Raoul had a power to him, a commanding presence.

"Please, Eric," Matthieu appeared beside Raoul and his huge blue eyes beseeched Eric. "We care about you, and we want to help. The mob... it is almost upon us."

The ringing in Eric's ears had faded and he listened.

Indeed, there was the noise of trampling, of voices. They had found one of the tunnels that would lead them here.

Perhaps the very entrance he had used to whisk Christophe off stage.

He couldn't let them find Christophe, Raoul and Matthieu in his presence.

He wanted, so much, to believe them when they said they desired him, wanted to stay with him, but he was so afraid.

"How can I trust that you won't feel differently in time?" he said, finally, his voice weak.

Christophe

CHRISTOPHE STEPPED FORWARD, taking one of Eric's hands. Raoul had let go of one of his arms, but held the other, perhaps afraid he would bolt. Christophe squeezed his hand and willed him to believe.

"We are right here with you and we'll do whatever you need to prove it to you," Christophe said. "I promise, and I know the others do too."

"And we will escape with you tonight," Matthieu said. "It might take time to fully understand how it will all work, but I believe we are all devoted to you. We want forever."

"I will fight for what I want," Raoul said. "And I want you. As Matty says, now and forever."

Christophe held his breath.

Eric took a long moment to look into each of their eyes, and Christophe knew he was searching for something he was utterly unfamiliar with - sincerity.

Finally, he nodded once. When he spoke again all evidence of his hurt was gone and replaced with decisiveness, although there was a hoarseness to his tone which made Christophe's heart twist with compassion.

"There's a tunnel to the street, it's long and narrow, but passable. I just need a few of my things, and we can escape that way." Eric broke away from Raoul and Christophe's holds, and hauled a worn out leather satchel from under the bed and started stashing things into it.

"But where do we go from there?" Christophe wondered. "We cannot take him back to the apartments."

"You and Raoul need to meet the mob, Chris, show them that you're safe," Matthieu said. "They will not stop chasing if they think he has stolen you."

"We will go back and meet them. We will tell them I killed the Phantom. After it's all sorted out, I'll call my carriage, and we will come around the back of the theatre to collect you," Raoul said. "After that, we shall go to the countryside. I have a chateau near a forest, a half day's ride away. We can be there before the sun rises."

Christophe chewed their lip and nodded. "That sounds perfect."

<hr />

Matthieu

MATTHIEU DIDN'T ENJOY the clamber through the ill-used passage that led into the street behind the theatre, but it was a relief to get into the night air and see the distant stars again.

Eric seemed rather moved as well, he had a satchel full of music compositions strapped across his chest, and a suitcase of clothing which he lugged behind him. Matthieu had been given a bag with a few of Eric's more fun inventions inside it and he followed behind as closely as he could.

When they made it out to the back alley, Eric closed the door behind them and locked it with a padlock he produced from a pocket. They hid behind a stack of old boxes just to be prudent.

Time moved slowly, and they didn't speak for fear of drawing attention, but Eric held Matthieu's hand and his grip was steady.

Presently, a carriage came up the alley and came to a stop. Raoul opened the door and escorted them both inside. Eric and Matthieu found seats, Raoul gave instruction to the driver, and quickly they were leaving Paris behind entirely.

Christophe told them of how they had met the mob, and watched as they tore through Eric's former residence. They'd trampled his porcelain mask underfoot and found nothing at all.

Raoul had claimed to run him through with his sword, and he had vanished entirely, a true phantom.

Eric snorted. "And I expect the fools believed that?"

"They did," Raoul said. "They had no reason to doubt me, when Christophe agreed that's how it happened."

"I think they were quite pleased to think he was truly a ghost," Christophe said. "At any rate, they all calmed down and the theatre will reopen again in a few days, once I'm rested."

There was a pause as they all considered the narrowness of their escape.

"This chateau of yours," Matthieu said. "Is it a safe place for Eric to stay indefinitely?"

"It is," Raoul said. He was sitting with his arm around Christophe, Matthieu and Eric sat opposite, and Matthieu had ensured that his leg was pressed against Eric's as a gentle reassurance. "There are only a few servants there, and they are loyal, they knew my parents, and would never betray any secret we have. They have never spread word of any of my previous dalliances, perhaps there will be a little more adjustment this time, but I shall explain things to them and ensure they understand the need for utmost discretion."

Eric sniffed a little, but his eyes were turned to the small carriage window, quite focused on the view as it changed from Paris buildings to less built up areas.

"You're so generous, Raoul," Christophe said. They turned their head and fluttered their eyelashes at him. Matthieu smiled, feeling endeared by the both of them.

"And, just so we're all in agreement and on exactly the same understanding," Matthieu said. "Are all four of us going to be in a relationship with one another?"

Eric turned away from the window then, and his hand found Matthieu's thigh, squeezing it rather tightly.

"I thought that was rather obvious, Matty," Christophe said. They looked at Eric and then Matthieu. "Isn't it?"

"I would feel better if we all agreed on it out loud, I think," Matthieu said. He placed his hand over Eric's. "Perhaps I'm being insecure, but I would like to hear it."

"Yes," Raoul said. "It's very strange, but well, we're nearing the turn of the century, I expect it won't be so shocking at all in a few years."

Christophe nodded. "And I couldn't live without each of you. I need you all, and I love you all."

"I cannot guarantee my behaviour will always be what it should be," Eric said softly. "But perhaps, in a quiet place such as the countryside, with no society fools or music critics around, I will be able to be more civilised."

"I have no doubt of that," Christophe said. They leaned forward, bracing one hand on Matthieu's knee to plant a kiss on the unmasked side of Eric's face. "You need a new start, and our darling Raoul has been able to provide it."

"You can work on your compositions," Raoul said. He gave a small smile. "There's a very fine piano sitting unused for some years now."

Eric's eyes lit up at that prospect. "I am honoured that the three of you would devote yourselves to me, and to each other. I hope to be worthy of it, and to serve you as the best possible Master that I can be."

"I hope there's a room that Eric can use as a torture chamber, as well," Matthieu said. He pressed a little closer to Eric and fiddled with the golden cuff. "I definitely need more training to be a good pet, I think. I'm very new to it after all."

Raoul's cheeks pinked and he nodded. "Of course, we can convert one of the guest rooms easily enough."

"Perfect." Christophe flopped back into Raoul's arms and half over his lap. "Now, I think I need to sleep."

"We probably all should," Matthieu said.

Eric pulled Matthieu into his arms, and stroked his back gently. Matthieu felt all the tension in his body ease away with each touch. "Rest then, Kitten. I believe it will take me some time to relax, but I will keep you safe."

IO

SIX MONTHS LATER

Christophe

Christophe went down to breakfast after waking up in their own room. Each of them had their own rooms in the Chateau de Chagny so that if they chose to have time to themselves they could. It also made it easier for comings and goings, since Matthieu and Christophe had rehearsal and performance schedules, and Eric was up at all sorts of odd hours, working whenever his muse took him.

Raoul, for his part, split his time between the chateau and Paris depending on where he was needed. His work, Christophe had observed, seemed to revolve around appearing at luncheons and dinners to show his support of the businesses he had stocks in, or patronised in some other way. Sometimes he had extended family that needed to be visited, and more recently he had taken to donating to charitable causes, and appearing at dinners and luncheons for the poor and needy.

During performance season Matthieu and Christophe stayed in Paris of course.

At this time, they had a four-day break after the preview performance for the new opera, the one that Eric had himself penned, and had both returned to the country to be with Eric and Raoul. Soon they would return to Paris and the season would start properly, and Eric and Raoul might spend some time in Raoul's townhouse, so as to view the opera themselves, and be close at hand.

Christophe had enjoyed the night alone in their bed and felt very well rested. When they arrived at the breakfast table there was no one else there but a newspaper was folded on the place that Christophe usually sat at.

The front page of the paper showed Christophe, in costume as the Angel of Music, the title role in Eric's opera. The feathered wings looked rather becoming, Christophe noticed. The headline was under the fold, so they opened out the paper to read *Opera La Rêve's Diva Shines in Ambitious New Show*

Despite the strange affairs at the Opera La Rêve, and the murders which occured there, the Opera has risen phoenix-like to new and astounding heights. The new writing talent behind the Angel of Music - a new opera by a mysterious foreigner by the name of Enrico Fantasma, is undoubtedly a success.

Christophe Daaé has proved a true star, performing in various roles over the last six months to great acclaim. The transcendent confidence of Christophe's performance is unmatched by any this reviewer has seen. One also notes that many audience members have come away as enthusiastic fans of the young diva.

The review went on like that, raving about the show. Christophe read it while eating a croissant, and was soon joined by Matthieu, who poured himself a large cup of coffee and piled his plate with fruit and pastries. He sat down in his customary place, opposite Christophe.

"Look at this," Christophe handed the paper to Matthieu.

"Well, they're right, you are a transcendent performer," Matthieu said, after a moment. "I'm glad they noticed."

Raoul joined them next, dressed in his riding gear. "Good morning you two," he said. He kissed them both on the forehead and took his usual seat next to Christophe.

"How was the hunting this morning?" Matthieu asked.

"Very good," Raoul said. "Three pheasants to have for dinner. I've given them to Mrs Dubois to sort out."

Mrs Dubois was the head of the household, and when they had arrived in the early hours of the morning, tired and bedraggled all those months ago, she had taken one look at them and welcomed them into the warmth of the kitchen. She'd provided hot coffee, freshly baked pastries and all but adopted Eric as her own child, for all the attention and care she gave him from the first. If any of the other servants had any misgivings over Eric and his appearance, Mrs Dubois sorted it out instantly. Eric, for his part, adored Mrs Dubois, and Christophe reckoned that his behaviour had begun to improve instantly because of wishing to please her.

"Has anyone seen Eric this morning?" Christophe asked.

"He was working on a new song last night," Raoul said. "I believe he was up late."

Just at that moment, Eric walked in. He looked a little dishevelled, perhaps having been awake the entire night. He had stopped wearing a makeshift mask after the first month of settling into the chateau and Christophe had come to love each scar and imperfection on his face, just as they loved the imperfections of their other two lovers.

"Good morning, Master," Christophe said. Their heart

filled with joy, the way it always did when the four of them were reunited.

"Good morning, Angel." Eric kissed Christophe and settled at the head of the table, smiling at them all with a familiar sparkle in his eyes. Christophe felt butterflies in their chest. The fact they had been together for months, and they still felt excited to be around each other was something magical indeed.

———◆———

Raoul

RAOUL HAD SELECTED a guest bedroom on the second floor to be the designated torture chamber. He'd had wood, building supplies and tools brought in, and Eric had spent a week renovating it. Once it was done, Christophe had renamed it the Play Room and they had been using it fairly frequently ever since.

Now, as he led Matthieu and Christophe there at Eric's order, Raoul's mind wandered back to his days before he had been reunited with Christophe. He reflected briefly on the summarily disappointing sexual encounters he had experienced before then. The kind of encounter seemed unfathomable now.

Eric had ordered him to take the other two up there, and undress them. They were all three instructed to be waiting, collared and kneeling for Eric when he arrived. Christophe and Matthieu didn't seem to mind at all when Raoul appointed him as a sort of second in command, and he enjoyed the chance to be the bossy one every so often, but they all three knew that it was Eric who was their Master, even if Raoul was sometimes also holding a leash, or a whip.

Raoul had no idea what to expect, beyond pleasure.

He had learned so much about obedience and patience from Eric over the last six months. Although he did sometimes still like to act up and push back, it was usually because he needed to be put in his place.

Or because he could see that Eric needed to get some anger out, and Raoul enjoyed the more painful punishments more than the other two did.

In some of their early training sessions together, Eric had explained that some people were naturally dominant, like he was. Some were naturally submissive like Christophe and Matthieu, and some people fell somewhere in between. Raoul was one of those who liked control some of the time, and liked to give it up other times. Eric, having studied humankind from the outside, was a genius at interpreting people's needs. Raoul was glad for it, and for the trust Eric put in him to be the dominant one over Chris and Matty, some of the time.

Beside him, Christophe was breathing slowly, smiling softly, their eyes half-lidded.

On the other side, Matthieu was the opposite. His chest heaved with quick breaths, no doubt anticipating what was to come, just as Raoul was.

The three of them had individual collars. Raoul's was the same one Eric had locked on him months ago, although he had some periods of time without it when he had to do business or travel, and in those times Eric had made modifications to it, namely making it thicker and putting more rings on it for more complex bondage.

Christophe's collar was a piece of art. A white leather collar with two rings that fit around the neck, and a vertical column connecting them in front and back. Each side of the collar was decorated with feathery leather wings that laid flat against their throat. It was delicate, artistic, and beautiful, just like Christophe.

Matthieu's was similarly beautiful while also being the most utilitarian of them all. Eric had a fondness for putting gold on Matthieu, so his collar was a gold plated metal piece that sat low on the neck, curved gently to a low swoop in the hollow of his throat. A ring sat there, waiting for the long gold chain that Eric liked to wrap around Matthieu's body.

At the sound of footsteps in the hallway all three of them tensed. Sat up straighter, spread their knees apart just a little more and put their hands behind their backs, as Eric liked them to pose as they waited for him.

Eric pushed the door open, his shirt unbuttoned. The country air and the company of Mrs Dubois had been good for him. There was a golden tinge to his skin from regular time in the sun. His body had become more muscular from the good, regular food that Raoul's staff served. But the biggest change had been the one in Eric's mind. Out in the quiet he had found a stillness he told them he had never known, and his own fears of rejection had been assuaged. He had relaxed in every sense of the word. Dominating the three of them had given him an outlet for his anger and his impulses, and he had thrown himself into writing his first full-length opera.

He paused in the door and looked between them.

"Such good pets, waiting for me so nicely. Just how you've been trained. I'm very pleased with my angelic bunny, my good dog and my pretty kitten."

Raoul felt a smile come to his face, but he knew better than to say anything unless specifically asked.

"Today we are all back together for the first time in some weeks," Eric continued. "So, we are all going to enjoy each other. First, Puppy, heel." Raoul went to his hands and knees and crawled to Eric's feet. "You may stand, Pup. You're going to help me bind these two."

"Thank you, Master," Raoul said as he got to his feet.

Eric went to the shelves of supplies and picked up a bamboo cane and a long coil of rope. He picked up Matthieu's golden chain and handed that to Raoul. "Use Kitten's bracelet to bind his hands behind his back, then fasten the chain to his collar."

Raoul nodded and turned to do as he said, but felt the cane whip his ass without warning. Raoul froze.

"You didn't answer me," Eric said.

Raoul felt the harsh sting of the cane melt into pleasure and the shock of it sped his heart up pleasantly. "I'm sorry Master." Raoul turned back and bowed his head. "I understand your instructions, Master."

"Much better." Eric raised the cane to press under Raoul's chin, forcing him to look up. Eric's eyes were sparkling, hungry, pleased and exciting all at once. Raoul's mouth went dry and tingles of excitement shot through his body. His cock was already hard and with Eric's cane under his chin he started to leak. Eric held him like that for a moment, and then let the cane drop, releasing him.

Raoul got to work. By this time they all knew the trick to turning Matthieu's cuff into handcuffs, so it was quick work to secure him. Raoul took a moment to stroke his fingertips up Matthieu's arms, caressing the lean muscles and smiling when Matthieu pressed back against him, encouraging him to take a little more. Raoul looked up to see Eric had lifted

Christophe to their feet and was therefore distracted, not watching to ensure Raoul was working as fast as possible. The spark of rebellion in Raoul flared up again and he leaned in to kiss Matthieu's shoulder, then up his neck, and was rewarded with a deep moan.

Matthieu turned his head and Raoul kissed him on the mouth, his hands circling around to tease at Matthieu's nipples in the way that always had him trembling.

"Well, isn't that a pretty sight?" Eric said. Raoul looked up from where he was sucking a mark into Matthieu's shoulder and grinned. Eric was in the midst of tying Christophe into a rope harness, and had turned them so they could both watch Raoul and Matthieu.

Matthieu moaned a little louder, they had discovered he had particular enjoyment for being watched, and Raoul tugged on his nipples with a tight pinch.

"However, your orders were quite clear, Puppy. If you don't wish to feel the cane, you'll be more obedient."

Raoul's cock twitched, so he pressed against Matthieu's ass, groaning at the friction. He wanted to be corrected, and Eric had given him the opportunity.

Eric tutted his tongue. "The leash, Pup. Or you get the cane."

Raoul whined like the disobedient puppy he was, and pulled back so he could pick up the chain, and clip it to Matthieu's collar. Then he went right back to teasing Matthieu and grinding himself against him so they were both panting and moaning.

There was a sharp tug on Raoul's hair and his head was forced back. "Hands to yourself, Puppy. I know our kitten is desperately beautiful, but you must only do what you are instructed."

Eric's eyes sparkled even more, and with a hand fisted in his hair, Raoul was pulled upright.

"I *was* going to suspend Christophe so that we could all have a turn fucking their hole and their mouth, but if you're going to be a recalcitrant pet then perhaps I shouldn't give you such a lovely treat."

That snapped Raoul to attention and the spark of rebellion quelled instantly. "No, please, Master. I'll be good, I'll do anything you say."

Eric hummed, disbelieving. "Well, that remains to be seen. But I suppose I can give you one more chance to behave."

He tugged Raoul by the hair to help with Christophe. Christophe's eyes were pleasantly unfocused, and Raoul recognised the special fuzziness of the mind that came from submitting to Eric's ministrations.

He wanted to lean in and kiss Christophe, but he was determined now to obey and not do anything he hadn't been ordered to.

Christophe

CHRISTOPHE'S HEART WAS THUNDERING.

Eric had spoken of suspension before, even made sketches and shown them to Christophe, but he had never actually done it before. On top of that, Eric had said they would be taking turns with Christophe, which further aroused them.

Between Eric and Raoul they soon had Christophe suspended from the exposed rafter by many ropes. The ropes looped around the tops of Christophe's thighs and their lower torso, complicated knots that distributed the weight evenly and reduced the amount of pain, although there was still some pain, it was endurable.

There were ropes around their chest as well, binding their folded arms tightly behind their back, and stringing from their shoulders up to the ceiling.

Their legs were tied bent in half, spreading them wide open and ready and Christophe's entire body felt on fire, ready to be used.

Once Eric had tied the last knot on their ankle, he called Matthieu over.

"Kitten, lick the angel open while they fly for us." Christophe moaned at the order, rolling their hips uselessly as there was no friction to be found to ease their need.

Christophe swung gently back and forth, moaning, as Matthieu got to work. He had shuffled over on his knees, chest pushed out, arms cuffed behind him. Matthieu's tongue was sinfully good, circling Christophe's hole and then dipping inside, quick and gentle. Kitten was exactly the correct nickname for him.

Eric caught Christophe's attention again, as he walked around to their head. He wound their hair into a thick cord and bound that with rope too, fixing it in such a way that Christophe was forced to look up, throat extended, although their body was parallel to the floor.

They were now utterly exposed and helpless, and their mind soared with the joy of it. The anticipation of what was about to happen made them moan almost as much as the way Matthieu was tonguing them.

"Please, Master," Christophe moaned, their voice cracked with need. "I can't take more teasing. I need to be filled, please!"

Eric hummed, always a little more indulgent with Christophe than he was with the others. "Very well, Angel. Let me just secure our puppy first..."

Christophe watched as Eric pulled Raoul to him, kissed him hard and then bound his hands in front of him with rope. Christophe moaned as Matthieu pressed his tongue deep inside and almost sobbed with need. The sight of their kissing had only increased their need for more.

"Please!"

Matthieu

"So DEMANDING," Eric said. He didn't sound at all annoyed though. Matthieu knew he was about to give in and give Christophe everything they asked for. "Here, you can lick Pup."

He positioned Raoul in front of their face and Christophe immediately started to lick from the sounds Raoul was making. Matthieu pressed harder with his mouth, hoping for a reward for being so obedient.

Eric moved into sight and smiled down at Matthieu. "Such a good Kitten, licking so nicely, got Christophe nice and open for us, didn't you?"

He reached for Matthieu's leash and gently pulled him back. "I'm very pleased with you, Kitten. You may fuck Christophe first for your reward."

He tugged Matthieu into standing, retrieved a pot of oil

from nearby and gently oiled Christophe up, and then slicked Matthieu's cock with it as well.

"Thank you, Master," Matthieu said. His voice was always came out a little softer, more breathy than usual when they played like this. Eric leaned in and kissed Matthieu hard, another reward, and one that he melted into. He yearned to reach out and wrap his arms around Eric, but he couldn't deny he loved being bound, as well. The knowledge that what happened was entirely up to someone else was endlessly arousing to him.

Eric gripped Matthieu's hips and moved him into place, helping to guide his cock inside Christophe and slapping both their asses once Matthieu was deep inside.

"Fuck Christophe until you come, Kitten," Eric commanded. Matthieu nodded, very happy to carry out that particular order.

"Thank you, Master."

Eric stalked back around to Christophe's head, where Raoul was holding onto the ropes connecting Christophe to the rafters and rolling his hips as he fucked their mouth.

"Are you close to coming, Pup?" Eric asked. He had the cane back in his hand now, and he drew it across Raoul's chest, causing him to pause his movements.

"Y-yes, Master," Raoul panted. His eyes were wide, afraid of being corrected, perhaps.

"Hold it. Pull out, and watch. You may not come yet."

Matthieu moaned, knowing what exquisite torture it was to be close and not allowed to fulfil oneself.

Eric tugged Raoul back by the collar, and took his place. Christophe eagerly sucked on him, eyes closed and moaning around his length.

Matthieu pumped his hips and came quickly, crying out, unable to hold back when he was already so aroused from

Raoul's earlier teasing, and from licking Christophe as well as fucking them.

"Good Kitten," Eric said. "And good Bunny." He caressed Christophe's jaw as he fucked into them. "Raoul, you take Matthieu's place and come inside Christophe, I want to feel both of you in there when I take my turn."

Matthieu moaned with the sheer filthiness of it all, and eased out as Raoul came up beside him. It was easier for Raoul to guide himself in with his hands bound in front, and Matthieu stepped back, uncertain of what to do next. Eric beckoned. "Here, Kitten." Matthieu went to Eric's side and moaned, watching his cock pump in and out of Christophe was almost enough to make him come again. Eric took hold of Matthieu's leash and pulled him in to kiss him, messy and rough, biting his lower lip. Christophe was a mess, moaning and writhing in the ropes, filled from both ends.

With a deep cry, Raoul filled Christophe and Eric broke the kiss with a grin. "You take the mouth now, and I'll finish off in Christophe. Do you want to come, Bunny?" Eric pulled out and Christophe took a quick breath before responding.

"Yes, please Master, I'm so hot."

"You may come when I fill you and not a moment before," Eric said. He pulled Matthieu close to Christophe's mouth. "Clean him up."

Matthieu moaned again as Christophe's tongue found his limp cock and licked it gently, retrieving every drop of mess.

Eric filled Christophe from behind and sent Raoul to kiss Matthieu and pet him. Matthieu was pleased with this, and leaned some of his weight on Raoul, who slipped his bound arms over Matthieu's head to encircle him and let him lean against him easier.

Eric gripped Christophe's hips and moaned, only thrusting a few times before he was coming as well. Matthieu watched with a fullness of heart he had never expected to experience.

He had Christophe's tongue on him, he had Raoul's arms around him, and soon Eric would begin the delightful spoiling and soothing that he did once their play was over, which was another reward as well.

Matthieu was full of love, and he felt truly loved in return.

His needs, even the ones he hadn't realised he had, were absolutely fulfilled. There had been so many changes in the six months, but now he knew he had stability. Christophe loved him back, and so did Raoul and Eric. Eric, who had changed so much with the new environment, who had mellowed, and become more himself and not a monster.

And of course, the special training.

Eric had given him a constant way to improve himself and his art, while also experiencing immense amounts of physical and emotional satisfaction. It wasn't simply obedience, but also self-control and self-knowledge, exploring the full range of what his body was capable of, and then extending himself further.

Eric untied Raoul and Matthieu, and got them both to assist in bringing Christophe back to the ground. Then he led them all to the massive bathtub Raoul had installed and began to care for their bodies, praising them all, and promising Raoul the caning he so clearly desired later in the day, if they were all up for it.

As he sank into the gently scented bathwater and leaned against Christophe, Raoul on his other side, and Eric on the other side of him, Matthieu knew that he was truly happy.

~ Fin

MONSTERS & MAYHEM
A CELEBRATION OF MM HORROR

A Delicious Descent

A Dracula Retelling by Amanda Meuwissen

M.M. Scrooge

A Christmas Carol Retelling by Lee Colgin

Also by Drake

Garden of Secrets

Alistair Lennox is disagreeable.

Isolated and miserable, with parents who don't care about him, his life has been equal parts privilege and loneliness.

But when his parents die, his life is turned upside down. In order to gain his inheritance, Alistair is forced to attend a college he's never heard of - for good reason. Misselthwaite College is a school for the magically gifted

Alistair has no magical gifts - unless being magically inept counts. What were his parents thinking? And what is the mysterious affliction plaguing William Carlisle, the affluent and arrogant heir to Misselthwaite? Is there a connection to the strange key Alistair discovers in a book, the stranger noises in the night, and, strangest of all, the multiple men who desire his friendship? Misselthwaite has no end of secrets.

But if being disagreeable is good for anything, it's for getting to the bottom of mysteries.

--

Garden of Secrets is book one in a duology, and the first installment in a magical new universe. A Secret Garden retelling with a queer twist and featuring MMMM polyamory.

Cabin Boy

I've never been what I was supposed to be. Wealthy sons of Port Governors aren't supposed to be ejected from the British Navy after less than a year, they're not supposed to like pulp romances or daydream about the handsome heroes of the stories instead of the heroines.

When my Father issued me an order to marry a woman, I knew I had no choice but to make my own way in the world, and I found a berth on the first ship out of Jamaica.

I didn't mean to join a pirate ship, and I certainly didn't intend to find myself the cabin boy to an incredibly charming Pirate Captain. Or that I'd also be attracted to the mysterious First Mate, or that both of them would show me all sorts of unspeakable and salacious pleasures while on board. How can I choose just one of them when I want both?

In addition to confusion on board the ship, there's also enchanting genderfluid merfolk, a cat which seems to understand a lot more than it should, an unseasonable storm and a sea witch with a serious grudge... and with all these complications, I am definitely in over my head.

--

Come and meet the crew:

Gideon: an innocent with a lot of forbidden desires and a lot of love to give

Tate: a huge, muscular ship's captain with a sweet side

Ezra: a dominant and closed off first mate

Ora: a genderqueer, curious and affectionate merman

Cabin Boy is a male/male paranormal gay harem romance featuring a naive hero with a gigantic heart (and anxiety) and one very smart ship's cat. First-person pov. This book is the first in a series and is not standalone. The entire series is published. HFN, with a HEA at the end of the series No cheating, high heat, lots of love.

All characters are 18 or older

Kidnapped by the Gentleman

Cedric has been kidnapped by pirates....

they have no idea how much trouble they're in for.

Cedric was living his best life, partying in the colonies, bedding whomever he pleased and trusting that his parents' money and affluence would get him out of any unfortunate scrapes. Until he was kidnapped by the fearsome pirate Lucifer, who planned to trade him for a hefty ransom. Unfortunately, he's not the only one after Cedric, and the strange secret society who have Cedric in their sights might just be more dangerous than Captain Lucifer.

Now Cedric is trapped on a pirate ship with a dashingly handsome captain, a quartermaster who won't stop staring at him and an overwhelming desire to find some fun, all while saving his hide from an unknown organisation who will stop at nothing to track him down.

This is the first book in a new gay pirate harem series from Drake LaMarque. Set in the same world as the His Piratical Harem series, this book features a plucky new main character, a new pirate ship and a Lovecraftesque new threat.

NOT a standalone, it ends on an HFN. All four books in the series are published and there's a HEA at the end.

Dark Attraction

Brand: A pansexual college surfer dude looking for love in all the wrong places

Gage: A mysterious goth with something to hide who will do anything to keep what's his

When they meet at a party, there's an instant attraction but between Gage's dominant hunger and Brand's need to submit to him... the fire may be all-consuming.

an MM vampire/human romance featuring lots of spice - start of a series!

#punkygothvampire #instalovekinda #consensualkink #spankinghappens #spicygames #justalotofrope #pwpkinda #liketheresomeplotbuteh

ABOUT THE AUTHOR

Thanks for reading, it's been a real blast retelling one of my favourite classic stories as part of the Monsters and Mayhem project. Please make sure you check out the other books in this project, there are so many incredible titles!

If you'd like to know more about me and what I write, please join my reader's group and follow me on social media.

twitter.com/DrakeLamarque

bookbub.com/profile/drake-lamarque

instagram.com/drakelamarque

tiktok.com/@jamiesandswriter

amazon.com/Drake-LaMarque/e/B07Y2FQGLR